WINTER
BLOOM

WINTER BLOOM

Tara Heavey

GALLERY BOOKS

NEW YORK   LONDON   TORONTO   SYDNEY

G

Gallery Books
A Division of Simon & Schuster, Inc.
1230 Avenue of the Americas
New York, NY 10020

Originally published in different form in the United Kingdom by Penguin Ireland as *Sowing the Seeds of Love*.

First Gallery Books trade paperback edition October 2010

GALLERY BOOKS and colophon are trademarks of Simon & Schuster, Inc.

For information about special discounts for bulk purchases, please contact Simon & Schuster Special Sales at 1-866-506-1949 or business@simonandschuster.com.

The Simon & Schuster Speakers Bureau can bring authors to your live event. For more information or to book an event contact the Simon & Schuster Speakers Bureau at 1-866-248-3049 or visit our website at www.simonspeakers.com.

Designed by Davina Mock-Maniscalco

Manufactured in the United States of America

10 9 8 7 6 5 4 3 2 1

Library of Congress Cataloging-in-Publication Data

Heavey, Tara.
  [Sowing the seeds of love.]
  Winter bloom / Tara Heavey.—1st Gallery Books trade paperback ed.
    p. cm.
  Previous title: Sowing the seeds of love.
  1. Gardening—Fiction. 2. Single mothers—Fiction. 3. Widows—Fiction.
4. Friendship—Fiction. 5. Dublin (Ireland)—Fiction. I. Title.
  PR6108.E18S69 2010
  823'.92—dc22   2010009735

ISBN 978-1-4391-7793-8
ISBN 978-1-4391-7794-5 (ebook)

For Georgia Grace

The Winter Garden

And the trees were so glad to have the children back again that they had covered themselves with blossoms, and were waving their arms gently above the children's heads. The birds were flying about and twittering with delight, and the flowers were looking up through the green grass and laughing.

—Oscar Wilde, "The Selfish Giant"

*E*VA HAD BEEN here before in her dreams. This magical place. Where the tunnels of roses go on and on. Every hue imaginable. Every scent known to humankind.

Reds. Deep and dark. Familiar to her as her own blood. She bows her head and steals the scent, buries her nose in its folds. She is taken aback as her senses flood—the confectionary aroma—the cola cubes of her youth, sweets crammed with sugar and nostalgia.

She moves to the yellows. She cups one in her hands and the colors swirl and unfurl, capture and enrapture. Good enough to eat, so she does. One petal at a time, imbibing the whole, nectar of the gods.

Then she's immersed in the pinks, the petals smooth and satiny. When she crowds into them, the scent is less heady but sweeter, more innocent, stays with her longer. She brushes the petals with her fingertips. It's like touching the cheeks of a thousand babies and her body wells up with a bittersweet happiness. And she can't stop touching them.

The delicate, delectable whites, more subtle in fragrance but no less lovely. Her beautiful, flowery girls that she can't quite reach because her vision is fading and blurring and crumbling as reality dawns and wakefulness crashes down. Real life blots out everything. Eva wakes newly bereft.

1

*I*T WAS A sunny, Saturday morning of freedom. The sky shone ice blue. Liam skipped alongside Eva, his entire body grinning up at her. She looked back down at her son, crimson scarf wrapped several times around his scrawny, little neck, and couldn't help but smile. It was that kind of day and Liam was that kind of boy. His childish antennae seemed to be tuning in to her newfound sense of optimism. It felt good, this feeling. The first time she'd felt it in she didn't know how long. Certainly not since moving to Dublin.

The move had been tougher than she would ever have anticipated or would ever admit. She put on the bright smile, the happy voice when she spoke to her mother on the phone. But there were times when the isolation threatened to overwhelm her. It was as if she were looking at the world from behind glass.

Her neighbors seemed impossible to get to know. She barely even saw them, barricaded as they all were behind their individual front doors. Maybe it was just the wrong time of year—late October—dark evenings, autumn electricity in the air.

But today. There was something different about today.

Today felt like hope.

"Here we are."

She stopped and dragged Liam to a halt beside her.

"This isn't the sweets shop."

"It's a different type of sweets shop. A very special one."

This pacified him and he allowed himself to be led into the shady interior. The lady behind the counter gave Eva a nod of recognition and her heart rose even higher.

The shop was like something you might expect to find in the old town of Barcelona. The type of store you might stumble across by accident, having become lost down a series of narrow, winding streets. You might have missed it if you hadn't had to leap out of the path of a manic young Catalan on his moped. And *what* you would have missed. It certainly wasn't the type of place Eva would have expected to find on the outskirts of the city center. But each day she was discovering anew how much Dublin had changed since her childhood visits. How much of the heart had been ripped out of the city. Timeless Georgian buildings knocked down to make way for fast-food outlets and coffee-shop chains. Faceless plate glass where graceful archways and doorways had once looked out.

Progress.

This, at least, was a positive change.

It was a treasure trove of goodies. They had gourmet sausages, artisanal biscuits, organic salmon, farmyard cheeses, handcrafted chocolates, homemade preserves, and luxury shortbread.

Her mother would love an Irish porter cake. Together with an Irish breakfast tea in a presentation caddy. She herself wouldn't mind the strawberries in Belgian chocolate. She could feel herself starting to salivate.

And then there were the sweets. Jar upon jar and row upon row of nostalgia: gobstoppers, bon bons, apple sours, licorice laces, chocolate mice, iced caramels, bulls-eyes, aniseed balls, flying saucers, pear drops, striped humbugs, butter humbugs, clove rocks.

The only thing missing was candy cigarettes. Presumably now illegal.

Liam's mouth was agape.

"Can I have whatever I want?"

"Tell me what you want first. You can have five things."

"Only five! I want—"

"Do you want the sweets or not?"

"Yes, I do."

Liam clung to the back of Eva's leg and twisted himself from one foot to the other.

"Those ones."

He pointed decisively at the chocolate mice.

"Just them. Nothing else?"

He nodded vigorously and held up his palm, fingers outstretched.

"Five."

"Five what?"

"Five mouses."

"Five mouses what?"

"Please."

One other customer stood between them and the counter. An older woman, perhaps seventy. Eva couldn't help noticing how well groomed she was. Such elegance. Such coordination. She looked down at her own navy fleece and jeans and felt ashamed. The woman was buying Earl Grey tea and fancy biscuits. How fitting. She examined the woman's face in profile. Her skin was like rice paper but her jawline barely sagged. "Well preserved" was how Eva's father would have described her. The woman completed her purchase and left the shop, whereupon the lady behind the counter turned her attention to Eva. The look she gave her was mischievous. Like a kid with a secret. She leaned forward ever so slightly.

"You'd never guess she'd murdered her own husband."

"Pardon?" Perhaps she'd misheard.

The woman inclined her head toward the exit door.

"Mrs. Prendergast. You'd never guess."

"You mean that old woman who was just in here now."

"That's the one."

"You mean she was convicted and everything?"

"Well, no." Here the story started to flounder. "They never found the body. If you don't have a body, you can't have a trial, apparently. But everyone around here knows that she did it."

"How do they know?"

"Well. There's that garden of hers for a start. Hasn't been touched since the day he disappeared thirty years ago. That gate was padlocked and it hasn't been opened since."

Eva laughed. "I'd hardly call that proof."

The other woman's face closed down and Eva regretted her words. She'd been enjoying this impromptu conversation.

"What can I get you?" The woman was suddenly businesslike.

"I'll have five chocolate mice, please. And two flying saucers for old time's sake."

THAT NIGHT, LIAM couldn't sleep, so she let him into her bed. She knew she shouldn't and that it was setting a bad precedent. But a large part of her didn't care. The part that was empty and lonely and homeless. She needed the closeness as much as he did.

Although there was an entire double bed in which to expand, Liam's sleeping body invariably gravitated toward hers. She was lying on her back, staring into the dark, when:

"Mummy."

She'd thought he was asleep.

"Yes, Liam."

"If Daddy was still here, would I be allowed into your bed?"

"Of course you would. Don't you remember coming into bed with me and Daddy? When you had a bad dream or when you were sick?"

"No."

"Well, you did. All the time."

"Oh."

They were quiet for a while.

"Night night, Mummy."

"Night night, Liam."

A few breaths later he was asleep. His knees sticking into her lower back. As if he were trying to burrow back into her womb.

2

*M*ONDAY MORNING AND a nine o'clock lecture. Not a good combination. As Eva watched her students strolling casually into the lecture theater at ten past the hour, yawning and scratching, she had to stifle the urge to yell. Still. What else could you expect from a bunch of eighteen-year-old college students. There was no point in starting without them and lecturing to an empty theater. Having said that, when they arrived, they just sat there like a pack of zombies anyhow. She'd only been working here a few weeks, but already this Monday-morning routine was starting to get old.

Irish people were late for everything, she knew that. The knowledge didn't stop it from infuriating her. Maybe she was just too English.

At last. A reasonable complement of students had arrived and it was worth her while speaking. She cleared her throat, hoping they'd shut up straightaway.

"Right. Today, people. We're going to continue our discussion on the Romantic poets."

She could sense some of them zoning out already.

"Now. John Keats. I'm sure many of you are familiar with his famous odes."

If they were, they were keeping it to themselves.

"'Ode to a Nightingale' and 'Ode to a Grecian Urn' are

the most famous of these, of course. But right now we're going to focus on 'Ode to Psyche.' "

They looked positively thrilled at the prospect.

"Can anyone tell me about the legend of Cupid and Psyche?"

She looked out at the sea of young faces. Some were studying the blank pages of their notebooks lest she should suddenly spring on them. Others, to whom her words had barely registered, stared blankly into space, their faces gray from too much alcohol and not enough sleep.

"Anyone?"

No one. She sighed.

"Venus, the goddess of Love, becomes insanely jealous of this mortal woman called Psyche, who's rumored to be better looking than she is. So she asks her son, Cupid, to shoot Psyche with one of his golden arrows and cause her to fall in love with the vilest creature on earth. The trouble is, as soon as Cupid set eyes on Psyche, he falls in love with her himself. So, he abducts her and keeps her imprisoned in his walled garden. Not that she minds all that much, seeing that he's the best-looking winged man in mythology."

This at least got a few appreciative smiles from some of the girls.

"The image of the walled garden is interesting in itself, because thoughout the Victorian era—an era in which the legend of Cupid and Psyche was rehashed many times—the walled garden was used as a symbol of female sexuality."

Some of the boys looked amused—or was it bemused—as she related this fact. As if she were far too old to be concerning herself with such matters. She supposed that, technically, she was old enough to be their mother—if she had given birth in her teens. Which was hard to wrap her head around given that Liam was hardly more than a baby still.

A new sound was emanating from the back of the theater, unmistakable in its rise and fall.

Someone had started to snore.

3

*T*HEY WERE ON another of their weekend expeditions, getting to know their new neighborhood. When Eva saw something that she hadn't witnessed in all her time living in London.

"Mummy, what's that man doing to that lady?"

"Oh, Jesus Christ. Hey!" she yelled at the height of her voice and started to run.

A woman was being dragged along the pavement by a younger man. More accurately, he was attempting to relieve her of her handbag and she was hanging on for dear life. The man, clearly startled by Eva's intervention, let go of the bag and sprinted in the opposite direction. She reached the woman and crouched down beside her.

"Are you all right?"

"Do I look all right?" The woman pulled herself up into a sitting position. Eva was as surprised by the woman's response as she was by her upper-class English accent. And even more surprised to discover that she was the woman she'd seen the previous week in the Good Food Store. Mrs. Prendergast, wasn't that it? She held out her hand. The older woman ignored it and struggled to her feet, unaided but shaken.

"I'll take you home. Where do you live?"

"There's absolutely no need."

"I insist." Eva took hold of the woman's elbow, but the

latter gave her a look of such ferocity that she withdrew it immediately. No wonder her neighbors thought her capable of murder.

"I'm quite able to walk, thank you very much."

"Okay. I'll ring the police then." Eva reached for her mobile.

"You will not. I'll not have a plethora of PC Plods trampling all over my carpets. I've got my bag and all my belongings. I just want to put the whole unpleasant business behind me. So if you don't mind . . ."

"Actually, I do. I'm walking you home and that's the end of it."

Eva held her own as the older woman attempted to stare her down, her eyes unnaturally bright. Eventually, she uttered a kind of snort and began to cross the street. Eva followed a few paces behind, hand in hand with a wide-eyed Liam.

"Where are we going, Mummy?"

"We're walking this lady home."

"Why?"

"To make sure she gets there safely."

"Where does she live?"

"I don't know."

"Will there be any little boys there?"

"I don't know, Liam. I shouldn't think so."

"But why—"

"Here. Have a sweetie."

Mrs. Prendergast had turned into the driveway of an elegant, old redbrick. A corner house.

Eva hoisted Liam up the steps to the plum-colored front door and stood behind the tall, slim, almost ramrod-straight figure of Mrs. Prendergast. Eva imagined her collapsing the moment she was alone.

The older woman stood inside her hall now, facing Eva.

"As you can see, I'm home in one piece." She swallowed. "Thank you."

"You're welcome. Would you like me to call a doctor for you?"

"No I would not. Now good-bye."

The door was already closing when Liam started to run in place.

"Pee-pee Mummy. I need to do a pee-pee."

Oh crap. She looked at Mrs Prendergast.

"I don't suppose . . ."

Mrs. Prendergast rolled her eyes theatrically and opened the door just wide enough for Liam to dart through. She wasn't seriously going to leave her standing there. Ungracious old cow.

"I strongly suggest you let me in too, unless you want piss all over your floor."

Mrs. Prendergast glared at Eva before flinging the door wide open.

"Thank you. Where . . . ?"

"Up the stairs and on your left."

The older woman's voice was like fine bone china.

As Eva ran up the stairs, two steps at a time, dragging Liam in her wake, she felt a pang of guilt. This poor lady had just been mugged and here she was being mean to her. But by God, there was something about her. Something so irresistibly antagonistic.

The interior of the house was beautiful. From the graceful curve of the mahogany banister to the jeweled patterns that the stained glass threw on the burnished wood floor. Once safely inside the bathroom, Eva stared absently at the pure white blind as Liam tinkled into the toilet bowl. She inched the blind away from the window and found herself, to her complete surprise, looking down at the remnants of a walled garden. She could see it quite clearly. The way it used to be. The paths, now overgrown, all around the edges and bisecting the center of the garden in a crisscross pattern. Stunted old apple trees choking with ivy. A tumbledown archway. Eva imagined it as it might have been in its heyday, swathed in rambling roses. Soft pink, she thought. And the body of Mr. Prendergast reclining in his shallow grave . . .

"Mummy, I can't reach the towel."

She handed the towel down to Liam and replaced it when he'd finished, trying but failing to leave it exactly as they'd found it.

Mrs. Prendergast was waiting for them by the front door. Quite pointedly, it had to be said. Eva would have loved to have had a good nose around. A door leading off the hallway stood ajar, offering a tantalizing view of a room crammed with antiques. But Mrs. Prendergast wasn't holding any guided tours. Instead, she was holding the door open, nice and wide.

"Thank you very much, Mrs. Prendergast. We're sorry for troubling you. What do you say, Liam?"

"You've got a cut on your knee."

Liam looked up at Mrs. Prendergast from his knee-high vantage point.

"You should get your mummy to put a plaster on it."

"Thank you, I will. Now if you don't mind . . ."

"Yes, of course. Bye now."

The door shut behind them before they'd even reached the top step.

On the way home, Eva couldn't resist taking a closer look at the garden. She skirted the outer perimiter of the wall, oblivious to Liam's complaints. Almost a perfect square. About an acre in size. Then she came across a wrought-iron gate, tall and forbidding. Black paint peeling and flaking off in lumps. It was locked tight, of course. The padlock looked as if it had been designed to keep out a marauding army, the heavy chain wrapped around itself many times.

Oblivious to passersby, Eva pressed her right cheek up against the cold metal and swiveled her eyes as far as they could go to the left. She thought how comical she must look to anyone on the other side. But there was nobody on the other side. Nothing much, in fact, other than dense undergrowth. And the walls of course, which encompassed the entire property and was an attractive, reddish brown color. Much of it was scrambled with dark green ivy. It was striking, how beautifully the two colors complemented each other. Gazing within, she was just able to detect a pattern in the planting, a pattern only discernible because the garden lay sleeping in its winter sparseness.

There were two lines of unruly shrubs bisecting the garden. Every so often, a larger bush loomed upward like a lopsided skeleton. These two lines met in the middle by virtue of a stagnant old pond. At least she presumed there was water underneath. So much chickweed grew on the surface that it looked solid green. If it hadn't been for the aeriel view out of Mrs. Prendergast's bathroom, she might not have guessed that what she was looking at was an old-fashioned—perhaps Victorian—walled garden. Funny that she'd only been talking about it the other day in class.

There was something magical—romantic—about the concept of a walled garden. Eva had always loved them. But she hadn't expected to find one here, so close to her new Dublin home. Still intact if a little ragged around the edges. There was one next to her childhood London home. Her mother used to take her there. Her own secret garden. It was small, but contained many possibilities.

Buried treasure.

She felt as if she were the first person ever to see the garden. As in *really* see it. Or at least the first person in a very long time.

She went home.

But the garden stayed with her.

4

$\mathcal{I}$T WAS A week later to the day. Almost to the hour.

Mrs. Prendergast's front garden was mainly gravel, bordered by a few well-spaced, orderly, low-maintenance shrubs. The appearance of the front of the house bore no relation to the wilderness out in the back. A grand succession of somber, stone steps led up to the front door, which was impressive and imposing and swirled with stained glass. She was standing right in front of it. Somehow her feet had led her up to the top of the steps where she stood regarding the tarnished brass knocker. No bell. What had brought her to this point? This wasn't usual behavior for her. Maybe it was because she was starting a new life. Possibilities had awakened within her.

"Can I knock, Mummy?"

She lifted Liam up and he rapped the brass against the wood. Nothing happened. After an appropriate interval, she lifted him up and he knocked again.

Still nothing.

"Shall I try again, Mummy?"

"No. She mustn't be in. Let's go."

Feeling foolish, she descended the steps, then crossed the gravel briskly, anxious now to get out of there and put the folly behind her, convinced that Mrs. Prendergast was peering out of an upstairs window, mocking her.

But behind her, the front door opened. Liam heard it too.

"Look, Mummy, she's in!"

Mrs. Prendergast stood looking down at them, her demeanor more forbidding than Eva remembered. She was regretting this already. But she followed her feet back up the steps until she was standing, once again, at the entrance to the house. Mrs. Prendergast raised a quizzical eyebrow.

"In need of my facilities again?"

Eva smiled nervously. "We came to see how you were?"

"Couldn't be better."

An awkward silence ensued.

"Was that it?"

"Look, Mummy, a doggy."

A wet muzzle pushed past Mrs. Prendergast's legs, followed by a canine face, as friendly as its owner's was frigid. A rotund body, a frenetic tail. The unmistakable pong of elderly, female dog. A retriever, to be precise. She smiled openmouthedly at Liam, as at a long-lost friend, her breath coming in hot, pungent waves.

"What's its name?" said Liam.

"Harriet."

"Is it a boy doggy or a girl doggy?"

"A girl, of course. Harriet is a girl's name."

Eva looked sternly at Mrs. Prendergast. How on earth was a four-year-old boy supposed to know that? But she checked herself. Now was not the time. Instead, "Beautiful day, isn't it."

"Hmph." Or that's what it sounded like.

"Look, Mrs. Prendergast. Since you're obviously in no mood for a conversation, I'll come straight to the point."

"So you do want something."

"It's about your garden."

"What about my garden?" Her bearing became rigid, her expression more guarded.

"It must be hard for you to manage such a large area by yourself."

Mrs. Prendergast stared at Eva from beneath dramatically hooded lids, looking at her as if she were something small and insignificant. Something that she might like to squash.

"What I mean is, it could be so lovely."

"What is your point, my dear?"

Eva guessed that the use of the word "dear" was ironic.

So preoccupied were the two women with each other that they didn't notice Liam and Harriet inching farther into the hall.

"My point is, I could help you with it."

"No thank you. Harriet!" Mrs. Prendergast looked around for her smelly mutt.

"What I mean is, not just you and me doing a bit of weeding. I mean, get a few people together to work on it."

"What people?"

"I don't know yet. I was thinking I could advertise."

"Absolutely not. Harriet!"

Mrs. Prendergast craned her neck past Eva.

"I think they went that way."

Eva indicated indoors. Mrs. Prendergast turned and disappeared into a door leading off the hall. Eva could hear Liam's high-pitched giggles coming from inside. Should she . . . ? She wasn't strictly invited. She wasn't invited at all. But if Mrs. Prendergast wanted Liam out, well then, she was the woman for the job.

She stepped over the threshold and stood behind Mrs. Prendergast at the entrance to the living room.

Liam was hunkered down on the floor beside Harriet, who was lying on her back, her nose stretched out to the ultimate. Liam rubbed her belly while the dog rotated one of her back legs in the air as if riding half of an invisible bicycle. Eva glanced quickly at Mrs. Prendergast. She didn't look as stern as before. And they said never to work with children or animals.

"What's that smell?" Liam lifted his head and wrinkled his nose up into the air.

"Liam!" The mortification.

"Oh, that'll be Harriet. She farts a lot."

Liam rolled around on the floor beside the dog, his little-boy laugh full bodied and infectious. Mrs. Prendergast's lips twitched slightly at one corner. Eva knew an opportunity when she saw one.

"I really wish you'd reconsider. It could be wonderful. Imagine the garden restored to its former glory. We could grow fruit, veg, herbs. You could have all the fresh produce you could eat—"

"What is your name?"

"Pardon? Oh my God. I didn't realize, I'm so sorry. I'm Eva. Eva Madigan. And this is Liam."

"You're English." For once it wasn't an accusation.

"Yes, I am."

"Where are you from?"

"London. As I—"

"Are you married?"

"Used to be. Are you?"

"Used to be. But I expect you know that already."

Eva felt herself starting to blush but Mrs. Prendergast didn't appear to notice.

"Are you Church of England?"

"No, Catholic."

"Oh. Pity. The Mother's Union is always looking for new blood. Like a pack of vampires they are."

"No, sorry."

Sorry? What was she doing apologizing for her own religion?

"And I take it you have lots of gardening experience."

"Oh yes, lots."

Growing sunflowers in the garden in Upper Norward when she was nine.

"Anyhow, I'm selling it."

"What?"

"The garden. I'm selling it for development."

"You can't do that."

"I beg your pardon?"

"I mean . . . I didn't mean . . ."

"I think you'll find I'm entitled to do whatever I like with my own property."

"I know, I know. Of course you are. It just seems such a terrible shame. It could be so beautiful. I'm sure it was once."

She looked searchingly into Mrs. Prendergast's face but found no response. Not even a flicker.

Eva sighed.

"Come on, Liam."

Liam righted himself and looked up at Mrs. Prendergast.

"Please can me and my mummy have your garden? I want to grow her some pretty flowers."

The silence was as embarassing as it was deafening.

"Let's go."

Eva scooped up her son before he had a chance to say anything else and headed out the front door. Once on the step, she turned to speak but the door was already closed. She felt heartbroken and she didn't quite know why.

5

*S*HE TRIED TO put it out of her mind. Because really. What was the point?

Then one day, not so very long afterward, she was in the Good Food Store. She was rooting around for something that would taste homemade but really wasn't when she felt a tap on her shoulder. She looked around in surprise. She didn't know enough people to expect a shoulder tapping.

"Oh. Hello, Mrs. Prendergast."

"You can have the garden."

"What?"

"It's 'pardon.' I said you can have the garden. Do what you like with it, I don't care. I'll still own it of course."

"Of course."

"Just let me know when you intend starting."

"I will. Thank you."

The older woman nodded curtly and was gone.

Eva floated home. It was only when she got back to her kitchen that she discovered she'd forgotten all her groceries.

SHE HAD NO idea why this garden meant so much to her. Was it because it was a perfect, desolate reflection of herself? Laid bare by a long, hard winter and years of neglect. Pruned by the harsh frosts and the icy winds and the months of darkness.

Where once all was lush, green with growth and optimism. Now all was gray and dense with stagnation. But still.

Still.

Just below the surface.

New life was waiting. To push out of the darkness and into the light. Just as she had always known it to be, in a place deep inside that she'd forgotten about.

It gave her such a feeling of excitement. If she could only help it to grow again—well then—it would be as if all things were possible.

So it was in this frame of mind that she set out one blowy morning in mid-December, down to the Good Food Store, her hand firmly clasping a stiff white piece of notepaper, folded down the middle in one sharp crease. She was relieved to see that there was a different woman behind the counter. Girl, really. She couldn't have been more than twenty. Slight, with shoulder-length dark hair. The kind of girl who absorbed the light rather than reflected it. Looking terribly miserable for someone who spent her working day surrounded by such glorious produce. But she of all people shouldn't judge.

"Can I put a notice up?" Eva gestured toward the notice board.

The girl took a break from staring into space.

"Go right ahead."

She recommenced staring. Eva would have loved to know what she was looking at. She stole a thumbtack from a poster for Pilates and secured her own notice in as advantageous a position as possible. Then she stood back to read it for the fiftieth time that morning:

Local garden in urgent need
of care and attention.
Community effort required.
All those interested,

PLEASE BRING YOUR GREEN FINGERS ALONG.
AT 8:30 PM NEXT MONDAY NIGHT,
THE 16TH OF DECEMBER TO . . .

SHE SUPPLIED HER address. She'd even drawn a few flowers in the top right-hand corner. What an idiot. Was she really going through with this? Yes, she was. She turned away before she changed her mind again. On to more mundane matters: dinner. She checked out the miniscule vegetable department.

"Do you have any green beans?"

She almost felt bad for dragging the girl back to a reality in which she clearly did not want to exist.

"We try to stock only Irish produce and we can't get Irish green beans this time of the year. Actually, we can't get them for most of the year. They all seem to be from Kenya."

Eva nodded and left the shop. She pulled her woolen hat tighter down around her ears, as if to contain all the thoughts that were colliding inside her head. So they couldn't get Irish-grown green beans. How interesting. How very interesting indeed. She pulled on her gloves and stifled a small smile. If she didn't know any better, she'd think that she was happy.

6

*I*T WAS 8:31 PM on the evening of the six-
teenth. So where were they? The milling throngs. Was all the
cushion plumping, crumb sweeping, coffee brewing, biscuit
buying, notice tacking to be to no avail? She'd even bought a
few potted plants to look the part. Devised ways to stop them
from looking new and out of place in her new and out of place
home.

The doorbell rang and her heart almost leaped out of her
body. She rushed out of the kitchen, slowing her steps as she
neared the front door. Calm. She opened the door. A man.

"Hello."

"Hello." He doffed his hat, delighting and surprising her
at the same time.

"Have you come about the garden?"

"I have."

"Please come in."

Someone. It was someone.

She stood aside to let him pass. He was short. Shorter than
she was. Neat and dapper looking. Closely trimmed beard—
dark even though he must be more than seventy.

He took off his pristine coat, his movements deft and
quick, to reveal an immaculate black pin-striped suit underneath. She felt messy and ungainly beside him. Too much time
concentrating on her house and not enough on her hair, which

was in the same ponytail she'd gathered it into that morning. She had kidded herself that the strands that had come loose were softening tendrils. In reality, they were just straggly bits of hair. Her nut brown hair, as Michael used to call it. Taking his coat, she ushered him into the sitting room.

"You're the first to arrive." She felt stupid and nervous. Small talk always made her feel that way. "Would you like some coffee?"

"That would be lovely."

She thought she detected the faintest trace of an accent, but it was too early to say. She busied herself in the kitchen with his hot beverage, transferring biscuits onto a plate, fumbling with the wrapper. Fussing about with milk and a sugar bowl. They were certain. Something on which she could rely, on this evening that fanned out before her in all its uncertainty.

She carried everything back into the sitting room on a large tray. The man leaped up when she entered, took the tray from her, and laid it on the coffee table.

"Thank you . . ."

"Uri."

"Thank you, Uri. I'm Eva. Sorry, I should have mentioned that before."

The doorbell. Someone else! She ran out to the door and opened it.

Her eyes widened in surprise. It was the sad girl from the food store.

"Hello."

"Hello."

"Come in."

She came in.

"Can I take your coat?" She took her coat and led her into the sitting room.

"I'm Eva, by the way."

"Emily." The girl kind of half smiled.

"Coffee?"

"Yes, please."

"Mummy."

Oh shit. Liam was still awake. Not only that, he was standing at the top of the stairs.

"Get back into bed."

"Who is it?"

"Just someone to see Mummy."

"Who?"

"Nobody you know. Now go back to sleep."

"But I wasn't asleep."

"Well, go to sleep now."

"I'm hungwy."

In desperation, she closed the sitting room door on this popular ploy. Inside, Uri was putting milk in Emily's coffee. They both looked up at her expectantly. She smiled tightly and looked at the clock: 8:45.

"I suppose we'd better make a start." She settled herself in an armchair. "I can go over things again if someone else comes."

No one else came. Apart from Liam, whom Eva could hear descending the stairs step by step. It was only a matter of seconds before the door swung open and there he stood, resplendent in Spider-Man pyjamas. His confidence deserted him as soon as his eyes alighted on the strangers and he ran onto his mother's lap, wrapping his legs around her waist and burying his face in the soft, warm place where her neck met her shoulder. The irritation Eva had anticipated didn't materialize. Instead, she felt the tension melt from her body.

"So. We have the opportunity to restore a walled garden."

"Really." Uri sat forward in his seat, his face intent.

"Yes. The owner has very kindly agreed to let us do what we like with it."

"Where is this garden?"

"Close by. About a five minutes' walk from here."

"Have you had plans drawn up?"

"Um. No. Not yet. I was waiting to see if I could generate enough interest first."

"Do you have photos?"

"No."

"How big is it?"

"About an acre."

"An acre in this part of the city. It's a wonder no one's built an apartment block on top of it."

"Yes. I think the owner was thinking about it, but she seems to have had a change of heart."

"What do you envisage for the garden?" Again, Uri asked the question. Emily had yet to speak.

"I see it as a community garden. Anyone who's interested can come and help. Try and restore it to its former glory. Flowers, vegetables, herbs, fruit trees."

"We could grow figs—vines even." Uri was smiling broadly now.

"Yes, I suppose we might be able to get a greenhouse."

He was looking at her carefully. Choosing his words carefully.

"Well, as you know, the temperature in a walled garden is always several degrees higher than that of a normal garden. So it should be possible to grow such fruit against the walls, where the heat is retained."

Eva nodded and looked at the carpet. She could feel herself blushing to her roots.

As you know.

She looked up and met Uri's eyes briefly. He was still looking at her, not unkindly, she had to admit. She could have kicked herself for being so unprepared. For not having done more research. She of all people. Professional lecturer. Some professional *she was.*

"Can we see it?" It was the first time Emily had spoken.

"The garden?"

"Yes."

"Now?" She hadn't anticipated this.

Emily nodded.

"But it's dark."

"I have a torch," said Uri.

You would, thought Eva, somewhat bitterly. Then she checked herself. She was damn lucky that someone had shown up who knew what they were talking about. Because she clearly didn't.

"What if someone else shows up . . ."

Her voice trailed off. Her two visitors looked at the clock then back at her. Nine o'clock. There was no need for them to say anything.

"What about Liam?"

"I can come too, Mummy." Liam's words were moist against her throat.

Why not? she thought. He was wide awake anyway.

"Okay."

"Yippee!" Liam climbed off her lap and ran out to the hall, presumably to get his boots.

"But I don't have the key yet."

She addressed the other two.

"Can we ask the owner?" said Uri.

"I suppose we could. But I wouldn't like to disturb her. It's a bit late."

"Of course. You're right. But is there a way to see in anyway?"

"Yes. There's a gate we can look through."

"Okay." He got up.

And they all put their coats on and went outside.

It felt wierd. Walking along with these two strangers, close in the darkness, Liam's hand clinging to her own. They crunched along the pavement, leaf-crackling sweetness, their breaths solid and white in the winter air. They were silent mostly, Liam's intermittent questions easing the tension. When they were almost there, Uri drew alongside her.

"Are you a gardener?" he said.

The question she'd been dreading.

"No. I'm a lecturer."

"In horticulture?"

"No. English."

She looked across at him. He was looking at the ground.

"Are you?" she said.

"A gardener?"

"Yes."

"No. Just a keen amateur. I'm a tailor by trade."

"Oh."

That would explain his immaculate appearance. Could he tell she'd bought her clothes ready-made and off the peg in Dunnes Stores?

"Here we are."

"Oh, I know this place," said Emily.

They arrived at the gate and peered into the darkness. The nearest streetlight was quite a distance away. Then Uri switched on his torch and shone the powerful beam within. They all followed the arc of light as it illuminated various parts of the garden. She watched their faces. They both looked suitably spellbound. Good. Good.

"Can I have a go?"

Uri handed the torch to Liam, who swung the beam erratically around the whole neighborhood.

"Well," said Eva. "What do you think?"

"I'm in," said Uri.

"Me too," said Emily.

Good.

Good.

7

*I*T WAS REALLY happening, then. She was really going to do this. She and her army of two volunteers. Thus she found herself, for the third time, on Mrs. Prendergast's doorstep one drizzly morning in late December. Her fingers had barely made contact with the brass knocker before the door was pulled open.

"I was wondering when you'd show up again."

Charming.

"Good morning, Mrs. Prendergast. I've come to let you know that I've decided to take you up on your offer. We'll be starting work on the garden directly after Christmas."

"We?"

"Me and the other volunteers."

"Will there be many?"

"Only a few at first . . ."

"All right then."

She started to close the door.

"Mrs. Prendergast."

"What?"

"I'm going to need a key."

The woman nodded and disappeared into the interior again. Eva could hear a drawer being opened and some riffling around. Mrs. Prendergast returned bearing a massive, rusty-looking thing.

"Here we are. I dug it up in case you came back. It's for the padlock on the gate. I don't even know if it works anymore."

She handed Eva the cool, metal object, then gave her a strange look, as if she couldn't figure her out. Then she shut the door. As Eva descended the steps, she could feel the joy soaring into her throat. She felt like singing. Bouncing along the pavement, she rounded the corner and headed for the gate. The key fit. But that was as far as it went. She wriggled, she pushed, she twisted, and she turned. Nothing. She cursed her weak, feminine hands. Michael could have opened it.

Angering herself with this thought, she tried again, more forcefully this time, making grunting noises worthy of a Wimbledon champion. She was on the verge of giving up when she felt something give. A subtle twisting into place. She felt a kind of elation as the padlock came undone, the cold chunk of metal falling into her palm. She unwrapped the chain—once, twice, three times. The gate emitted a creak reminiscent of a slasher film. How long since it was last opened? She stepped quickly inside and secured the gate from within.

How quiet. How eerie. How suddenly cut off she felt from the outside world. The traffic whizzing past. The pedestrians rushing by. Here, all was still. Timeless. Untouched for nigh on thirty years. She walked silently to the center, feeling as if she'd suddenly become invisible. She bent and touched the chickweed on the pond. It separated out from itself, revealing the dank, dark green water beneath. Water that you couldn't see to the bottom of. It was probably only a foot deep, but to Eva, in that moment, it could have gone on forever. The ground was soft with rainfall. The air was still. She almost felt as if the garden were breathing all around her. The plants, silently growing.

She sank down onto her knees and started to cry.

8

CHRISTMAS WAS OVER. The less said about that the better. It was time to make a new start. Onward and upward in the garden.

She had spent the duration of the holidays in her mother's house in England, taking advantage of the two-week-long Christmas vacation. And now she was back in the staff room at college, as if she'd never been away. Looking in far better shape than most of her colleagues, it had to be said.

"Oh God." Philip, a fifty-something lecturer in engineering, eased himself into the sagging armchair. He was clutching a mug of coffee as if it contained the very essence of life. "I hate the first day back after Christmas," he said, his eyes squeezed shut dramatically. "I always feel I should be home in front of the TV, stuffing myself with chocolates. Any other state seems unnatural."

Eva smiled across at Philip. She liked him. Could allow herself to do so because he was middle aged and safe. But she didn't sympathize with his point of view. The last place she wanted to be was at home. Devoid of adult company. Wallowing. She had missed the activity of college. She had even missed her laconic, zombielike students. And of course, she had her work on the garden to look forward to.

Eva had asked all her family for garden implements that Christmas, ignoring their comments and strange looks. The looks would have been decidedly stranger had they known that her back garden was no more than a yard with a few well-scattered pots. She now had: a spade, a big fork, a trowel, a little fork, a thing for pruning low branches and another thing for lopping off high branches. She'd been studying too, having realized that an in-depth knowledge of the legend of Cupid and Psyche wasn't going to get her far in a real-life walled garden. Not that she had a hope of fooling Uri. She had a feeling that she'd already been rumbled there.

They were both waiting for her at the gate that first morning. She saw them before they saw her. Uri had his hands dug deep inside his overcoat and his face pressed up against the wrought iron. It must be freezing. Emily was staring into the middle distance, in what Eva was beginning to think of as her habitual pose.

"Sorry I'm late. Liam wouldn't let me leave the nursery school. He must have known something was up."

She reached them, slightly breathless and pink cheeked. The cold air was making her nose run and she wiped it surreptitiously with a ragged piece of toilet tissue. Uri smiled at her broadly and Emily gave her a little nod. She noticed they had tools with them too. All the better for digging.

She struggled a little less with the gate this time and they all entered the garden. Emily walked off by herself a few paces and looked all around. Uri took himself off to explore the farthest reaches of the garden, bending and prodding and muttering to himself. Eva gave them a few minutes to familiarize themselves, allowing them to wander back to her in their own time. Uri seemed excited. Emily, expectant.

"Where do you want us to start?"

This was a truly critical moment as far as Eva was concerned. Uri clearly knew far more about gardening than she did—they both knew it. Yet he was deferring to her. She wasn't sure how she would have handled it if he had tried to take over. She may have been half inclined to let him. But he hadn't. So . . .

"Well. The place is a bit of a mess, so the first thing that has to be done, I think, is to clear it."

"I agree totally," said Uri, nodding his head at her and smiling as if she'd said something really intelligent rather than blindingly obvious. "Of course, it would have been better if we could have started the clearing in the autumn but not to worry."

"Of course," said Eva, experiencing a surge of excitement. She knew that, thanks to all her studying. "Now, we may find some plants that are salvageable, so be careful what you pull out."

She directed this comment to Emily, who, for all she knew, was as clueless as herself.

"So," she continued. "Let's get gardening."

And so it was that Eva, Emily, and Uri spent three successive days pulling, yanking, chopping, and hacking in the walled winter garden. On the second day there was a light snowfall. Uri brought along a yard brush and beat the snow from the upper branches of the evergreens.

"But it looks so pretty up there," said Eva.

"It might damage the trees if we leave it."

"Oh."

"I've been thinking," he said. "We might be eligible for a grant for the garden."

"Really?"

"Yes. If we billed it as a community project. It could help with the planting costs. Would you like me to look into it?"

"Yes, please!"

"In the meantime I can bring in plenty of cuttings."

"That'd be great, Uri."

It *was* great. He was great—with his ridiculous yet charming deferral to her authority. If she didn't have him helping her, she'd be well and truly up a creek. The reality was that stark.

It was as if somebody had sent him. Ordered him from some magic mail order catalog.

Liam came along with the snow, speeding up and down the partially cleared paths on his yellow tractor. Eva hoped the others didn't mind his presence. They didn't appear to. She had noticed Emily watching her son intently at times, but she didn't seem annoyed. Intrigued almost. Uri told him stories. Long, convoluted tales, mostly involving dragons, with Liam invariably the hero of the piece. They didn't talk much, the three adults. There didn't seem to be much need, apart from "pass the pruning shears" and such like. Rather, they settled into a silence that Eva found strangely companionable, seeing as how they hardly knew one another. It must have been something to do with their common cause.

On the third day—a Sunday—they all agreed to stay on for the afternoon. Sunday lunch consisted of goat cheese and green tomato chutney on ciabatta bread, and organic apples, all washed down with sparkling elderflower cordial. This came courtesy of Emily, whose aunt happened to be the proprietor of the Good Food Store. Touched by the girl's generosity, Eva brought hot tea in a flask and Uri supplied the cups. Liam had his first gobstopper, under the close supervision of his mother. He stuck his tongue out at intervals.

"What color is it now?"

"Red," said Eva.

"Green," said Uri.

"Blue," said Emily.

It was late on Sunday afternoon and the light was beginning to fail.

"Shall we call it a day?" asked Eva.

"I think so," said Uri.

They both stood back to admire the progress that had been made. It was getting easier to discern the original shape of the garden.

"Of course," Uri was saying, "we'll have our work cut out

for us in the spring when the new growth starts. Keeping down the weeds."

Eva nodded solemnly, but inside she felt something close to jubilation. What did she care about a few weeds? Look at what they'd achieved in three days alone.

"Over here. Quick." It was Emily. Shouting! Emily who scarcely raised her voice above a whisper. The two rushed over, expecting a pruned finger at the very least. But when they got there, Emily was crouched on the ground, looking up at them, her face shining as if she'd seen a vision.

"Look."

Eva and Uri looked down at the small patch of ground that Emily had been clearing.

There, in the fading light, in all its smallness and all its whiteness, was a snowdrop.

9

$\mathcal{E}$MILY'S FUTURE SPREAD out before her like a vast expanse of Montana grassland. Endless. Limitless in its possibilities. She'd never been to Montana, although she had seen *The Horse Whisperer*. Nevertheless, this was the image she'd pressed to herself ever since she'd left home and started college.

Maybe it was because her family was so large, so overwhelming. And the family home so small in comparison. Always having to share a room. Never being on your own. Which was why, growing up, she had learned how to spend so much time in the spacious, beautifully furnished room of her imagination. And why her current, one-bedroom flat, lit by one tiny window, was to her the glittering, multimirrored palace of Versailles. She would lie on her bed on a sunshiny morning and feel the weight of the sun press down on her eyelids, rendering everything blood colored. She would stretch out her bare toes and fling her arms back on either side of her head. She would imagine her dark hair fanned out on the white pillow and luxuriate in her aloneness, knowing what it was to be young and free, with the space to grow into herself at last.

Emily knew she'd be lying to herself if she pretended she'd felt like this from her very first day of college. On the contrary—she'd been terrified. And even worse, horrified by the dichotomy between her own confidence and that of her female classmates. These city girls seemed so unbelievably sure of themselves. They made her feel like such a dork. It wasn't so much what they said or what they did. It was just the way they were. So to deal with this, Emily had adopted a kind of strategy. She'd lain low for a couple of weeks and studied these women. The way they moved, the way they gesticulated, but mostly, the way they wore their clothes. By Monday of the third week she was ready. This is how she looked:

Her haircut was gamine, dark and sleek. Then from the bottom up: nude Ugg boots; black diamond tights; denim miniskirt; and short, black leather jacket, cinched at the waist. Around her neck, tied in the manner of a necktie, was a scarf she'd bought secondhand in Temple Bar. Her bag was vintage and so was her jewelry. She especially loved her chandelier earrings. They made her feel like Queen Nefertiti. She was confident that she looked nothing like the farmer's daughter she truly was and felt ready to insinuate herself into the company of her female classmates. During lectures, she would sit beside a likely looking girl and one or the other of them would strike up a conversation.

Her strategy worked. Before long, she was part of a magic circle of girls who; in their quest for individuality, wore identical clothes and held identical views. Part of her knew that this setup was shallow. But so far nobody had noticed that she wasn't cool, so mission accomplished as far as she was concerned.

The boys were another matter. They were everywhere she looked, in every conceivable incarnation, their voices and laughter overloud with exaggerated self-confidence. She was in awe. Although her air of nonchalance belied her awestruckness. She felt as she had as a child when she fantasized about being locked in a sweets shop overnight. Although so far she hadn't so much as stolen a kiss. She didn't want to make a

mistake and choose the wrong one. It was far too important a
selection to make.

So it was that she sat in the college bar one night, sometime around the beginning of second term. It was freezing outside and the bar held a welcome glow. She was surrounded by
five or six of her gal pals, variously chatting and texting and
going out for a Marlboro Light. A group of lads sat across the
way, drinking pints of Bavaria lager and pretending not to
look over. One of the boys, Joe, noticed Emily before she noticed him. It was his friend Niall who first brought her to his
attention. He nudged Joe in the arm.

"What do you think of her?"

"Which one?"

"Twelve o'clock. Dark hair, legs crossed."

He stole a casual glance before returning to his pint.

"Looks like a librarian."

"Yeah, but a hot librarian. Like she'd whip off her glasses
and do you across the desk."

"She's not wearing glasses."

"You know what I mean."

"You've been watching too much porn."

"No such thing as too much porn."

Joe looked again. She was nice. Small and dark and neat.
Pretty in a quiet, not too obvious way. And she looked like
she'd be a tough nut to crack. Which was always appealing.

"Want to meet her?"

"What? Just like that?"

"I know one of her friends. She was in my sister's class in
school. They must be first years. Come on."

And so it happened that the two boys traversed the great
divide and introduced themselves. Joe sat as close to Emily as
propriety would allow.

"Hi, I'm Joe."

"Emily."

"Lovely name."

"Thanks."

"Are you a first year, Emily?"

She nodded her head.

"What are you studying?"

"Pure English."

Joe thought it fitting that she should be studying something pure. It suited her primness of being.

"I'm in engineering. Third year," he said, volunteering the information himself as he judged, quite rightly, that she was unlikely to ask him for it. As it was, she just nodded. Other young men might have been put off by her reticence. Not Joe. Being not in the least bit self-contained himself, he was impressed by the quality in other people. Especially women.

"So. Do you drink here much?"

"Sometimes."

"Why don't we meet up here Thursday night. Just you and me," he added, lest there be any confusion.

Emily lowered her eyes and said nothing, which made Joe considerably keener.

"About eight."

"Okay."

"You will?"

"Yes."

Joe beamed, and before long the two men sidled back from whence they had come. Emily's friend Rebecca, the one who knew Niall's sister, slid over into the chair that Joe had just vacated.

"That looked very cozy."

Emily grinned. She couldn't help herself.

"He asked me out."

"What?!"

"Keep your voice down, they're only over there."

The two girls looked over at Joe and Niall, who had rejoined the rugby scrum of mates, all huddled together around their table.

"They're probably talking about you."

"Stop!"

"I'm only teasing. Where's he taking you?"

Emily's crest fell a little as it struck her that he hadn't asked her out for a fancy dinner.

"We're meeting here for a drink." She could see Rebecca having the same thought she had just had.

"Oh well, it's a start," said the other girl.

It was the start. Of Emily's first love affair.

10

*I*T WAS THURSDAY night and Emily was mid-conniption. Only twenty more minutes to go, she said, peering into her bathroom mirror, her breath making little clouds on the glass. What if he stood her up? The thought cannoned into her belly. God, what would she do? To be stood up in the college bar of all places, in full view of people she might actually know. Even if the place was full of strangers, she'd still have to report back to the women (she thought of them in her head as "the wimmin"). Rebecca had made short shrift of letting all and sundry know about her "date." If, indeed, that was what it was. God, she didn't think she could handle the humiliation of being stood up. Would such a happening pierce her armor of cool to such an extent that her new friends would see her for who she really was? She couldn't have that.

She had to adopt a strategy. She'd bring a book. Someone had just loaned her *The Unbearable Lightness of Being*. Better still, she'd arrive ten minutes late. If he wasn't there, she'd merely keep on walking, as if she was just passing through, and nobody there would be any the wiser. Of course, this meant an extra ten minutes in which to lose her mind. How on earth was she to occupy herself? She tried to read, but the pages might as well have been blank. She jumped up on her bed, in an effort to quell her churning stomach, and bounced for a full minute. Then she jumped back down and performed a handstand against the wall. Her giggles were muffled by the maroon material of her gypsy skirt, which covered her face and made her feel twelve again. Upside down. A different perspective on the world. And the last time tonight that her underwear would be exposed, of that she was determined. She uprighted herself, all red faced and breathless, and looked at the clock. The hands appeared to have ground to a halt.

But time hadn't stood still, despite all appearances to the contrary. Because it was now ten minutes past eight and she was walking into the college bar, head erect, shoulders back, heart in mouth. There he was! At least she thought it was him. The boy had his back to her. He was leaning forward, his elbows on his knees, hands clasped loosely together. The hunched shoulders were wide and his build stocky. His black hair was tightly curled and cut close to his head. As she reached his side, she recognized the dark, brooding sideburns and noticed him checking his watch, with any luck, slightly uneasy.

"Joe?" She stood not directly in front of him and inclined her head slightly, as if looking around a corner.

"Emily." He stood up, like a well-brought-up young man, and his smile only slightly betrayed his relief. He gestured to the seat across from him, whereupon Emily promptly sat down and crossed her legs neatly.

"You came," said Joe.

"Yes, I did."

"Can I get you a drink?"

"Bottle of Corona please."

Joe purchased the drinks, set them down, and grappled around for something to say.

"So. Pure English. You must like to read."

"Yes, I love books."

"Any particular kind?"

"Anything and everything."

She wasn't giving him much to go on but he plowed on regardless.

"I like books too. Mainly thrillers. Dan Browne, John Grisham—that kind of thing."

There was no response.

"Do you read thrillers?"

"Not really."

"What, not at all? You must have read *The Da Vinci Code,* everyone's read that."

"I have read that one, yes."

"And what did you think?"

"I thought it was badly written."

"Well, I liked it," Joe finished weakly and tried another tack.

"How are you finding college life?"

"Okay. Yeah. I like it."

"Do you live on campus?"

"No, I have a bedsit."

Emily could almost see the thoughts running through Joe's head: country girl—didn't live at home—a point in her favor perhaps?

"Where is it you're from again?" he said.

"Kilkenny."

"Oh yeah." Another dead end. Clearly Joe knew diddly-squat about the place.

Emily sat anxiously in her seat and watched Joe struggle. She didn't mean to be such hard work. What other people mistook for aloofness was in fact shyness. And although this impression could be handy at times, at other times—such as now—it was a downright nuisance. She had to throw him a lifeline before they both drowned in silence and awkwardness.

"What's your second name, Joe?"

He was Joseph Francis after his two grandfathers and he'd taken Luke for his confirmation after Skywalker.

She wondered briefly if he was thick, then instantly dismissed the thought. He couldn't be if he was studying engineering. He was probably a whiz at physics and maths and that sort of thing. Emily had been terrible at maths in school and therefore had great respect for those who were not.

"I mean your second name. Your surname."

"Joe Devine."

Joe tried not to imagine her imagining his name tacked on to the end of hers. He knew what girls were like.

"And you?"

"Emily Harte."

Joe held out his hand and grinned.

"Pleased to meet you, Emily Harte."

Emily took his hand and shook. They locked eyes and stayed that way, fingers and gazes intertwined for longer than either had intended. They broke away finally and each party took a nervous sip from their drinks. But the ice was broken, contact had been made, and they both smiled.

EMILY THREW HERSELF down on her bed and luxuriated in the night that had just been.

Emily Harte-Devine. Emily Devine-Harte. Oh, it was too good to be true. She wouldn't even have to change her name if she became a romantic novelist. Although no one would believe that such a name could be real. And she couldn't believe Joe was real. Joe Devine. Devine Joe. The Devine Mr. J. She made a halfhearted attempt to check herself. She was aware of her tendency to imbue the boys she liked with romantic qualities they did not possess. To see past the spots to the Byron within. But she was confident that she wasn't doing that now. She hadn't felt this way since—well—since ever.

Emily lay on her bed and wondered if Joe was good marriage material.

IN A BEDSIT not very far away, Joe lay on his bed and wondered what color Emily's nipples were.

11

*T*HEY'D BEEN TOGETHER for two whole weeks now. And how deeply in love certain parties had fallen in that time. Emily would have had to be in a very honest mood to have admitted, not least to herself, that she was partly in love with the image that she and Joe presented to the world—or to college life at least. They looked so well together. He was exactly a head taller than she was. Her head fit exactly into the crook of his neck, should she be so inclined to place it there, which she did often. If he had any objections to her doing so, he never voiced them. For his part, she was exactly the right height for him to sling his arm around her shoulder in a casual yet possessive, masculine gesture. And they could walk along in this pose quite comfortably together—he the leading man and she the lady—trying on their new adult roles for size and liking the fit. They each felt they complemented the other well, right down to their respective coloring and the clothes they wore. Emily liked Joe's style, even if it was a little bit rugger-bugger for her taste. And Joe liked Emily's arty look. He felt it lent them elegance as a couple, and him, a touch of panache.

In other words, they were ideally suited.

So it was only a matter of time before, you know, they both felt ready to move the relationship on to the next level. Certain parties were more ready than others.

Joe had done it lots of times. He hadn't told Emily this.

He didn't have to. She felt the pressure of it just the same. She never had. She hadn't told him but she felt he knew it just the same. How glad she was now that she had waited, until an age that many of her contemporaries considered geriatric. She could have chosen to get it over with years earlier, in a sticky, clumsy fumble. But instead she had this precious gift that she and Joe could unwrap together. The prospect thrilled her, set all her senses to jangling. She literally could not think of anything else. Her lectures went by in a wordy blur—even those given by the good professors, the interesting ones, the leave-you-breathless ones. Her inability to concentrate was complete. Unless, of course, she was concentrating on the dress she was going to wear on the night. The night in question being this Friday. Her designated deflowering. It was unspoken between them but they both knew.

The dress was rainbow colored and gossamer light and made her feel as if she were wearing butterfly wings. Something lurched inside Joe as he watched her walking toward him across the cobblestones. She was smiling shyly. Looking beautiful. They didn't say anything as their hands connected. Just looked at each other deeply. Then Joe bent down and kissed her mouth.

"Let's go."

They had booked a table at a nearby Chinese restaurant. A rare treat. Mostly they just sat and looked at each other. Emily ate almost nothing at all. Joe ate too much, wolfing down his food so fast that he couldn't taste it. So much so that sweat broke out on his forehead. He wiped it away with his napkin, embarrassed. He was meant to be the one in control tonight. The one who knew what he was doing. And there was Emily, sitting calmly across the table from him, looking at him with those eyes of hers. Under the table, he ran his hand up the back of her calf. Emily felt her heartbeat throbbing throughout her entire body.

"Let's go," he said again.

It was her bedsit they chose. Her place. On the basis that it was neater, less smelly, and had a greater variety of atmospheric candles. Once they were inside, Emily found that she could barely look at Joe, let alone take off her clothes. So she let him do it for her. He undressed her slowly. Reverently. When she was fully naked, he laid her out on the bed. The trust that he saw in her eyes as she looked up at him filled him with awe and guilt. He knew himself to be unworthy even as she did not. Emily held her arms out, feeling herself open, exposed. This is my body, which I have given up for you.

When it was over, she lay on the bed, her sheet drawn up to her chin—underwhelmed by the physical sensation of what she'd just experienced, but overwhelmed by the emotions she felt for Joe. Joe took himself off to the bathroom. It was only then that he realized the condom had split. He toyed with the idea of telling her but decided against it. Why spoil the night? The chances of anything happening were miniscule. He flushed the evidence away, wishing he could join the lads in Doyle's. But he supposed he'd better go and cuddle her for a bit. Wasn't that what all the birds wanted?

EMILY FELT A little odd. She put it down to stress. Joe-induced stress. Things hadn't been the same since their night together. It wasn't any one thing that she could put her finger on. But she could sense his interest waning and it filled her with panic. She couldn't have him withdraw from her now. Not after she'd given herself to him body and soul. Some of the other girls had noticed it too. She'd had to endure a few snide comments. About how he'd never used to keep her waiting. Twenty minutes of torture under the all-seeing eye of the big blue clock. And she could see his mind wandering when she spoke to him, his eyes straying over her shoulder. She did most of the talking nowadays, always trying to engage his ever elusive attention. She just couldn't understand it. She'd given him what he wanted, hadn't she?

THE STRESS OF it all was taking its toll, making her physically ill. The very sight of meat or fish made her want to vomit, not to mention the extrasensory smell of it. Especially in the morning.

Especially in the morning.

Ding.

Emily went to the chemist's.

HOW REMARKABLE THAT the mere act of peeing on a piece of white plastic could alter the trajectory of your life forever. The thin blue line that separates your old life from your new. A line that might as well have been a yawning chasm. As she stared at the definitive evidence of her condition, Emily felt as if she were falling down into such a chasm. Maybe the toilet would just swallow her up, like a giant mouth.

Her mind couldn't wrap itself around the improbability of the situation she found herself in. Ohmigod. This isn't happening. Ohmigod. This isn't happening. He used a condom, it isn't happening. Ohmigod.

She took the second test and it told her the same unpalatable truth. Then she went back to the chemist's and blew the rest of her weekly budget on a second pack. The third time wasn't a charm and neither was the fourth. She paced her bedsit like a big cat in a zoo, sinking down onto her bed every now and then, burying her face in her pillow, wrapping herself in her duvet, only to get up and begin pacing again. Eventually she broke the cycle and left her flat. There was only one person who could help her now. And he was in the college bar meeting his mates. She ran down the street, realizing too late that she should have brought her coat, hugging her arms across her chest as she ran. Then she stopped abruptly. What if she was hurting the baby by running? She had a terrifying premonition of how her life was going to be from now on. Always putting another person's needs before her own. She wasn't ready for that. She was only nineteen. She could scarcely look after herself.

She began running again and didn't stop until she reached the entrance to the bar. She was inside now and the music helped to mask the thudding in her head. She looked around wildly for Joe, oblivious to the strange looks she was receiving. At last she found him, sitting not with his friends but in a booth, with Rebecca, Emily's friend. They looked very pally-wally, their heads huddled together, his arm resting across the back of her seat. Emily stood in front of them and stared at Rebecca stonily. The other girl gave her an arch look.

"I'm going to the bar," she said before slinking off.

Emily took her place, the wood still warm. Joe's body language alarmed her. He didn't even try to touch her.

"I have to talk to you."

"What is it?" His look, his tone, his manner—all wary.

She handed him the final test, discreetly, under the table. He looked down in confusion.

"What's this?"

He looked at her. She said nothing.

"Is this what I think it is?"

She nodded.

"Oh, Jesus Christ."

He brought his hand up to his face and covered his eyes. It was only then that Emily started to cry. She buried her face in his neck, sobbing quietly. She waited a long time for him to gather her up in his arms. It never quite happened. What he did do was pat her awkwardly on the shoulder.

"Don't worry. It'll be all right."

12

*J*OE'S VERSION OF all right and Emily's version of all right turned out to be two very different things. It was Emily's misfortune that she'd thought of Joe as her savior.

They were sitting on a bench in St. Stephen's Green the next day, staring blankly at the ducks. It was a beautiful setting. Leaves rustled gently above their heads. The water rippled. In the distance, Emily could see drifts of golden daffodils interspersed with scarlet tulips. The sight salved her soul somewhat.

The purpose of this meeting was to discuss the position they found themselves in. That's what Joe had said. As if they were running a small corporation. Emily didn't know what to feel. Joe was still here. That was good. Vital. But where was the joy? The excitement one usually associated with new life? There was none. She understood this, logically. But her heart . . .

It wasn't what she'd ever imagined for herself. She had vivid memories of her mother announcing her pregnancies with Emily's younger siblings. How happy they'd all been. The sense of anticipation in the house.

None of this horrible numbness.

"Have you given any thought to what you're going to do?" said Joe, looking at his shoes.

"What do you mean 'do'?"

It was already done.

"I mean, have you thought of all the options?" His voice was level but she sensed that anger wasn't very far away.

"Such as?"

She wouldn't give him the satisfaction of saying it for him.

"Come on, Emily. You know what I mean. There are clinics you can go to in England."

She said nothing. Her face was impassive, but inside she was falling apart.

"It happened to Niall a couple of years back with a girl from home. She just took a flight over. She was home the next day. All over and done with."

The silence now screamed out between them.

"Don't you want us?"

She heard her voice, tiny and pathetic. She hated herself for saying it, knew it was the worst thing she could possibly say, but still she couldn't help herself. Joe sighed an exasperated sigh and closed his eyes.

"It's not that I don't want you. It's just . . . You must see, Emily, what a disaster this is. For both of us. Neither of us has finished college. I've got another year and a half to go. You've got three and a half, for fuck's sake. It's going to be years before either of us is going to be earning halfway decent money. And what about this course you say means so much to you? How are you going to carry on with your studies with a baby to look after?"

"There's a nursery school on campus."

He struck his forehead with the palm of his hand.

"What about the rest of the time?"

"We could manage, between the two of us."

The words hung suspended in the air.

The two of us.

He tried a different tack, his voice newly reasonable.

"It's only early days. What are you? Six weeks? It's not even a baby yet. It's a pinprick."

"It has a heartbeat."

He looked at her properly for the first time.

"You're not going to do this, are you?"

"I won't have an abortion, no."

"Give me one good reason why not."

"You don't know much about my family, do you?"

"I know there's six of you."

"Yes. Six kids. As in good Catholic family. My father's a eucharistic minister and my mother's always going on about good family values and the right to life of the unborn, that kind of stuff."

"Your family doesn't have to know a thing. And you don't even go to mass."

"Not up here I don't. But that's not the point, Joe. They might not know, but I would. I couldn't live with myself."

"Jesus Christ. You'll be wanting us to get married next." He looked at her in alarm. "You don't want . . ."

"Of course not."

"Thank fuck for that."

Her heart plummeted to her feet. Now she knew where she stood. Her place in Joe's affections. Swampland.

He turned away from her again and leaned forward on the bench, his elbows on his knees, his face in his hands.

"Would you not even consider it?"

She tried but failed to keep the tremor out of her voice.

"Joe. This is our baby. Part of you and me. I will not kill it."

Emily gazed straight ahead. She kept her eyes focused on a single tree—a weeping willow. The irony wasn't lost on her as her vision blurred.

"Are you going to break up with me?" She looked up at him then.

Joe looked back down at her in despair. If only she wouldn't keep looking up at him with those big weepy eyes of hers. He put his arms around her.

"Of course I'm not going to break up with you."

Emily wept gratefully into his sweater.

It wasn't too bad for a while. She couldn't claim that Joe was as keen as he had been in those first few weeks. But he did start turning up on time to meet her. And he showed concern when she was unwell—one time even buying her a pack of ginger biscuits because he'd heard they were good for nausea. But every time she tried to talk about the baby, he fell silent. They'd agreed not to tell any of their college friends for the time being. Why add to the pressure? But when Emily was nearing sixteen weeks, her waistline disappearing, she felt it was time to bring up the thorny topic of their parents. She'd almost told her own mother twice, but her courage had failed her at the critical moment. Her parents weren't much keener on premarital sex than they were on abortion. Quite frankly, she dreaded their reaction. But she couldn't hide it forever. She was going to have a baby. Her heart flooded with happiness at the thought. She really had amazed herself. In the beginning, the pregnancy had seemed such a tragedy, her career plans scuppered, her relationship with Joe threatened. But now they were going to be a family.

She announced her plans to Joe over coffee. They could go to his house and tell his parents this Friday night, then get the bus down to Kilkenny on Saturday morning to tell her parents.

"Okay," he said finally.

She smiled and squeezed his hand. It was all going to be "official."

So she dressed in her best clothes that Friday evening, not taking as much care as she usually did to hide her slight bump. She'd been dying to meet Joe's parents, to be introduced as "the girlfriend."

She arrived at their designated meeting place outside the library five minutes early, so she wasn't too concerned that he had yet to arrive. She watched college life whiz happily by, everyone in good form, preparing to go out for the start of the weekend. She didn't envy them. What she had was even better.

It wasn't until ten past that she started to get worried. She texted Joe.

Where are you?

The response came about five minutes later.

I'm sorry. I can't do this anymore.

Panicked, she rang his number but it went straight to voice mail. What did he mean? That he couldn't go through with telling his parents? Or he couldn't go through with any of it? Ever again. She sat rigid for a couple of minutes, then she got up and walked decisively over to the public telephone. She bypassed the queue and headed for the telephone directory that hung suspended from the wall. The *D*s. Devine. There they were. Joseph and Martha at an address in Ranelagh. She walked quickly outside to College Green and hailed a taxi she couldn't afford. If Joe was too chickenshit to tell his parents, she'd have to do it for him. They had the right to know that they were going to be grandparents.

They were at the house already. She paid the taxi driver and got out. No point in asking him to wait. She sat on a wall opposite and stared at the house. Passersby looked at her curiously. She supposed she might look a bit unhinged. Someone turned a light on in a downstairs room. A woman in her fifties. She was tall, with flicky, ash blond hair. Emily watched her as she picked up a newspaper, put on a pair of reading glasses, and sat in an armchair beside the window. Her future mother-in-law. After a while, she got up again and drew the curtains. Emily saw her shadow sitting down. They had a nice garden, she thought dispassionately. She wondered if Joe's father was a keen gardener. Did his wife call him Joseph or Joe? She'd never know. After about an hour, the owner of the wall on which she was sitting came out and stood in front of her.

"Can I help you?" she said, her tone and expression lacking warmth.

"I was just leaving." Emily got up. Her buttocks were ice cold anyway.

She might as well go.

The Spring Garden

*Whoever loves and understands a garden
will find contentment within.*

—Chinese proverb

13

$\mathcal{E}$VA WAS AMAZED by how satisfying it was; all that digging. Slicing through the earth with the blade of the shovel. Feeling it give. Like sticking a fork into a moist piece of chocolate cake. And then overturning the soil, all black and crumbly and teeming with earthworms. Worms that hadn't been disturbed for the best part of three decades—they and their great-grand worms before them. She did feel guilty about the worms, but it was all for the greater good. She was lucky that her ad hoc schedule at the college allowed her daytime hours in the garden. Any free time she had, down she would come, Liam happily ensconced in his nursery school. Uri probably put in the most time, semiretired as he was. With Emily turning up at whatever odd hours her lectures and schedule at the Good Food Store would allow.

Like all activities you could carry out on autopilot, such as walking, driving, and taking a shower, digging had an uncanny way of helping Eva sort out her problems without her consciously trying. Organizing her life as she organized the piles of earth. Uri came up behind her.

"It's coming on."

She stopped digging and leaned against her shovel, slightly puffing.

"It is, isn't it? I thought we'd start with a bed of nasturtiums, followed by a row of spuds along there, then a row of carrots, the Swiss chard, the corn, the turnips, and finish up over there with the cornflowers."

Uri nodded. Then he crouched down and scooped up a handful of black earth, rubbing it through his fingers.

"This is good stuff. Very good stuff."

"I know."

There was a time when Eva would have considered an activity such as the enthusiastic fondling of earth quite alarming. Now she understood. Something caught her eye.

"Look, there she is again."

Uri followed her line of sight toward an upper window at the back of the house. He was just in time to discern the twitch of a curtain.

"Missed her again. What a shame she doesn't just come down and say hello."

"Yes. Pity."

Privately, Eva was quite pleased that she didn't have to deal with any interference on Mrs. Prendergast's part.

She watched Uri as he returned to his apple trees, stopping now and then to tug at a weed, like a garden gnome come to life. The weeds were a problem. A problem that had only fully revealed itself come spring. In particular, a weed that Eva thought of as "the pernicious weed" until Uri told her that it was called ground elder, which had taken over almost half the garden during the long years of neglect. The discussion about a chemical solution to the problem had been brief:

Eva: "We could always use weedkiller. Just this once."

Emily: "No."

Uri: "Absolutely not."

Eva: "All right then. Let's get weeding."

She felt that they were winning the battle. Just about.

Eva resumed digging. And then something wholly unexpected happened. There was a wooden door at the top end of the garden. A door that none of them used because it opened out on to Mrs. Prendergast's private garden. But this morning the door opened. Enter Mrs. Prendergast bearing a tray of tea things and a plate of posh biscuits. They all stopped what they were doing and stared at her. Before anyone could approach, Mrs. Prendergast had laid down the tray, head down at all times, and exited the way she had come, closing the door behind her. The three looked at each other and approached the tray cautiously, as if it had been left there by fairies. It was laid out as if the queen were coming to visit—delicate china cups and saucers and a doily on the plate. Uri laughed as he bit into a biscuit. He gestured to the teapot.

"Will you be mother?" he said to Emily.

LATER THAT DAY, at going-home time, Eva opened the wooden door and approached the back of the house. She knocked three times. When she got no response, she laid the tray down on the doorstep and walked away. She hesitated after the first few steps then turned.

"Thank you," she called into the silence.

THIS PATTERN WAS repeated on every day they worked in the garden. At first, either Uri or Eva would try and approach her, to thank her or engage her in conversation. But she was too quick for them. Sometimes they didn't even hear her. They would stumble across the tray at some point, the temperature of the tea indicating how long it had been there. Then, one day, the pattern was broken. Mrs. Prendergast appeared at the door, earlier than usual, minus a tray. On her head she wore a straw hat tied with a pink ribbon. On her hands she wore worn, brown-leather gloves. In her right hand she carried pruning shears, in her left, a wicker basket such as one might use for gathering cut flowers. She brushed past Eva without looking at her.

"I'll do the roses," she said. "You're making a mess of them."

Eva approached her later that morning.

"Hello, Mrs. Prendergast. How are you keeping?"

"I've decided to put the garden on the market."

"What?"

"It's 'pardon.' I said I'm selling the garden."

"But you can't!"

Mrs. Prendergast turned abruptly and gave Eva a look that was designed to intimidate.

"I didn't mean . . . I mean . . . what about the roses? Why . . . ?"

"My son needs the money for a business venture."

"But . . ."

"I'm afraid my decision is final."

Eva nodded weakly and withdrew. What was she going to do?

For three whole weeks she wrestled with her concience. Should she tell the others? She frequently woke in the night in a sweat, the weight of not telling them pressing down heavily on her chest. But she still had hope. She had to have hope. It must be a good thing, musn't it? Mrs. Prendergast working on the garden. Surely she'd be less inclined to destroy something she'd helped to create. And maybe nobody would want to buy a prime piece of development land so close to the city.

Her concern grew as relentlessly as the pernicious weed, and was even harder to uproot. She bit her nails to the quick as she observed those first fledgling conversations between Uri and Mrs. Prendergast. What were they talking about? She pretended to work a piece of ground closer to where they stood, heads huddled together. She heard snippets.

"David Austen roses . . . the best . . . richest colors . . . headiest fragrances . . . catalog." And was she hearing things or were they discussing tailoring as well? Why on earth not? They were two of the best-turned-out people she'd ever met. "Pinking shears." Or was that some strange gardening implement? She wasn't sure. But so far so good. Nothing about apartment blocks or evil developers. But she had to, had to, had to say something to Uri tonight. She owed it to him. And besides, she was going to lose her mind.

They were packing up that evening. Emily had already left for her shift in the Good Food Store and Liam was playing quietly with his toy excavator in the newly dug herbaceous border. Her golden opportunity. Except it didn't feel golden. She approached Uri as he was putting away his tools meticulously in the little makeshift shed.

"I have something to tell you."

"I already know. And yes, you should have told me."

This unbalanced her. Were they talking about the same thing? She didn't want to put her foot in it.

"You mean . . . ?"

"Mrs. Prendergast's plan to sell the land, yes."

Eva felt her whole being deflate.

"I'm sorry. You're right. I should have told you sooner. All the work you've done over the last couple of weeks."

Uri stared at her for a few moments.

"It's all right."

She stared back at him.

"But I more or less lied to you. What if it's all concreted over by this time next year? All this work will be for nothing."

Uri observed her closely, his body still, his face composed.

"But it might not be."

He picked up his bag and started walking toward the gate. He turned just before he reached it.

"You still should have told me."

THEY AGREED TO tell Emily together the very next day.

The girl was hunkered down in the earth, humming softly to herself as she worked it with her trowel. She jumped when Eva spoke, as if being caught doing something she shouldn't.

"Emily. Can we have a word?"

"Of course." The girl looked wary, as was her custom.

"We—I—have something to tell you. It's about the garden. Something I should have told you a while ago."

Emily looked alarmed.

"You know how I told you before that Mrs. P said we could have the garden and do whatever we liked with it?"

Emily nodded.

"And you know how she still actually owns it?"

"Yes."

"Well, she's decided to sell."

"Sell . . . I don't understand."

"She's selling it for development."

"When?"

"As soon as she can get a buyer."

"What? But that could be tomorrow. Today even."

"Hopefully it'll take longer than that. Maybe even a year or more."

Eva looked on in dismay as the younger woman's face crumpled right in front of her. Emily hid her elfin features with her delicate little hands and started to sob.

Uri and Eva exchanged a look.

Eva reached over and tried to hold on to her wrist, but Emily jerked away, mumbling something incoherent.

"What?"

"How could you?"

Eva thought she had never been on the receiving end of such a look, such an expression of hurt and betrayal. Maybe once. Her face burned with the intensity of her shame.

"I'm sorry," she whispered. "Really sorry."

Uri approached Emily and put an arm around the girl's heaving shoulders. To Eva's chagrin, she didn't try to shake him off. He uttered strange, foreign-sounding soothing noises, reminding Eva that he was not from these shores any more than she was. Emily kept repeating the same thing over and over. Eva strained to hear. Something about how they couldn't take this away from her too. Finally the heaving and the sobbing came to an end. But Eva was not entirely off the hook.

"How long have you known?"

"Three weeks."

"Three weeks! And you never said anything!"

"I'm sorry."

"And you? How long have you known?" She looked imploringly at Uri, eyes widened, willing him not to have betrayed her too.

"I found out yesterday."

Emily nodded, clearly relieved that she had nothing to forgive him for. She swiped at her eyes with her knuckles.

"What are we going to do?"

"We're going to continue to do what we've been doing," said Uri.

"But Mrs. Prendergast . . ."

"Don't you worry about Mrs. Prendergast."

"Why?" Eva was suddenly interested. "What are you going to do?"

"I'm not going to do anything. I won't have to. I'll let the garden do it."

"Do what?"

"Work its magic."

The two women stared at Uri. He laughed.

"Don't you know that gardens are magic?" He squeezed Emily's shoulder. "Especially this one."

THE SCENE WITH Emily had really floored Eva. She had known all along how much the garden meant to her personally. But she'd had no idea how much it meant to Emily. How it seemed to go to her very core. Eva had never so much as had a semipersonal conversation with the girl, sensing her very real desire to be left alone. Or was this just fear on her part? *If she tells me her stuff, I'll have to tell her mine.* Because when she thought about it, it really wasn't all that normal. A pretty, twenty-year-old girl practically dedicating her life to a garden. Why wasn't she out boozing and sleeping around? It was okay for Eva. She was past it—not to mention a single parent. No one could expect her to have a life. But Emily? No. It just wasn't normal. Eva took a silent vow to keep more of an eye on her from now on. She couldn't believe it really. Two people as insanely obsessed with this garden as she was. This lost cause, underdog of a garden. Perhaps they were all as mad as each other. She felt light as helium for a few days, no longer weighed down by the burden of her guilty secret. But this feeling was to be short-lived.

14

$\mathscr{E}$MILY DID GO home to her parents, on the weekend that Joe abandoned her.

But she didn't tell them about the baby. How could she? They looked at her with such pride. Their eldest daughter, the first in the family to go to college.

She wore baggy sweaters, not knowing how long she'd be able to get away with it. She had her meals prepared for her, got her laundry done, and let her mother wrap her love around her like an old patchwork quilt. She'd need it to sustain her through the coming weeks.

She took to waiting for Joe outside his lectures. He never showed up. She saw Niall noticing her. At the end of day three, he came over to her.

"If you're waiting for Joe, don't bother."

"I'm entitled to wait for him if I want to."

"No. You're not getting me. He's not here."

"Where is he then?"

"London."

"What?"

"He left college. He won't be coming back."

"What? But what about his exams . . . his . . . everything?"

"He might repeat third year. But he won't be back anytime soon."

Niall was accusing. Aggressive as he addressed the little

trollop who'd ruined Joe's life. He turned and walked back to his friends. Joe's friends. Did they all know?

SHE WAS HALFWAY through her pregnancy now. Horror had given way to despondency. She went about her business, attending lectures, handing in essays, going home at weekends. It was characteristic of Emily that her bump was small and neat. It was still barely perceptible and easily hidden beneath loose-fitting clothes. Sometimes she felt as if she was holding it in by a sheer act of will. Her mother commented once that she was very quiet. Emily brushed away her concerns and the matter was dropped. She *was* quiet. That's what happened when you had a lot of thinking to do. But she reckoned she'd decided now. Arrived at a solution that would suit all parties concerned.

SHE'D DONE HER research. She was confident that she'd selected the most reputable agency.

"You must be Emily."

The woman was holding out her hand. She was in her thirties. Smiley. Glasses and curly hair. Emily shook her hand and followed her into her small office. It was warm and feminine, designed to inspire security and confidence.

ONCE SHE'D MADE the decision, it wasn't so bad. In a funny way, she was able to pretend it wasn't happening. She began to socialize a little more. She studied for her exams and sat them. It was actually working out quite well. She'd elected to stay in Dublin for the summer and work—but obviously not in her aunt's shop. Her parents would be disappointed that she wasn't spending the time at home. But not half as disappointed as they'd be if they knew the truth. The baby was due at the end of September, so she could start the new college year as if nothing had happened. Then, next summer she could go to the States, as she'd originally planned for this year. Visit Montana. Get her degree. Do an MA. Maybe even a Phd. Professor Emily Harte! Yes. Once again, her life was going perfectly to plan.

EMILY HAD HER first contraction in the supermarket, meandering down the aisles, her trolley full of ice cream. Braxton Hicks? Another one. Maybe not. She abandoned her trolley beside the cereals and walked rapidly out of the sliding doors. She didn't think of it again until she was well into labor. Had all the ice cream melted? She stood outside and breathed in great big gulps of Dublin city air. Was this it? Or not. She still had a week to go. How could she tell if her labor was really starting? If only she had someone to ask. The truth was, she did have someone to ask. Plenty of people in fact. She'd just chosen not to. Her friends back home. She'd deliberately kept her distance since she'd found out about her pregancy. They thought she'd gone all snobby on them since moving to Dublin. Her classmates in college—she wasn't even sure if she could call them friends. And that, she supposed, was why she hadn't told them, absenting herself from college life toward the end, only attending vital lectures and tutorials, perpetually wrapped up in her multilayers. If anyone suspected, nobody said. Her mother. God, no. Her aunts and cousins—they'd just tell her mother. Her sisters were too young and silly. No. The only people she spoke to about her pregnancy and the increasingly abstract concept of the baby were her doctor and the lady at the adoption agency. Emily had always been self-contained. But in this she was taking her self-containment to a whole new level.

The truth was, she didn't want anyone talking her out of it.

So it was, several contractions later, that she rang the hospital. The midwife on duty told her that, yes, they were probably contractions, but as it was only her first baby, she most likely had hours, if not days, to go, and that she'd be better off staying at home and getting hubby to run her a bath and make her a nice cup of tea. She stuck it out for another half hour before heading to the hospital. Let's get this over with.

She liked the midwife who first examined her. Or maybe she just wanted to like her, so desperate just to latch on to anyone. And this woman was gentle. Soft, warm hands; quiet, measured movements.

"You're only one centimeter," the gentle lady was saying. "You may as well go home. It'll be a long time yet."

Please don't send me home.

The gentle one was leaving the room.

"Please don't send me home."

The midwife came back and leaned over the bed, her arm clasping Emily's forearm.

"Are you on your own?"

Emily nodded, somehow unable to speak.

"Would you like me to call someone for you?"

Emily shook her head and bit her lip.

"Your mother? A sister? A friend?"

"I'm having the baby adopted. Nobody can know."

The midwife squeezed Emily's arm.

"You can stay here as long as you like. You might get moved around a bit though. You try and get some rest and I'll be back to check on you in a while."

Emily sagged back into the bed. Thank you, God.

And that was the last thing she felt inclined to thank God for for the next twenty-four hours.

The pain was bad enough.

The terror of the unknown worse.

But the sense of aloneness.

That's what really unhinged her.

The gentle midwife was with her for the first half, holding her hand, massaging her shoulders and feet. The sense of betrayal when this woman's shift ended was enormous. But she had to pick up her children. She promised she'd call in the next day.

"Would you not give your mam a call?" was the last thing she said.

Emily shook her head, tears gathering momentum at the corners of her eyes. She couldn't. Not now. Not like this.

And as for Joe . . .

In her weaker moments, those moments of agony toward the end, her want of him was ferocious. As if he'd only just left her and the last few months of her hardening her heart against him had never happened.

Her new midwife was briskly efficient and lacked the bedside manner of her colleague. In a funny way, this was an unexpected relief. Emily stopped being tearful and focused on the matter at hand. Let's get this done. And the woman was there when it was crucial: Push. Pant. Rest. Push again. Until at half past three that morning, Emily's baby was born. Six pounds, eleven ounces. They laid the baby on Emily's chest, inside her nightdress, where it lay snuffling and covered in sticky stuff. It only started to cry when they took it away to clean it up. Later, when they were both sanitized and wheeled back out to the ward, Emily eased herself into a sitting position and reached for her mobile. She rang the last—the only—number she had for Joe Devine. The mobile number that had remained resolutely unanswered for a whole week after he'd left, before she'd given up trying to contact him. It went straight to voice mail. Her throat tightened at the sound of his voice. She waited for the beep: "I thought you should know. You have a baby daughter."

Then she switched off her phone, lay down on her side, and stared at her baby.

She looked just like her father.

LATER THAT MORNING, Emily's daughter lay cradled in her arms as she fed her from a bottle. She was wrapped in a pink blanket that some nurse had given her and dressed in a borrowed baby onesie and nappy. Emily hadn't thought of these things. She hadn't packed a bag. Why should she when it wasn't really happening? It had been over an hour since she'd rung the woman from the adoption agency. The foster family should be here by now. She heard footsteps coming toward her bed and saw a shadow behind her curtain—she hadn't wanted to talk to the other mothers. It was the gentle one. She approached Emily's bed cautiously.

"They're here."

Emily nodded.

"Do you want to meet them?"

She shook her head.

"I'll just give you a minute." She went back out and Emily could hear her footsteps receding down the corridor.

For a long time she looked down at the baby, who had finished feeding and was now sleeping, her tiny face puckered and closed. Emily brushed her daughter's cheek with the back of her finger. Then she bent low and breathed in the scent emanating from her head. Then, as she heard footsteps approaching, she stuck out the tip of her tongue and licked her baby's temple. The midwife emerged.

"Ready?"

The woman approached and held out her arms. Emily handed her the baby, who squealed in protest at being taken away from the habitual warmth and scent.

Then they were gone. Footsteps receding. Voices. Gone.

Emily sat there for a while. Then she lay down and faced the wall.

Her breasts ached, her stitches stung.

And in her heart there was a hollow place where the baby used to be.

15

THE NEXT TIME Mrs. Prendergast emerged from her little wooden door, she was accompanied, not by a tray or a trowel, but by a tall, dark-haired man in his thirties. He had a bearing so princely and a carriage so erect that he could be none other than Mrs. Prendergast's son. Mother and son stood talking together for some minutes, just inside the door. The other three exchanged brief glances and pretended not to notice. The two eventually wandered over to Eva, Mrs. Prendergast a few paces ahead. Eva laid down her hoe and rubbed the worst of the muck off her hands and onto the arse of her jeans. Nobody would be looking there anyway. She was touched by the pride and the pleasure in the old woman's eyes as she introduced her son.

"Eva Madigan. I'd like to introduce you to my son, Lance Prendergast."

Lance stepped forward and held out his hand.

"Pleased to meet you, Eva."

Eva shook his hand, no doubt leaving behind an earthy residue, which he had the good manners to ignore. His handshake was cool and firm, his smile unwavering, and his eye contact excellent. Shit. He was even quite good looking, if you liked that kind of thing. He was dressed, very snazzily, in a dark suit, and looked very much the businessman.

"My mother told me all about the Trojan work you people were doing on the garden, so I decided I'd have to come along and see for myself."

"Oh. Well. That's . . . kind of you."

"What is it you're doing here, exactly?" He pointed to the patch of ground beneath them.

"Potatoes. I'm planting seed potatoes. Should have a crop sometime in July."

He was looking hard at her, as if trying to evaluate something. Then he smiled.

"Excellent. My mother tells me she's been promised all the fresh fruit and veg she can eat."

"That's right."

He smiled at his mother and she beamed back at him. Eva was quite taken aback. She had never seen Mrs. Prendergast beam before, didn't think she had it in her. Even Liam, the most regular beneficiary of the the older woman's smiles, never got that full-wattage treatment. Would she be like that when Liam was older? Who was she kidding. She was like that now.

"I'll be looking forward to some spectacular dinners this summer, then," Lance was saying. They all laughed politely.

"There's someone else I must introduce you to. Mr. Rosenberg!"

Uri didn't hear her call, so Mrs. Prendergast commenced walking toward the far corner of the garden where he was laboring. Leaving Eva and Lance alone. He drew a step closer, so that he was standing squarely in front of her, quite intimidating in all his tallness and smartness.

"What the hell do you think you're doing?" he said.

"I beg your pardon?"

Eva genuinely thought she'd misheard. He was still smiling at her, but the words coming out of his mouth didn't match his expression. Until she looked properly into his eyes.

"I said, what the hell do you think you're doing? Taking advantage of a helpless old lady like this?"

What? Who? Helpless old lady? Eva almost laughed when she realized he was referring to Mrs. Prendergast.

"I can assure you that I'm doing no such thing."

"You know full well that my mother has all but agreed to sell this land. I'll not have a bunch of"— he searched for an appropriate phrase—"hippie misfits mess it all up for her."

She nearly laughed again. "Hippie misfits." Was that the best he could come up with? But she didn't quite laugh. Because there was something in his eyes that was really quite horrible. He continued: "We—she—is set to make a lot of money out of this transaction. I'm sure you wouldn't like to stand in the way of a comfortable retirement for my mother."

Or a whopping great inheritance for you, thought Eva.

"Of course not," she said, forcing herself to maintain eye contact.

"Lance. Come and meet Mr. Rosenberg."

One more warning look and Lance turned away from her, baring his smile at Uri instead. She heard Uri admiring his suit.

The son wanted the garden sold.

The mother adored the son.

They were toast.

LATER, AFTER HE'D gone, Mrs. Prendergast came back out in her gardening gear. She stood beside Eva as she casually pulled on her gloves.

"My goodness. That weed really does get everywhere, doesn't it."

Eva straightened up and looked at her suspiciously. Was she actually making conversation?

"You know, he's single," said Mrs. Prendergast.

"Who?"

"My son. Lance. He's single."

"Oh. Really."

"Yes. He's handsome, isn't he?" She had a faraway look in her eyes.

"Um, yes. Very handsome."

Mrs. Prendergast smiled, then she looked at Eva critically.

"You know, dear, you might be quite pretty if you made a little effort."

And off she went to tend to her roses.

16

$\mathcal{E}$VA LOOKED DOWN into her palm. She was holding a handful of possibilities. Myriad microcosms of worlds. Worlds that she could so easily let slip through her fingers. In other words—tomato seeds. Dozens of them. Each one capable of great things. But not one of them capable of being anything other than a tomato plant. Not a carrot nor a zucchini nor a cauliflower. Just as she was incapable of growing into anything other than Eva Madigan.

It was early in the morning. Ridiculously so. Not even half past seven. She'd come to the garden because Liam was on a sleepover, his first. With a little boy he'd become friendly with at the nursery school. The boy's mother had offered to take them both to the school that morning. Such a sensible idea. It took every ounce of willpower that Eva had not to go over to their house right now and hug the very breath out of her son. She hadn't been able to sleep without his knees sticking into the small of her back. And now, with no lecture to give until eleven, and no little boy to prepare for the day, she felt utterly redundant. Which was why she had come to the garden. At least here, she could do something useful. Plant things. Things that would grow into food. Which no one could deny was a useful commodity.

She knelt down on the earth that springtime morning and slowly, painstakingly, following to the letter the instructions on the back of the seed packet, sowed her tomatoes. In cute little seed trays for the time being. It was still too early to trust them to the soil. Then she sowed lettuce. She imagined the rows and rows of succulent green plants they were to become, like something out of a Peter Rabbit book.

She wasn't alone. A robin was perched in the uppermost branches of the tallest, oldest, most gnarled apple tree, singing his beautiful song. Eva felt blessed. As if the song was for her ears alone. A private recital.

"Won't you promise to eat any slugs that come near my lettuces?" she said to him. He continued to trill away. She smiled and returned to her task.

She must have spent a full hour, sifting through the soil with a thing like a giant sieve, discarding stones and old roots, her hair dusted with misty rain, overcoming her fear of spiders. When a thought came unbidden: all she needed was a man to come up behind her and kiss the nape of her neck, where the soft downiness of her hair met the cool creaminess of her skin. The thought startled her and she shivered. She swung around and looked back over her shoulder, as if to surprise somebody.

"Michael?"

But there was no one there. Nothing, in fact, but the brute force of her loneliness.

URI ARRIVED AT nine o'clock as expected. He was semiretired now and dedicated most of his mornings to the garden. But this morning he wasn't alone. He had with him a younger man, mid to late thirties judging by the web of lines around his eyes.

"This is Seth. My son. Seth, this is Eva."

"Hi."

"Hello."

"Seth is a gardener. He'd like to help."

"Really?"

A gardener! Uri had never said. He'd mentioned his sons all right. He had two of them. But a gardener . . .

"That's if it's okay with you."

"Of course it's okay," Eva said quickly. "Absolutely. I mean, when can you start?"

He smiled and held his hands out from his body.

"Right now?"

She never would have pegged him for Uri's son. He must favor his mother, she thought. He was taller than his father but by no means gigantic. His hair was brown, graying at the temples. She couldn't tell what color his eyes were because they were screwed up against the sun. His skin had the weatherbeaten texture of someone who spent a lot of time outdoors and his arms were freckled, like speckled birds' eggs.

"You do know that the future of the garden is looking very grim, don't you?"

"I know. But I don't see any fat ladies singing just yet."

"No." She laughed. Funny.

"So, Eva. What can I do for you?"

The answers crowded inside her head.

"Well. No one's really gone near the pond yet. You could give that a go."

"Right you are."

She watched him go, his steps jaunty, as if he had a spring in him.

She approached Uri.

"Why didn't you tell me your son was a gardener?"

"He's had a rough time of it lately. I wanted to wait. I didn't want to put him under any pressure."

They both watched Seth work, straight into it already, his movements fluid, very unlike how Eva imagined her own movements to be, awkward and stuttering. Amateurish. He was going to be such a help.

And he might even have a few spare plants knocking around.

LATER THAT NIGHT, after Liam had gone to bed and before she climbed into a well-deserved bath, Eva did something she hadn't done for a while. She looked at herself in the mirror. Really, *really* looked. Peered. Examined. Things had certainly changed since the last time she'd looked and she got quite a shock. Her hair, with its silver roots and faded, colored ends, resembled an ice pop with part of the juice sucked out of it. God, she'd really let herself go. She'd never thought that her appearance mattered that much to her, but she had to admit that now, staring at her haggard reflection, at this woman old beyond her thirty-five years, she did care. What had happened to that laid-back, smiling person Michael had fallen in love with and married? She could remember a time when the only thing that ever got her down was gravity. Now look at her. All dragged down and disheveled. It was time to drag herself back up again. She owed it to Liam and she owed it to herself.

17

*T*HE FOR SALE sign was up now. They tried their hardest to ignore it, but it still cast it's long shadow over the garden. March came in like a lion and went out like a lamb. The gales blew the sign down. They all cheered. The onset of April's showers cooled them, enchanted them, soaked them to the skin.

Liam had his own patch now. Sunflowers. He watered them diligently every day with his Winnie the Pooh watering can. The little boy was in a state of high excitement over the introduction of fish into the pond. Seth had brought along some minnows one Saturday morning, allowing them to rest for a while, their plastic bags floating as they became acclimatized to their new home. And then releasing them. Liam particularly loved this part. Seth had brought another minnow with him that morning—his four-year-old daughter, Kathy. She was two months younger than Liam and one head taller. And, Eva discovered as she lifted the little girl up into the arms of the apple tree, at least a ton heavier.

"I thought they could play together," said Seth. "Keep each other out of trouble. You don't mind, do you?"

"Why should I mind?"

"You just seem surprised."

"Only because I didn't know you had a daughter."

"Well, I do."

"So I see."

She smiled at him and he averted his eyes.

"Are you using those shears, Eva?"

"No. Work away."

"I like your hair," said Emily, wandering by with a wheel-barrow.

"Thanks."

They smiled at each other. They'd been having the odd conversation of late, mainly about books, and Eva felt she was making some progress. Emily still wore her sadness like a cloak, but sometimes you could find an opening. She watched her trundle the wheelbarrow along the path. Then her heart caught.

"Liam!"

She began to run.

"Liam!" she screamed. "Get down from there now."

Her screams caused the others to stop what they were doing and stare. First at her and then at what she was running toward: Liam—hanging upside down from his knees from the branch of an apple tree. She reached him.

"Jesus Christ, come here!"

She dragged him off the branch, turned him the right way up, and hugged him to her.

"You're all right, you're all right," she muttered over and over, kissing the top of his head repeatedly.

"Ow. You're hurting me," said Liam, squirming to be let go.

She reluctantly released him to the ground.

"What's wrong? What happened?"

"We were only pretending to be bats, Daddy," said Kathy, giving Eva a resentful look.

They were all looking at her now. All gathered around and staring. She realized with embarrassment that she'd overreacted.

"Sorry, everyone, it was nothing. I just got a fright, that's all. I thought he was going to fall."

People murmered and returned to their tasks. Eva mentally kicked herself. Just when she thought she was getting back to normal, something like this happened to remind her that she was still mad after all.

THAT SATURDAY AFTERNOON was magical. For a start, the sun shone magnificently. It was the first day they'd been able to wear T-shirts—apart from Mrs. Prendergast, who wore a white, embroidered, short-sleeved blouse. The robin had found a mate and they'd decided to build a nest. When they didn't have twigs in their mouths, they both sang their heads off. Seth had introduced some frog spawn into the pond earlier that spring and the water was alive with tadpoles. Liam and Kathy were forever capturing them in jam jars and staring at them for hours on end, willing their little froggy legs to appear. Harriet, the fat old retriever, snuffled around, wagging her geriatric tail before eventually flopping down in a panting heap on the newly planted herbs. The old dog farted to her heart's content, and nobody minded because she just added to the aromas.

They drew quite a crowd some days. Passersby staring in at the gate, pausing in their rush-hour rush. Occasionally, somebody would call one of them over and ask them what they were doing.

Defying logic?

They had a definite plan now and the planting was gathering momentum. Each gardener had his or her own tasks and they physically and mentally divided the garden into four quadrants: the kitchen garden, the rose garden, the orchard, and what they called the secret garden, because Emily wouldn't tell them what she was doing in her section. At first, Eva thought it was a cottage garden, but there seemed to be more to it than that. Seth minded the pond and was, as he said himself, general dogsbody. He was also in charge of wheelbarrow rides. Liam and Kathy would get into the wheelbarrow and he would zoom up and down the paths, making race-car noises, swerving just in time to avoid trees and pretending to tip them into the pond. The children would giggle wildly. It made Eva's heart ache to see the neediness in her son for a bit of male attention. The longing in him.

Mrs. Prendergast was less impressed with the great wheelbarrow races.

"*Must* you make that infernal racket?"

"Why don't you hop in yourself Mrs. P. Give it a lash."

Seth tilted the barrow toward her. She gave him a withering look. She didn't have much time for him. Eva imagined she thought him uncouth.

Eva was mainly in charge of the kitchen garden, although "in charge" wasn't the right way to put it. The arrangement was more relaxed than that. But she spent more time there than anyone else. There was something about growing food that appealed to the practical side of her nature. What could be more fundamental to life? More important? She liked to feel she wasn't squandering her time. Of course, she was making mistakes constantly, not having done it before. Take the tomatoes. She was only transplanting them from the seed trays to their little pots now. She knew she'd left it too late and that they'd be lagging behind. But she pressed the compost down with her bare finges and sprayed their roots.

"Grow, little ones, grow," she whispered, then looked around furtively to make sure that no one had heard her. She had made a start on the green beans too, erecting cane pyramids, anticipating their ascent, their little orange flowers. Kneeling in the muck, she felt a ridiculous level of contentment. She didn't hear Emily come up behind her.

"I'm ready now."

Eva jumped.

"Emily. I didn't see you there."

Had Emily heard her talking to the plants?

"I'm ready to tell you now."

"What. You mean . . . ?"

"To tell you what I've been planning for my part of the garden."

"Oh." Eva scrambled to her feet. "Let's go."

"I didn't want to say anything before, because I wasn't sure how it was going to work out."

"That's okay."

She searched the girl's face. She'd never seen her so animated.

"Anyway. What I was hoping to do was a sensory garden." She was looking at Eva as if seeking approval.

"Go on."

"Imagine a garden that was a total feast for the senses. You enter here. Honeysuckle on one side. Jasmine on the other. I was going to ask Seth to help me put up a pergola."

She looked at Eva, who nodded at her to continue.

"We could put a little swing seat underneath. A person could sit there and just absorb the fragrance. Then I want to put a pebble path here. You walk along barefoot first thing in the morning. It's a reflexology thing. At the end of the path is a bubble fountain. The idea of the soothing sound of water. I'm going to hang wind chimes from the branch of that tree and I'll plant some tall, ornamental grasses to the right. The breeze will rustle through them. Color. I want lots of color."

Eva said nothing as she watched Emily's hand movements become more expansive.

"A green area—like the green room in a theater. Lots of lovely, relaxing foilage. Then pink—to relieve tension—a blossoming cherry, I think. Crimsons and golds and coppers to raise energy levels. Think daffodils and tulips in the spring. Wallflowers! Maybe Liam could plant me a row of sunflowers. And then we have to have some herbs." Her voice was getting faster and faster.

"Lavender lining that pathway—French lavender—it has a better fragrance than English. No offense."

"None taken."

"And I want to place troughs of herbs on either side of a bench right—there."

Emily looked at Eva expectantly.

"Is that it?"

"Oh, and I want to put a row of fairy lights around the pergola beams, and hang colored lanterns from the branches of the bushes. Oh, and plant a chamomile lawn. That's it. For now. What do you think?"

"What do I think?"

"Yes."

"I think you're either a madwoman or a genius."

She saw the doubt cloud the girl's features and amended her words quickly.

"What I really mean is, I think you're inspired. A true artist."

"Really?" The girl's cheeks bloomed.

"Yes, really. Only, Emily. You know as well as I do that the garden probably isn't—"

"Don't say it!" Emily held up her hand as if warding off a curse, startling Eva with the ferocity of her emotion. "I can't bare to think about it. I think the garden deserves"—she searched around for the right words—"one last hurrah. And we're the ones that have to give it to her."

Eva liked that, "last hurrah." Yes, why not. Why the hell not.

"Okay, Emily. Do your worst."

SETH WAS PUTTING up an archway for Mrs. Prendergast's roses, the erection of which she was supervising with much derision.

"Not like that. Look at it, for God's sake. It's all lop-sided."

"Do you want to have a go?"

"Don't be ridiculous. Not with my arthritis."

"Well, would you mind letting me get on with it then?"

"What? And let you arse it up?"

"Hi there." Eva joined them.

"Great. Another woman to tell me what to do." But when he looked at her, his eyes were smiling. She couldn't get a handle on his eyes. The color, that is. They seemed to change in accordance with the landscape. Today, they mirrored the sky in their blueness.

Mrs. Prendergast sighed a theatrical sigh. "I could murder a cup of tea."

"Would you like me to . . ." began Eva.

"No thank you, dear." Mrs. Prendergast still didn't allow any of them within the confines of her home. They had to use the toilet in the Good Food Store. Apart from Liam and Kathy, who were allowed to go in the nettles, tinkling and squatting accordingly.

"I suppose *you* want a mug of that revolting coffee," she addressed Seth.

"That'd be marvelous, Mrs. P."

"Stop calling me that."

"Well, if you insist on not telling me your name . . ."

Mrs. Prendergast snorted with disgust as she walked off to prepare their elevenses.

"She loves me really." Seth grinned.

"You know, I'm beginning to think she does. She just hasn't realized it yet."

He recommended hammering the archway into place, Eva handing him nails at intervals, working in silence. She was reminded again of how much she enjoyed his presence in the garden. Just to watch the way he carried out his tasks. To be with him. After a time, she sat on the ground, her arms wrapped around her knees. She desperately wanted to know more about him.

"So. Kathy seems to be a very well-adjusted little girl."

Seth looked up instinctively from what he was doing and across at his daughter, who appeared to be teaching Liam how to make daisy chains. She took the lead in most of their games.

"She's great."

"She's a credit to you and her mother."

He shrugged. "Thanks. She's a tough little thing really. She's been through a lot."

"Like what?"

Eva instantly wished she could take it back. She didn't know how far she could push it. Seth seemed such an odd mixture of confidence and reticence. He was standing upright now, his hands on his hips. He looked at Eva as if working out whether he could trust her or not.

"You know her mother and I are divorced."

"No, I didn't know. I thought . . . well, no, I didn't know."

There was a silence. Seth appeared to be examining the mud on his boots.

"Does she see her mother?"

"Oh yes. God yes. She spends part of the week with her mother and part of it with me. It's just a bit confusing for Kathy at the moment."

"Is there another . . . ?"

"Tea, everybody!"

18

*I*T WAS QUITE a burden. Being an Irish teenager named Seth Rosenberg in the 1980s. He kind of stood out
among the Seamus Brennans and the Paddy Maloneys. But his
bald penis gave him quite a rarity value during his twenties.

Seth liked girls and they liked him. He didn't know why this
should be the case, but he was glad that it was. He had been ac-
cused more than once of having "a way with the laydeez." He
didn't know about that. All Seth knew was that he was himself
and that seemed to work. His sense of security came from several sources. Not least his parents' deep, unshakeable, unmov-
able, unstoppable love for him. His mother loved her two boys
with every ounce of her considerable being. Although Seth
knew that it was he she loved best. Or maybe his brother felt
this way too. It was a thought that had only occurred to him of
late. Just as many other previously unthought-of thoughts had
only just occurred to him. He supposed that's what happened to
you when your world got turned on its head.

His relationship with his father had been more turbulent.
Whereas Seth's mother was pure indulgence, Uri's love was
borne out of discipline, a determination that his sons would
make something of themselves. Although, to Uri's credit, as it
became obvious that Seth would never travel down an aca-
demic route, he had the wisdom to let him go his own way,
serving his apprenticeship as a gardener and eventually build-

ing up his own successful landscaping business. Growing up, Seth had found his father's dark moods oppressive, the aura of blackness that surrounded the man at times. Seth had to get away from him. Being not in the least bit broody or introspective himself, he couldn't handle the trait in another.

And he didn't want to think about it.

But as he'd gotten older, he'd deepened in understanding. Just as his impatience toward his father's faith had matured into respect.

So. His parents' love. His innate likability. His popularity with women. The knowledge since a young boy that he'd wanted to work with plants. The successful realization of his ambitions. It could be said that Seth had led a charmed life. Of course he had his bad days. But really, they were few and far between.

Seth was twenty-nine years old when he met Megan. He fell hard. Harder than he would have thought possible. He'd assumed he'd been in love before. But he realized now that he'd only ever been in like. He'd said "I love you" several times. He hadn't really meant to lie to those women, but the moment he met Megan, he knew he'd been lying all along. She was just pure, golden, unadulterated gorgeousness. She bowled him over.

The night they met had seemed inauspicious enough. In the pub, with the lads. She was the friend of a friend of somebody's girlfriend. The link tenuous, but just enough to merit an introduction. He'd wanted to say something glib. Something to make her laugh. But he'd just sat there like a fool. She had been kind, bailing him out, asking him questions about himself until he'd regained the power of speech. But he'd never really recovered. Not from Megan.

They got married almost two years to the day from their first meeting. As he watched her walk up the aisle toward him, he felt as if his heart was going to explode out of his chest.

Had it all been a lie?

"It's so nice living with your best friend," said Megan.

She was sitting up in bed, propped against Seth's pillow and her own. They weren't long back from their honeymoon, one of their first weekends of married life. She was watching Seth as he shaved in the connecting bathroom. Seth stopped scraping the white foam off his jawline with his new razor and gazed back at the reflection in the mirror. She looked so incredibly contented. He padded back out to her, fresh from his shower, white towel draped around his waist, and stood over her body, dripping foam.

"Am I your best friend?" he said.

"You know you are."

She patted the space beside her and he sat down on the edge of the bed.

"You're my best friend too and I love living with you," he said.

She smiled at him and he admired her adorable dimples.

"God, you're gorgeous," he said, reaching up to stroke her cheek. She leaned her face down into his palm. He still couldn't believe at times that he was permitted to touch her. But he was. He even had the papers to prove it now. He wiped the rest of his shaving foam off with the edge of his towel and leaned in to kiss her mouth. Softly at first. Then he cupped her face with his hands and kissed her deeply. He opened his eyes just in time to see her look of panic. And even if he hadn't seen it, he'd felt her pull back.

"What's wrong?"

"Nothing."

"Don't you want . . . ?"

"It's not that. It's just that I've planned a special breakfast for you."

"We can have it later."

"I'm starving right now."

She flung back the covers and sprang out of bed. He watched as she put on her dressing gown and drew the belt tight around her waist.

"I'm making bacon and scrambled eggs. Your favorite. And freshly squeezed orange juice."

"Sounds great."

She kissed his cheek and he listened to her dainty clop-cloppings down the stairs. She was right. They were best friends.

Except he already had a best friend. His name was Barry and he'd known him since he was six. But he didn't want to have sex with Barry. He wanted to have sex with his wife. But he was beginning to form the distinct impression that his wife didn't want to have sex with him.

They'd abstained before marriage. He felt stupid admitting it now. It had been her idea.

"Imagine how special our wedding night will be."

And he had gone along with it. Because he would have done anything for Megan. To keep her happy. To keep her. But the wedding night had come and gone and he had yet to see a marked change in her enthusiasm. Sure, they did it sometimes, but he always had to initiate proceedings, and hard as he tried, he could never shake the feeling that she was just letting him do things to her. It didn't really feel as if they were doing it together. Making love. He would have laughed once at this phrase, but now he understood. He loved her. She loved him. What was the problem? A couple of months into their marriage, he'd decided to broach the subject. They were in bed again. Seth was lying on his side, propped up on his elbow, his head resting in his palm. Megan was sitting bolt upright as he ran his fingers delicately up and down her forearm. She looked almost virginal, sitting there in her white nightgown.

"Is there something wrong, Meg?"

She looked surprised.

"Wrong? No. What do you mean?"

"I mean you never seem to want to have sex."

He tried carefully to read the expression on her face. Uncomfortable maybe. As if she wished he wouldn't bring up such a distasteful matter.

"We do have sex."

"Yes, but not very often. And I feel like I'm—I don't know—forcing you or something."

"That's just silly."

"Maybe it is. But that's the way I feel."

Neither of them said anything for a while. He noticed she'd pulled her arm away.

"Don't you fancy me anymore?" He hated himself for saying it, feeling pathetic and unmanly. Megan rolled her eyes.

"Of course I do." She sounded almost angry. Her tone, her body language—all screamed "go away."

"Did something happen to you?"

"What do you mean?"

"I mean, when you were younger. Did something traumatic happen to you? Did someone hurt you . . . ?"

"Oh, don't be so ridiculous, Seth. You're blowing this way out of proportion."

Was he? He couldn't tell.

"Am I?"

"Yes, you are. Look. As a man, your libido is stronger than mine, that's all. You just naturally want it more than I do. It's perfectly normal. Probably all husbands feel the same way."

Did they? Perhaps. He allowed himself to be soothed, wanting to believe it, although a small niggle of doubt still remained.

"Now come here and give me a cuddle." She pulled him close to her so that his head was resting on her chest. More cuddling.

"Do you realize how lucky we are, Seth, to have each other? I don't know any other girls who get on so well with their husbands or boyfriends. I mean, we do everything together."

It was true. They did. Except . . .

"And there's no one else I'd rather spend my time with."

"Me neither."

It was true. There wasn't.

"So let's just appreciate what we have." She stroked his hair.

She was right as usual. Seth lay there and did his best to feel appreciative. Although mostly he just felt horny.

THEN SOMETHING HAPPENED the following month that changed things drastically. They were eating out one night, on the occasion of Megan's twenty-ninth birthday. Seth had ordered champagne. He watched his wife as she sparkled across the table from him. They were waiting for their desserts to arrive when she covered his hand with her own. He felt a surge of happiness at her touch.

"Seth," she said. "I've been doing a lot of thinking lately."

"Oh yeah? About what?"

"Well, I think it might be time," she paused to take a sip of champagne, "for us to try for a baby."

"What?" Seth was genuinely gobsmacked. He hadn't seen this one coming.

"A baby, Seth. You heard what I said. What do you think?" Her voice was gentle but her eyes were full of concern.

"Jesus, Megan. Of all the things to spring on a person."

"You can't be that surprised. We have talked about this before. You said you wanted kids."

"I do, I do. Someday. Not right away."

"Why not?"

"We're barely married. We still have loads of things to get for the house . . ."

"You think furniture is more important than family?"

"No! No, of course not. I didn't mean that. I just mean—what's the big rush all of a sudden?"

"It's not a 'big rush.'"

He was pissing her off. He could tell.

"I suppose it's because I'm twenty-nine now. It's made me think. I can see thirty looming. The younger a woman has her babies, the better it is for her physically."

Babies! They had gone from baby to babies in under a minute. How many sprogs did the woman want?

"I just don't see the point in waiting," she continued. "We have each other, we're married, we have our house. We're both bringing in an income."

He looked at her. She was making perfect sense of course. As usual. He smiled at her and covered her small, perfect, feminine hand with his big calloused one.

"I suppose I was hoping to keep you to myself for as long as possible."

Megan smiled, sensing victory. "You'll still have me," she said. "I'm not going anywhere."

"When did you want to start trying?"

"We could start tonight if you like."

That sealed the deal.

FROM THAT NIGHT on, everything became wonderful and rose colored in Seth's world. The one thing that had been missing from his life he now had. The sight of his wife bouncing up and down on top of him, milky breasts jiggling, hair flying, became a common occurrence. He couldn't get enough of her. He felt as if he'd struck gold. He had a willing participant at last. When she wasn't having sex with him, she was reading books about fertility—most favorable positions, foods to eat. She even had him taking zinc tablets. One a day, every morning with his breakfast. She made him laugh, supervising his taking of them like a matron in a hospital. He wasn't allowed to carry his mobile in his front pocket anymore. And he was under strict instructions not to put his laptop on his lap. Something about heating up the testicles. He was glad enough to go along with it all, just as he always did everything in his power to make Megan happy. His best mate Barry pulled him up on it. They were having a drink one night, in what used to be their local. Seth had just told Barry—still a bachelor and proud of it—that they were trying for a baby.

"So you could be looking at a daddy before long."

"Is that really what you want?"

"Of course it's what I want."

"Who came up with the idea?"

"Well—Megan, I suppose."

"Ah yes. What Megan wants, Megan gets."

"What the fuck is that supposed to mean?"

"Nothing, nothing. I didn't mean anything." Barry held up his hands defensively.

Seth took a gulp of his pint.

"Look. You're not even married. You don't know what you're talking about."

"True. You're absolutely right. What do I know about having a wife?"

"Exactly. Fuck all."

"I'm just looking out for you, that's all. Making sure it's what you want too."

"It is."

"Well then, I'm happy for you."

"Thanks."

"You're welcome."

They dropped the matter and spent the rest of the night discussing soccer. Neither one of them wanted to jeopardize their friendship.

But the conversation had made Seth think. He spoke to his brother, Aaron. The two of them were in their parents' house the following week, fixing a leak under the kitchen sink.

"What do you think of Megan?" Seth said suddenly, as if trying to catch his brother off guard. His brother looked across at him through the P-trap, a puzzled expression on his face.

"What do I think of her?"

"Yes."

"What are you asking me that for?"

"Just answer the question."

His brother considered the matter for a few moments.

"Well. She's a fine-looking bird and she makes a mean shepherd's pie."

Seth laughed, comforted by his brother's lack of depth. But he knew it would be a cop-out to end the investigation there. He should take it to a higher court. To the people who loved him best in the world.

Except he didn't ask his mother. He was pretty sure he already had a handle on her feelings for Megan. She liked her as well as she could like any woman who had taken Seth away from her. He believed she thought Megan pretty, intelligent, and personable—decent daughter-in-law material if one had to have such a creature in one's life. This is what he believed. He lacked the courage to put these beliefs to the test. So he asked his father.

He and Uri were clearing up together after one of his mother's delectable roasts. It was just the two of them.

"Da. Can I ask you something?"

"Of course."

"What do you think—I mean *really* think—of Megan?"

His father looked at him for a very long time. Then he spoke.

"I believe you are very much in love with her."

Seth nodded. He wouldn't have expected anything less from the Zen master. Uri had hit the nail on the head. It didn't matter what anybody else thought of her. He loved Megan and that was the beginning and the end of it. The alpha and the omega. It was irrelevant now anyway, because after three months, during which time Seth had watched his wife's jiggling turn from enthusiastic to desperate, Megan had succeeded in becoming pregnant. They were pregnant—as she was prone to say, making him cringe.

He didn't know how he felt about it really. He knew she was thrilled and he knew that they had stopped doing the wild thing. She didn't want to hurt the baby. Truth be told, he couldn't relate to this thing that was growing inside his wife's belly. She still looked exactly the same to him. Apart from a funny look around her eyes at times.

Megan threw herself into "their" pregnancy with much gusto. And Seth went along with it. Painting the nursery. Putting up a jungle-animal border and hanging a matching mobile over the crib. They went on shopping trips to Mothercare and bought tiny white baby onesies and hats—they reminded him of miniature skullcaps. And then there were the interminable conversations about names. She never seemed to tire of that one.

In time, the pregnancy started to show. Megan had already bought a lifetime's supply of maternity clothes. Seth kept waiting for the baby to feel more real to him, but it never happened. He did, however, like to look at his pregnant wife, thinking her incredibly voluptuous, with her full breasts resting neatly on her swollen belly. He dutifully held his hand on her bump every time she alerted him to a kick. And tried hard not to think "so what?" What she was feeling at her end was clearly more profound than what he was feeling at his. But the days turned into weeks, the weeks turned into months. Until the unbelievable became inevitable and his wife was full term. As in, he could become a father at any second. And still the enormity of it all escaped him.

Then one day he was out on a job. He'd just returned to his Jeep, having spent the morning planting a grove of native trees, when his mobile rang. It was his brother, Aaron.

"Where the hell have you been?"

"Nowhere. Here. What's wrong?"

"You're wife's gone into labor. We've been trying to contact you for the last two hours. You'd better get to the hospital pretty sharpish if you know what's good for you."

"Is she okay?"

"Far as I know." Aaron laughed. "You'd better hurry."

Seth cut Aaron off only to discover he had fifteen missed calls and eight messages on his phone. He didn't stop to check them. Just hot-rodded it to the hospital.

When Megan saw him she yelled, "Where were you?" then dissolved into tears. "Seth." She held out her arms. "I'm so scared."

"It's okay, love. I'm here now."

And he felt a greater bond with his wife at that moment than he had in the past nine months.

Over the next few hours, it seemed to Seth that some primeval creature, its face contorted with pain, had taken over his wife's body. All he could do was watch.

Their daughter was born a few minutes after midnight, a swirl of black hair on her red, angry, pointed little head. Seth had never seen or felt anything like it. She was real at last, this child of his.

"What'll we call her?"

"After what you've been through, I think you should get to choose."

"I want to call her Kathy."

"Kathy it is."

"Do you like it?"

"I love it."

"I love you, Seth."

"I love you too, Megan."

SHE MOVED OUT of their bedroom shortly after her return from the hospital. It was so Seth could get some sleep, what with the baby crying all night. She didn't want him to fall asleep at the wheel and crash the Jeep due to pure exhaustion. He was grateful for this, as Kathy did cry a lot. Although he did miss his wife's presence in their bed. Looking back, he was too overwhelmed at the time with new fatherhood to give it much thought. Because overwhelmed he was, mostly with feelings he could never have anticipated. Who was this tiny blob who had taken over his entire existence? This red-faced, screaming despot who, for some unfathomable reason, he loved to distraction. Everyone said she was the spitting image of him. He couldn't see it himself. To him she looked, oddly, like Uri. This minute bundle of femininity reminding him of a bearded old man. He hoped she'd grow out of it. Knew she would. Knew she'd grow up to be the most beautiful woman ever to walk the planet. Apart from her mother.

A year passed and Seth was still sleeping alone. It couldn't be the crying anymore. Kathy had stopped crying. And she'd dropped her nighttime feeding. So what was it?

It was breakfast time. Kathy was in her high chair. Megan was feeding her baby gloop. Seth stood at the counter with his mug of coffee.

"When are you moving back in, Meg?"

The spoon of baby gloop hung suspended in midair. Kathy's mouth gaped open, like a baby bird's.

"Moving back in where?"

"You know where. Into our bedroom."

Megan sighed. "Are we not fine the way we are?"

"No, Megan, I don't think we are. I want you to move back in."

"But, Seth, darling, you snore." She laughed prettily.

"I'll buy you a set of earplugs." Seth was grim.

Kathy began to protest and Megan shoveled the food into her mouth.

"Look, Seth. I've been giving this some thought and I think it would be best if we could . . ."

"If we could what?"

"If we could—well—live like brother and sister."

Seth felt something dangerous well up inside him.

"I mean," Megan continued, sounding ever more confident, "essentially that's what we've been doing for the past year and it's worked out pretty well, don't you think?"

Seth could contain himself no longer.

"I don't want a fucking sister," he roared. "I want a wife. You're supposed to be my fucking wife."

There was a terrible silence in the kitchen. The two women in Seth's life stared at him in horror. Then one by one, they began to cry. First Megan, her face crumpling. Then Kathy, wailing inconsolably. Seth lifted his daughter out of her high chair, sickened that he'd managed to frighten her to tears.

"It's okay, it's okay," he murmured, over and over, stroking her hair and kissing her on the forehead. "It's okay, it's okay."

When the child finally calmed down, he handed her back to her mother.

"I won't be home tonight," was all that he said.

SETH GOT WELL and truly plastered that night. He met up with Barry and the lads and fooled himself into thinking that it was just like old times. Most of his friends were unmarried. No wives, no kids, no responsibilities. After the pub, they got the DART into town and went to a club. Once inside, Seth felt like a fish out of water. So he drank like a fish. To forget about that and to forget about everything else. A girl came up to him. She had overprocessed hair and a strong Dublin accent. She was forward. Tarty. The exact opposite of Megan. Seth went back to her flat and shagged her brains out.

He woke the next morning feeling sicker than he'd ever remembered feeling. The girl was in the shower. At least the other side of the rumpled bed was empty and he could hear water running somewhere close by. He pulled on his clothes and left the flat, closing the door quietly behind him, wanting to put the whole sordid business behind him. He was in a part of town that he didn't recognize. He caught a glimpse of his reflection in a shop window. He didn't recognize that either. He looked rough. He hailed a taxi and got the hell out of Dodge.

Once home, and miraculously still in possession of his keys, he let himself in and walked straight up the stairs. He knew Megan was home because her car was parked outside, but he didn't look for her. He dragged his clothes off and left them in a murky puddle on the bedroom floor. Then he stepped into the shower and attempted to wash away the excesses of the night. Feeling marginally better, he grabbed a towel and walked back into the bedroom. Megan was sitting on the bed, looking at him coldly. He stood directly in front of her, toweling himself viciously, almost taunting her with his naked body.

"Where were you last night?"

"I told you I wouldn't be home."

"I asked you a question, Seth."

He took a step closer to her, bearing down now.

"You want to know where I was last night?" His voice was an angry hiss. "Fucking some tart, that's where."

Megan's lower lip started to tremble. Seth threw his towel down on the bed and began tugging out drawers, looking for clean clothes.

"How could you do that?" She was openly sobbing now.

"It was easy."

Something had shifted. She was crying and he didn't even care. He had reduced his beloved wife to tears yet he didn't give a shit. What kind of cold bastard was he? Later there would be guilt. Self-hatred and shame. But for now . . . perhaps he was still drunk. He was fully dressed.

"I'm going to work."

"What, now? Just like that? You can't—"

But he was already gone.

On his way out of the house, he heard a noise coming from the sitting room. He paused and looked in at the door. Kathy was in her playpen, gurgling at her teddy bears. She looked up, and seeing Seth, her face broke into smiles. She held her arms up to him. He went inside and picked her up, hugging her fiercely until she squealed. He lifted her away and looked into her face. She was rubbing the side of her cheek, which was red and raw looking. He automatically touched his own cheek with his fingertips. Rough and unshaven. He'd given his little girl razor burn. He hugged her again, more carefully this time.

"That's the last time I'll ever hurt you, Kathy."

Then he began to cry.

19

Subtle changes were occurring in the neighborhood: a conspicuous lack of litter on the streets surrounding the garden; the saplings that the local council planted along the roadside, routinely snapped every couple of months by the local yobbos, remained unsnapped. The gardeners became accustomed to faces pressed up against the wrought iron of the gate, as if starved for beauty. Eva tried to convince Mrs. Prendergast to leave the gate open, but she wouldn't hear of it.

There were subtle changes occurring within the garden too. And not just to the plant life. Walls within the walled garden were starting to crumble. Among those who worked there and around some of their hearts.

Seth was helping Eva plant her tomatoes. Into the soil this time. Into their final home. It was a glorious May morning as they knelt together before the south-facing wall. Mrs. Prendergast floated by carrying her new pruning shears with the flowered handle.

"You're planting them out too early."

Seth looked up at her. "Do you think so, Mrs. P?"

"Yes. We may have more frost."

"I don't think so."

"I think we will."

"I think we won't."

"Have it your way."

"I will."

Mrs. Prendergast stalked off, her expression thunderous.

"Why do you always have to antagonize her?"

"Because it's fun."

Eva laughed. "You obviously haven't heard the rumors about her."

"What rumors?"

She lowered her voice. "That she murdered her husband and buried him in the garden."

"This garden?"

"Yes."

"Is that why she won't let us dig by the back wall?"

"Could be."

They resumed working the soil.

"It wouldn't surprise me. I'd say the old grump has it in her all right. She frightens the shite out of me."

"She's just an old woman."

"All women are terrifying. Didn't you know?" Seth grinned at her. "Hand me the first plant, would you?"

Eva turned the tender little plant upside down above her palm and shook it free. It came loose in a little shower of compost. She paused to examine the intricate root system, like delicate white threads, only alive. She felt as if she were looking into the plant's soul, staring at its innards. Learning its secrets. She almost felt she should ask its permission first.

"I *am* waiting."

"Sorry." She handed the plant to Seth, who settled it into its new home—the hole he'd prepared for it—and firmed the soil around it with his fingers. They both knelt back and admired it proudly.

"Do you want to do the next one?"

"Yes, please."

Eva began to dig.

"You know," said Seth, "it wouldn't surprise me if she started the rumor herself."

"What? Mrs. Prendergast?"

"Yeah."

"Why would she do that?"

"To frighten little children."

"But she's great with children."

"So are you."

Eva, embarrassed, paused momentarily in her digging.

"I'm not that great."

"You are. It must be hard bringing up Liam on your own. His father—"

"Mummy, Mummy. You said I could water the 'matoes." The little boy charged over with his Winnie the Pooh watering can, bored in the absence of Kathy, who was spending the day with her mother.

" 'Course you can water them. We haven't planted them all yet."

He plunked himself down on Eva's lap and she wrapped her arms around him like a seat belt.

"I can finish up here, Seth. I'm sure you have other stuff you want to be getting on with."

"Right then." He stood up and wiped his hands on the sides of his jeans. "Catch you later."

She hoped she hadn't hurt his feelings. But she just wasn't ready.

20

THE THING THAT really got to Seth was that to the outside world, it looked like they had everything. He was handsome. She was pretty. He had his own thriving business. She was the attentive mother, famed for her superb home cooking. They had a lovely home, a garden that people crossed the road especially to see. And the most beautiful baby girl anyone had ever set eyes on. Yet behind closed doors and behind closed hearts, they had nothing. Nothing except Kathy. She was everything they amounted to now and the only reason Seth stayed.

He didn't have any more one-night stands. His level of self-disgust was already at an all-time high—he didn't need to add to it. Since "that night," he and Megan had settled into an uneasy truce. They each did their own thing mostly. If they were invited to friends' for dinner, they went along and everybody commented on what a lovely couple they were after they'd gone. The pretense made him despair. It also made him wonder how many other people were living a lie, cozied up in their sham marriages. In truth, Seth was at a loss. He didn't know what to do, and for the moment at least, it was easiest to go along with the charade. He was petrified by the thought of losing his daughter. No court was going to take a one-year-old away from its mother. He'd have to move out into some grotty bedsit, unable to hold his girl first thing in the morning and bathe her last thing at night. The thought gave him such a pain in his chest that he sometimes feared for his life. So he avoided thinking about it at all. Instead he sat and drank his beer in front of the telly while Megan trotted off to the gym. She said she wanted to lose the baby weight. He couldn't tell if she had or not because he made a point of not looking at her anymore. His life became work and Kathy, Kathy and work. And it continued that way for a whole year.

HE SENSED A change in Megan. She breezed in and out of the house, her demeanor airy, her conversation light. She chatted to him as if they were friends. As if she almost had sympathy for him or something. And she started giggling again, that girlish giggle he used to love. Now it annoyed the fuck out of him. What business did she have being happy when she'd made his life a bloody misery? He began to suspect her of having an affair. Though why he should care what she did was beyond him. But he was damned if she was going to start a new life while he was still stuck in the old one. He began to look at his wife again, as he would a woman. Appraise her. She certainly looked well. She'd gotten her figure back. Her tiny waist restored. And she'd done something to her hair— got yellow stripes in it or something. It looked blonder. And of course, when a person was happy, they looked better. They just did.

"What's his name?"

It was dinnertime and they were all in the kitchen. Seth sat at the table, nonchalantly playing with his mash. Megan swung around to look at him, suspending her search for ketchup in the upper cabinet.

"What did you say?"

"I asked you what his name was."

She laughed without humor. "Yes, that's what I thought you said. Who are you referring to exactly?"

"I don't know. You tell me." He sat back in his chair and folded his arms, staring at his wife while his dinner began its steady decline into congealment.

She shook her head and looked away.

"You think I have another man."

"Well—don't you?"

They both watched their daughter as she transferred sticky handfuls of mashed potato from her bowl to the floor, delighting every time in the splatting noise it made.

"I can assure you, Seth, that the last thing I want in my life is another man."

"Well, what are you so goddamn happy about all the time?"

"I've just got my life back, that's all."

He examined Megan's face. Was it true? He couldn't tell. On the one hand, it wasn't as if he could accuse her of being a nymphomaniac. On the other, it didn't quite ring true. No person could be so transformed just by "getting their life back."

So he transformed himself too. Into a suspicious, paranoid obsessive. He began watching her. Analyzing everything she said. He checked her bedside drawers when she was out. He didn't even know what he was looking for. Wasn't it the wife who was supposed to behave like this? And then one day he followed her. No sooner had she pulled out of the driveway than he leaped into his Jeep and sped after her, just catching a glimpse of her car turning right down at the end of the road. She'd dropped Kathy at her mother's earlier, so she'd be free to meet whoever. And he could have sworn she was wearing lipstick. He weaved in and out of the traffic in an effort to keep up with her. She was going at some speed. Couldn't wait to get to him, he thought bitterly. Then Megan indicated and Seth indicated too, and they both pulled into the local Spar. Seth parked at a discreet distance from his wife's car and craned his neck to see her. He could see her selecting her items and taking them up to the cashier's desk. Probably buying condoms. And whipped cream.

He slid down into his seat as she reemerged. He tried to see what she'd bought. It looked like a newspaper and a sliced pan of bread, but she could have other items concealed under the newspaper. She tore off again and he was right behind her, just two cars between them. He'd get her now. But—what was she doing? She was heading back home. Shit. He waited five minutes before entering the front door himself. She looked up as he walked into the sitting room.

"I didn't know you were going out." Her voice was mild.

"I just went to buy a Lotto ticket. There's a rollover tonight. Big jackpot."

She laughed. "I just did the same thing. I was afraid I'd be too late. The draw's on in a minute. Want to watch it together?"

"No thanks."

He turned and walked out to the hall. He stood there for a few moments with his hands in his pockets. What an idiot. It was time he moved on.

SO HE DID. Normal life was resumed. He couldn't exactly claim to be happy, but he was pretty much coasting along in neutral, finding his joy in his daughter and his plants.

Then one day he forgot his phone.

He was expecting an important call at midday, so he had no option but to go home and get it. He could see it in his mind's eye, on the nightstand beside his bed. When he got home, Megan's car was parked outside the house. This was strange because she normally worked Tuesday mornings, ever since she'd gone back to her job parttime as part of the great "getting her life back" extravaganza. There was another car outside the house too. One he didn't recognize. Could be somebody visiting the neighbors.

He let himself into the house and bounded up the stairs

two steps at a time. All was quiet. His bedroom door was ajar. He pushed it open. His phone was on his bedside nightstand, as he'd remembered. Except, he didn't see his phone. Instead he saw Megan, lying in the bed they hadn't shared for over two years. She was naked from the waist up. She had a sheet covering her bottom half, but he presumed she was naked from the waist down too. One milky, pink-tipped breast was exposed. The other was covered by the sleeping head of a dark-haired woman. The woman was beautiful in repose, long curly hair and a generous bosom. Megan was awake, looking at him levelly. Without a word, she ever so gently extricated herself from the other woman's embrace. The woman murmered and shifted her position but remained asleep. Megan put on a robe—Seth's robe, because it was his room—and, still wordless, walked past him and out to the hall, closing the bedroom door carefully behind her.

She went downstairs and he followed her to the kitchen where she commenced filling up the kettle.

"Coffee?"

He didn't reply. Just slid into the nearest chair and, elbows resting heavily on the table, held his head in his hands. It was some time before he could lift his head.

"How long?"

"Siobhan and I got together about five months ago."

Siobhan. So that was the other woman's name.

"No. How long have you known?"

Seth watched Megan as she shoveled three times the usual amount of sugar into his mug and stirred it vigorously. She placed it down in front of him and he followed the foam as it swirled around on top of the dark brown liquid. He knew he wouldn't be able to touch it. Megan sat down opposite him and husband and wife faced each other. Her expression was completely without artifice. So much so that he hardly recognized her. He knew that he was going to get the truth, and the prospect terrified him. "Something happened when I was pregnant with Kathy. Something to do with carrying a girl. I can't really explain it."

"Try."

"It was like, I don't know. I was filled with femaleness or something and it made me realize that I needed to be with a woman. To share my life with one. And that I couldn't be with a man anymore. Seth, don't look at me like that, please."

"What do you expect?"

She swallowed and raked her hands through her hair. He thought she looked ashamed. Good.

"I was afraid to do anything about it at the time. We'd just had Kathy and I was all over the place as it was. I suppose part of me hoped it would go away. Although I knew that it wouldn't. So I just tried to get along with life the best that I could. Then Kathy got older and a bit easier and I started to get out and about a little bit more and feel better about myself. I met Siobhan at the gym and," here her voice got smaller, "we made a connection."

Seth winced.

"We were just friends at first. For ages, that's all it was. Then this one time. Well, I'm sure you don't want to know the details. I'm sorry, Seth. I was building up to telling you."

"You should have told me the second you knew."

"I know, I know. You're right. I should have told you a long time ago."

"You let me waste the last two—more—years on you, when all the time you knew you could never—"

He broke off and stood up. He walked around the kitchen table, put his hands in his pockets, and stared out the window at his much admired garden. He supposed he'd have to leave it now.

"And the whole time you never loved me." He hated how choked he sounded.

"Oh, Seth. That's not true." Megan got up and stood behind him. "I did love you."

"No you didn't. How could you? Not properly."

"I loved you as much as it was possible for me to love any man, Seth. How could I not love you?"

"Spare me."

"It's true. I thought I was in love. I didn't know any better. I guess I thought everyone felt the way I did."

"What? Fancied women?"

"No. It's not that I was going around fancying women all the time. I had the odd feeling every now and then but I thought it was normal. You hear about women having lesbian fantasies and I assumed that's all it was. I had boyfriends growing up. You weren't the first man I'd been with. And it was different with you, Seth. I thought I'd found—my soul mate, I suppose."

"So did I."

The silence hung in the air between them and started to buzz in Seth's ears. He longed to put on the radio and turn to some inane talk show. Anything to block it out. The morning was clouding over outside and he felt that nothing in his life was ever going to be right again.

"I'm sorry," said Megan. "I really and truly am. For everything I've put you through and for being too much of a coward to tell you before."

"I'm sorry too. That the last five years of my life have been a joke. A lie. A big, fucking waste of my time." He could feel the anger building now and he turned and looked at her.

"Tell me, Megan. Were you just using me for the sperm? Is that what it was? You decided you wanted a baby and I had the one thing you couldn't get from a woman. You used me, was that it?"

"No, Seth. It wasn't like that at all. And can you please keep your voice down?"

"Don't tell me what to do, you lying bitch."

"Don't call me that."

"I can call you whatever the hell I like." He was shouting

now. "Sneaking around behind my back. Having your affair."

"I wasn't the only one."

"That was one night, Megan. One lousy night out of years of—nothing. Nothing, Megan."

"Are you all right, Meg?"

Nobody had noticed Siobhan opening the kitchen door. They both swung around now to look at her, framed in the doorway, fully dressed.

"I'm fine, Siobhan."

"Oh, Siobhan, is it? I didn't recognize you with your clothes on. I'm Seth, Megan's husband. Or is that 'Meg' to you? Come on in and join the party. Oh, I forgot. You already had a party. Up in my bed."

"I think you'd better go, love."

Love.

"Yes. Even better idea. Why don't you go? Get the hell out of my home and don't come back."

Seth started to advance toward Siobhan, his eyes blazing. Megan held on to him, one hand on his chest, as Siobhan retreated.

"Stop it, Seth."

Seth heard the front door being opened.

"Nice tits, by the way," he shouted.

The front door slammed.

Seth slumped back down into a kitchen chair before his legs had the chance to buckle. He folded his arms on the table and rested his head down on top of them. Nobody said anything for quite a while. Then: "Can I get you anything?"

Megan's voice was small. With great difficulty, he lifted his head.

"How about the last five years back?" He groaned. "What a waste."

"Don't say that, Seth. We have Kathy, don't we?"

Yes, there was always Kathy. Fear overtook him.

"You're not taking her away from me. She's all I've got."

He felt tears stinging the back of his eyes and he covered them with his hand. His wife sat down beside him and laid her hand on his shoulder. When he didn't shrug her off, she squeezed it gently. It was the tenderest touch he'd felt in years.

"I'd never do that to you, Seth. Never."

As it turned out, Seth didn't have to move out of the family home. Megan moved in with Siobhan instead. True to her word, she agreed to a joint-custody arrangement. Maybe she too was afraid of losing Kathy. Luckily, Kathy was too young to understand what was going on and, to everyone's relief, adapted beautifully to her new living arrangements. Which was more than could be said for Seth.

The house felt overlarge and echoey when Kathy wasn't around. And although he'd barely admit it to himself, he missed Megan too. He would have sold and moved out but he didn't want to cause his daughter further disruption. Besides, the house wasn't just his to sell. Instead, he spent as little time there as possible, and when Kathy was with her mother, sat anesthetized with booze in front of the telly, his eyes bloodshot, his cheeks unshaven, well on his way to developing a beer gut. A lot of the time, he didn't bother going to bed at all. He'd fall asleep in front of the box and wake up with a crick in his neck sometime in the early hours, with a mad infomercial blaring at him. He'd turn down the volume, rest his head on a cushion, and cover himself with his jacket. He'd wake up sometime in the morning, judging the time by the brightness in the sky, and turn the volume back up. Then he'd have his coffee and, if he was feeling up to it, a vitamin pill. Sometimes he'd shower, sometimes he wouldn't. Sometimes he changed his clothes and sometimes he wore the same outfit three days in a row. He couldn't even consider another woman. He felt so completely emasculated that he doubted he'd ever be able to get it up again. He went to work, thanking his lucky stars that he didn't have a boss, because if he did, he would have been well and truly sacked.

Then his mother died. And it was like someone pulling an awful cosmic rug out from under him. Let's all laugh as Seth falls flat on his back again. Let's see if he can make it up this time. He barely made it the last.

But Seth did make it. Just about. He and his father and his brother, united in their grief, making each other strong, making their dead mother proud. And life went on. And the separation came through. And Seth started to shave again and change his underwear on a more regular basis. And then one day his father rang him up and told him about this garden.

21

ALL MONTH LONG they came—the men in suits. The speculators. They paced around the garden, looking incongruous in their formal garb. Sometimes they came in twos and threes, oftentimes alone. Sometimes one of them would inadvertently step on a plant. "Sorry," they would say. So you should be. The odd time, one of them might even inquire about the garden, about the work they were doing. "Such a shame," they might say as they walked away, pressing down the newly dug topsoil with their shiny shoes. "Well, don't build on it then," Eva would scream silently in her head. But never out loud. Because she was used to keeping things in.

Someone else who was accustomed to keeping things in was Emily. But even she couldn't do it any longer. She appeared one morning looking as if she'd been in a fight. Hay fever? But as the morning wore on, it became evident that there was more to it than that. Emily cried silently as she worked the same piece of earth over and over, her tears dampening the soil, unseeing. She had wiped her tear-stained face so many times that it had become mud streaked. Uri and Eva exchanged concerned glances

"Should we do something?"

"Ask her what's wrong. She talks to you," said Uri.

So Eva approached Emily. Hesitantly. Not wanting to

frighten or offend this private young girl. She came up behind her and laid her hand gently on her shoulder.

"Emily?"

Emily turned around and, wordlessly, barely looking at Eva, buried her face in her shoulder and sobbed openly. Eva put her arms around her and they both sank to the ground and sat there in the mud. Everyone else pretended not to look while Eva absorbed Emily's pain, feeling oddly privileged to be chosen in this way. The tears became lighter, the sobs more shallow. Emily lifted her head, rooted around in her pocket for a tissue, and blew her nose lustily. Eva thought she'd never seen anyone look so forlorn. She tucked a stray piece of hair behind Emily's ear.

"What is it, Emily? What happened to you?"

There was a long silence. So long that Eva didn't think she was going to get an answer.

"I had a baby."

Eva was taken aback. She hadn't been expecting this. Her guess had been that Emily had been dumped. She collected herself.

"When was this?"

"Eight months ago." Emily sniffed. "She's eight months old."

"A little girl."

Emily nodded, the picture of misery.

"Where is she?"

For one terrible second, Eva feared that Emily was going to tell her she'd left the newborn baby in a Dumpster.

"I put her up for adoption. She's been with a foster family. But"—fresh tears were starting to flow—"they've found a family for her. They want me to go in and sign the consent papers."

Emily began to sob again. Oh God. Eva searched her pockets frantically for something resembling a tissue. Emily's own had disintegrated into a sodden ribbon. Not that she seemed to care. She seemed oblivious to everyone and everything as she cried with abandon. Eva looked around at the others in concern. They were huddled together, whispering.

"Hush now. It's okay. Everything's going to be okay." Eva rubbed Emily's arm, starting to feel uncomfortable at this very public show of emotion, but mostly just so desperately sorry for this young girl. She waited until Emily had calmed down a little before speaking again.

"And you say the baby's still with foster parents. She hasn't gone to a family yet."

"No."

"Are you going to sign the papers?"

"I don't know. I can't decide."

"Surely the adoption people provide some sort of counseling."

"They do. I still can't decide. I mean, how could I look after a baby? I've got no boyfriend, no money, no job. I'm not even close to finishing my degree."

"What about your family?"

"They're really religious. They wouldn't understand."

"You mean they don't even know?"

Emily shook her head.

"You mean you never told them!"

"No."

"Did you tell anyone?"

"You're the first person I've told. Apart from the woman in the adoption agency. And the father."

"And I take it . . ."

"He didn't want to know."

"Oh, Emily." Eva put her arm around Emily's shoulders and drew her close, trying but failing to imagine what it must have been like for her.

They stayed like that for a while. Emily, her wet face buried in Eva's shoulder, didn't notice Mrs. Prendergast tiptoeing over and placing a mug of steaming tea on the ground in front of her. Eva and Mrs. Prendergast looked at each other. Then Eva nodded and Mrs. Prendergast tiptoed away again.

"Here," Eva said after a while. "Your tea's getting cold."

Emily looked up. "Where did that come from?"

"The fairies left it."

Emily picked up the mug with her frail-looking hands, the tips of her fingers poking out from under her sweater. She closed her eyes and drank deeply, as if the mug contained the elixir of life.

After a while, "Better?"

"A little."

"You know, you might not be giving your family enough credit."

Emily shrugged.

"How do you get on with your mother?"

"Okay. Well, I suppose."

"There you go, then. She might surprise you. But she can't help if she doesn't even know."

Emily showed no reaction.

"And how do you feel about the baby?" Eva looked searchingly into Emily's pink, swollen face.

"I don't know. I just don't know." She gnawed at her fingernails.

Eva took a deep breath. The deepest she could find.

"I have something to tell you," she said. "It might help you decide."

22

*T*HE FIRST TIME I gave my little girl choco-
late, she laughed out loud. I'd made her mouth happy. It was a
chocolate button on the occasion of her first birthday. Her dad
caught it all on the camcorder—he the Hollywood dad, we the
Hollywood family. I've watched it so many times I know it by
heart. But I've never managed to catch the deceit in my eyes.
Michael never caught it either. Even though I was in the thick
of it by then.

We were as entranced as she was, as the chocolate melted
on her tongue, then stuck to the roof of her mouth. As her
mouth filled up with brown goo, her ridiculously large blue
eyes filled with surprise, then delight.

"She's just like her mother," said Michael, still filming.

I wasn't sure if he was referring to her looks or to her
newfound love of chocolate. Because she did indeed resemble
me closely in each respect. It was gratifying at last to have a
child who looked like me. Liam was so unlike me he could
have fallen from the clouds. Which didn't diminish my love
for him. He was my firstborn, my finest achievement thus far
in life. He'd stopped growing inside the womb and had to be
cut out of me early. So my overprotectiveness was in overdrive, right from the start. It meant he was always small for
his age. Some would say puny, I would say delicate. I had worried he'd be jealous of the new baby, having had the dubious

benefit of my fierce attention all his young life. But he seemed thrilled by her and laughed along with us at her reaction to the chocolate button before demanding, quite rightly, one for himself.

"Come on, Liam. Give us a smile." Michael trained the camera on him.

"Cheese," said Liam, the chocolate making brown lines between the divisions in his teeth.

"How old is Katie today?"

"One." Liam held up a decisive finger.

"And what do we have to say to her?"

"Happy birthday, Katie." He started to clap and Katie copied him.

Michael and I looked fondly at each other. Our clever, beautiful children. Then he laid down the camera and walked over to me. He put his arms around me and spoke warmly into my neck.

"I love you, Eva."

I closed my eyes. "I love you too." It wasn't a lie. I remember that moment exactly, even though it wasn't recorded. The feel of his arms supporting my body, his breath against my skin. The mixture of happiness and guilt. I had everything in that moment. Absolutely everything. Except, I was such a stupid fool I didn't even know it. Always wanting more. Forever yearning for something I didn't have. Later, I blamed myself for my lack of gratitude: if you're not sufficiently grateful, we will take it all away.

How can I describe Michael? He was always Michael to me, although his friends called him Mick. Only his mother and I used his true name. We knew it suited him best. He worked as a quantity surveyor. Off he'd go every weekday morning to survey his quantities, laptop under his arm, hard hat on his head.

The first thing people noticed about him was his hair: red, ginger. He hated it, declared himself a lifelong victim of "gingerism," I loved it. Its silkiness, its floppiness. I think I nearly convinced him to love it too.

We met at this really tacky party in Camden Town. I—unbeknownst to myself—was meant for the host. I can't even remember his name now. Michael had been earmarked for the flatmate's sister, an unfortunate girl who got so inebriated that it took two men to carry her to bed. She was probably a respectable married lady now, who cringed at the memory. If she did have a memory.

Michael was sitting opposite me. His general lack of drunkenness marked him out. He sat back in his chair and sipped his wine gently, casually surveying the chaos surrounding him. I was doing much the same at the other side of the kitchen table. Although part of me wanted to get roaring drunk too, my desire to impress Michael stopped me.

"What's your name?" he said. It wasn't the type of party at which formal introductions had been made.

"Eva."

"That's beautiful," was all he said.

I was sold.

And from that moment, merely counting the seconds before I could ditch all the other turkeys and have him to myself. He must have felt the same way because, less than an hour later, the room having descended into drink-sodden chaos, he looked at his watch and then pointedly at me.

"Let's get out of here."

They never even saw us leave.

So we escaped together, the night blessedly cool and high after the claustrophobia of the flat, our laughter soaring like night birds into the starry sky, where it remained suspended on the air currents. Sometimes I imagine it up there still.

We went to an all-night café and talked all night. His name was Michael O'Brien and he was London Irish too. His parents were from County Mayo and he'd spent many the rain-sodden summer there. We compared tales of Irish grandmothers and laughed uproariously.

"Mine says 'feck.'"

"Mine too!"

"Does she get up at six every morning to bake soda bread?"

"I think she buys hers in Londis."

"Oh." Slight disappointment. "Mine told me she cuts the cross on the top to let the fairies out. For years I believed her."

"Mine's called Kathleen."

"Mine too!"

"They can't all be called Kathleen."

"No, I think some of them are called Mary."

It made it easy to agree on our daughter's name when the time came.

The London child of Irish immigrants, I had never considered myself English. My Irish cousins had never considered me Irish. In their eyes, I was forever the plastic Paddy. I preferred to think of myself as a rare kind of hybrid.

I had spent all my summer holidays at the home of my Dublin grandparents, marveling anew each year at their strange vernacular. The delicious shock the first time my devout granny—holy water font in the front porch—said "feck." The pure joy of it! Had I misheard? Trying the word out for size back in London on my schoolmates. Being made to stand in the corner.

The memories were visceral. As if they'd seeped into my cells. Even now, on certain mornings in late June, I was back in my parents' Ford Cortina, being driven on empty back roads from the ferry to my grandparents' house. Birdsong and hedgerows. Then the joy of arrival. Grandparents unable to wait behind the confines of their front porch. Spilling out of the house to meet us, down the front steps, through the roses, the snapdragons, the Michaelmas daisies. My grandfather and his pipe. Mellow Virginia. For years after his departure, the scent lingered in the drawer beside his chair. My granny. Hair newly colored and permed. Tattooing our cheeks with her red, heart-shaped kisses. We would run up the path, lured by the smell of Irish bacon and sausages slit up the middle. Soda bread and black-and-white pudding. The white spread thick and smooth on the soda bread. The black, born of pig's blood, spurned for reasons of morality and disgust. Then later, the potato cakes sizzling, salty butter melting. The tea cake for tea. The aunties dropping in. *The Benny Hill Show* on the telly. Photos of grandchildren on every surface. Love.

My grandparents were gone now. My grandfather had died when I was nineteen. My grandmother, just a few years ago. The house had been sold and the memories divvied up. I myself had received a battered gold locket that I lost intermittently, only to refind with great joy every time.

When I first moved to Ireland, I used to drive by their house, tripping myself up on my own nostalgia. I'd had to stop. Too much pathos can drag at the soul.

We compared notes for what seemed like hours: the luridly Technicolored photo of John Paul II in the hall; the sacred heart in the kitchen, the fake red candle perpetually aglow—all the babies named and blessed, including the ones who'd died at birth. Jesus offering his heart to share. Our grandmothers offering their limitless love. We didn't exactly say that, but the feeling was understood and acknowledged. It made Michael seem dear to me already. Familiar and safe. Like family.

He proved himself later that night when he escorted me to the front door of my block of flats.

"Which is yours?"

"See that window up there?" I pointed to a small pane on the third floor.

"When you're in, turn on the light and look down and wave at me. I'll be waiting."

"For what?"

"To make sure you got in safe."

I gave him a quick, shy kiss on the cheek and ran inside, not waiting for the lift, taking the stairs two steps at a time, wings on my heels. I got inside and turned on the light. Breathless from the flight of stairs and my emotions, I looked out of the window. There he was. A lone figure in a dark coat. He waved and I thought I saw him smile. He walked away and I watched his glorious red hair glint as he passed beneath a streetlight.

That was it really. We hardly spent a night apart until the one before our wedding two years later, the two Kathleens crying copiously in the church. I had no doubts. If Michael had them, he hid them well. I loved my gingerbread man and he loved me. And we lived in our gingerbread house. Because that's what it felt like—as if we were playing at being grown-ups. I thought I'd feel the same when our first baby was born, that we'd be playing at being mummies and daddies. But the advent of Liam into our lives catapulted us into adulthood and, suddenly, life wasn't a game anymore. It was very real, very serious. What if something happened to him? Suddenly we were gambling on a planet that didn't always seem like such a good bet. We started to fight more. Nothing serious, only bickering. But the halcyon days were over. Reality had bitten us on the arse and life would never be the same again.

I didn't regret motherhood, not for one second. But I did regret failing to appreciate my freedom when I'd had it. I realized with a jolt that my ambitious travel plans would have to be curtailed. That I no longer had just myself and Michael to think about. Simple things like taking my time in the shower, spending precious minutes slathering myself with body lotion afterward. Such experiences were now a thing of the past. My gray hairs multiplied from stress and lack of care, and the tiny lines on my face multiplied from lack of care and sleep. I no longer cleansed, toned, and moisturized. I was lucky if I managed to pass a baby wipe across my face at nighttime, before falling into bed like a stone. Although these were only simple things, they made me feel less human, less of a person and a woman in my own right. I was now "mother" and all other aspects of my identity were secondary. As far as Michael was concerned, I believe he felt more stuck in a job he wasn't too crazy about. As far as our relationship was concerned, we couldn't—wouldn't—take these pressures out on Liam, so we took them out on each other. It sometimes felt as though we were rivals rather than batting for the same team.

"You go up to him. I'm knackered."

"What do you think I am? I've been working all day."

"Oh, and I haven't, I suppose."

"I didn't say that."

"You implied it."

"Don't be so bloody sensitive."

"I'm not being sensitive. You're being inconsiderate."

"I went up last time."

"And I went up twice before that."

And so on.

It was a competition: who was the tiredest?

Nevertheless, we took another gamble on the planet and on ourselves, and not long after Liam's first birthday, Katie was born. Again my love was outrageous, but different. With Liam, the funny little person with body parts I didn't possess, I was excited but fearful, setting out on the strange odyssey of motherhood. With Katie, I was already home. She was a perfect fit inside my heart. I understood her tiny woman's brain and watched with joy her joy at flowers and animals and chocolate. She loved the things that I loved: her brother and her daddy.

Michael and I grew to inhabit our roles, and for a time, we grew in the same direction. Looking back, he kept on shooting upward. It was me who veered off course.

I had known Peter for years, since I'd started work at the

college in my midtwenties, fresh from my own degree in pure English and my MA in romantic poetry. He lectured in physics. I'd always liked the way his mind worked, so different from mine. But that had been it. He was friends with Michael too. We went to each other's houses for dinner and stuck together at boring work functions. They had a son who was slightly older than Liam and the two boys would play together. Peter's wife—Lara—a home economics teacher—crocheted Katie the most beautiful blanket when she was born. I used it on her crib at first. Later, I would shove it down the back of the airing cupboard so I didn't have to look at it.

I went back to work when Katie turned six months, weepy at her easy withdrawal from my breast. I settled back into my coffee-break routine, a group of us huddled around our habitual table with the wonky legs in the canteen. Peter was always there.

"Would you like more milk, Eva?"

Always solicitous. At first I thought it was because I'd had a baby, but it continued. One day, seemingly from out of nowhere, it dawned on me that his eyes always sought out mine in a group. It was my opinion he looked for. My approval. As if I were special to him. It made me think.

It had been years since it had even dawned on me to fancy another man. Michael had been enough for me since the night we'd met. Of course, I still noticed a good-looking man on the street or the screen, but in a dispassionate way, as if admiring a beautiful piece of art. And I suppose I'd always thought of Peter as good looking in that same, dispassionate way. It had never occurred to me to imagine what it would be like to actually be with him.

Looking back, I don't know if I can put it down to anything more exalted than boredom. My life, my identity, had become so subsumed with being a wife and mother, so taken up with the humdrum details of my family's existence, that something in me yearned for escape. To become the heroine of my own romantic novel—the more Harlequin the better. Instead of trying to fix what I already had in my own home— which wasn't even that badly broken, just a few hairline cracks—I looked for something new and whole on the outside. In a way, I was being lazy. Another unthinking participant in our disposable, throwaway society. My marriage just needed a little recycling. And my children were far too precious for me to even contemplate throwing away their happiness and security.

It was a day like any other. Unremarkable weather. Drizzly. Nothing to inspire. I had seen Michael that morning of course, we had moved around each other, not saying much. This wasn't significant. Just a usual workaday morning, people rushing to get ready. He had kissed me on the way out the door, on the cheek, mouth full of toast, leaving behind a fine residue of crumbs. I wiped them away.

I dropped the children off at the childminder's, Liam battling the constraints of his car seat, me battling the traffic. The childminder—Shiela—was a woman in her fifties who had raised a family of her own. My children adored her, which made me illogically resentful, something I chided myself for every morning. It was my choice to go back to work. Choice: the curse of the modern woman. Liam ran straight in through the front door the second it was opened.

"Look at my new twuck, Shiela." He held up his latest toy for her inspection.

"Oh, that's lovely, dear."

Katie held out her arms to Shiela, almost leaping from my own in her enthusiasm to get to the other woman. For God's sake. She'd only known Shiela for three months. I'd carried her in my womb for nine months, etc., etc.

"I'll see you later," I said.

"See you later, dear. Liam. Come and give your mummy a good-bye kiss."

But Liam had already been swallowed up into the dark interior of the house.

"Oh, it's fine. Don't bother him. I'm late anyway. Bye, Katie."

I kissed my daughter on her indifferent, satin cheek and got back into the car. I pulled away, the image of Shiela trying unsuccessfully to get her to wave to me in my rearview mirror. I asked myself for the millionth time if I was doing the right thing. The right thing. What was that? I supposed I was lucky I didn't have children who clung to me, wailing inconsolably whenever I tried to leave them. I switched on the radio in my car and my thoughts were subsumed in the traffic. By the time I got to the college, I was more than ready for a grand latte. So I went straight to the canteen and who should be there . . .

I was immediately self-conscious. How ridiculous after all this time.

"Is this seat taken?"

Peter smiled and gestured to the seat opposite him.

"You're in early," I said, striving for normality.

"Papers to mark."

It was hardly a romantic setting. The college canteen. Sipping from polystyrene cups. Then why did I feel like I was on a date? I wished I could shake this infernal crush. Was it wishful thinking on my part, to even suspect that he was feeling anything remotely similar? I knew he liked me. But maybe not as much as I liked him. And maybe not in the same way. I was projecting my feelings on to him, something I used to do all the time with men before Michael—always with disastrous results. It was quite distressing to learn that I hadn't progressed beyond the romantic mental age of nineteen. Had my third-level education, my marriage, my career, childbirth times two not taught me anything? Apparently not. The sophistication that I thought I'd garnered was proved to be nothing more than the most fragile of veneers.

"How's Lara?" When in doubt, mention the wife. It proves you have no designs on him.

"Okay, I think. Haven't seen much of her lately."

What does that mean? That you're not getting on? Doesn't your wife understand you?

"How come?"

He shrugged. "Both just busy I guess."

How was it that I never before appreciated the shape of his mouth? The unabashed sensuality of the upper lip. The squared-off curve of the lower. I tried not to stare. I took a sip of coffee and winced as it burned my mouth.

"Are you okay?"

"It's just hot."

"Here. Have some of this."

He leaned over and pressed his glass of water against my lips. I took a gulp, annoyed by how refreshing it felt. He took the glass away and a dribble of water ran down my chin. Embarrassed, I wiped it away with my sleeve, my eyes lowered, rattled by the strange intimacy of the situation. I got up to leave.

"I'd better go." Backing my chair awkwardly behind me, I gathered up my papers and walked past him toward the exit. He stood up and grabbed my arm as I went by.

"I will see you later?"

I was completely taken aback. I felt my color deepen, his fingers sinking into my flesh, his eyes boring into mine.

"I'll be around at lunchtime."

He nodded and released me and I walked out of the canteen on legs that seemed to belong to another woman, my head and heart full of confusion.

THAT NIGHT I snapped at Michael, even though he'd done nothing. And when he came to bed, I pretended to be asleep.

I WAS JUST playing, really. The fantasy was in my head. Just trying to make life a little less boring. To feel alive, for God's sake.

THAT WEEKEND WE visited a garden. The whole family. I consider it my last, pure weekend, the memory of which was to shine out like a beacon in darker times. The sun shone—in reality—and even brighter in memory. In reality, I'm sure there were clouds, occasionally and momentarily blotting out the light. In memory, there were none. In reality, I had a sore back, from lugging Liam around and from picking up Katie as she tripped again and again over her newly found feet. Of course, Daddy was willing and capable of doing this too. It's just that so often, my name was called: Mummy, center of their tiny universe. In memory, my back is pain free. I experience no tiredness as I lift my children up into the soft air and swing them around. They squeal with delight and the afternoon resonates with their laughter. Bees buzz, birds trill, butterflies flutter by. The scent of sunscreen, our picnic lunch. Pâté and Bakewell tart for the grown-ups. Cocktail sausages and puréed fruit for the children. Warm, fizzy 7-Up in plastic cups. Katie fell over herself to get to the flowers. Liam ran manically around the borders as if in a maze. Michael and I reveled in the magic.

"It doesn't get much better than this." He was lying out on the checkered blanket, propped up on one elbow, his legs crossed at the ankles, a supremely contented expression on his face.

"No, it doesn't," I concurred, meaning every word. I lay on my back and shielded my eyes with my arm, blocking out the light but not the heat. It was impossible not to feel totally relaxed under the benign force of the sun. I felt Michael move closer to me and anticipated his touch. Welcomed it. He whispered into my ear and his breath tickled.

"I love being here with you," he said.

"I love being here with you too."

"You know you're the center of my universe, don't you?"

"Am I?"

"You know you are."

I did know.

"I don't know what I'd do without you, Eva."

"You won't have to do without me."

"Promise?"

"Of course I promise. What is this, Michael? This isn't like you."

"You just seem so distant lately. Like you're here but not here."

I was shocked that he'd noticed. I thought I'd hidden it so well. Locked in my private fantasy world, locking him out. Telling myself that what were only thoughts couldn't possibly affect him. But in reality they were. The evidence was breathing in my very own ear. The guilt was immediate and heavy, my enjoyment of the day eliminated. I propped myself up on my elbow and looked Michael in the eyes.

"I'm sorry if I've seemed preoccupied lately. I promise I'll change."

I meant it too. What need had I for sordid, tawdry affairs when I had all this? This perfect love. This perfect family life. I vowed there and then to stay away from Peter, to make sure we were never alone, to always keep about me the protection of company, to keep temptation at arm's length, and not a hair's breadth away as it had been last week. Only a madwoman would jeopardize all this—all the gifts I had in my life. This goodness.

Michael did a quick check all around to see where the children were and to see if anyone else was close enough to see. Satisfied, he cupped my breast with his hand and kissed my lips. I giggled against his mouth. As it was in the beginning.

But I couldn't help it. It was as if I was two different people living two different lives. In one, the devoted wife and mother. In the other, the traitorous whore. Which is how I thought of myself at moments, even though I hadn't actually done anything. But I knew what my intentions were and they weren't good—every time I saw Peter. The thought of a different pair of hands on my naked skin was so unutterably exciting that I couldn't let it go. I did send him packing once. He came all the way to my front door, when he knew Michael and the children were out. He knew because they were out with his wife and child, all at the Fun Factory together. I opened the door and he stood there looking at me. What had remained unspoken had become undeniable, through eye contact and body language. Through something strange and indefinable in the ether between us. The air we jointly breathed had become souplike and vaguely tangible. It seemed incredible to me that nobody else was conscious of it. I stepped back and he stepped inside the hall. I was still in my dressing gown, luxuriating as I was in a rare morning to myself. I crossed my arms over my chest, acutely aware that beneath my dressing gown I was wearing the lightest of nighties and no underwear. I couldn't speak. I felt absolute terror. Like that time on the motorway when I was convinced a lorry was going to plow right into me. Yet it was only Peter standing in front of me. Peter, my friend. Peter who, for some strange reason, had become the most attractive man in the universe. When I wasn't with him, I could deny it, discount it. But when I *was* in his presence, the attractiveness seemed to radiate off him in waves, pulling me toward him, an irresistible force. Again, I resisted. He took a step closer, I took a step back.

"This is a surprise. I'm not even dressed."

I'd deny what was happening with normal talk. Again, he wouldn't speak. Speak, goddamnit. Help me break this spell. I was genuinely scared. I turned and went into the kitchen, heading straight for my trusty kettle and switching it on.

"Tea or coffee?"

"Eva . . ." He came up to me and stroked the side of my arm with his big, familiar but unfamiliar hand. His face was close to mine now, his eyes imploring, pleading. I shook him off.

"On second thought, I don't have time for tea. I think you'd better leave."

He drew back and stared at me for a few interminable seconds.

"Is that what you want?"

"Yes." I wouldn't look at him.

He left silently. I barely heard the click of the front door.

I don't know why I refused him that time. Maybe the venue was wrong. My home. Photos of my babies on the wall. Maybe the knowledge that our spouses and children were out innocently together. Perhaps as banal as the fact that I hadn't yet brushed my teeth that morning. I'd like to think it was the strength of my morals but I was soon to learn that my morals were weak indeed. When he left that morning, I felt so bereft. He was gone. It was over. I had nothing left but banal reality. I didn't want it. Next time, I went to him.

FEARING IT WAS too late, I arrived at his office that Monday. A soft knock on the door.

"Come in."

He looked amazed. I was the last person he'd expected to see. I stood for a long while, my hand stuck to the door handle, my eyes lowered. When at last I looked up at him, he was staring wordlessly. He dropped his pen on his desk and pushed his chair out, his body language open to me. I clambered onto his lap, avoiding his eyes, closing my own, focusing on his lips, covering them with my kisses, his cheeks and his forehead, finally knowing what it felt like, my questions answered. His taste, so different, so dark. It was magical, ecstatic. Like the first time in the universe. We smothered each other with ourselves, slathered each other. Entered each other. It was urgent and vital and somehow inevitable. Maybe if one of us had had the willpower. But neither one of us did. In the moment, I was exultant. Ten seconds later I was remorseful, guilt ridden, devastated. I gathered myself up and made to leave.

"Don't go, Eva. Stay and talk."

"I don't want to talk. I have to go."

"But . . ."

"I have to."

I was never going back there again. Except I was.

I THOUGHT MY guilt was at its pinnacle. I had no idea. That evening, I went home and threw myself into my role as earth mother and hearth goddess with greater gusto than I ever had before. I collected the children and spoke to them with great animation, all the way home in the car. When we got in the door, I didn't begin picking up the morning's detritus as I normally did. Instead—and this was revolutionary—I played with them. To hell with the house. I got down on my hands and knees, down on that floor, and I played with all my might. Every one of Liam's requests, I acquiesced to. He lit up as I moved cars up and down endless ramps, drove trains backward and forward across infinite tracks, and picked up imaginary loads with pint-size diggers. For Katie, I did whooshing in the air. Up over my head and down again between my legs. Up. And down. Again. And again. For the first time, she tired of the game before I did. Maybe there was a touch of the manic about it all, but my children didn't seem to care. They reveled in the attention. Once I'd dispensed with their tea, I set to work on Michael's favorite dinner of all time: steak fried with mushrooms and onions and homemade chips.

"What's all this?" He came through the kitchen door, his face holding delight, having scented his meal out in the hall.

"I thought you deserved a treat, that's all."

He put his arms around me and I allowed myself to be kissed.

"How lucky am I?" he said.

I hugged him tight and closed my eyes tighter.

"To come home to a wife like this, to food like this. Two beautiful children. I don't deserve it."

No, you don't, I thought.

"Does this mean I might get lucky?"

He smiled at me with such warmth, his eyes full of love.

"Might do."

While he read Liam his bedtime story, I jumped in the shower and scrubbed myself furiously—especially the important bits. He was already in bed waiting for me when I came out.

"You don't have to wash on my account."

"I know. I was just feeling grimy."

He turned the sheet down. "Come on in."

The phone rang.

"I'll just get that."

I rushed to pick it up. "Hello?"

"Eva."

My heart began to pound in my ears and my mouth lost all moisture. I could hear him breathing into the other end of the phone, rhythmically, like the waves crashing against the shoreline.

"I'm sorry. You have the wrong number."

I put the phone back in its cradle.

"Good," said Michael. "Now come to bed."

I got into bed with my husband and put out. At least, one half of me did. Good Eva. Bad Eva was very far away indeed.

PERHAPS I COULD be like a sophisticated Frenchwoman. I could take a lover between eating *salade* and smoking Gauloises. That's presuming real-life Frenchwomen actually did such things, outside the genre of film noir. Occasionally, I would attempt to justify my actions. But my excuses were paltry and pathetic and did nothing to convince myself. I couldn't just blame my bad self. It was my whole self, and my whole self was wrong. I did my best to keep away from him after that first afternoon in his office, but unfortunately, he didn't try to keep away from me, his marriage being, I think, already in a genuinely bad place at the time. He may have felt he had nothing to lose, whereas I had everything. I was the truly stupid one. But I thought I was in love. Felt I was. Although I loved Michael too. It was all so confused. Maybe I just loved Michael in the manner of a best friend but I was actually "in love" with Peter. If only it were permissible for a woman to have two husbands. If only Michael would go and have an affair with another woman. Then I wouldn't have to be the baddie anymore. If only he'd run off with Peter's wife, Lara, then all our problems would be solved. But he wasn't going to do any of that. Because he loved me. Properly "in loved" me. It was exquisite torture. How could I be so happy yet so unhappy at the same time? Happy to the power of infinity when I was in bed with Peter, and miserable as soon as my conscience got the better of me. We couldn't go on like this indefinitely, we both knew that, but we avoided talking about the future, both hoping, I think, that events would overtake us and that we'd be spared making any horrible, definitive decisions.

IT WAS AN evening like any other. Dinner had been eaten and the dishes cleared away. Liam was tucked up in bed, Thomas the Tank Engine stories read to his satisfaction. Katie was restless. She fretted and she fussed. She was unhappy up in my arms and unhappy down. I rocked her to no avail and fancied that she was absorbing my own agitated state. We were knackered and she was knackered but she was still no closer to sleep.

"Maybe it's her teeth." I tried the Teetha, I tried the Calpol. I considered downing the bottle myself. Frustrated, I eventually handed her over to Michael.

"Here. You take her."

"What can I do?"

"I don't know. Take her out for a drive or something. It might knock her out."

When Katie was younger, the rhythmic rocking of the car used to lull her to sleep. It was worth a try.

"Okay." Michael grabbed up his keys and a blanket for Katie. "I'll give it a go. See you in a few minutes."

Except I didn't see him in a few minutes.

My husband and daughter went out for a drive and they never came back.

And just like that, my family was halved.

23

EMILY HAD STOPPED crying. Eva had started. Then stopped again. The two women were silent for quite a while. Until Eva spoke: "A truck plowed right into them. The driver had a heart attack at the wheel."

"I'm so sorry, Eva. I had no clue."

Eva shrugged.

"I told you for a reason. And I wouldn't have told you if I didn't think I knew what you were already thinking." She looked at Emily in all seriousness.

"I've lost my baby forever. But you have a chance to get yours back."

The Summer Garden

A sensitive plant in a garden grew,
And the young winds fed it with silver dew,
And it opened its fan-like leaves to the light.
And closed them beneath the kisses of night.

—Percy Bysshe Shelley, "The Sensitive Plant"

24

URI COULD BARELY keep up with his lawns. Each quadrant of the garden had its own small, central, grassy area to which he attended assiduously. Every week he was out there with his handheld mower. Mrs. Prendergast's roses were clusters of light-filled beauty, among which she floated in a selection of floral dresses, trailing her hands dreamily against the delicate petals, taking full credit for their glory. Even though it was Seth who had put up the trellises, Seth who had kept down the weeds, and Seth who had fed them well-rotted manure—much to Mrs. Prendergast's disgust at the time.

"Must you?" she said. "It stinks to high heaven."

"Look. Do you want them to grow or don't you?"

"There's no need to take that tone."

"If you want roses, you gotta have shit."

"Honestly!"

But he didn't say a word now, surprising Eva as he let Mrs. Prendergast take full credit. Although on second thought, she wasn't really that surprised. There was a new atmosphere in the garden—an atmosphere of joy. A sense of hard work paying off at last. In such a beautiful, life-affirming setting, it was virtually impossible to be anything but entirely pleasant to every other soul. Why would you want to be anything otherwise? It hadn't always felt this way—not to Eva. There had been times when she felt that nothing was happening, times when it felt that the earth was intent on retaining all her secrets. The morning she had arrived to find her Peter Rabbit lettuces devoured by slugs. The times she had knelt on the earth and willed her veggies to grow.

"Grow, goddamnit," she would hiss, peering into the furrows of the soil, her brow furrowed, scouring for signs of green. She agonized over everything, every blade of grass. The tomatoes weren't ripening quickly enough and she feared that there wasn't enough sunshine left in the season to redden them sufficiently. As for the apple trees—a very poor showing considering all the pruning that had gone into them.

"We have an apple tree at home," said Emily. "An ancient thing. And she produces an incredible crop every second year."

Maybe that was it. This wasn't their year.

Uri approached her on one such day, her anxiety visible to the naked eye as she peered into the soil. He bent low over her. She could almost feel his beard brushing her cheek. He whispered into her ear.

"Each blade of grass has its angel that bends over it and whispers, 'Grow, grow.'"

Eva looked up into his face.

"It's not all about you, you know," he said, quietly and definitively, before smiling and walking away from her again.

Eva felt her arrogance. Then she straightenend up and relaxed her shoulders, experiencing a new lightness. It wasn't all up to her, thank God. And she felt that with a new humility, more quickly than she would have imagined.

"I'M A BIT concerned about my potatoes. Would you have a look at them, please, Seth?" she said one day.

"Sure. What's the problem?"

"Look at the leaves. They've all gone yellowy and withery. I'm afraid it might be potato blight."

"Hmmm." He bent over and examined a leaf. "I think you might be right."

"Oh no. What are we going to do?"

"There's only one thing for it."

"What?"

"We're going to have to emigrate to America."

"Seth!"

He laughed. "When the leaves turn yellow like that, it means it's time to dig them up."

"What? The spuds? You mean they're ready for eating?"

"No, for juggling."

"Stop!"

"Here," he said, handing her the shovel he'd been leaning against. "I think it's only right that you should do the honors."

She hesitated.

"Go on," he urged.

She took the shovel from him, feeling quite a ridiculous level of excitement and anticipation. They were spuds, for God's sake. She sliced the blade into the earth beside the plant closest to her, then she placed her booted foot above it and stepped down hard. The soil gave way easily. Then she bent low over the plant and tugged it with both hands. She felt it give and pulled up hard. Nothing. Nothing but a compact little network of roots. She looked at Seth in dismay.

"That doesn't mean anything," he said. "Look in the ground."

Eva hunkered down and sifted through the soil with her fingers. She couldn't believe it. Nestled in the soil, for all the world like precious jewels, were three, lifesize, perfect pink potatoes. She couldn't believe it.

"They're pink!" she said, holding one up for inspection.

"They are."

"Incredible," she said, brushing away the earth with her thumb. "They look just like something you'd get in a shop."

Seth laughed. "What were you expecting?"

"I don't know. I just didn't think that they'd be so—perfect."

She had an overwhelming urge to ask Seth if he'd bought them in a supermarket the night before and buried them especially for her to find, like a bizarre adult Easter-egg hunt. She rifled around and found three more potatoes. Then she dug up another plant. Then another. It was almost addictive, the thrill so unexpected. It made everything somehow worth it—the impossible seem possible. The proof that everyday miracles could occur.

And then she caught Seth looking at her. The meaning behind his eyes was obvious. She looked away.

"You know, this is great for me," he said.

"What is?" She stiffened.

"Witnessing a conversion."

"A conversion?" She straightened up and chanced looking over.

"Yes. To plants. Gardening."

"Oh." She smiled. Relaxed. "You make it sound like a religious experience."

"Isn't that what it is? A return to your basic nature. It's my religion anyway.' He commenced digging.

She regarded him curiously. Feeling free to do so, now that he was no longer staring at her. She'd never heard him talk like this before. He was usually so glib. As if it was his mission to keep everything light between them.

"I didn't know you had such hidden depths, Seth."

He leaned on his spade and looked at her seriously again. "There's a lot you don't know about me, Eva Madigan."

Again, his expression was way too frank for Eva, who reddened and averted her gaze once more.

"Come on," she said. "These potatoes aren't going to dig themselves."

25

*M*ICHAEL WAS KILLED instantly. I like to think he felt nothing. I don't like to think of the terror he must have experienced as he saw the truck skidding toward him, out of control, on the wrong side of the road. The driver's heart attack was fatal for everyone. Katie died in the ambulance on the way to the hospital, her little heart fluttering in her chest like a butterfly. Then still. Alone in the ambulance with no Mummy. Not even her daddy's inert, smashed-up body, which stayed behind in the tangled-up hunk of metal that used to be a Ford Focus, waiting to be cut out by the firemen. I like to think she was already gone. That only the mechanics of her body were still ticking over. That she was up with the two other Kathleens, who'd finally gotten to rock and to hold and to cradle their posthumous great-grandchild. Because she needed someone to look after her.

I didn't think I'd ever get through the pain. It immobilized me. Crushed me. I couldn't believe it at first, couldn't take it in. How could they be with me one minute, and the next, completely obliterated? Where was my Michael—the essence of him. His soul. And my baby. All that potential locked up inside that chubby little body. Where did it go? It couldn't have vanished, just like that. Yet it was nowhere to be found.

The morning of the funeral had an air of unreality about it. I wasn't in my own body. I didn't want to be. I was only aware of Liam's small hand, a permanent fixture in my own. He wouldn't let go and I wouldn't let him. But I could scarcely look at his white, pinched face, permanently upturned toward my own. His large, questioning eyes. When I saw the tiny white coffin I lost all reason and my mother took charge of him. I held Katie on my lap one last time on the way to the graveyard. No need to worry about car seats any more. Her car seat hadn't saved her anyway. I believe what I did was keen—loud, openmouthed wailing while I rocked over the body of my dead child. It was unbearable. Indescribable. I wanted to throw myself into the grave and be buried along with them. I thought I'd die anyway, from the grief alone. Nobody could feel what I was feeling and keep on living. Nor would they want to.

All the arms that encircled me, the arms of the living. All the voices that said sorry, the voices of the living. It was all a blur of black and flesh and tears. My family rallied around me, a human shield, as did Michael's family. Would they have been so understanding if they had known the truth?

Peter didn't attend the funeral, but Lara did. She embraced me fiercely, not attempting to disguise the rivulets of tears flowing freely down her cheeks. I presumed that Peter had elected to stay at home and mind their son. I was grateful for his absence. He rang me two days later.

"Eva."

"Hello, Peter."

"I don't know what to say. I'm so sorry."

"Thank you."

"How's Liam?"

"Coping, I think."

"That's good."

There was a brief silence.

"Do you want me to come over?"

"No."

"Are you sure?"

"Yes."

Silence again.

"What happens now?"

"You go and be with your wife."

I heard his sharp intake of breath.

"Is that what you want?"

"Yes."

"Forever?"

"Forever."

"I'll call you again in a few—"

"Don't."

"But just as a friend."

"No. I don't want that. I need you to respect my wishes. Please, Peter."

"Okay."

"Good-bye, Peter."

"Bye, Eva."

I was letting him off the hook.

And that was the last time I ever spoke to him. It was the last time I ever saw him too. He and Lara moved away shortly after that, right out of London to the countryside, to make a new start. Lara sent me a beautiful card around that time. I have it somewhere still. I sometimes wonder if what happened to my family made them value their own all the more.

I didn't miss Peter. Not once. Events had thrown every-thing into stark perspective. What I'd had with him meant nothing. It had been meaningless lust. A petty excitement. A sordid betrayal. I couldn't understand how I'd been so blind. So deluded. My emotions were not to be trusted, I—clearly—was not to be trusted. I missed Michael like a hollow ache that wouldn't go away. Our bed was cold and empty and huge. I'd spent the last couple of months of our life together trying to escape his embraces. Thank God he never found out why. Did he know now? Up in heaven looking down.

"Forgive me, Michael," I whispered over and over. But I

didn't think I'd ever be able to forgive myself. I knew I was being punished, for my lust and my betrayal. I hadn't valued them enough, so they'd been taken away from me. My Michael and my Katie. My baby girl. When I wasn't in our bed, wrapped in Michael's dressing gown, I was in Katie's room, kneeling down on the floor in front of her chest of drawers as if it were a shrine. I would take out her tiny pink clothes and smell them. Then I'd fold them and refold them and rearrange them until they were perfection. I'd always loved to see her rainbow-colored garments lined up in neat rows, despite the disregard in which I held the neatness of my own wardrobe. It was just such a treat after having a boy. I would spend hours doing that. When I'd finished, I'd start all over again. It may have been meaningless, but so was life. And it gave me comfort. Afterward, I'd curl up into a ball on the floor beside her crib and fall asleep. I slept a lot in those first few weeks. I think it was the drugs the doctors were giving me. Or maybe I just didn't want to be conscious. My mother took over Liam. I was useless to anyone. So much so that she eventually had to say something to me.

She called around one day to find me on the couch wearing Michael's socks and dressing gown, a cold cup of tea in my hand, staring blankly at the blank TV screen.

"Why don't you come back to my house with me, love?"

"I'm okay here, Mum."

"But you need to be with people."

"I'd rather be on my own."

My mother knelt down in front of me and forced me to look her in the eye.

"Listen to me, Eva. I know you're feeling—just awful. I know your heart has been broken. God knows, we're all shattered. I remember how I felt when your dad died and I know that this is much, much worse. But, my darling, it's not all about you. If it was I'd say fine, wallow in your misery for as long as you need to. But you have a little boy to think of. Your son. Liam needs you. He's missing his mummy desperately and there's only so much I can say or do. It's you he needs. You have to pull yourself together for him, love. I know it feels impossible but you have to try."

The tears were back. Pouring down my face as usual. Hadn't I cried enough already? No wonder I was dehydrated, my skin dessicated—this constant deluge of salty water on my cheeks. I nodded and blew my nose.

"Okay."

"Okay, you will? You'll come home with me?"

"Yes."

"Good girl. Jump into the shower first. You'll feel the better for it."

But I was in no condition for jumping into anything. Instead, my mother helped me up the stairs, linking me all the way. Then she turned on the shower and, encountering some resistance, removed Michael's robe.

"Now," she said. "Will you be okay from here on in?"

I nodded.

"Good girl. See you in a few minutes. I'm going to go down and make a fresh pot of tea."

My mother shut the door behind her and I removed my pajamas. It was like shedding a second skin, I'd been wearing them so long. I looked down at my body. My skin seemed gray. Tired looking. I was skinnier than I remembered. I seemed to have shrunk. Maybe I could disappear altogether.

I stood under the hot jets and willed them to wash it all away.

I did feel slightly better once I was clean and wearing new clothes. Immediately I felt worse for feeling better. What right had I to feel anything but despair? My husband and child were dead and it was all my fault. If I hadn't sent them out on the roads in the dark. If I hadn't submitted to my lust. If I had been a better mother, a better wife, a better person . . . the downward spiral that kept on spiraling downward.

Downstairs, I allowed my mother to fill me with hot, sweet tea.

"That's better," she said, stroking my damp hair.

She drove me to her home, a few miles away. I kept thinking that every car was going to career into us. I half-wished they would.

Liam was sitting on the floor in the middle of the sitting room with my aunt, surrounded by miniature diggers, consolation toys. Everything leaped when he saw me—his body, his expression, his heart. He ran toward me and I knelt on the floor and opened my arms out to him.

"Mummy!" He flung his arms around my neck and clung on for dear life. "I yuv you, Mummy."

"I love you too, Liam."

It was a minute before I tried to extricate myself, but he clung on even harder.

"Don't go, Mummy."

"I won't, darling. I won't."

THE FIRST ANNIVERSARY was brutal. But the day after I felt a kind of relief. At least I'd no longer be thinking "this time last year."

When I saw a toddler girl on the street, I averted my eyes.

I had returned to work for a spell, my colleagues kind yet awkward. But I found I no longer had the heart for it. Too many reminders of a life that was gone. So I left.

Liam became my everything. The whole universe focused into his dear little face. He was the reason I ate, slept, lived.

The house was mine now. Michael's death had canceled out the mortgage on this mausoleum for my memories. It was cold comfort. For a long while I was just existing, putting one foot in front of the other, putting each day behind me with the relief that I was that little bit further away from the source of all my pain. But I had to think of our future.

Liam would be school age soon. Did I want to keep on living here?

Then one night I had a dream. It was a dream like no other I'd had before or since. A perfect record of a conversation I'd once had with Michael. I dreamed about him often, but this dream was so vivid, so real, that I woke up newly bereft, the feeling so strong that he was with me still. I could almost smell the coffee he was making in the kitchen, could almost hear the shower as he stood under its jets. But the house echoed with nothingness. And that's when I knew I had to leave.

He was never coming back.

The memory was this: it was midmorning on a Saturday. The sun shone through the window as we sat at the kitchen table, the morning papers spread out in front of us, the children playing at our feet.

"You know," said Michael, suddenly putting down the part of the paper that he'd been reading. "We should move to Ireland."

"What?"

"It's the perfect time to do it. The economy there is strong. I'd get a job, no problem."

"What about my job?"

"You'd get one too. It might just take you a little longer."

"But I like the job I have." Peter was there.

"The kids could start school over there. Just think. They'd have Irish accents."

We both smiled at the thought.

"Are you serious about this?"

"Yes. Why not?"

"It's a really big step."

"I know. But what have we got to lose? It'd be a better quality of life for us. Just think about it."

I hadn't really thought about it, my mind taken up with other matters at the time. But I thought about it now, sitting up in my empty bed, enveloped by the warm feelings the dream had engendered. Why not? There was nothing for me here. Well, that wasn't strictly true. There was my mother. Liam's nana. Who'd been such a support in the last year or so. But I was stronger now. And she could visit. Dublin was only a short plane ride away. Because it was always Dublin for me. That was my home away from home. And it would make Michael happy, I thought, smiling to myself, sitting up in our bed. His son growing up to be an Irishman. A proper Paddy, not a plastic one like Michael and I had been. It was settled then. That's what we were doing. For better or for worse.

26

$\mathcal{I}$T DIDN'T TAKE Emily long to make up her mind. Not after she'd heard Eva's story. Or at least those parts Eva had deemed fit for her delicate young ears.

Eva had been right. Emily had made up her mind already. She rang the woman in the adoption agency later that afternoon, sitting on the swing seat in her sensory garden, the beginnings of honeysuckle to her left, the stirrings of jasmine to her right. She rocked herself gently as she cradled the phone to her ear, one leg tucked up under her, her boots kicked off.

"Hello. Can I speak to Stephanie, please?"

"Certainly. Can I say who's calling?"

"Emily Harte."

"Hold the line please."

The seconds ticked slowly by as Emily rocked to and fro, waiting for the opportunity to rock her world. To transform her future.

"Emily. Stephanie here."

"Hi, Stephanie."

There was a short silence during which each waited for the other to make the first move. Stephanie broke it first. She was used to this. Awkward pauses were part of her daily round.

"Are you calling to make an appointment, Emily? To sign the consent papers?"

Emily noted the professional compassion in the other woman's tone and was grateful for it.

"I've changed my mind," she said, feeling as if her heart was going to jump right out of her mouth and land on the ground in front of her. She pictured it rolling and coming to rest on the chamomile lawn.

"About what exactly?" Stepanie's voice was cautious.

"I want to keep my baby." Emily was exultant, the adrenaline racing around her body and forcing her to her feet. She began to pace as Stephanie breathed at the other end of the phone.

"Are you quite sure about this, Emily?"

"I'm one hundred percent certain."

"You don't need more time?"

"No more time. I've had enough time. Too much."

"Okay, then. I'll put the arrangements in place."

"What does that mean?"

"That I'll organize a handover for a few days from now."

"You mean I can have my baby back?"

"Of course you can have your baby back. She's still your baby."

She was her baby. Her baby.

My baby.

Once the phone call was over, Emily was beside herself.

"Oh my God, oh my God." She paced up and down, holding her face in her hands. She had to see someone, tell someone, touch someone. She ran out to the main part of the garden. Eva wasn't there. She'd gone to lectures. Seth wasn't there. He was out working on a proper job. Uri was nowhere to be found. Only Mrs. Prendergast was present, walking slowly back up to her house, oblivious to everything around her. Emily ran to her.

"Mrs. Prendergast!"

Mrs. Prendergast stopped walking toward the house and turned around, startled. Emily sensed that she'd thought herself alone in the garden. Emily reached her and flung her arms around the older woman's neck, startling her even further. Emily squeezed the woman, then released her, amazed by how fragile she felt in her embrace. How vulnerable. She drew back and looked at Mrs. Prendergast as if for the first time. A woman she'd always viewed as formidable rather than frail. Mrs. Prendergast's face was uncertain, her cheeks slightly flushed.

"What is it, my dear?"

"I'm getting my baby back. They're giving her back to me."

"Your baby?" Mrs. Prendergast was looking at her as if she had two heads.

"Yes. She's mine. My baby." Emily started to cry. Big, fat, happy tears, completely devoid of shame.

The older woman looked at her, amazement and something strange in her eyes that Emily was too preoccupied to register.

"That's wonderful, my dear. I'm very happy for you."

"Thank you." Emily laughed through her tears, like a summer shower, and hugged Mrs. Prendergast again.

"Can I get you anything? Do you want to come into the house and sit down?"

"No thanks. I'd better get back home and start organizing myself." Emily moved toward the gate, half walking, half running.

"Bye, Mrs. Prendergast."

"Bye, my dear."

Mrs. Prendergast watched Emily until she was really alone in the garden. Then she wrapped her shawl tight around her shoulders, hugging her own body, even though the day was warm. She was no longer ramrod straight with no one to watch her, a tiny figure passing beneath the shade of the ancient apple trees, back into the house that had sheltered her secrets for most of her adult life.

THE HANDOVER WAS organized for Friday morning. Emily arrived ten minutes early and Stephanie drove them both to the foster family's home. Emily was ready. At least she thought she was. The house wasn't at all what she'd been expecting, although she hadn't even known that she'd been expecting anything. It was small and neat and modest. Emily realized that she was put out because they hadn't housed her daughter in something more palatial. Her next thought was that it was a damn sight more than she herself could offer. Oh God.

The car drew to a halt and it was time to get out. Incredibly, her legs were still functioning and she accompanied Stephanie to the front door. They rang the bell and waited. A man of about sixty answered the door. He nodded at Stephanie, clearly recognizing her, and stood aside to let them enter. He stared at Emily, averting his gaze as she caught him. They were ushered into a living room, where a woman sat in the center of a couch, an infant asleep in her arms. She looked more grandmother than mother. This surprised Emily, but she didn't dwell on it much as she was far to busy staring at her daughter. Everyone whispered, in deference to the sleeping child.

"You must be Emily," said the woman.

Emily nodded.

"I'm Marie. Why don't you sit down beside us."

Emily did so, perching on the edge of the couch, her eyes fixed on the baby's face.

"I'd know you anywhere," said Marie. "She's the image of you."

"Is she?" Emily allowed herself a smile. Was it true? She couldn't see it. But she recognized her daughter, or at least she felt she did.

"Wouldn't you like to hold her?"

"Won't she wake?"

"Here. Sit back."

Emily eased herself back into the couch and accepted the warm, floppy weight of her daughter. The baby stirred but remained sleeping. The minutes passed. It had been eight months since she'd last held her. Last tasted her. Her daughter now had a full set of eyelashes. They fanned out into two black crescents, casting delicate shadows on her cheeks. Her mouth was a perfect rosebud. This, Emily remembered. She looked at Marie.

"Have you done this before?"

"Thirty-nine times now, including this little one," said Marie. "And each time it's like giving up one of my own."

Emily looked at her properly for the first time.

"I'm sorry."

The woman touched her arm.

"Don't be. I'm happy for you both. Very happy."

"Are you ready?" said Stephanie gently.

Emily nodded and eased herself up off the couch.

"Here are all her things." Marie handed an oversize bag to Stephanie while she addressed Emily. "You've got nappies, wipes, baby onesies, and clothes. The little teddy she sleeps with and a bottle for later."

"Thank you."

"You're more than welcome. Take good care of each other."

"We will. I'll send you photos. Let you know how she's getting on."

"Will you?"

"Of course."

"I'd really love that." Marie planted a swift kiss on the baby's forehead and turned away.

Emily stepped out of the house feeling as if she were stealing her own baby.

OF COURSE, THE baby woke up and started to scream as soon as they attempted to strap her into her car seat. Emily sat in the back beside her and held a bottle to her lips. It kind of worked.

"I'll take you home," Stephanie said.

"Would you mind taking me somewhere else instead?"

STEPHANIE HELPED EMILY lug the buggy out of the boot and assemble it on the footpath, then click the car seat into the buggy. There was so much to know, and that was even before you got to the baby.

Although the day was balmy, Emily placed a blanket over the once again sleeping form of her daughter. Then she let herself in through the wrought-iron gate, which had been newly painted by Uri. Who was the first person to see her.

He approached her, smiling. "We were wondering where you'd got to. Doing a little babysitting?"

"You could say that."

Uri peered into the buggy. "Where did this little one come from, then?"

"Me."

"Pardon?"

"She came from me, Uri. This is my daughter."

Uri looked from Emily to the baby and back again.

"Really?"

"Yes."

She could see the questions passing across Uri's face, but he contained them all. Instead, he stepped up to Emily, held her by the upper arms, and kissed her warmly on each cheek.

"Mazel tov."

Emily felt close to tears at his touch. Then Eva came rushing over and she *was* in tears as the other woman overwhelmed her with emotion.

"Emily! You're here. You're both here." She leaned into the buggy. "Oh, she's so like you, Emily. I'm not just saying that." Then she embraced Emily with abandon, rocking her back and forth in her arms, both women laughing through their tears.

Seth and Mrs. Prendergast approached with some caution. They both stared at the baby, then at Emily.

"Is she yours?" Seth said eventually.

"She is."

"Congratulations."

"Thanks."

"What's her name?" said Mrs. Prendergast, unable to resist reaching out and touching the child's cheek with her dry fingers.

"Rose," said Emily, looking down at her daughter. "Her name's Rose."

Mrs. Prendergast nodded, before turning and walking away.

Eva insisted that Rose and Emily stay with her for that first night. She didn't have to do much persuading. Rose screamed well into the early hours, waking up even Liam. He snuggled into his mother's warmth, half asleep.

"Has Katie come back to us, Mummy?"

Eva hugged him close. "Go to sleep, my darling."

THE NEXT DAY, Eva drove mother and daughter to Kilkenny.

"What time are they expecting you?" They were almost there.

"They're not."

"What?"

"I didn't tell them I was coming."

"Why not?"

"I wanted to surprise them."

Eva had a horrible thought as she glanced across at Emily's impassive profile.

"You did tell them about Rose."

"Not yet."

"What?"

Luckily, there was a lay-by coming up for Eva to skid into.

"Jesus Christ, Emily. What were you thinking?"

"I couldn't bring myself to tell them over the phone. And besides. They're less likely to reject her if they see her in the flesh. I mean, she's beautiful, isn't she?"

"Of course she's beautiful. But, Emily. You should have told me that they didn't know. What do I do when we get there? Do I come inside the house or do I just drop you off. Or do I wait outside in the car in case . . ."

"In case they kick me out."

"Well, I wasn't going to put it like that. But . . . you don't think they will, do you?"

"I don't know. I hope not."

"So do I."

They sat there quietly for a while, staring out of the windscreen in unison, lorries whizzing by at intervals and shaking the car in their wake.

"Will you come in with me?" Emily looked across at Eva.

"I don't see how I have any choice."

"I'm sorry, Eva. I didn't mean for you to feel emotionally blackmailed."

"It's not that. I just need to pee. Really badly. And it's all your fault for making that tea before we left."

IT WAS A traditional farmhouse. Nothing cutesy about it. Just functional. Some effort had been made—there were rambling roses up the side wall. And it was neat. But it was what it was.

They arrived close to lunchtime, and to Eva's untrained eye, it looked like no one was around. But, said Emily, given the location and given the time, this scenario was impossible. Emily removed the sleeping Rose, complete with car seat, and carried her into the house. Eva followed close behind.

The large kitchen was empty but clearly showed signs of

life, pots bubbling and steaming on an old Aga. Emily placed Rose and her car seat carefully in a vacant corner, facing the wall. Footsteps approached from the hall and the two women looked at each other. A third woman entered, an overflowing laundry basket under one arm. She looked just like Emily, only her colors were less vivid. She stopped dead.

"Emily!" Her face creased into smiles. "This is a lovely surprise. What are you doing here?" She laid her washing basket down on the massive kitchen table and hugged her daughter.

"Hiya, Mammy." Eva watched Emily sink into her mother as if she was afraid it was to be for the last time. Mrs. Harte met Eva's eye over her daughter's shoulder.

"Hello."

Eva nodded. Emily disengaged herself.

"Mammy. This is Eva, a good friend of mine. She drove me down. Eva started the whole garden thing, remember, I was telling you?"

"Oh yes. It's very nice to meet you. I'm Emily's mother in case you didn't guess. Why don't you sit down and take the weight off?"

Eva nodded and proceeded to sit down in one of the kitchen chairs.

"Nice to meet you, Mrs. Harte."

"Oh, none of that. Call me Bridget."

Eva was amazed by how young she was—no more than midforties—and realized how inaccurate her vision of Emily's mother had been. She was only about a decade older than herself.

Rose chose this exact moment to whimper. It was a delicious sound—not ready to wake up yet, just settling back into her dreams. Three sets of eyes swung toward the car seat in the corner.

"You have a baby!" exclaimed Bridget, rushing over for an examination. "Ah, would you look at her. How old?" She addressed Eva.

"Um. Eight months, but . . ."

"Eight months. What a gorgeous age. What's her name?"

"Rose," said Emily. "Mammy. You have the wrong end of the stick."

Bridget looked up at her daughter in confusion.

"What do you mean?"

Eva watched Emily draw herself up to her full height.

"She's mine."

Understanding and denial fought for dominance on Mrs. Harte's face.

"What are you talking about?"

"The baby. She's mine."

Eva was sure the clock hadn't been ticking as loudly in the seconds beforehand. But now it was all she could hear, as if signaling the imminent detonation of a bomb.

She and Emily watched as Bridget's complexion turned from cream to flush to puce.

"Mammy, are you all right?"

Bridget was holding on to the side of a dresser as if to support herself. Wordlessly, Eva took the woman by her free arm and walked her to a kitchen chair, where she sat her down. Then she searched for a kettle and switched it on.

"Mammy. Say something."

Bridget was gripping the side of the kitchen table. The table that had been scarred by a thousand coffee cups. She appeared to be whispering something to herself.

"What did you say?"

"I don't understand." Bridget turned and looked at her daughter, her face now a somewhat normal color. "How could you possibly have a baby?"

"Well, I did it the old-fashioned way. It wasn't a virgin birth, if that's what you mean." Emily's words were defiant, but Eva noticed that she kept her eyes lowered.

"No. I mean, she's eight months old. Where has she been all this time?"

Emily sighed and sat down heavily in the chair beside her mother.

"She was in a foster home. I was going to have her adopted but I couldn't go through with it."

"But your pregnancy . . ." Bridget was shaking her head slowly.

"I was small. I wore baggy clothes. And then when I was heavily pregnant, I just didn't come home. Remember last summer when you were put out that I wasn't coming home for the weekends?"

Bridget nodded as if in a trance. Then all of a sudden, she seemed to come to.

"Who's the father?"

"A boy in college. He's not important. He didn't want to know."

"So when you had the baby. Rose. In hospital?"

"I had her in hospital, yes."

"Who was with you?"

"No one."

The words reverberated around the kitchen as their impact resonated with all three women. Bridget clamped her hand over her mouth and her face began to crumple.

"Why didn't you tell me?"

"I didn't think you'd understand."

As both women began to cry, Eva slipped out of the kitchen and closed the door quietly behind her. She found herself in a long hallway. At the end of the hallway was a porch. On the porch was a young boy—around eight or nine—in the process of kicking off a pair of mucky shoes and simultaneously shrugging a schoolbag off his back.

"Hello," said Eva, walking toward him.

"Well." He nodded at her. She presumed that "well" passed for "hello" in these parts.

"I take it you're Emily's brother."

He nodded briefly. "Who are you?"

"I'm Eva, a friend of Emily's."

He nodded, apparently uninterested, and walked past her toward the kitchen door.

"I wouldn't go in there if I were you."

"Why not?"

"Because Emily and your mother are in there and they need some privacy."

"But I came home for me dinner."

"Just give them five minutes. Go and watch some cartoons or something."

The boy eyed her resentfully.

"What are you doing here anyway?"

"Actually, I was looking for a toilet."

27

*T*HEY DIDN'T SEE Emily for the rest of the summer. She was on maternity leave. It was strange without her at first. But the others grew to fill in the gap.

There were reminders of her everywhere. In the purple spikes of lavender—French, not English. When a breeze or a childish hand jangled the wind chimes. Eva would sit in the evenings by Emily's night-scented stock like a woman intoxicated. Sometimes Seth would sit with her and they would talk until nightfall, the children playing around them, well past their bedtime. It was only a matter of time before they both asked the questions they'd been aching to ask. Until they did, these questions would remain an unspoken barrier between them.

Eva went first. Having faced more in life, she was less fearful. It was like a confession box, that clump of night-scented stock.

"Do you see much of your wife, Seth?"

The question appeared sudden, but they both knew it had been a long time in coming.

"Yes. Every time I pick Kathy up or drop her off."

"Of course. What's that like?"

"All right. It was weird at first, but we're both used to it now."

"Is she in another relationship?"

"Yes."

"That must be strange. Knowing that Kathy has another father figure in her life."

"Mother figure."

"Pardon?"

Seth turned his head so that he was looking at her. She could clearly see his eyes now. Hazel, flecked with blue and green.

"She has another mother figure. Megan left me for a woman."

Several heartbeats were missed.

"Really?"

"Yes, really."

"That must have been tough."

He shrugged and looked down at his feet.

"Did you feel—I don't know—emasculated or something?"

"If you mean did I feel like she'd cut off my balls, then the answer is yes."

"Ouch."

"Ouch is right. It didn't help that she was so open about it. She still lives in the same neighborhood and doesn't try to hide it. I'm not saying she should or anything. It would just be easier for me if everyone didn't know. Can you imagine the lads down the pub? It doesn't really go with my macho image."

"No, I don't suppose it does."

They were both quiet for a while.

"Have they grown back then?"

"What?"

"Your balls."

He laughed. She liked making him laugh.

"I almost have a full set." He looked at her. "Your turn."

"What?"

"You know. You got my sordid details. Now you tell me yours."

He was smiling, but she could see that his eyes were serious. Had he been as curious about her as she had been about him? It took a while for her to speak. He didn't say anything, sensing she was building up to it.

"My husband died," she said eventually. "A little over two years ago."

"I'm sorry," he said.

"Did you already know?"

"How would I know?"

"I told Emily a while back. I wasn't sure if she'd said anything to anyone."

"Not to me she didn't. Although I did wonder why Liam didn't seem to have anything to do with his father. That would explain it."

She nodded.

"How did he die?"

"Car accident."

"Jesus. That must have been terrible. For you and for Liam."

They both watched Liam as he and Kathy raced his extensive collection of tractors up and down the path, their commentary enthusiastic and bizarre.

"I sent him out."

"How do you mean?"

She breathed deeply. "We had a little girl too. Katie. She was one. She couldn't get to sleep one night, so I suggested he take her out for a drive."

Eva felt Seth's hand enclosing hers. His skin rough. His sympathy complete.

For a long time, neither of them said anything. Then: "What was she like? Katie."

He watched Eva's face closely as she smiled, her eyes filling up with tears.

"Oh, you know. She was a one-year-old girl. She was gorgeous. Always smiling. Massive blue eyes, reddish gold hair—

her daddy was a redhead. Chubby little arms and legs. You just wanted to eat her. She'd only just learned to walk. She was delighted with herself, toddling around, pulling the house apart. She was just—brilliant."

"I'm so, so sorry, Eva."

She nodded her head in acknowledgment and they both just sat there for ages, watching the children, laughing intermittently at their antics, Eva's hand in Seth's.

"Almost the worst thing has been the guilt," said Eva at last, staring straight ahead.

"It wasn't your fault. When I think of the number of times I drove Kathy around when she was a baby, trying to get her to sleep."

"It's not just that."

"What is it, then?"

Eva didn't know why she was telling him this. She was just struck by the urge to be absolutely honest.

"I was having a—a kind of affair when they died."

"Oh."

"It was stupid. I thought it was serious, but it wasn't. It took Michael dying to make me realize how little it meant."

She looked over at Seth, trying to gauge his reaction, but he was consulting his shoes. She thought she sensed a withdrawal of sympathy, but it may just have been her guilty conscience.

"The one good thing was that he never found out about it."

"That you know of."

"Pardon?"

"As far as you know he never found out about it."

"I would have known."

"Not necessarily."

Seth was sitting forward now, looking away from her. At some point he had withdrawn his hand.

"What's that supposed to mean?"

"It's like when Megan—my ex—started to see Siobhan,

her girlfriend. I suspected for months before I actually found out about it."

"Thanks, Seth."

"What? I'm just being honest."

"Don't you think I feel bad enough as it is? I know what I did was wrong. Unforgivable even. But believe me, I've paid a price for it. Jesus Christ." She stood up, angry now.

"Where are you going?"

"Home. Liam! Packing-up time."

She looked back at him and found that he was staring at her, his expression hard. She knew what it was: she'd disappointed him. Failed to live up to the image he had of her in his head. Well, fuck him. She'd never told him to put her on a pedestal.

She gathered up Liam's belongings and turned to look at him again. He was stony faced.

"Do you know what it took for me to confide in you?" she said, struggling to keep the tremor out of her voice. "I never thought you'd throw it back in my face. You might have thought better of me, but I thought better of you too, Seth."

She turned and walked away from him, muttering, "Arsehole," under her breath, just loudly enough for him to hear.

IT WAS JULY and the garden was by now producing far too many fruits and vegetables for the gardeners alone to consume: potatoes, peas, sugarsnaps, spring onions, cabbage, and lettuce. Not to mention the soft fruits: raspberries, strawberries, black currants, and red currants. An emergency meeting was called. This consisted of Eva, Uri, Seth, and Mrs. Prendergast standing around in a rough circle, leaning on various forks and shovels.

"We have to decide what to do with the leftover veggies. We can't let them go to waste."

"No. Absolutely not," said Uri.

"We could have a harvest festival," said Seth.

"Don't be so ridiculous," said Mrs. Prendergast. "It's far too early in the year to have a harvest festival."

"But we have the produce now."

"A harvest festival isn't held until the autumn."

"We'll call it something different, then."

"A harvest festival is a very good idea. Maybe we can plan one for a couple of months down the line. But in the meantime, I have another proposal."

They all looked at Eva expectantly.

"How about seeing if the Good Food Store would sell it for us? I'm sure Emily's aunt would agree. She's a very accomodating woman and they have a little fruit and veg section already. What do you think?"

The others all nodded enthusiastically.

"It's worth a try," said Mrs. Prendergast.

"It's an excellent idea," said Uri.

"What would we do with the profits?" said Seth. "There's hardly any point in plowing it back into the garden."

He found himself at the receiving end of three dirty looks.

"What?" He held up his hands. "Well, there isn't, is there?"

Eva, who still wasn't really talking to him, addressed him coolly.

"We can decide what to do with any profits we make at a later date. Let's just see if she'll agree to it first. Uri, will you come with me? Mrs. Prendergast, I think I'm right in saying you don't get on with her particularly well and Seth would just annoy her."

"How would I annoy her?"

"You're just annoying."

"Thanks."

"Of course I'll come with you," said Uri.

They spent the rest of the morning putting together a selection of their finest produce. When it was assembled, Eva and Uri carried the box over to the store. As luck would have

it, Emily's aunt, her father's sister-in-law, happened to be behind the counter when they called.

"Ah, Eva. What can I do for you today?"

Amongst the Hartes, Eva was widely credited with getting
Emily back on the straight and narrow again. This was a card
she was prepared to play if she had to.

"It's more," said Eva, plonking the wooden crate down on
the counter in front of her, "a question of what we can do for
you."

"Is that so?"

"Yes, it is. You do know Uri—Mr. Rosenberg?"

"Of course. Morning, Uri."

"Good morning, Mrs. Harte."

"What I have in this box is an example of the food we've
been producing in the community garden—you know—Mrs.
Prendergast's old walled garden."

"I do indeed."

"We were wondering if you'd be interested in selling it
for us."

The woman looked as if she needed convincing.

"A percentage of the profits to go to the shop, of course,"
said Uri.

"Of course," echoed Eva. "And you can't get fresher fruit
and veg than this. Handpicked in the last hour. Local produce
grown by local people. It fits in with the whole ethos of the
shop: food for the community, grown by the community, no
air miles, no pesticides . . ." She trailed off, looking to see if
her words were having any impact.

"I'll tell you what," said Mrs. Harte. "I'll give this lot a
try, and if it sells, I'll take some more off your hands."

It was all sold by that evening. They were in business.

EVA ARRIVED IN the garden first thing and carried out her
usual tour of inspection. She'd had a busy week marking exam

papers and hadn't visted for days. She was heading toward the runner beans when she spotted it—one perfect, plump, shiny, voluptuous tomato. Bright red. Tomato red even. She caressed it gently, loath to disturb such perfection. It looked so delicious. Nobody would know . . .

"Hi there."

She jumped. It was Seth. "What are you doing here?"

He gave her a look.

"Same as you."

"You gave me a fright."

"Why, what are you up to?"

"Nothing."

She had quickly withdrawn her hand from the red-hot tomato, but she hadn't been quick enough in averting her gaze. Seth leaned over to the plant.

"Is it—a tomato. Brilliant."

He rubbed the fruit between his thumb and forefinger.

"Eva Madigan. You weren't thinking of—eating it—were you?"

"Of course not."

"Are you sure?" He was mocking her now.

Eva felt herself redden. Tomato red?

"Something, something, something . . . money can't buy except true love—oh, you know the song, homegrown tomatoes." He delivered this in the most appalling American southern accent, pronouncing "tomatoes" the American way.

"What?"

"It's a song. Guy Clark, I think. Country and western."

Eva laughed in spite of herself.

"I like it. Only please don't say it again in that terrible accent."

Seth laughed too, relieved that she was talking to him.

"Do you think it's true?" he said.

"I don't know."

"Why don't you give it a try?" He took a step closer to her.

"What do you mean?"

"Try it." He leaned across her and touched the plant.

"Oh, the tomato."

"Why, what did you think I meant?"

"Nothing. I can't eat it."

"Why not? That's what it's for."

"But it's not mine to eat. It belongs to everybody."

"There'll be other tomatoes. You started this thing. It seems only fair that you should get the first taste."

"You think so?"

"Go on," he urged.

Eva gripped the tomato, prepared to give it a good tug, but it fell into her hand as if it had been waiting for her. She looked at Seth again. He nodded and smiled. Then she bit deep into the tender flesh, the unimaginable sweetness bursting onto her tongue.

"Mmmm." She closed her eyes.

Seth laughed delightedly.

"Here," she said, holding it up to his mouth.

Seth, his eyes not leaving hers, held Eva's hand in his own as he bit into the fruit. He continued to hold her hand long after he'd finished chewing, all the while staring at her.

"I'm sorry, Eva," he said. "You were right. I am an arsehole and I apologize."

"I'm sorry too."

"Yoo-hoo!" It was Mrs. Prendergast. Seth withdrew his hand and the two stepped away from each other.

THEY WERE DIGGING a new flower bed, Seth and Eva. It was experimental, a wildflower patch. Eva imagined a heady mix of borage, poppies, and marigolds. Except she felt as if she were just making up the numbers, Seth being able to dig three times faster and deeper than she was, no matter how hard she worked. Liam and Kathy were helping too. Kathy, with her pink Barbie shovel. Since meeting Kathy, Eva had discovered that they made just about a Barbie everything. The girl had Barbie wellies too and a pink Barbie bicycle. She wouldn't be surprised if they made Barbie tampons for older girls. Liam was using his favorite yellow digger, scooping up minute particles of earth and moving them a few centimeters along. If it wasn't for Seth, they would have been digging until Christmas.

It was pleasant, satisfying work, despite or perhaps because of the hard physical labor involved. The children nattered aimlessly and asked all sorts of irrelevant questions. Such as:

"Eva."

"Yes, Kathy."

"Are you going to be my new mammy?"

The rhythm of Seth's digging was disturbed for a barely discernible nanosecond. Eva didn't dare look at him.

"Why are you asking me that?"

"Because I already have two mammies and if I had you as well, then I'd have three."

"Well, I think two mammies are plenty for any girl. And I'm already Liam's mammy. I'm pretty busy doing that."

"You're not Liam's mammy. You're his mummy."

"That's very true."

"Well, if you're not going to be my mammy, why were you holding my daddy's hand the other day?"

Silence. Eva could feel her face growing hot.

"Kathy. Leave Eva alone now. She's trying to work."

"But I want to know why she was holding your hand." Kathy's voice became whiny.

"Your daddy was holding my hand to make me feel better because I was sad."

"Why were you sad?"

"I can't remember. But I'm better now."

"Were you sad that Liam's daddy has gone away?"

Seth and Eva glanced at each other. Eva thought he looked as alarmed as she felt.

"Did you tell her?" she asked him.

"No! It must have been Liam."

"My daddy's up in heaven with Holy God and all the angels," announced Liam. "And Katie is with him and she has wings too."

"Where's heaven, Daddy?"

"It's a very long way from here."

"Like Bray?"

"A bit like Bray, yes."

"Can we go there tomorrow, after play school?"

"No, Kathy. It's a really, really long way away."

"We can get the bus."

"No, Kathy."

"Oh why not? It's not fair." She started to bash the earth with her Barbie shovel.

"I know. Who'd like some chocolate?"

"Me!"

"Me!"

Eva delved into the pocket of her fleece for the few squares of Dairy Milk she hoped she hadn't eaten already. No, they were still there.

"Here we go."

"Yippee!"

"Yippee!"

She glanced quickly across at Seth. He wasn't looking at her but was instead focusing hard on pulling up a stubborn piece of old root. She recommended digging, concentrating on the far end of the bed, a piece of land hitherto unworked. The blade of the shovel hit something hard. Must be a rock, and a big one at that, judging by the feel of it. She attempted to go around it, digging elsewhere, but she kept reconnecting with the rock.

"You got something there?" Seth was behind her.

"Yes. I can't shift it."

"Here. Let me have a go."

Seth sliced into the piece of earth she'd been digging and came up against the same hard object.

"I don't think that's a rock."

Eva grabbed at his sleeve, her eyes wide.

"You don't think it's—a bone, do you?" She instinctively looked around for Mrs. Prendergast.

"No. No, I wouldn't say so." He laughed. "You don't seriously believe that story, do you?"

"I don't know. No. Of course not."

"She may be a mad old trout but she's not a murderer."

"She might have been driven to it."

"How?"

"He might have been an annoying bastard."

Seth laughed. "Here. I'll prove it to you. It's not bone, it's metal."

He began digging again in a more frenzied manner, then started tugging at something with his hands. Seth lifted the object out of the dirt. It was an old, square, rusty metal box. Liam and Kathy had finished their chocolate.

"What is it, Daddy?"

"It's a box."

"What kind of box?"

"I don't know, Kathy."

"Open it, open it." The children jumped up and down in an excited manner.

"It's not mine to open," said Seth. "It might belong to Mrs. Prendergast. We'll have to ask her first."

Gathering Uri to them as they went, they trooped en masse to the back door of Mrs. Prendergast's house and knocked. They heard her advancing steps.

"His teeth might be in there," whispered Seth, just as the door was opening, leaving Eva to bite down on her giggles.

"Mrs. P." He held the box with outstretched hands. "Look what we found. Does it mean anything to you?"

Mrs. Prendergast wore an unfamiliar expression on her face. She took the box wordlessly out of Seth's hands and turned and walked back into her house. The remaining adults looked at one another. Uri nodded and they followed Mrs. Prendergast into her hallowed living quarters.

The back door led them into a kind of coat and mucky boot area that opened out into the kitchen. Seated at the surprisingly rustic-looking kitchen table was Lance, Mrs. Prendergast's son, a half-drunk mug of coffee in front of him. He was slumped back in his chair, in his shirtsleeves, the top button of his shirt open, his tie loosened. He straightened up as they entered, his expression shifting from tired to surprised to wary.

"Lance, look at this. Do you remember?"

She proferred the box and Lance took it out of her hands and examined it. Eva could see now that it was an old biscuit tin, badly rusted over. The brand was Jacobs USA and the recognition brought her whizzing back to the 1970s—a child in her grandmother's Dublin home at Christmastime. *Oliver Twist* on the telly. A brown-gray furry toy rabbit called Strawberry on her lap, her favorite present of that year.

"Have a biscuit, Eva, love."

Selecting a fluorescent pink wafer sandwich, her grandmother smiling at her indulgently, equating as she did even illuminated food with love. Eva was suddenly nostalgic for the Irish foods of her childhood: Galtee and Calvita cheeses; Tayto crisps; Lemon's sweets; Kimberley, Mikado, and coconut cream biscuits. All of them you could probably still get, although she hadn't tasted most of them for years. She resolved to remedy this as soon as possible. Could you still get USA biscuits . . . ?

Lance and his mother were searching each other's faces.

"The time capsule," said Lance. Then he laughed and attempted to prize it open.

"What's a time capsule?" said Liam.

Eva scooped him up into her arms and held him to her.

"It's when you put some things in a box and bury them and leave them for somebody else to find years later. You put things in the box to show the person who finds it what life was like when they buried the box. Sometimes it might not be found for hundreds of years. But this one wouldn't be that old."

"How old is it?"

"Twenty-eight years old," said Lance, who had opened the box and was unfolding a newspaper. It was slightly damp and some of the pages were stuck together. Eva took a few steps closer to peer at the date on the front of the *Irish Times*.

"The twenty-sixth of June 1979," she read. As she leaned in, she breathed in the mustiness of the last twenty-eight years and the scent transported her instantly back to her childhood for the second time that day.

When she was a little kid, her family used to take weekend breaks in Eastbourne, in a trailer belonging to friends of her parents. Each time they opened up the trailer anew, months of mustiness would invade their collective nostrils. It was a scent peculiar and exotic to Eva, and exactly the same as that which was now emanating from the newspaper. She had only experienced it one other time and that was when she purchased a secondhand book from a little bookshop in Notting Hill. She opened it up and whoosh, she was back in the trailer, six years old again. She looked into her son's four-year-old face. Would this moment become a memory for him?

Lance was reading out headlines from the paper. They all crowded around and peered in. It did occur to Eva that perhaps they should give Lance and his mother some privacy but, quite frankly, she was too nosy. And Liam would have a fit if she took him away now. And they had buried it with the intention of somebody else finding it, so it couldn't have been that private. And besides, nobody else looked as if they had any intention of budging.

It appeared, from the headlines, as if not much had

changed in the past twenty-eight years, a thought that was either comforting or depressing, depending on which way you looked at it.

"What else is in there?" said Kathy, standing on her tiptoes, her body tense with impatience. Lance folded the newspaper and put it to one side. He delved into the box and pulled out a clear plastic package.

"Money."

He emptied out coins representative of every denomination and an old pound note.

"What else?" said Kathy, unimpressed.

Mrs. Prendergast reached down and took out what appeared to be an old photograph. She stared at it for a good two minutes before handing it silently to Uri, who was standing beside her. After several seconds, his face broke into a smile.

"The apple tree."

They all crowded around him, except Mrs. Prendergast, who sat down on one of the kitchen chairs, her face masklike.

Trust Uri to notice the apple tree. Eva barely registered it, recognizable as it was, although less gnarled and more tender. Instead, she was focusing on the three people standing in front of the tree, smiling for the camera and squinting into the sun. A young boy—Lance presumably—dark haired and skinny, wearing seventies-style short shorts and a Band-Aid on each bony knee. Standing behind him, a protective hand on his shoulder, was none other than a young Mrs. Prendergast. It had to be her. The same narrow figure, the tiny waist. Only her bearing was less stiff, as was her hair, pale gold and wavy, tied into a ponytail that cascaded over her left shoulder like a keratin waterfall.

"Kathy, look at Mrs. P," said Seth. "Wasn't she a fine thing?"

"That's not Mrs. Prendergast," said Kathy, her tone full of derision.

"Yes it is."

"Then how come she looks so different?"

"It was taken a long time ago."

Eva could see that Seth was regretting bringing the matter up. But she was far too interested in the photo to pay much heed. The third figure was a man. He stood a little apart from what presumably were his wife and son. He was large, attractive, muscular, his face and smile not unlike Lance's. His hands were on his hips and his shirtsleeves were rolled up. The famous Mr. Prendergast she presumed.

"Is that your father?" Uri addressed Lance.

"Yes." Lance sat down again, his face closed.

"Look, roses!" Eva's attention was momentarily distracted by a cloud of pale pink in the left of the photo. It was tremendously exciting to see this picture of how the garden once was, if only in part.

One last thing remained in the box. Lance took it out now. He handed it to his mother and she turned it over in her hands, smoothing its face with her fingers.

"Do you remember this, Lance?" She was smiling now.

"Vaguely."

It was a ceramic angel, faded and old looking, like something you might put on a Christmas tree. It was blue and white.

"Your father brought this back from Amsterdam."

"It's a fairy," said Kathy.

"Actually, no, Kathy, it's an angel," said Uri.

"I didn't know you Jews believed in angels."

It wasn't what Lance said so much as the way he said it. Indefinable. Yet unmistakable. The way he spat the word out instantaneously transformed the atmosphere in the room from one of wonder to one of hostility. Eva felt as if she'd been slapped in the face. She could only imagine how Uri and Seth felt. It was horrible. With great dignity, Uri placed the photo back down on the table.

"You'd be surprised by what us Jews believe in," he said, before walking out of the kitchen, out of the house, and into the garden. The silence in the kitchen grew. Eva could feel something mounting up in Seth, beside her. She willed him not to say anything, not to thump Lance. He didn't. Instead, he glared at Lance with great intensity, before following his father out to the garden. Eva was left in the kitchen with Lance, Mrs. Prendergast, and the two children, who were examining the angel in great detail.

"How could you, Lance?" Mrs. Prendergast said, turning to her son.

This time they needed their privacy.

"Come on, kids. It's nearly lunchtime. Let's go and get something to eat."

"I'm not hungry."

"Me neither."

"I've got treats."

"Yippee! Treats!"

"What are they?"

"Come outside and I'll show you."

They left mother and son alone to discuss whatever it was they had to discuss.

EVA HATED THE way the garden felt that afternoon, Seth and Uri so quiet. As if the very air itself had been tainted. She wanted to say something but they both seemed so unapproachable, each man working in his own private space. It was so awful though. She had to do something. She eventually walked over to Seth, who had finished digging the bed. He was loading up his wheelbarrow with an assortment of rocks. It was about an hour after the incident.

"Hi, Seth."

"Eva." He nodded at her and continued loading up the rocks.

"How are you?"

"Grand."

"Are you sure?"

"Why wouldn't I be?" He stopped what he was doing and looked at her, his hands on his hips.

"It's just that I thought, you know, what happened inside . . ."

"I wouldn't let an ignorant prick like that get to me."

Except it was clear that he had.

She let the silence settle between them for a while. Then: "It must have been strange for you. Growing up Jewish in Dublin."

"Not really. Most of the time it made no difference at all. I barely thought about it until my bar mitzvah."

"So you had that, then?"

"Oh yes."

"And were you . . . ?"

"Yes, Eva, I am circumcised."

She gave an embarrassed little laugh.

"I suppose everyone wants to know that."

"Pretty much."

"You must get sick of people asking?"

"Depends on who's doing the asking."

He smiled at her then. Right into the pit of her stomach.

"What was Uri like, when you were growing up?"

"He was pretty strict. A lot stricter than he is with his grandkids. He wanted Aaron and me to 'make something of ourselves.'"

"Well, he got his wish."

Seth smiled again and cast his eyes downward, almost bashfully. Eva was surprised. She hadn't known he did bashful.

"Ah, you know. We had our moments. Mostly when I was a teenager. Didn't want to go to synagogue. Wouldn't study. Gave back cheek. The usual pain in the arse stuff."

"You! A pain in the arse. I don't believe it."

"Yeah, well. It's true."

"And how do you feel about it now? The religious side of things."

"Well, it doesn't do all that much for me, but it means a lot to him. So I respect that. Respect him. More than anyone else, really. He's been through a lot, my da. And he's come out of it one of the best people I know. If I can be half the man he is, half the father to Kathy that he was to me and Aaron. Well. I'd be doing pretty well."

Seth, who seemed to have lost himself in this reverie, came back sharply into focus.

"Anyway, what are we doing standing around here, woman? There's work to be done."

He handed her a shovel.

"Get digging."

He walked away then. To fetch a bag of compost, or so he said.

Eva watched him go.

A thought came unbidden: I could love this man.

She was momentarily distracted by the sight of Mrs. Prendergast coming across the garden. She didn't look at Eva. Instead, she headed straight for Uri. She watched as he stopped what he was doing and turned to face her. Mrs. Prendergast spoke earnestly to him, beseechingly, her body tense and bent slightly forward, her arms crossed tightly over her chest. When she'd finished speaking, Uri looked at her for a few long seconds. Then he embraced her warmly and the two of them linked arms and walked toward the house, disappearing together through the wooden door.

"Did you see that?" said Seth, coming to stand by her side.

"I did."

"What do you reckon that was all about?"

"She was probably apologizing for Lance."

"She shouldn't have to."

"Well. Maybe she wanted to. Unless . . ."

"What?"

"There could be more to it."

"Like what?"

"Maybe you're getting a new mammy."

They both laughed. And everything felt okay again. At least to Seth. To Eva, it was as if the entire universe had been flipped on its head.

28

*I*T WAS SO odd. So unfathomable to her. That moment in time when everything switched. The inner shift in consciousness that altered her world.

One minute Seth was a friend. Objectively attractive, undeniably useful, mildly annoying. And now here she was thinking about him every second of the day. Obsessing about him. Could he tell? Could he feel the desire radiating off her in waves? Her wanton want?

Was it just like Peter all over again? Nature, her body, her emotions tricking her when ultimately all was an illusion. A house of cards that came tumbling down in the face of reality.

She didn't know. So she tried to ignore it and took refuge in what she did know. The garden.

It was mid-July and this is what the garden looked like, in four quadrants. The kitchen garden—tomatoes, lettuces, runner beans, spuds, Swiss chard, zucchini, cabbages, and carrots. Eva was particularly entranced by the carrots. You could see their broad, orange tops poking up through the soil, as if somebody had bought them in a shop and shoved them whole into the ground. She was insanely proud of all her veggies and privately thought them even more beautiful than the riotous flowers in Emily's sensory garden, although she had to admit that the young girl had accomplished quite a feat. None of her colors clashed, even where you might have expected them to do so. Shaggy yellow daisies along-side violet alium. Bright orange lilies against deep blue del-phiniums. Who would have thought it? It was like a grand experiment to prove that everything in nature worked in harmony.

Mrs. Prendergast's roses were like something out of a dream—tunnels of them, archways and trellises. Uri's fan-shaped fig tree dominated the back wall of the orchard. The apple trees sported their little green orbs. Alpine strawberries, rows of them, raspberry canes, gooseberry bushes, cultivated bramble. The dividing herbaceous border grew tall and pow-erful. The pond teemed with life. Everywhere there were patches of glory, yet the garden, still in its infancy, as gardens went, had yet to obtain an all-important unity. A vital matu-rity. All the elements hadn't quite come together, although they were working on it, nature and the gardeners in their di-vine collaboration. All it would take was time. Time they didn't have. Because one day, it happened.

It was a Saturday morning.

"What's that man doing to the sign, Mummy?"

A man, presumably from the estate agents, was up on a ladder hammering the words SALE AGREED across the FOR SALE sign. Eva stood stock-still.

"What is it, Mummy?"

"Nothing."

She was grateful he couldn't yet read. Eva walked rapidly over to the man, sorely tempted to kick the ladder out from under him.

"What do you think you're doing?"

"My job," he said mildly, jumping lightly to the ground and lifting up the ladder as if it were made of air. He walked away from Eva, whistling maddeningly. She experienced an ir-rational surge of anger toward him, which the logical side of her brain knew was misdirected. But she had to direct it some-where, because it was about to consume her. She entered the garden. Seth stood in the center, in front of the pond, gazing up at the sign.

She went up to him, her newfound feelings pushed to the side.

"You've seen it, then."

"Yeah."

"What are we going to do?"

"What can we do?"

"Try and talk her out of it. Convince her not to sell."

"But she's already accepted an offer."

"The sale hasn't gone through yet."

"Eva . . ."

"We can't just give up."

He didn't say anything. Just looked at her calmly. She found this even more infuriating than the whistling.

"Seth, don't tell me you're going to stand by and let this happen."

"Eva. You always knew this was going to happen one day. We all did."

"I know. But I always held out a little bit of hope. Didn't you?"

"Not really, no."

"Then why did you help us?"

"Maybe I have a weakness for lost causes."

"This is not a lost cause. Don't you dare call this garden a lost cause." She could hear the level of her voice rising dangerously high. A few seconds more and she'd be out of control.

"Calm down, Eva."

"Don't tell me to calm down. Patronizing git."

Seth looked taken aback. Then he laughed, thus angering Eva even more.

"How dare you laugh at me."

"I'm not laughing at you, Eva. I know you're upset, but it's happened. You have to let it go."

"Let it go! How can I do that? How can you?"

"We have no choice."

"There's always a choice. Always something you can do. I'll do up a petition. We can go door-to-door. I'm sure local people will support the garden."

"But it's private land."

"Why are you being so negative?"

"I'm not. I'm being realistic."

"I can't just do nothing. Can't you see that? I can't let this all have been for nothing." Her voice was starting to crack.

Seth took her by the shoulders and turned her around to face the garden.

"It hasn't been for nothing," he said. "Never say that. Just look at what you've achieved. Look at it. You've created something out of nothing. This beautiful garden out of a . . . wilderness. Never say that it's been for nothing, Eva. You're incredible, what you've done. You're nothing short of a goddess." He squeeeezed her shoulders. "A green goddess."

She could feel his breath on the side of her face, the very warmth of it. His body stood directly behind hers, so solid, so reassuring. It would be so easy just to yield. To sink back into him. Why didn't she?

"Eva." It was Mrs. Prendergast.

At the sound of the older woman's voice, Eva's body became rigid again and she swung around to face her, twisting Seth's hands off her shoulders in the process. At last. A worthy target for her rage.

"How could you do that?"

"I take it you've seen the sign."

"It's hard to miss."

"I understand that you're upset, but I never misled you."

"Not with your words, but with your actions you did."

"What are you talking about?"

"Getting so involved in the garden. Encouraging us. Your bloody roses. Have you thought about that? Your precious roses. They'll all be ripped up."

"We'll find good homes for all the plants, Eva." Seth laid a steadying hand on her arm but she shook it off, angry with the whole world.

"Of course I've thought about it," said Mrs. Prendergast, her tone and expression cold. "What I actually came over to ask you both was whether you'd like to come to the house for dinner tonight. I've already asked your father, Seth, and he can make it."

"I'd love to, thanks," said Seth, sounding remarkably gracious.

"Eva?"

"I'm afraid I'm washing my hair," said Eva, sounding remarkably ungracious.

"There's no need to be like that, my dear. I'm planning to make a special dinner, using mainly produce from the garden."

"You're going to use *my* vegetables to make your—your last supper. Unbelievable!"

"I'd just like a chance to explain—"

"What's the point? Will you be sitting there counting your money? Go to hell, Mrs. Prendergast."

She turned and walked away from them both and out of the garden, not wanting either of them to see the tears that were crowding at the corners of her eyes. She'd had so much work planned for today. But now it all seemed pointless.

A COUPLE OF hours later, she was curled up on the couch feeling sorry for herself. She had given up the pretense of marking papers and was flicking from one channel to the next. Liam was at a friend's house, so she was all alone. The doorbell rang.

"Oh go away," she murmured, making no attempt to answer it.

After a spell, it rang again.

"Piss off." She covered her face with a big furry cushion and willed whoever it was to go away.

The doorbell rang again.

"Oh, for fuck's sake." Flinging the cushion to the side, she jumped off the couch and marched out to the hall. It better not be someone trying to sell her something. She flung the front door open. Seth. Leaning up against her wall, his arms and ankles crossed, his expression sardonic.

"For a second there, I thought you weren't going to answer."

"What do you want?"

"You'll have to work on your Irish welcome, now that you're back on the Ould Sod."

"Sod off."

She turned and walked back into her sitting room. Seth closed the door behind himself and followed her in.

Eva was immediately conscious of several things. Her appearance, for a start. Had her face calmed down yet after her prolonged bout of sobbing? Were her eyes still swollen, her nose still red? Then there was the matter of the mound of used tissues on her coffee table. She leaned down and shoved the bulk of them into her pocket, just as Seth was walking into the room. As for the tasteless interior décor she had inherited from the previous inhabitants of the house, she didn't have time to do anything about that. He'd just have to suffer it.

It occurred to her that Seth had never been to her house before.

"How did you know where I live?"

"I didn't realize it was a state secret."

"It's not."

She sank back down on the couch and folded her legs up under her. Seth sat himself down in the armchair opposite. It unsettled her. Having him in her home.

"Nice wallpaper."

"Have you come here to mock me?"

"No. I've come here to stop you from making such a fecking eejit out of yourself."

"I'm not!"

"Yes, you are. The old bag is trying to apologize and you're throwing it back in her face."

"What does she expect?"

"Did she ever tell you she wasn't going to sell the garden?"

"No."

"Well, then."

"I just didn't think she'd actually go through with it. I see that now. After all the work we've put into it. After all the work *she's* put into it, for God's sake. I don't understand."

"Maybe she needs the money."

"Her! You're joking. The woman's minted."

"You don't know that."

"Yes I do. Have you never seen her clothes? All her stuff? It's the best of everything."

"Well, why don't you come along anyway and see what she has to say for herself. Maybe it'll help you understand."

"I don't think I could stomach it."

"She probably wants to thank you too."

"She needn't bother."

"And you could always give her another piece of your mind."

"I could, couldn't I?"

So that was how Liam and Eva ended up at Mrs. Prendergast's at half past seven that evening. Eva marched right up to the front door and knocked aggressively. She was damned if she was going to use the tradesmen's entrance tonight.

"Why don't we just go through the gate, Mummy?"

"I forgot my key."

And she couldn't bring herself to walk through the garden on such a rare and beautiful balmy summer's evening, when she knew it would be at its glorious best. Eva closed her eyes and tried not to imagine. To imagine it there and imagine it gone. As far as she was concerned, her garden and everything in it was about to be murdered.

The door opened and there stood the murderer.

"Eva. So glad you could make it. And Liam. Come on in. Kathy's already here."

Eva tried to hide the hostility in her eyes, but it was impossible. It was as much as she could do to keep her mouth shut. Mrs. Prendergast's own eyes were hooded and wary. Eva thought she detected ironic amusement also. She looked away. She couldn't afford to become more annoyed than she already was.

"We brought you some wine." Liam was jumping up and down on the spot, as was his tendency when excited. He smiled openly at the woman who had become to him a kind of surrogate grandmother. How on earth was Eva going to explain to him that they wouldn't be seeing her anymore? The little boy had had too many loved ones taken away from him already during the course of his tiny life. But she honestly couldn't see how they could go on seeing Mrs. Prendergast under the circumstances.

Eva handed her the bottle of wine.

"Oh, how very kind. Wolf Blass. One of my favorites."

Mrs. Prendergast's manners were impeccable. She had to give her that. But then again, so were Hannibal Lecter's.

Eva and Liam walked into Mrs. Prendergast's hall for only the second time in their acquaintance. Eva recalled the first time vividly. Who could have predicted all that had happened since then?

She led them through a small reception room at the back of the house. It had an air of unlivability about it. But it opened out into the most spectacular sunroom. Eva had heard Mrs. Prendergast refer to it many times, but she'd never been inside. It was a conservatory, really, of the curvaceous, domed variety. The furniture was wicker and the plants numerous. The color scheme was all reds, oranges, and yellows, sun colors. A cushioned window seat ran around the sides of the room and a long oak table dominated the center. The table was set with crystal goblets, silver cutlery, delicate china, and linen napkins. At least ten tea lights were scattered about the table in various pretty glass holders and the centerpiece was a crystal bowl filled with water in which five bosomy, blossomy, blousy yellow roses floated demurely. But by far the most beautiful thing about this beautiful room was the view of the garden through the open wooden door. Which tonight did nothing but add insult to injury.

Seated at the table were Uri and Seth. Kathy was sitting on the floor, tying a sunbonnet onto Harriet's uncomplaining head. Liam ran over and knelt beside them. Uri was his usual impeccable self. He stood up when Eva entered the room and inclined his head toward her.

"You look lovely," he said.

"Thank you." She loved his old-world manners.

Seth stood up too, more awkwardly than his father and nodded at her.

"You look very nice," he said.

"Thanks."

She had actually dressed up for once. She was wearing a red dress with sparkly bits that she'd got in Monsoon. It might have been the first time that any of them had seen her in anything other than jeans and wellies. Seth had dressed up too. She'd never seen him so clean. He was wearing chinos and a spotless white linen shirt. He washed up well. She felt the full force of it.

It was strange. Being with the same people she saw week in, week out, but wearing unfamiliar clothes. And being in the same location but in an unfamiliar room with an unfamiliar view of the garden. A different perspective on everyone and everything. It made Eva feel shy suddenly and at a loss for what to say.

"Wine?"

"Yes. White please."

Uri poured her a glass of wine and a goblet of sparkling water. She sipped at them both, grateful to have something to do with her hands and mouth. Grateful also that Mrs. Prendergast chose that moment to bring out the starter.

"Onion tarts with goat cheese," she announced. "The onions and the tarragon are from the garden."

"Mummy, I don't like them."

"Don't worry, Liam. I have fish fingers and chips for you and Kathy."

"Yippee."

Liam returned to the floor and the ongoing tormenting of Harriet.

"Oh my God. These are exquisite." Eva hadn't meant to be so effusive in her compliments to Mrs. Prendergast that evening, but she couldn't help herself. The tarts were divine. "I didn't know you could cook like this."

Mrs. Prendergast shrugged but real pleasure showed on her face. "I seldom get the chance to cook for anyone nowadays."

Eva quizzed her as to the recipe, but only half-listened to the response. She was thinking about how glad she was that they had the food to talk about. Normally, they mostly talked about gardening, but that topic now seemed redundant. Eva ate too fast in her nervousness and washed down the food with too many overlarge gulps of wine. She could already feel her head becoming light and that familiar heaviness in her thighs. She was glad. Being slightly drunk was the only way she could envision getting through this evening.

"I think," said Uri, "that a toast to absent friends is in order. To Emily."

They all raised their glasses.

"To Emily."

Eva clicked her glass with Mrs. Prendergast's.

She had to admit that the older woman was being extremely nice to her, given her behavior earlier on. She hadn't even apologized for being so rude. It was too early for her to say sorry. She didn't feel it yet. Someday she would and she'd say it then. Perhaps Mrs. Prendergast's attack of niceness had been brought on by guilt. Or maybe she was thinking about her lovely pile of cash. Eva swallowed her recurrent anger with another gulp of wine.

Mrs. Prendergast brought out the kids' food next and they all watched them slathering everything in tomato ketchup and listened to them chattering mindlessly. Harriet sat under the table hopefully, her ears pricked up, anticipating falling debris. Seth was quiet, she noticed. But not so Uri and Mrs. Prendergast, who both seemed remarkably cheerful and relaxed. Didn't they care? More anger. More wine. The warning voice inside her head was ignored. If she didn't know better, she'd think that Uri and old hatchet head were flirting with each other. Mrs. Prendergast wasn't so much laughing at whatever it was Uri was saying to her as giggling. Something that, in Eva's opinion, she should have grown out of a good fifty years ago.

The children's plates were cleared away and the main course presented.

"Broccoli and chicken lasagna, baby potatoes, and salad. All the vegetables, herbs, spuds, and salad are from the garden."

"Good for you," Eva muttered under her breath. If anyone heard her, they chose to ignore her.

There was no denying that the food looked and smelled superb. Mrs. Prendergast had even decorated the salad with pansies. The taste almost made Eva forgive her. Dessert was white chocolate and raspberry cheesecake ("raspberries courtesy of Uri"). Finishing up, they all sat there, officially stuffed, sipping Earl Grey tea.

"I'd like to propose a toast," said Uri. "To Mrs. Prendergast, for making us this magnificent feast."

"Mrs. Prendergast." They all raised their glasses and clinked with one another.

"And to Eva. For growing most of the ingredients."

"Not anymore," said Eva, failing to clink. She was sick of it now. Uri's cheeriness. Mrs. Prendergast's girlish giddiness.

"How can you both act this way? As if this is some sort of celebration. We have nothing to celebrate. Nothing! You'd be better off having a funeral mass."

"Don't you think that's a tad overdramatic, my dear?"

Mrs. Prendergast smiled at her. To Eva she looked incredibly smug.

"No, I do not. I don't know how you have the gall to sit there smiling when you're destroying everything we've done, everything we've worked toward. And for what? For money! Money that you don't even need. You can't eat money, you know. Don't you know that what you already have is way more precious by far? Priceless even. It's an act of desecration. To dig up those apple trees—they're even older than you are."

"Eva. That's enough now."

But she couldn't be stopped.

"The roses. Emily's garden that she poured her heart and soul into. What about the insects, the bees, the butterflies? The robins! Where are they going to nest next year? You're just going to let them pour concrete over the whole lot. Destroy it all. Well, it's nothing short of sacrilege."

Eva's heart was beating wildly now as she stared down Mrs. Prendergast. She knew she was quite drunk but she didn't care. She was glad, in fact. Glad that the wine had given her the Dutch courage to say what she felt she had to say. They were all looking at her. All except Mrs. Prendergast, who took a demure sip from her teacup and placed it daintily back in its saucer.

"You know, my dear, I couldn't agree more." Mrs. Prendergast looked across at Eva, her expression imperious. "That's why I've sold it to Uri."

There were a few seconds of silence, then everything erupted.

"Did you just say you sold it to Uri?"

"That's exactly what I said."

"Dad. Is this true?" Seth looked at his father.

"Yes, it is."

Eva covered her face with her hands.

"Yes!" Seth punched the air and leaped to his feet. Then he grabbed his father, who was sitting beside him, and hugged him to his chest. "Nice one, Da."

Uri laughed.

"And Mrs. P." Seth held out his arms to her in an expansive gesture. He advanced slowly around the table, not taking his eyes off her. Mrs. Prendergast shrank back into her chair as Seth went down on one knee on the floor beside her.

"Mrs. P," he said again. Then he hugged her so tight that Eva was afraid he might break one of her ribs. Then he planted a big, noisy kiss on her right cheek.

"Mrs. P, you're a legend."

"Oh good Lord," said Mrs. Prendergast, her face pink.

"I can't believe it. This is fantastic," said Eva. "Oh, Mrs. Prendergast—I am so, so sorry. I've said some awful things. Please, can you forgive me?"

Mrs. Prendergast looked at Eva, her eyebrows raised.

"I'll think about it."

But Eva knew she was already forgiven.

"Why didn't you tell us before?" asked Seth.

"We wanted to surprise you."

"Well, it worked."

A terrible thought occurred to Eva.

"You're not going to . . . I mean . . . you wouldn't consider building on it, would you?"

"Absolutely not," said Uri. "It's going to stay a garden for as long as I have breath in my body. And hopefully a long time after that." He looked at Seth, for whom the possibility that the garden would one day be his, at least in part, was just beginning to dawn.

"I'd like to propose another toast," said Mrs. Prendergast. She raised her glass. "To the garden."

They all held up their glasses.

"The garden."

There was a knock on the front door. Loud, angry, insistent. As if the knocker had been standing there unheard for quite some time. Which was quite possible, given the level of commotion in the sunroom.

"I'd better go and answer that," said Mrs. Prendergast, throwing down her napkin, her face flushed, her eyes bright as she left the room.

"Are you sure you can afford it, Da?" said Seth when she'd gone.

"Yes. I see it as an investment for the future."

"But it's only an investment if you plan to sell it sometime down the line."

"I don't mean an investment for my future. I mean an investment for everyone's future."

They heard voices at the front door. Mrs. Prendergast's and that of a man. They were too far away to make out what they were saying. Then snippets of conversation floated into the sunroom, although at first it wasn't clear if this was because the voices were getting louder or closer. After a while, it became evident that both those things were happening.

"How much? Jesus Christ, you are joking."

"Lance, please. I have guests for dinner."

He entered the sunroom and took in the scene.

"I should have bloody well known."

Lance's white shirtsleeves were rolled up and his formal tie was askew and no longer looking formal. His dark hair was sticking up, as if he'd raked his hand through it repeatedly. He looked like he'd been drinking. The atmosphere in the room changed instantly.

"Who the fuck do you think you are, ripping my mother off like that?"

Lance glared at Uri. He looked and sounded furious.

"Lance!"

Uri's expression and posture remained calm and still, as if he'd faced a lot worse in his time.

"I offered your mother considerably more, but she refused to take it." His voice was quiet but it carried. Uri's dignified, almost regal manner was totally at odds with that of Lance, who turned angrily to his mother.

"Is this true?"

"Mr. Rosenberg paid full market value."

"You could have got double that, you stupid bitch."

There was a sharp intake of breath all round.

"Don't you speak to your mother like that," said Uri, his face thunderous.

"What's it to you, you sly Jewish bastard?"

There was a moment's silence, then all hell broke loose. Seth was on his feet so fast that his chair fell backward onto the floor. His face was contorted with anger and it was clear that he intended to launch himself at Lance.

"Seth, no!" Uri was on his feet too and grabbing Seth's arm. Eva got up, intending to head him off.

"Come over here and say that," Seth was roaring, his face puce.

"Daddy, what's wrong?" Kathy and Liam were standing at the door to the sunroom, two little pairs of eyes wide, like saucers. They'd been inside watching a DVD. They must have heard the raised voices and come to see what was going on. The sight of his daughter seemed to bring Seth to his senses. His rigid body visibly relaxed and the amount of red in his face was reduced to an acceptable level of pink.

"Nothing's wrong, sweetheart. Go back inside."

"Daddy, why is your chair on the floor?"

"I just knocked it over by mistake, Kathy. Come on back inside with me and we'll watch the rest of the film."

"It's over, Daddy."

"Then we'll watch another one."

Seth herded the two children out of the room, not even looking at Lance as he walked past him. The four remaining adults stood looking at one another, the tension almost sickening to the stomach.

"You won't get away with this." Lance was looking at Uri, his voice quieter now, yet somehow more menacing. Then he looked over at his mother.

"This transaction isn't going through. I won't allow it."

Then he was gone, as if he'd never happened, except that everything in the room was altered. None of them spoke, moved even, until they heard the front door slamming. Mrs. Prendergast emitted a peculiar high-pitched sound and sank into the nearest chair. Uri was at her side instantly. Eva noted with alarm that the other woman was trembling. She wasn't surprised. If Liam ever grew up and spoke to her like that . . . it didn't bear thinking about.

"Here. Drink this."

Uri poured some brandy out of a bottle that was standing in the middle of the table. He held the glass up to Mrs. Prendergast's lips. She took it in one shaking hand and sipped. Eva began to lift dirty plates from the table.

"Leave that, Eva," said Uri.

"But hadn't somebody better clear up?"

"I'll take care of all that. You and Seth take the children home. I don't want them seeing her like this. I'll stay here."

"You sure?"

"Quite sure."

Eva put down the plates and went to find the others. She followed the squeals of the Disney DVD. The children were transfixed, their faces lit up by the swirling colors on the screen. Seth was sitting on the edge of an armchair, his elbows on his knees, his head in his hands.

"Seth." Eva's voice was soft. He didn't hear her, so she walked over to him and touched his hand. He jumped and looked up. As if by instinct, he took her hand and held it against his cheek, brushing her palm with his lips as he did so. Eva pulled her hand away.

"Come on, kids. Time to go."

"I don't want to."

"But, Mummy, it's only just started."

"Come on. You can watch the rest tomorrow."

She ignored their squeals of protest as she ejected the DVD and put it back in its case.

"Come on, Kathy. It's way past your bedtime."

They bundled the children out into the night air. It was ten o'clock and still bright. "How are you getting home?" said Seth.

"On foot."

"We'll walk you there."

"There's no need."

"I insist."

"Okay."

They walked in silence for a while, at least the two adults did. Kathy and Liam skipped ahead, hand in hand, singing nonsense songs.

"Do you get that kind of thing a lot?" said Eva.

"What?"

"Anti-Jewish stuff."

"Not really. But it does rear its ugly head every now and then. Some prick like that."

Eva nodded. "Poor Mrs. Prendergast."

"I know."

They watched the children for a while. Then Seth said: "I like your dress."

"Thanks."

"The color suits you."

"Thank you." Eva felt pleased and embarrassed at the same time.

"I was beginning to think you didn't have legs."

She smiled. "They've been there the whole time."

"So I see. They're quite long, aren't they?"

"Yes, they go all the way to the ground. Here we are."

They slowed down and stopped outside her front door.

"How are you getting home?"

"I have the Jeep. It's parked opposite Mrs. P's."

"Are you okay to drive?"

"I only had one glass."

Eva nodded. She'd been so busy knocking it back herself that she hadn't noticed what anyone else was doing.

"Good night, then. Thanks for walking us home."

"But, Mummy. I want to show Kathy my new excavator."

"You can show her the next time."

"But I said I'd show her now. Please, Mummy."

"Please, Eva."

"Okay. Hurry up though. You both need to get to bed."

Eva opened the door and the children ran inside, talking and laughing. She felt awkward.

"Do you want to come inside and wait?"

"No, it's all right. It's nice out here."

It was a lovely night. Eva didn't like the way Seth was looking at her. It was making her feel flustered. He took a few steps forward and she looked hard at the pavement. What happened next was what she wanted but at the same time didn't want. He put his arms around her waist and pulled her close. He stroked her lower back with the tips of his fingers.

"Eva. Look at me."

With huge difficulty, she looked up into his eyes. They seemed to go on forever. And then he was kissing her. And she felt as if she was falling, down into a bottomless tunnel, spinning out of control. She broke away and stepped inside the safety of her front door.

"Kathy! Liam! Come on now."

Sounding like a stampede of buffalo rather than two small children, Kathy and Liam ran back into the hall.

"Ready, Kathy?"

"Yes." She went outside and joined her father.

Eva went to close the door.

"Thanks again for walking us home." She didn't look at him.

"Eva."

"What?" This time she looked up.

"You can't punish yourself forever, you know."

"Good night, Seth." She shut the door.

"Mummy, what's a punish?"

"It's what'll happen to you if you don't get into bed now. Come on. Up the stairs."

The man didn't know what he was talking about.

29

*T*HE SUNLIGHT POURED in through the gap in the curtains, bathing Emily's eyelids, compelling them to flicker. This was her favorite way to wake up, from one dreamlike state to another. She lay there for some time, semiconscious, believing herself to be back in her bedsit. And then the tiniest whimper. Her eyelids flew open. She sat up in the bed she'd slept in since she was a girl, in the room that had sheltered her childhood dreams: ponies and gymkhanas, her teenage fantasies of Westlife and Gary O'Connor. All that giving way now to adult reality. (She must get rid of that ridiculous poster.)

Rose had settled herself back to sleep, although her restlessness indicated imminent wakefulness. Emily knew it would be wise to go downstairs and prepare a bottle, but she really couldn't drag herself away. Her reality now was so unreal. So magical.

"Wow," she said to her sleeping daughter.

"Wow," she said to herself, countless times a day. Because she loved it all. Every second of it. Even when Rose bawled her head off. Even when she did it in the middle of the night. It gave Emily the excuse to take her into her bed and hold her close. Breathe her in.

Now Rose slumbered in the crib her mother had slept in. As had all the other Harte babies. There was a baby-shaped indentation in the mattress, and Rose fit snugly into this. There was a gentle rap on the bedroom door. "Come in."

The door opened to reveal her father. He was dressed in his outdoor clothes and had the air of someone who'd been up for hours. He'd probably sorted the cows already.

"Is madam awake?" he said.

"Not yet. But she will be soon."

"Will I bring you up a bottle?"

"That'd be great, Dad."

He nodded and disappeared. She listened to his footfall descending the stairs and marveled anew at this miraculous turn of events.

THE DAY SHE'D brought Rose home had been a seminal day in the Harte household. Her mother had been wonderful, coddling her. Forgiving her instantly. If anything, she blamed herself for not being there for her daughter. Although what she thought she could have done when she didn't know a thing about it . . .

One by one, the Hartes came home. Reactions varied, from shock to joy to indifference. Until the only one left was Emily's father. Thomas Harte. Home from the fields. Innocent of all that had occurred in his absence.

The house fell silent as the back door opened. They were gathered in the kitchen, all of the Hartes, including the newest arrival. They listened collectively as he took off his boots and removed his jacket, whistling tunelessly as was his habit. He entered the kitchen and drew back in surprise. His entire family looking at him so strangely. And then he saw Emily and his face opened up in delight.

"Well, hello, stranger. What are you doing here?"

Emily gave her father a nervous half smile.

He noticed Rose for the first time, currently nestling in his wife's arms.

"Where did the baby come from? Don't tell me someone else has roped you into babysitting. You're too much of a soft touch, woman. Would you ever tell them you've enough of your own to be getting on with? What's for tea? I'm starved."

He looked at his wife expectantly, wondering mildly why she wasn't responding to his words. Then his eyes swept over his family. He hadn't been imagining it. Something was definitely up. He stopped rolling up his sleeves.

"What is it?"

A couple of the younger siblings looked at Emily. The others looked at the ground. His eldest daughter cleared her throat. But still her voice came out like a squeak.

"She's mine."

What did she mean "she's mine"? That she was minding her for someone else? But a part of his brain, the part that was reluctantly clicking into gear, knew that this wasn't true. The strange atmosphere in his kitchen told him this, if nothing else.

"What do you mean, girl?"

Emily swallowed visibly.

"She's my baby, Dad. I had her last September."

Each second was a year. Many a member of the family wished they weren't present. They were soon to get their wish.

"Kids. Leave the room now, please."

There was a scramble for the door. Emily longed to join in, but guessed she was no longer classified as one of the "kids."

Emily, her mother, and her father remained. And Rose. Oblivious to all the fuss she was causing. Emily braced herself. Her father spoke.

"How could you, of all the girls in the world, be so bloody stupid?"

"I'm sorry, Daddy."

She felt her eyes fill with saltwater. This was it. The moment she'd been dreading ever since she'd peed on that plastic stick. Her father's rejection. The casting out from the warmth of the family fold.

Thomas advanced slowly. Every footfall dreadful to Emily. He stopped in front of Bridget and Rose and stared down at them for what seemed like an age. Then he reached down and scooped up the baby with the practiced ease of a father of six. He held her up in the air and appeared to examine her. Rose's limbs flailed in the open air, reminding Emily of an insect stuck on its back.

"Begod, she's a Harte through and through. Would you look at the cut of her." He laughed out loud. "Bridget. Have you seen the nose?"

Emily almost swooned with relief. She closed her eyes and allowed herself a small smile, which her father caught.

"And don't think for one second, miss, that this means you've gotten away with it."

"No, Daddy." Her voice was small. Humble. She knew she'd gotten away with it. As did all the younger Hartes, who were listening on the far side of the kitchen door.

"And when any of your brothers and sisters ask, I gave you the bollocking of a lifetime. Is that clear?"

"Yes, Daddy."

He laughed again and cradled baby Rose in the top right-hand corner of his chest. Rose rested her head in the crook of his neck. Then she vomited delicately down the back of her grandfather's shoulder.

THE NEXT DAY was Sunday. Emily spent most of the morning in her room, feeding and dressing and luxuriating in Rose as the rest of the family got ready for mass in their noisy, haphazard, familiar way. Emily was confident she'd be excused from this Sunday-morning ritual. There was a knock on her door.

"Come in."

Her father entered.

"Are you not even dressed yet?"

"I've been minding Rose. I thought—"

"It's nearly time for mass. Here. Hand me the baby while you get yourself ready."

"But I thought—"

"You know this family always goes to mass together. Now get a move on, girl."

She should have known better. There was no point in putting up an argument, as he was gone already. God. The thought of facing her neighbors. The people she'd grown up with. She pulled on the least-wrinkled clothes she could find. Pride, rather than vanity, dragged a comb across her head.

"Emily!"

They were all waiting for her in the kitchen. Then off they went to the church, two cars needed to contain the entire clan.

She felt her father feeling her misgivings at the entrance to the church. He bent low and whispered in her ear.

"Best to get it over with," he said.

They sat in their usual pew, a little distance from the top on the left-hand side. Emily saw all the familiar faces. Felt all the eyes on her and Rose. Knew she'd be the hot topic of gossip in the parish for the week. That little upstart got her come-uppance. Thought she was better than us. Look at her now.

Then the mass was over. Emily kept her head down as they all filed out of the church, flanked by family on every side. But then something happened. Something wholly unexpected.

"Ah, would you look at her. Isn't she a dote? Is she yours, Emily?"

"She is. Yes."

It was Mrs. Brennan, a woman Emily had known most of her life. Her daughter had been in the same class at school.

"How old?"

"Almost nine months."

"Nine months. What a gorgeous age. Marie, come and have a look at this little one."

Marie Dowling, a woman of similar vintage, came and stood with them.

"Ah, look. She's a stunner all right. What's her name?"

"Rose."

"Rose. Oh, it suits her. Can I have a little hold?"

"Of course."

As Emily handed over her child, the heart that had been hammering in her chest slowed down to a dull thud.

Before long, she and Rose were encircled by the women of the parish. Cooing. Petting. Loving.

Emily smiled a watery smile.

It was their turn to shake hands with the priest, a gentle man she'd known since childhood. Her anxiety returned. Her father went ahead of her.

"Father. How are you this fine morning?"

"Keeping well, Tommy. And yourself?"

"Father. I'd like to introduce you to my grandaughter, Rose."

He nodded at Emily to come forward. Emily did so. Holding up Rose for inspection.

"Well, would you look at her. Isn't she a beauty. The apple didn't fall too far from the tree. She's the picture of her mother."

Emily smiled in acknowledgment and relief.

"We'll be off now, Father. Enjoy the sunshine."

"I will surely, Tommy."

"Father Curran. Can I ask you something?"

All eyes were on Emily in surprise. That she would voluntarily prolong this encounter.

"Rose hasn't been baptized yet. I wonder if you'd be kind enough to do the honors."

"I'd be delighted, Emily. Give me a ring in the morning and we'll work out a suitable date."

Emily looked across at her parents. They were looking at each other and smiling. She thought her mother might cry.

In this at least, she could do the right thing by them.

AND THAT HAD been three months ago. And not one of the Hartes could imagine their family without Rose. Emily could take no credit for it. It was all down to Rose and the spell she'd woven around them all. And to her parents. Their love for her overriding every abstract principle they'd ever held. What a stupid girl she'd been—doubting them the way she had. When she thought back now on that first day in mass and the guts it must have taken. Pillars of the church, both of them. Proudly displaying for their fellow pillars of the church to see, their fallen woman of a daughter, their illegitimate granddaughter. They must have been up half the night before, agonizing over it.

Rose was fully awake now, giving out to her mother for allowing her to go hungry for all of two seconds. Emily picked up her daughter and held her close, relishing the way she snuggled into her, those sweet little snuffling noises. There was a knock on the door, closely followed by her father, bearing a bottle.

"Here's Granddad," said Emily, turning Rose around so she could see him.

"There's a phone call for you. That girl Eva. Will I feed Rose while you take it?"

"Okay. Thanks."

Emily went down to the hall and picked up the phone.

"Hello?"

She listened while Eva talked nonstop for two minutes flat, barely pausing for breath. At last it was her turn to speak.

"I think it's a great idea. But surely we can come up with a better name than the Autumn Party."

30

$\mathscr{S}$HE THOUGHT SHE was alone in the garden. Early morning. It had been raining but it had stopped now and all the colors were magnified. Everything felt like a new beginning. Just Eva and the birds. Liam was on a sleepover. She had come here to think. The perfect place to do so. The bower beneath the yellow trumpets of honeysuckle and the white stars of jasmine. She made her way there now, all green and leafy, all dapple and shade. Blessed coolness. Balm on her soul. Peace of mind at long last.

But she wasn't alone. Someone else swung gently on the swing seat, wrapped in a plaid blanket, eyes softly closed. At first she was dismayed. To sit there had felt like her only hope. Then she felt glad for the other woman. She probably needed it more than she did. Feeling her intrusion, she turned silently to go.

"Eva."

She had been spotted.

"Mrs. Prendergast. I was just leaving."

"Why not stay?"

How could she turn down this surprising invitation?

Mrs. Prendergast moved along in the seat, making room for Eva, who felt she had no choice but to sit down, although the intimacy of the situation made her somewhat fearful. There truly was nowhere to hide in a place like this. The only saving grace was that they didn't have to look at each other. Sitting side by side felt easier than face-to-face. Less confrontational. They swung gently together, backward and forward, lulling each other. Eva began to relax. Just two women sitting in a garden together. For the first time, Eva didn't feel the age difference between them. Together, they could still be alone with their own thoughts. Eva was amazed by how easy and companionable the silence was between them. It was like a spell that spoken words would break. But after a while, words became inevitable. Necessary. Eva let Mrs. Prendergast do the honors.

"I'm sorry about the other night," the older woman said.

"Don't be. It was a marvelous night. The food was superb."

"You know what I mean."

Eva paused, trying to find the right words.

"That was hardly your fault. If anybody should apologize, it's me. I was so rude to you. I am sorry."

"You were just sticking up for your garden."

They swung for about a minute, not saying anything.

"He has gambling debts, you know."

"You mean . . . ?"

"Lance."

"I see."

"My brother told me. I rang him up the next day because I was still quite . . . upset. Lance had approached him, looking for a loan, and he'd got the truth out of him."

"That would explain why he was so angry."

"Yes. But it's no excuse for the way he spoke to me. To Uri." She sniffed.

"I suppose not."

Eva stole a glance at Mrs. Prendergast's profile. She wasn't crying, but she wasn't far from it.

She sighed. "I hope your son never speaks to you like that."

Privately, Eva fervently agreed. But she couldn't think of a way to say it that didn't sound rude or hurtful, so she said nothing. Neither did Mrs. Prendergast. But Eva could feel the pain radiating off her in waves. She desperately wanted to convey her sympathy to the other woman but she wasn't sure how. Had it been a woman of her own age or younger, she would have given her a hug. But Mrs. Prendergast wasn't the hugging type. At least, Eva felt it would be inappropriate. Instead, still staring straight ahead, she felt for the other woman's hand with her own and gave it a squeeze. Slowly, then released. There was no visible response, but Eva sensed Mrs. Prendergast's body relaxing beside her. So much so, apparently, that the older woman said: "What happened to your husband?"

"He was killed in a car accident."

"Ah. I'm sorry."

Eva nodded her acknowledgment.

"When did he die?"

"Two years, three and a half months ago."

A pause.

"Do you think you'll ever marry again?"

"Good God, I have no idea. It's too early to say."

"You think almost two and a half years is too early?"

"It is for me."

"I hope you don't always feel that way."

"Why not?"

Eva was beginning to feel slightly irritated.

"Well, for your own sake, but mainly because of Liam. It's better for a boy to grow up with a father. I sometimes think that if I'd married again. Well. Things might have worked out differently."

Eva resented the implication that she and her indomitable love were not enough for her son. At the same time, she felt a gnawing fear in her chest when she thought of his future.

"You know," said Mrs. Prendergast, her tone altered. "There was a time when I hoped that you and Lance, you know. But I don't suppose you'd have any interest now. He hasn't exactly shown you his best side. He can be lovely. Honestly he can."

"I really don't know him, Mrs. Prendergast. But I doubt we'd be on the same wavelength. I *am* flattered, though, that you thought of me in that way."

"Don't be. His girlfriend is an abomination. Awful, vulgar girl. Anybody would be better than her."

Eva smiled and shook her head. Good old Mrs. Prendergast. She must be feeling better. So no need to tread so carefully.

"Can I ask you a question?"

"What?"

"Why are you selling the land to Uri?"

Mrs. Prendergast sighed. "A number of reasons," she said. Then stopped talking.

Eva looked at her.

"Care to elaborate?"

Mrs. Prendergast sighed again.

"Well. He asked me, for one thing. At the start, I really just wanted to get rid of the land. It wasn't so much about the money—until Lance got wind of it. It reminded me too much of the past and it was weighing me down. And then, you know, I became fond of the garden again. And the roses. And finding the time capsule made me think of things in the past that weren't so bad. Then when Lance was so rude to Uri, I suppose I wanted to make it up to him."

"I think I understand."

Mrs. Prendergast stood up quite abruptly.

"Anyway. Back to work. I'm off to plant some myrtle."

"Where?"

"Don't worry. I'm staying within the confines of the rose garden."

"I'm not worried. But why would you plant myrtle in the middle of a rose garden?"

Mrs. Prendergast drew on a pair of gloves that had been hidden beneath the swing seat. At first, Eva didn't think she was going to get an answer. It wouldn't be atypical of a woman who was capable of unimpeachable politeness one minute and mind-blowing rudeness the next. Eva stood up and stretched, already thinking about what she was going to do next.

"It's my name," said Mrs. Prendergast.

"Excuse me?"

"Myrtle. It's my name."

"Really?"

"Really."

"What an . . . unusual name. It's lovely."

Mrs. Prendergast snorted. "Liar."

Both women smiled furtively. Eva watched the older woman as she walked away from her, straightening her back as she went. She called after her.

"Does this mean I can call you—"

"Mrs. Prendergast."

"Right."

31

$\mathcal{G}$OD, SHE LOVED it. Absolutely. Everything about it. The low ceilings. The thick swirls of cigarette smoke that hung in the air, having nowhere to escape. The hormones bouncing off the walls. The scent of Johnnie Walker on the breath of the men she danced with. Not as overpowering as it had once been, in the days when you were obliged to be squished against the man in the death grip of a slow waltz. She thanked God in heaven for whoever had invented jive. It made everything seem much lighter, much more free.

It was 1957 and London was booming. Rationing was out, prosperity was in. Harold Macmillan told his people that they'd never had it so good and they believed him. It was on the night of October 4, 1957, that Myrtle met Martin Prendergast. An auspicious date—that chosen by the Soviets to launch *Sputnik*, the first ever artificial satellite to be sent into space.

She'd noticed him from the very beginning. She'd heard his booming voice, watched him throw back his head and laugh voraciously. He had a natural lust for life that compelled her. And what he had, she wanted. She set her heart on it, fixed her gaze on it, made him notice her in her own quiet, determined way. She wasn't the prettiest girl there, she knew that. But she had something—she knew that too. And it was this certainty that drew Martin to her, he thought of his own volition. She held his gaze—just long enough. She then went back to being aloof, a role she inhabited well. She waited for him to make his inevitable move.

"Would you like to dance?"

He held out his larger-than-life hand. His eyes laughed at her, challenging her. She recognized his accent and her stomach lurched. Irish. Forbidden. As she stood up, she felt as if she were falling.

His hands were rough and she knew immediately that he worked with them. His face spent a lot of time outdoors, in all weathers. It creased at the corners every time he smiled, which was often and always at her.

"I'm Martin," he said, her blue felt skirt swishing against his legs.

"Marnie."

"Marnie?" It was a struggle to hear over the music.

"That's right."

"Is it short for something?"

"Just Marnie."

"Hello, Just Marnie."

She smiled demurely and looked away, anxious not to reveal the effect he was having on her.

In those days, she didn't call herself Myrtle. She disowned her own name and in the process her restrictive background. Marnie was her new persona, the person she aspired to be and believed she was when you peeled back the middle-class layers. Her parents, her upbringing, her education. Everything that had prepared her to be the person she now rejected. Martin was the passport out of herself. She recognized this instantly. Her parents would hate him. At least her father would.

He was tall. Head and shoulders above her. His hair was black and his eyes were blue. What she thought of as Irish blue. Vibrant, all-singing, all-dancing blue. Nothing like her own insipid slate blue grayness. Everything about him was so alive. He made *her* feel alive and it wasn't a feeling she was prepared to relinquish.

When the dance was over, they were reluctant to let go of each other.

"Can I buy you a drink?"

"That would be lovely, thank you."

He smiled at her, as if he found what she'd said both delightful and amusing. Which is how he made her feel in general. As if he saw the self she had always known herself to be, that had been clamoring its whole life to get out. How was she to know that he made every woman feel that way? And at that moment, how was she to care?

They had their drink, talking intermittently and smiling continuously. And then chaos was unleashed. The room in an uproar. A raid! The police in one door, Martin and Myrtle out the other. Out into the night, laughing and running, hand in hand. Then, without saying anything, Martin held open the door of a coffee shop and she ducked inside. It was one of the new breed of Soho espresso bars. Not the old, classic, Italian style. The décor was loud and shiny and tasteless—the epitome of cool. The clientele was a blend of beatniks and teddy boys, mods and art-college types. He ordered them two coffees while Tab Hunter's "Young Love" played on the jukebox.

"Where are you from?"

"County Mayo."

"Is that in Ireland?"

"It surely is."

He smiled at her again. His voice was a rich, deep baritone. She wondered if he could sing. Surely someone with a speaking voice so lilting, so lyrical . . .

"Where are you from?"

"I'm from here. London."

To Myrtle, this was embarrassingly boring. (To Martin, it—she—was impossibly exotic.) Each was what the other aspired to be.

"A genuine London girl. Next you're going to tell me you were born within the sound of Bow bells."

"Not exactly."

Not exactly was right. Myrtle—named for her paternal grandmother—had grown up in the affluent suburb of Woodford, with her parents and one younger brother. It seemed crucial right now to conceal this from Martin, whose background, she guessed correctly, was a million miles away from where he was right now.

"Tell me about County Mayo."

"Nothing much to tell."

"There must be something. What part of Ireland is it in? Is it near Dublin?"

"Miles away. On the west coast."

An image appeared in her mind, from her old grammar school geography book.

"Did you live in a thatched cottage?"

"I did."

She raised her shoulders to her ears and her expression became gleeful.

"How romantic."

His laugh was short and mirthless. "You wouldn't think that if you had to live in one."

"Why?"

He leaned back in his seat and put one foot up on the chair beside her, an action she found to be both intimate and cocky, although the move seemed totally unconscious on his part.

"We had nothing growing up. Nothing. And the only people left living in the thatched cottages now are the old people. The whole west of Ireland is empty."

"How do you mean, empty?"

"Emigration. I went home for my sister's wedding last summer and the priest said it was the first wedding in the parish in seven years. There are only two directions for the young to go and that's west to America or east to England."

She could tell he was trying to keep the bitterness out of his voice, but she could hear it still, biting at the edges of his words.

Martin went on to tell her how he chose the latter, lured by tales of ceaseless work to be got and money to be made by building on the ruins of blitzed-out London. He started out laboring—backbreaking work that might have broken the heart of a lesser man. But not Martin. He kept his head down and worked, listened, and learned. At night, he drank pints with the other Paddys on the Kilburn High Road. And it was those Paddys he recruited on to the first crew of Prendergast Construction. Contracts were hard to come by at first, but he persevered and built up his reputation as a reliable, hardworking professional. The jobs started rolling his way, and after a decade of hard work, he was rolling in it.

What he didn't tell her was that he was ready. Ready to take a wife. A wife in keeping with his new station in life. A wife to aspire to. A life to aspire to. Myrtle. Or Marnie, as he knew her then. He was looking to join that which she was chomping at the bit to escape: the Establishment. To him, she was an ethereal, Grace Kelly–type figure. A class act. He wanted some of that for himself. He knew he had her, just as she knew she wanted to be had.

As Myrtle listened to Martin's account of all that had gone before, something struck her quite forcefully. How brave of him to reveal so much of himself to her. So much that might easily have sent a nice, middle-class girl like herself running in the other direction. But his story was having the opposite effect, as Martin had instinctively known it would. She admired his courage. She admired his grit and determination. But most of all, she admired the muscles that were straining under the material of his suit. Straining to get to her.

Someone selected "All Shook Up" on the jukebox. They smiled at each other.

"Do you like Elvis?"

"I just love him."

"Do you want to come and see *Jailhouse Rock* tomorrow night?"

"All right."

YEARS LATER, WHEN Myrtle would hear the expression "whirlwind romance," she thought of her early days with Martin. Their courtship. Listening to Long John Baldry in the Soho coffeehouses. Jiving all over London to Buddy Holly and the Crickets, Andy Williams and Johnny Ray. Their day trip on the Flying Scotsman, inadvertently taking in a huge gulp of acrid smoke as she stuck her head enthusiastically out of the window. Their picnic on Margate beach, chasing their windbreaker, laughing like loons as it was carried off on a strong breeze. Everything was fun and games, drinking and partygoing. She knew he'd have to meet her family sooner or later. Later rather than sooner if she had her way. But Martin was pushing for it. She wasn't sure why. Curiosity? The misguided belief that he'd be accepted into the fold? She tried to explain to him what her father was like.

"He can be quite—difficult."

"How do you mean 'difficult'?"

She sighed. How to explain.

"He's very stern. Almost Victorian in his outlook. And you know he's Scots Presbyterian."

"So?"

"So he's not too keen on Catholics."

"Leave him to me. I'm good with parents."

Myrtle felt a painful sensation in her chest.

How many girlfriends had there been before her? How many sets of parents to charm? And how many girlfriends to come? That wasn't all that was troubling her. She doubted that her father would be the pushover Martin anticipated. She guessed how he would rate him: flashy, arrogant. An unreliable type.

"What's your mother like?"

"Pathetic. No mind of her own. Does everything he tells her to."

She resented the way Martin looked at her then, with disapproval in his eyes. Presumably for the disrespectful way she'd spoken about her female parent. He didn't know. The extent to which she'd felt let down—rejected—so many times. All the times she had looked to her mother for backup and it had never come. When she alone had had to stand up to the vagaries of her father's temper. She herself would never live like that. In fear of the man she was supposed to love.

"Mothers are my specialty," was all Martin said.

She remained doubtful. Anticipating that her younger brother, Roger, was the only member of the family likely to be impressed by Martin's worldliness.

IN ANY CASE, an invitation was procured for tea that Saturday. They turned into the cul-de-sac where Myrtle had spent her formative years.

"Stop!" she shouted.

Martin slammed on the brakes of his new Humber Hawk. "What?"

"I have to tell you something."

"Jesus, Marnie. What is it?"

"Stop the car."

"It is stopped."

"I mean turn off the engine."

He switched off the ignition and turned to look at her.

"You're not having second thoughts? About me meeting your parents."

"No. I mean. Yes, I am. Second, third, and fourth. But that's not it."

"What then?"

She sighed. "You'll probably find that my family call me Myrtle."

The corner of his mouth twitched.

"Why would they do that?"

Another sigh, deeper than the last.

"Because it's my name."

"Then why did you tell me your name was Marnie?"

"Myrtle! Wouldn't you lie if you had a name like that?"

He stared hard at her. Oh God, what must he think? To lie about something so fundamental. Then he started to laugh. Like it was the funniest thing he'd ever heard. He threw back his head. He even brought his hand down so hard on the steering wheel that the horn sounded.

"Careful!" She looked around, anxious that they didn't draw attention to themselves. She imagined all the twitching curtains.

When he'd composed himself, he took her face in his two hands and kissed her firmly on the mouth.

"You're something else," he said. Then he restarted the engine and drove slowly down the street to number 48.

"THESE ARE FOR you." He handed a bunch of peach-colored gladioli to Myrtle's mother. Myrtle could tell she was impressed, but that was irrelevant.

They were shown into the front room, where her father and brother were watching *Hancock's Half Hour*. The older man's eyes never left the TV screen. Martin advanced confidently, his hand outstretched.

"Pleased to meet you, Mr. Ferguson."

For one terrible moment, Myrtle thought her father would refuse Martin's hand. He certainly thought about it, of that she was sure. She could almost hear him thinking it. But at the last second he shook it perfunctorily, glancing up briefly from the television at which he stared with a fierce concentration. He didn't rise from his armchair. Myrtle knew this to be a slight. Her whole family knew it. If Martin recognized it as such, he didn't show it. Instead, he sat himself down in the remaining free armchair, not waiting for the invitation to sit that would never come. Myrtle perched uneasily on the arm of the settee. She glanced anxiously at the rigid form of her father, then at Martin. The chair in which he sat sagged low in the middle. He looked ludicrously large in it, his knees looming up to his chin. Myrtle thought he looked ridiculously out of place in the room as a whole. Something about the two worlds in which she co-existed coming together and clashing discordantly.

"I love this program," said Martin, nodding at the TV screen, in which they could all make out the figure of Tony Hancock through the snowy haze.

Roger grinned in agreement. Mr. Ferguson remained silent as a stone.

"Do you like *Double Your Money?*" Martin addressed Roger, who had just opened his mouth to reply when his father interjected.

"We don't appreciate that kind of American rubbish in this house."

The other occupants of the room shifted uncomfortably while Tony Hancock and his canned laughter filled the roaring silence.

"I see you drive a Simca, Mr. Ferguson."

Martin decided to change tack. Myrtle recognized, with a sinking feeling, that he still thought he had a chance.

"And what do *you* drive?"

"A Humber Hawk." The pride was evident in Martin's response.

Myrtle's father made a sound. Indefinable in nature. It could have been a snort. But its meaning was clear. Don't think much of that.

Myrtle's sense of uneasiness grew. She knew they shouldn't have come.

"You're Irish." It was an accusation.

"Yes, sir."

Martin's easy confidence was deserting him. She could see it and it pained her, even though she had known it to be inevitable.

"What's your full name?"

"Martin Prendergast."

"What class of a name is that?"

At this point, Roger excused himself and rapidly vacated the room. Myrtle longed desperately to follow him, dragging Martin by the arm as she went.

"I don't know what—"

"Are you a Catholic?"

"Yes."

Mr. Ferguson pursed his lips and took up the newspaper that had been residing on the table beside him. He opened it up with a snap, obliterating his face as he did so. Martin and Myrtle looked at each other, Myrtle with real dismay, Martin with evident growing anger.

"I don't see what—," he began to say.

"I suppose you work on a building site."

"I have my own construction company."

Martin stood up. His efforts to get out of the chair would have been comical in any other circumstances.

"Marnie," he said, his fury barely contained. "I think it's time we left."

He held out his hand.

When Myrtle looked back on this moment, she was to see it as a pivotal point in her history. Should she embrace Martin, embrace her future, become the Marnie she'd always longed to be? Or stay and be the Myrtle she'd always been, with this her family, her taciturn father, her submissive mother?

She took Martin's hand.

MARTIN SPED OUT of Woodford in his Humber Hawk, virtually skidding around the corners of Myrtle's neighborhood.

"Slow down!" She held on to the dashboard in alarm.

Thankfully, he brought the car to a shrieking halt at an old bomb site, minutes away. It was an area upon which several houses used to stand. In summer, it was lush and pink with fireweed. Now, it was stubbly and gray. Martin got out and slammed the door behind him. Myrtle watched him uncertainly as he viciously kicked an innocent rock several times before picking up a large branch and beating the rock continually until he'd got the rage out of his system. She was about to get out when he returned and sat back down beside her, his breath heavy and rasping. His normally perfect coif was all askew. She could smell the Brylcreem on him. From that day on, that smell would propel her back to this moment. She was afraid to speak. Afraid of what she'd just witnessed. But in an odd way, she felt even more drawn toward this man. His actions spoke to her of real passion.

"Are you all right?" she said.

He drummed his fingers on the steering wheel, not looking at her.

"I've been offered a big government contract."

"Oh. That's great, Martin."

"It's in Dublin."

"Oh."

She felt the fear like ice water down her spine. Had she misjudged the situation back at the house? Was he leaving her? She closed her eyes, leaned back in her seat, and felt an incredible rush of hatred toward her father. Why did that man have to ruin everything for her?

"Did you hear what I said?"

"I heard."

"What do you think?"

"I'm pleased for you, Martin."

"Marnie, you're not hearing me. I want you to come with me."

"You mean . . ."

"I want us to get married."

And there in the back of that Humber Hawke, their marriage was consummated before it had even begun.

MARTIN PRENDERGAST AND Myrtle Ferguson got married in Woodford Registry Office on as cold and inhospitable a day as that early January could muster. Myrtle stood nervously on the pavement in her ice pink two-piece, clutching her bouquet to her breast. Martin stood beside her, his suit crisp and black, smoking a rare cigarette that he ground out with his heel after peering impatiently down the street for the umpteenth time. Accompanying them was a girl named Gladys, to whom Myrtle referred as her friend. The two often went dancing together, although they had seen less of each other since Martin arrived on the scene.

Myrtle was aware that she didn't possess a talent for friendship. There was something about her that put other girls off. She liked to tell herself that they were jealous of her success with men, her ability to make the most of herself. But deep in her core, she knew it was her lack of warmth that put them off. From her father, she had inherited not just a pale blondness, but a glacial coolness. She didn't know how to be any other way, although she longed to open up. She hoped that Martin could perform this miracle for her.

So Gladys was the closest thing she had to a female friend, and today she was to be her witness and her maid of honor. The two women got on tolerably well. Gladys was a bookish girl who wore thick, black-rimmed glasses. An intellectual, it never occurred to her to be jealous of Myrtle. She appreciated an intelligent person with whom she could have a decent conversation. And besides, it was handy having someone to go dancing with. Once on the dance floor, Gladys had no problem attracting men herself, thanks to her generous bosom and a surprisingly sensual dance technique. Although today her bustline was hidden by a dark winter coat made of a thick serge material and buttoned up to her neck. Still, she shivered.

Three heads whipped around to the sound of running footsteps. It was Myrtle's brother, Roger, adjusting his tie as he ran.

"Where have you been?" Myrtle snapped at him involuntarily.

"Sorry. I had to run back home to put on my suit."

"Are they . . . ?"

"Sorry, Myrt. They're not coming."

She took a deep breath and it appeared to the others that her body shrank slightly. Roger looked anxiously at his sister. Newly eighteen, he felt a responsibility as the most senior Ferguson male present to say something, but words failed him.

"Right then," said Myrtle brightly. "Let's go in."

And so they were married. Myrtle resented the silent assumption in the registrar's eyes that theirs was a shotgun wedding. On second thought, maybe it was.

They adjourned to a nearby pub to celebrate. It was hardly the wedding that Myrtle, with her flawless taste and eye for detail, had meticulously planned since a young girl. But, she told herself repeatedly, she was Martin's wife now and that was what really mattered.

All day long she ignored the sick feeling in the pit of her stomach.

Some might have called it a gut feeling.

THEY BOARDED THE ferry to Dun Laoghaire that night. They were to have a honeymoon of sorts in the west of Ireland, during which time Myrtle was to be shown off to an assortment of Martin's relatives. She was under strict instructions to maintain the deception that they'd got married in a Catholic church. Myrtle didn't know what she'd say if someone asked her straight out if she was a Catholic.

It was a rough winter crossing and Myrtle was as sick as a dog. As she groaned in their cabin, Martin repaired to the bar where he commenced drinking with a motley crew of Irishmen who were returning to the Emerald Isle, the majority only on a temporary basis, to wives they scarcely knew anymore and children who'd grown up so much since their last visit that they barely recognized them. The drinking was serious and heavy. Songs were sung, increasingly maudlin as the night wore on. Myrtle lay tossing disconsolately in the top bunk, retching her guts up into a tin bucket. Her discontent was added to considerably by Martin's long and unexplained absence. Some wedding night this was turning out to be. Finally, the key turned clumsily and noisily in the lock and the groom materialized. Martin staggered into the cabin. At first Myrtle put his unsteady gait down to the rocking and rolling of the ship. She'd seen Martin with drink on him many times before and he was generally able to carry it well.

"Where the hell have you been?" She'd raised herself up on her elbow and addressed him angrily.

Martin stood looking at her, swaying slightly. He appeared to be having difficulty focusing. It was then that she realized he must be very drunk. His lip curled into a kind of snarl. Nothing like Elvis.

"Shut up, you stupid bitch."

Then he fell onto the lower bunk and began to snore almost instantaneously.

That was the day *Sputnik* fell to earth, after spending exactly three months in orbit.

32

$\mathcal{T}$HERE WAS SOMETHING so precious about late summer. The knowledge that the flowers would soon be gone made their beauty all the more intense in the eyes of their beholders. The butterfly garden that Emily had planted that spring now came into its own. It was as if the butterflies were having a farewell party. Every time Harriet gamboled past the buddleia, a host of tortoiseshells and painted ladies rose into the air, as if the very petals themselves had come to life and taken flight. The bees were in overdrive too, collecting the last of the pollen for their winter pantry. As for developments amongst the human inhabitants of the garden, they too proceeded at quite a pace.

Following the ill-fated dinner party, having discovered that Mrs. Prendergast was such a sublime cook, and in a bid to take her mind off her errant son, Eva convinced her to create a personalized range of pies to sell in the Good Food Store. Emily's aunt jumped at the idea, as did the customers, who couldn't get enough of "Mrs. Prendergast's Gourmet Pies"— their major selling point, apart from their obvious deliciousness, being the guaranteed use of fresh, local produce that went toward their creation. Spinach and goat cheese was Eva's favorite.

As for Eva herself, she was going through a weird time. Changes were taking place at a rate faster than she could han-

dle. Liam was starting "big school" the following month and
the prospect flooded her with a whole gamut of emotions—
most of them negative. She'd made two attempts so far to purchase his uniform, and each time had to vacate the store in an
embarrassment of tears. It pained her immeasurably that Michael wasn't here to see his son take his first real steps into
boyhood. And because Katie was no longer coming up behind
him, this might well be the one and only time she'd experience
such a monumental life step and this added to its poignancy.

She was also in a quandary over Seth. Since the night she
had rejected him on her doorstep, a polite but cool distance
had developed between them. She didn't know how to bridge
this gap or even if she wanted to. As for Seth, she couldn't
work out if he had lost interest or was just biding his time. She
hoped it was the latter, but that might have been her vanity
speaking.

Plans were under way for the harvest festival. The idea
was to open the gate and let the public flow through. They
were going to have guided tours around the garden and
there'd be stalls selling fruit and veg and homemade soup. Eva
was in quite a flap over it all. Mrs. Prendergast watched her
flapping with some amusement.

"If you like," she said, "I could ask some of the women
from the Mother's Union to help out."

"Really? Do you think they'd be useful?"

"Well, they're forever making jams and chutneys and
doing unspeakable things with doilies. I'd imagine that this
type of thing would be right up their alley."

"Do you think they'd mind?"

"Mind! You must be joking. That lot would sell their own
children for a chance to get a look inside my house. I have to
warn you though—some of them are insufferably bossy.
They'd probably give you a pain in the arse trying to take
over."

"I'd be delighted if somebody took over."

So it was decided.

The sale of the garden to Uri proceeded without a hitch. Uri busied himself in the meantime building a tree house in the apple tree for the children and nailing up a birdhouse to shelter the robins through the winter months.

And then one day the bombshell. It didn't look like a bombshell. Just a harmless piece of paper. It was the words that were written on it that were so incendiary.

"Can he do this?" Eva spoke in hushed tones to Uri. They were both watching Mrs. Prendergast, who was hunched over her kitchen table, her head in her hands, in a pose that was utterly at odds with her usually composed demeanor.

"According to my solicitor, yes, he can. Doesn't mean he'll succeed, of course. But he can slow things down."

"Bastard," said Eva, but in even more hushed tones. It wasn't for her to call Lance names, what with his poor wounded mother sitting a few short feet away. Lance was accusing Uri of duress, of forcing Mrs. Prendergast to sell the garden to him. It was almost laughable—the idea of anyone forcing Mrs. Prendergast to do anything. But it must feel to her like the ultimate betrayal. Lance literally turning around and biting the hand that had fed him since he was an infant. He must need the money very badly. Still . . .

Uri looked furious, in that particular way he had, his face concentrated and fiercely composed. He muttered something in a language that Eva didn't understand, before sitting down beside Mrs. Predergast and putting his arm around her shoulders, his face close to hers. Eva left them to it.

She walked out into the garden and straight into Seth. Typical.

"Have you heard?" she said. At least they had something constructive to discuss.

"Yes. What a bollocks."

"As usual, Seth, your descriptive powers are spot on."

She didn't like the way that Seth was smiling at her. In her

opinion, he wasn't trying hard enough to pretend that everything was normal between them. She was trying her hardest.

"I hope Mrs. P can cope with this." She spoke rapidly, not
wanting to leave any gaps for him to fill in with words she
didn't want to hear.

"Of course she'll cope. She's a tough old bird."

"You reckon?"

"Yeah. You can bet she's been through a lot more than
this in her life. You can see it in her. She's like one of those ladies the British Empire was founded upon."

She smiled in spite of herself and hoped that he was right.

"Have you seen my Da?"

"Yes. He's in there with her now. Which reminds me.
Where exactly is your dad originally from?"

"You mean you've never asked him?"

"I've wanted to but I get the impression he doesn't like
talking about his past."

"He's German. Anyway. I'd better leave them alone if she's
upset."

"They're getting close, aren't they?"

"I suppose they are."

"Are they 'an item' do you think?"

"Couldn't tell you."

"Would it bother you if they were?"

"Why would it bother me?"

"You know. Because he's your dad and she's not your
mum."

"If it makes him happy, then I'm happy. A person can't
mourn forever, you know."

This was said very pointedly and it annoyed Eva that she
had walked herself into it.

"I've got to go," she said, feeling his eyes bore into her
back as she walked away from him.

It wasn't just his mother who was affected by Lance's legal
action. The whole future of the garden was once again in jeop-

ardy. Eva and Uri had been in the middle of their autumn bulb selection. What now?

"It'll never work, what he's doing," said Uri. "No jury will believe it."

But Eva noticed that his enthusiasm for their proposed bulb-planting extravaganza had waned considerably. Maybe they'd all lost a bit of their zest.

But the plants didn't know what was going on, so they did what they always did and kept growing. There was a renewed poignancy to their loveliness. The grass was that little bit greener, the colors of the flowers more magnified, their scent more intense. Surely this was a change in the perception of those who beheld them and not a trick of nature.

33

MYRTLE FOUND THE landscape of the west of Ireland rugged. It reminded her somehow of Martin's dark features and it seemed fitting to her that he'd been nurtured by this land.

They arrived in the town a little before eleven on a Thursday morning. The main street was surprisingly dense with people and cattle.

"Fair day," said Martin. "I forgot all about it."

He seemed pleased though. They drove slowly behind a disparate herd of cows, their bony haunches swinging from side to side, surprisingly high. City girl Myrtle had never seen an udder so close, so heavily veined, so pendulous. Although the car windows were shut tight, the stench of excrement was vile. Martin revved at the last of the herd to scare her out of the way.

"Stop!" she said.

"What?"

The town's women were out in force, bearing buckets of water and stiff brushes, to scrub the dung off their walls. What men were left were scattered around in small groups. Conversations were stopped and heads turned as the Humber Hawke advanced slowly along the street. Several men nodded in Martin's direction and he raised his fingers from the steering wheel in salute.

The houses thinned out and the countryside deepened. The rain fell slantways now and Martin was quiet.

"How far now?"

"Not far."

He hadn't mentioned the incident on the boat. Neither had she. She doubted he remembered. She wished she didn't.

The land was bad here, Martin had told her that, the soil thin. The fields were small and uneven and bounded by low stone walls. Here and there, the murky green fields were interrrupted by the black and white of a cow. Apart from that— nothing much. Hedgerows and stones. A lowering gray sky.

"Bleak, isn't it?" Martin was looking at her, his eyes searching.

She chose her words carefully.

"I expect it's nice in the summertime."

He looked straight ahead, his expression gloomy.

"I'm never coming back."

BEFORE LONG AND without indicating, Martin turned abruptly down a narrow lane. The going got considerably bumpier as the car careened over numerous potholes. It wasn't much more than a dirt track with a rough line of grass growing up the center. And then a long, low, whitewashed cottage loomed before them.

"Is this it?"

"Yes."

"But it's not thatched."

She was amazed by how disappointed she felt.

"I bought my mother a new slate roof two summers ago." His pride was evident.

He stopped the car and they both got out and stretched. The rain felt like icy pinpricks on Myrtle's face and hands. As Martin got their bags out of the boot, the front door to the cottage—a half door like that in her old geography book—

opened inward. An old woman came out. Myrtle, feeling suddenly shy, stayed by the car door and let Martin greet the woman first. She was tiny, the top of her head only reaching Martin's chest. She had to raise her arms almost vertically in order to clasp his face in her own two hands. Evidently Martin's mother, although it seemed improbable that she could ever have borne such a hulk of a man, never mind his five other siblings. After a brief exchange, Martin turned and beckoned to her. She walked slowly toward them.

"Mom," he said. "This is Marnie."

It wasn't until much later that it dawned on her that he'd introduced her as Marnie. This was his name for her. She was his now.

As Myrtle drew close she tried not to look shocked by the woman's ancient appearance. She couldn't have been more than a decade older than her own mother, but the difference in years between them looked more like thirty. The lines on her face were many and deep and her smile showed that several of her teeth were missing. But it was warm and genuine and made Myrtle feel welcome. She was heartened and relieved as she entered the cottage and realized how pathetically she wanted this woman to like her.

It wasn't much warmer inside than out, despite the presence of a peat fire. Several chairs were huddled around it, which was wholly understandable.

"Sit yourself down, my dear. You're very welcome."

Myrtle was offered the one and only armchair in the room.

"Let me take your coat."

She would have dearly loved to keep her coat but, ever polite, she slipped it off and handed it to the older woman.

"You must be parched."

"Pardon?"

"I'm sure you'd love a cup of tea after your journey."

"That would be lovely, thank you."

Myrtle watched in fascination as Mrs. Prendergast re-moved a teapot from a hook above the open fire and poured tea into a cup.

"Bread?"

"Please."

She cut a thick, rough slice of soda bread and buttered it heavily before handing it to Myrtle.

"Thank you. Did you make this yourself?"

The other woman gave her a strange look.

"I did, of course."

Myrtle sipped her stewed tea, absorbing everything, while Martin and his mother conversed. The room was a fair size with a high, arched wooden ceiling. The furniture was sparse—a dresser with delft, a rough kitchen table with chairs, the arm-chair she sat in, and the rocking chair in which Mrs. Prendergast rocked, a black-and-white cat purring companion-ably on her lap. That was it. The floor was linoleum and the open fire appeared to be the only source for heating and cook-ing. Behind the rocking chair was an intriguing curtained alcove that Myrtle later discovered was where Martin's mother slept.

Photographs were handed around. A head-and-shoulders shot of a man in a police uniform—Martin's brother Joe in Boston. Various American grandchildren—the offspring of Vincent and Kevin in New York. A picture taken last summer on the occasion of Martin's sister marrying the solicitor from Castlebar.

"Oh, wait till I show you." Martin's mother got up from her seat in an excited manner, tipping the indignant cat onto the lino. Myrtle looked at Martin, who nodded at her, and she followed them out to the side of the house where a small, rough extension had been added. Martin's mother opened the door and stood aside.

"Look," she said, her eyes shining.

Martin stuck his head in first.

"That's great, Mom."

It was Myrtle's turn. She felt Mrs. Prendergast's expectant eyes on her as she peered inside. What to say?

"It's lovely."

The correct response apparently, as Mrs. Prendergast beamed before closing the door reverently and walking ahead of them back into the house.

Myrtle looked up at Martin.

"It's a toilet," she whispered, her face baffled.

"Think yourself lucky. Six months ago you would have had to go in a hole in the ground."

They had been back in the house only a few minutes when the front door opened again. In walked a man in his thirties, wearing wellies, a donkey jacket, an Aran sweater and a cloth cap. A couple of hens ran in with him and he whooshed them out again with his feet.

"Martin!" he said, taking off his cap and flinging it down on the table.

Martin got up and the two men shook hands warmly.

"Good to see you. How are you keeping?"

"I'm well. And you?"

"Mighty. Just sold a heifer down at the fair."

"Did you get a good price for her?" said Mrs. Prendergast.

"Begod, I did."

The man looked over Martin's shoulder at Myrtle. Martin followed his gaze.

"Sean. This is my wife, Marnie. Marnie. This is my brother Sean."

He nodded at her. "Pleased to meet you."

So this was the elder brother, Sean. The one who'd got the farm. He was similar to Martin but a shadow of him—his looks not as striking, the jawline a little less defined, the eyes a little less blue. He was shorter than his younger brother too. Less powerful looking. But he had the same outdoorsy, craggy look. Myrtle wondered how he'd got home from the fair and realized that he must have walked the whole way. At first, she expected him to be intimidated by her, imagining she must seem quite the sophisticate. But Sean possessed a quiet confidence and a certainty about who he was that made *her* feel gauche. He was a man completely comfortable in his own skin, a claim that she had never been able to make about herself.

The two men went out to admire the car while Mrs. Prendergast made preparations for dinner, Myrtle helping out when she was let. She was allowed to dig up the carrots, onions, and potatoes from the plot at the back of the house. It reminded her of the victory garden that her mother used to keep during the war. She brought back the veg and Martin's mother prepared it for the stew.

The day passed pleasantly and uneventfully. Myrtle was amazed by how relaxed she felt, staring into the flames of the peat fire as the short day darkened and closed in all around them. She gazed at her husband, who sat at the opposite side of the fire, staring into his own private flames. She felt such an overwhelming surge of love for him that she thought her heart would burst right open. That night in bed, the bed that as a child he'd shared with his brother Joe, Martin reached out for her, but only for reassurance, his mother on the other side of the wall.

"You don't think any less of me, do you, Marnie?"

It was safer saying this into the pitch-black darkness.

"Why would I think less of you?"

"Now that you've seen where I come from."

"If anything, I think more of you. I can see how far you've come."

He pulled her closer to him and she knew she'd said the right thing.

THEY LEFT EARLY the next morning, after a hearty breakfast of soda bread and eggs. Martin's mother waved them off until they were out of sight.

"How long ago since your father died?"

"Six years."

"What was he like?"

Because the silent specter of the man had hung over their entire visit.

"Let's just say he was handy with his fists," said Martin, his face closed, signifying that the subject was over.

After visiting Martin's sister in Castlebar, they spent a couple of days in Westport before heading down to Killala Bay. It was a wild day. The waves hurled themselves at the rocks and the wind whipped up mini sandstorms. Martin stared out to sea, his mood reflective, as it had been since the start of their honeymoon.

Together they explored the desolate beauty of Connemara, illuminated by the sun at rare intervals. The sight of two children with a donkey and a cart full of peat almost made up for Myrtle's disappointment at the lack of a thatched roof on Martin's mother's cottage. Then it was on to Galway City. Then Yeats country in Sligo. Then home to Dublin to start their new life together.

34

*I*T WAS SHOCKING really, how alone she felt. The acuteness of her loneliness bit into her soul, removing massive chunks of the Myrtle she used to be—the Marnie she used to be—whoever it was she used to be. It left her uncertain of herself in an uncertain world where everything seemed a pale imitation of her life in London. She had Martin of course. But Martin was never home. And she had no need of a job. Not now that she was a wife, comfortably looked after by her able husband. She was expected to be content with furnishing her new home on the outskirts of this pathetic little town that laughingly called itself a city. She threw herself into the task, bringing her considerable good taste to bear on what she had to admit was a most handsome Victorian redbrick. Martin was delighted with the result and bought her a newfangled Hotpoint washing machine as a reward. She would have enjoyed this present more had she had someone to show it to.

She had her prize though. Her man. Then why did she feel so hollow? She tried so hard to do everything that was expected of her. She checked her hair and makeup to ensure that she looked perfect for Martin when he came home. She cooked his favorite meals, timing them with precision. The trouble was, she never knew when to expect him anymore. He became impossible to predict. And all too often, his meals would slowly congeal in the latter half of the oven. She tried not to be annoyed. She knew how hard he worked and she didn't want to waste what little time she had with him arguing, especially since he was often the only person she spoke to all day. But in spite of this, or perhaps because of this, her well-kept anger began to fray at the edges. It didn't help that he came in most nights reeking of whiskey. They couldn't *all* be business meetings.

The first time she confronted him she stood, apron on, hands on hips, feeling like a fishwife from out of a movie. "What time do you call this?"

He didn't answer, instead choosing to walk past her into the living room. A decanter of whiskey sat on a silver tray on a side table. It was flanked by two upside-down, cut-glass whiskey tumblers. They hadn't been a wedding present. Almost everything in the house was handpicked by Myrtle and paid for by Martin. There'd been a dearth of presents on her side. On his, anything decent could scarcely be stretched to.

Martin turned one of the glasses the right way up and sloshed a generous helping of dark brown liquid into its interior. He downed it in one go. Was it normal for a man to drink this much? Myrtle had no idea. Her own father had been a teetotaler his entire life and she had no one else to compare Martin to. Martin had drunk a lot during their courtship, but she hadn't paid much heed since they were out socializing all the time anyway. Alcohol had been intrinsic to their lifestyle. And she'd always known that he loved going out. It was just that it had never occurred to her that once they were married, he'd be going out without her. The party was over. Or rather, she was no longer invited.

"Well?" She stood behind him now, hands still planted on hips, furious at being ignored.

"What's for dinner?" he said, still with his back to her.

"You mean what *was* for dinner. It *was* lamb chops but they've been burned to a crisp, so now there's nothing for dinner."

He turned to her then, having refilled his glass. He took a sip, appraising her thoughtfully.

"Well, you'd better make me something else, then."

He walked away from her, leaving her stranded on the rug in the living room. Once she'd got over her initial shock, she was in hot pursuit.

"How dare you walk away from me. I will *not* make you another dinner—"

The words were gasped out of her as he turned suddenly and grabbed her roughly by the chin. He brought his face down close to hers and hissed into it. "No wife of mine speaks to me like that. Now get me some food."

His features were contorted. When he'd finished speaking, he released her chin, pushing her back slightly as he did so. Myrtle stood there trembling with outrage and fear. How dare he. Never in all her born days . . . she'd never seen her father treat her mother like that . . . never had he laid a hand on her. She had always dismissed her parents' marriage as passionless. Now . . . She touched the tender skin on her chin. Then she covered her mouth with her hand as she started to cry. Big, silent, free-flowing, gut-wrenching tears. Her first instinct was to run and tell someone—preferably her mother. But the only person she had to tell was in the next room waiting to be fed. So she started cooking.

IN TIME, MYRTLE began to meet a few women of her own age. Mostly at her own dinner parties. Martin would announce that he had invited a few "associates" over. If she was lucky, she'd get twenty-four-hours' notice. More often than not, she'd have just a few hours to prepare.

The first time it happened, she rushed out to Easons and bought *Mrs Beeton's Book of Household Management* and Fanny Cradock's latest. She spent the afternoon cooking up a storm. She thought it had gone okay. Everyone had been quite rapturous over her sherry trifle. Still, you never knew with Irish people—they did tend to exaggerate. With an almost physical stab of longing, she wished she was back amongst her own people. Still, the women had been kind to her. At one stage, while the men were talking shop, one of them had leaned in to her and whispered: "Your husband is *so* handsome."

She had felt herself expanding with pride. Yes, Martin was handsome. And he was hers. She was proud too of the way he held court at the dinner table, entertaining everyone with his highly embellished stories, taking care of every awkward pause and empty glass. And he must have been pleased with her because he winked at her when no one was looking. It was a good night, which continued in the bedroom later.

She didn't know what to make of it really. Her new life. Her new role. Her new husband. It was all so hard to get her head around. What was normal, what was not. What was acceptable and what was not. If only she had a sounding board. Something or someone to judge it all against. But there was no one. This isolation was disconcerting. She'd always been sure of who she was—it had never occurred to her not to be. But now, uprooted as she was, she had to rediscover herself all over again. She wasn't certain she liked what she was finding, reflected as she was in the eyes of just one other. She was unsure now, when before she had been so sure. Of herself. Of him. An uneasiness began to seep into her soul. Had her father been right? The thought was summarily banished—because it wasn't something that was fit to be admitted.

She began to see that her husband had two sides: Public Martin and Private Martin. Public Martin was loud and gregarious, the craic all the way up to ninety. Private Martin was saturnine and introspective. He sat in the chair in the dark with five o'clock shadow. The only thing these two men had in common was that they were both drink fueled. It frightened her. This prospect of living in a strange land with a total stranger. She tiptoed around this dark side, not wanting to get on its wrong side. This is what she had chosen. Her bed to lie in. Her man to understand. She tried to.

MYRTLE WAS LYING in bed one morning listening to Martin getting ready. She lay on her right side, facing away from him. Her stillness, the absence of rhythmic breathing, betrayed her wakefulness. He came around to her side and sat on the edge of the bed, looking down thoughtfully at her listless form as he buttoned the cuffs of the blue shirt that she and her iron knew intimately. She turned over onto her back and looked up at him.

"What's wrong?" he said.

Don't you know?

"Nothing's wrong."

Not when he looked at her like this, there wasn't. The gentle, tender Martin.

"You know what you need?" he said, his eyes warm.

"What?"

"A baby."

"A baby!" Her voice was incredulous, although she didn't know why. Isn't that what married couples did? Breed.

"Yes, a baby. You know. Tiny little creatures. Squawk a lot."

"I know what a baby is."

"Think about it." He bent down and kissed the tip of her nose.

She lay there for a long time after he'd gone. A baby. It's not that she hadn't thought about it before. Martin's children. Part of her longed to have them. But the other part . . . She felt so empty. Of course, she wouldn't feel empty if she had a baby growing inside her. She rubbed her taut belly and tried to imagine. Maybe Martin would be home more often if they had a family. That thought sealed it, really. Her dream of what their life together would be like had been slipping away from her of late. But now it drew back into sharp focus—with embellishments. She with her swollen belly, wearing a charming maternity smock that she'd made herself. Martin, with his hand on the demure rise of the material. A laughing Martin bouncing a laughing baby boy on his lap. Because for some reason, her fantasy conjured up a boy, dark and dimpled and handsome like his father. She didn't know why this should be so, because in her heart she'd always wanted a girl. Something about having no sisters and a distant relationship with her mother. She could give birth to her own sister now. Or re-create the mother-daughter relationship that she'd always yearned for. But a boy is what she saw. Either sex would do the trick and change them from a struggling couple into a family. Complete. And there could be other babies, lots of them. As the glee took hold of her, she stretched her body to the max, her fingertips grazing the headboard, her toes flexed. Then she curled up abruptly into the fetal position, hugging herself and rocking gently. Maybe if they had a baby Martin wouldn't drink so much.

THE TROUBLE WITH family planning is that it's not an exact science. This can work either way. In Myrtle's case, what happened was nothing. A whole lot of trying and a whole lot of nothing. And the more nothing happened, the more anxious she became. It wasn't something she discussed with anyone, least of all Martin. He just went about his business as usual, and for all she knew, he'd forgotten about their conversation. She couldn't. It began to consume her, tensing up her shoulders and worrying her brow. She'd be sitting there and before she knew it, a thumbnail would be bitten to the quick. She also developed the habit of chewing on her lower lip. Barely four months had passed. No time at all in the great scheme of things.

One night, Martin came home extra late and extra drunk. She'd learned to read the signs at a glance. She placed the remains of his partially charred dinner before him. He chewed it slowly. His well-, well-, well-done steak.

"What's this crap?"

"I can make you an omelet if you like."

"I don't want an omelet. I want a steak. A decent fucking steak."

He stood abruptly, pushing back his chair with his calf muscles, causing it to screech against the kitchen floor. Myrtle winced.

"Stupid bloody woman. Can't do anything right. Can't cook. Can't even bloody well get pregnant."

He pushed past her, out of the kitchen and into the sitting room. She knew better than to follow him. But she could see him as clearly as if she had, sloshing the whiskey into the tumbler and knocking it back. She felt her cheeks burn with shame. He was right. She *was* useless. She'd never thought it before but she thought it now. Who was she to contradict what was ultimately the truth? She was a failure as a wife, she felt it in every nerve and sinew. To her shame, he felt it too.

It took another five months. Ten months altogether. In the words of Martin: "You could have given birth by now."

But she was pregnant. That was the thing. The triumph. And no one was going to take that away from her, least of all Martin, who she could tell was pleased, really.

She longed to tell her own parents. When the three-month danger period had elapsed, she wrote them a carefully crafted letter, informing them as to her condition and asking after their health. The letter contained no hint of recrimination. Neither did it contain an apology. She received no reply. And during the silent months that followed, something inside Myrtle withered and died.

But a new excitement colored her days. A life that had been dull and empty was now vibrant and full of possibilities. She had a nursery to decorate, clothes to make for herself and the baby, blankets to crochet. It was all down to her, just as she had always known it would be. She didn't mind. It was the way she preferred it, really. Myrtle had always been solitary in her pleasures. Alone didn't necessarily mean loneliness to her. And of course, now, she was never alone. She took to talking to the embryo, the fetus, the baby.

"What will we call him?" he asked.

"How do you know it's going to be a him?"

"How could it not be?"

She smiled. She felt the same way.

"How about Martin?" he said.

"Wouldn't that be a tad confusing?"

"It worked for my father and me." He was defensive.

She didn't care. There was no way her son was having such a Catholic name. But she'd save that argument for another day.

They'd been getting on quite well since they'd found out she was pregnant, both anticipating the difference it was going to make to their lives. But everything changed once she started to show. He would stare at her stomach, an odd, unfathomable expression on his face. He grew sullen and withdrawn and stopped touching her. She began to feel isolated again. Fearful. Were the early days of marriage so difficult for everyone? She'd never have guessed it could be so hard. If she didn't know better, she would have said that he resented the new life growing inside his wife. Was jealous even. As ridiculous as the notion sounded even to herself. How could someone be jealous of someone who didn't even exist yet? His own flesh and blood, for God's sake.

The late nights away from her grew more frequent. The heavy drinking, briefly suspended, began again in earnest. He would roll in spoiling for a fight and she, in her heightened emotional state, was increasingly willing to give him what he wanted. Ready, in fact, to more or less goad him. She felt that her vulnerable condition gave her a superior edge, made her, ironically, invulnerable.

"Here he is," she said one night, easing herself out of her chair in that way peculiar to heavily pregnant women. "Stinking of booze as usual. You should be ashamed of yourself, treating your wife this way. I am carrying your child, you know."

She was indignant. Self-righteous. Martin said nothing as he stood unsteadily in the hall, eyeing her warily.

"Is this how you're planning to behave when our child is born? A fine example you're going to be." She came right up to him, standing close. And her eyes widened with incredulity.

"What's that smell?"

"What smell?" He looked a bit scared.

"You know what smell. It's perfume! It is, isn't it? You've been with a woman."

"Don't be so bloody stupid."

"Don't you call me stupid. You have, haven't you? You're reeking of it."

Her voice rose several octaves, out of control, hysterical.

"How could you do that to me? I'm your wife. I'm having your baby."

She drew back her hand and slapped him across the face, again feeling as if her life had descended into some bad piece of melodrama. Without missing a beat, Martin slapped her back. Except his slap was in a different category. While he experienced a light sting, she was sent thundering into the wall. At first she didn't know what had happened. She'd never been struck before. She felt as if someone had tried to twist her head from her neck. For a few seconds, she remained flattened against the hall wall, dazed and stunned, before trickling down to the floor, her knees falling, defeated, to the side, her eyes blinking repeatedly. Martin was all over her in an instant.

"Oh Jesus, Jesus, I'm sorry. Are you all right? Can you get up? Oh Jesus. Here, I'll help you, you're all right, you're all right."

She focused on his unnaturally white face as he scooped her up off the ground and carried her into the living room. He laid her tenderly on the couch and placed cushions behind her back and head. She continued to focus on his face, his jawline twitching nervously. She couldn't fully comprehend what had happened. It was so far outside her usual frame of reference. Had she been naive? Should she have seen it coming after the previous incident, which, she realized now, she had successfully put at the back of her mind?

"Oh, my darling, you're all right, you're all right." Martin was muttering over and over, half to her and half to himself.

"The baby," she said.

"What about it? Is something wrong?"

"I don't know, but . . ."

"Do you feel any different?"

"Well, no. But I think I should be checked out by a doctor."

"No! No reason to bother a doctor. None at all. You're fine. I'll look after you.' He left the room like a man on a mission. She lay on the couch, shivering slightly. Then her teeth started to chatter, which caused a shooting pain in the bottom-left half of her face. She reached up with shaking fingers and touched her cheek. Her skin felt hot and she could feel it throbbing. Martin returned. He was carrying a frozen steak and the bedspread from upstairs.

"Here. Hold this against your face."

She did as she was instructed and felt some soothing. He arranged the bedspread all around her, tucking it up to her chin and around her feet, from which he gently removed her slippers.

"You hit me," she said, her eyes brimming, her teeth still chattering in her head.

"No I didn't."

"What do you mean, you—"

"I mean, I know I did, but it was only a slap. And you slapped me first." He attempted a sickly smile.

"And that makes it all right?" She started to cry properly.

"Oh God. I'm sorry, I'm sorry."

He cradled her, laying his cheek against her good side.

"I'll never do anything like that again. I swear to you, Marnie. I'll never hit you again. I'll change. It'll be all right. Everything's going to be all right, you and the baby." He rocked her back and forth and she cried piteously in his arms.

"The perfume," she said.

"There's no other woman, Marnie. I swear to God. There's only you. No other woman but you. I was in a club, that's all. You know how you get crushed up against everybody."

She desperately wanted to believe him, his tender words and sentiments balm to her aching spirit. The throbbing in her cheek subsided to a dull ache and she ceased to shake. Martin sat with his arms around her for an hour or more, the room, the house, growing dark around them. Until he felt she believed him.

IN TIME SHE was okay and the finger marks faded. Her cheek was no longer tender. Martin continued to be so. And attentive. Remorseful. No more late nights. He came home when he said he would. If there had been a woman, she was put on the back burner. The baby was okay too. He stayed intact until ten days before his due date. Martin wasn't present for the birth. He was relegated to the smoke-filled waiting room with all the other expectant fathers. But he came in as soon as he was let and allowed Myrtle to call their son Lance, either out of a sense of guilt or some upwardly mobile tendency within him.

LANCE HAD HIS father's hair but not his eyes. His eyes were Myrtle's—slate blue–gray eyes that saw the world for how it was and not how they wanted it to be. He was quite a sedate baby, which was just as well, because how would she have coped otherwise, what with everything else that the situation had thrown at her? Martin's strange moods. One minute, delighted with her and the new baby. The next, sulky and petulant, as if he were the older sibling instead of the father, jealous and vying for her attention. Up until this point she had only needed to be wary of his moods when he had drink taken. But now, as if aching nipples and eyes falling out of her head with tiredness weren't enough, she had his mercurial rantings to put up with.

"You're giving that child too much attention."

"You're spoiling him. Let him cry."

And "You care more about that baby than you do about me."

"Of course I bloody well do," Myrtle felt like screaming. "What do you expect?"

Because the love she'd had for Martin had almost run out. Like an egg timer with the tiniest trickle of sand left to run through. He'd squeezed the life out of it with his big, rough hands.

And she'd loved him so much.

She wept for her lost love, so strongly held. She missed it and she mourned it. And it could have been his forever if only he'd known how to keep it. All that she had now was resentment. Another dull ache to put up with. Perhaps it would get better as Lance got older and she wasn't so tired all the time. Nowadays, if someone commented on how handsome or entertaining her husband was, she didn't feel proud. Instead she felt anger and a powerful urge to blurt out the truth. She did this once. When the urge to unburden herself became too great.

The woman was named Frances. She was the wife of a colleague of Martin's. She and Myrtle often found themselves thrown together at dinner parties. She'd had a baby girl around the same time that Myrtle had given birth to Lance and the two women would visit each other's homes in a bid to stave off the madness that often besets the first-time mother, home alone with her baffling baby.

Myrtle was really just trying to find out if her marriage was normal. That's how it started.

"How's Bill adjusting to fatherhood?"

"Oh, he loves it. He's wonderful with her. I'm sure Martin's the same."

"Not really, no." She was sick of lying. Trotting out the accepted truth just to please.

Frances looked a little taken aback, as well she might. Myrtle clearly was not playing the game.

"Maybe he needs more time to get to know Lance." Her words were designed to reassure herself as much as Myrtle. "It doesn't come as easily to men as it does to us." She looked so smug and snug in her feminine role that Myrtle wanted to hit her. But she couldn't do that, so she verbally slapped her instead.

"I sometimes think that Martin's jealous of his own baby. Do you ever think that about your husband?"

Frances looked shocked. "No, I don't."

"He's jealous of all the attention I give him. He was even jealous of him when he was in the womb. He hit me once, you know. When I was pregnant."

"I'm sure—"

"He did, you know. Flattened me up against the wall. Did your husband ever do anything like that to you?"

"Jesus, Mary, and Joseph, no."

"So it's not normal, then?"

"Of course not. I'd better go." Frances began gathering up her things. It was clear that she didn't want to know, feared getting involved.

Myrtle didn't see much of her after that. She didn't tell anyone else. And the wound in her soul festered and turned into an oozing, weeping carbuncle.

IT WASN'T ALL bad. As Lance got older, the less wholly dependent he became on Myrtle and this suited Martin. He liked to play with the young boy—rough and tumble games, throwing, tickling, and flinging—causing him to squeal with delight. Myrtle was glad for Lance, that he had this alternative to her rather more sedate reading, coloring, and walking routine. It was clearly true that children needed two parents, a mother and a father. Although Martin never talked of his own father. And come to think of it, her brother Roger hated his. She hoped the cycle could be broken. Her more pressing concern right now was whether or not her son needed a sibling. She had never intended for him to be an only child. Given the amount of time it had taken for her to conceive Lance, maybe they shouldn't hang about too long. Her hemming and hawing came to an end one day when Martin announced gruffly: "Lance needs a little brother."

That was decided, then.

IT TOOK SIX months this time, a little less than before. Things were good. Martin was happy and so was Lance. Father and son patently adored each another. Myrtle felt content about her growing family and newly optimistic about the future. But this happy phase in her life was to be short-lived. Because, again, the problems began when her pregnancy started to show. She wasn't sure why this should be the case but it was. The constant reminder of her condition seemed too much for Martin to bear. He became surly again, eyeing her stomach suspiciously, as if it was an intruder in their home, as if he had had nothing to do with it in the first place and it was none of his doing. The drinking began again. The staying out. She accepted it all with a sense of dread, the tired inevitability of it all. Lance was the only recipient of his smiles—that was, when he saw him. More often than not, he'd been asleep for hours by the time Martin fell in the door. There was a new quality to his drinking. It was getting worse. *He* was getting worse. She wasn't sure if it was because he was drinking more or if he wasn't able to hold it as well as he once had. But it certainly seemed to have a hold on him.

SHE WAS FOUR months' pregnant. She liked to talk to the baby. To hold her hand on her stomach and feel its first flutterings. It had become her habit to go to bed early and feign sleep when Martin came in. The pregnancy gave her an excuse, and besides, she was exhausted anyway. Usually it worked and he left her alone. But not this night.

She tensed when she heard his footfall on the stair—heavy, uneven, ominous. Normally he stayed downstairs and drank some more before falling into a drunken stupor on the couch. She kept her eyelids resolutely closed as he entered the room and sat down heavily on the bed.

"Are you awake?"

She lay still as a stone.

"Marnie, wake up." He shook her shoulder.

Still she didn't react.

"Wake up, you stupid cunt."

And with one almighty shove, he pushed her out of the bed. She struck her forehead on the bedside table on the way down and lay there stunned for several seconds, vaguely aware that he was coming around to her side of the bed. She looked up at him in abject shock.

"What are you doing, Martin?"

"That'll teach you to ignore me, English bitch."

And he kicked her hard in the stomach.

IT WAS A girl. Tiny, perfectly formed, and dead. She would have called her Rose. She wouldn't be able to have any more children.

She stayed in the hospital for a week, staring at the wall as Martin sat on the bed and talked. He was the tender Martin she'd once known. Attentive. Above all, remorseful. While he unloaded his guilt, she weighed her options. By the end of the week, she concluded that she didn't have any. It was 1962. At that time, no one of Myrtle's acquaintance was separated, divorced, or a single parent. She hadn't spoken to her parents since she'd got married. She loved her brother, Roger, but he was still young, feckless, and broke. She was fond of Martin's mother and family, but they would hardly take her in if she left their son and brother. What female friendships she had forged since landing on this godforsaken isle were superficial. And Martin said he'd never harm her again. She didn't believe him, but it was all she had. On the seventh day, he brought Lance in to see her.

"When are you coming home, Mummy?"

"I'm coming home now."

She got out of the bed and started to dress. She met Martin's eye.

"Thank you," he mouthed.

35

*E*VA AND *S*ETH had spent the morning busily ignoring each other. Eva, digging up potatoes as if her life depended on it. Seth, messing around the pond and achieving very little. It was pretty uncomfortable. Eva would have left long before, but she was waiting for the two women from the Mother's Union. She had taken Mrs. Prendergast up on her offer. She'd been in such a tizzy at the prospect of organizing the Harvest Festival—or "the Autumn Party," as Kathy and Liam insisted on calling it—that the idea of two extra and experienced pairs of hands had been too tempting to turn down. She hoped that she hadn't been too hasty. She also hoped that Seth would clear off home. He wasn't even doing anything.

"You must be Eva."

She turned to see two middle-aged women picking their way daintily through her vegetable patch. They tiptoed around the turnips and greeted her at the garlic.

"You must be . . ."

"Joyce and Pearl." Joyce was the spokeswoman.

"Pearl, Joyce, delighted to meet you."

They all shook hands rather formally and Eva felt herself to be on familiar territory. She recognized these women, despite never having met them before in her life. They were the women of her childhood. The women who worked the stalls at church fetes. The women who ran whole committees single-handedly. And Joyce was a dead ringer for Eva's first headmistress. Despite her Catholic upbringing, she had attended the local Church of England school, for reasons of reputation and convenience. And these women were unmistakably and indisputably Protestant. She couldn't quite pinpoint what it was about them, but she knew that she was right.

"I must say, Eva. I've heard a lot about this garden but none of the descriptions did it justice. It's simply glorious. And the vegetable patch is magnificent. I can't remember the last time I saw such healthy-looking chard."

"Do you grow your own?"

"Oh yes. Have done for years."

Here was someone else who knew more about gardening than she did.

They all looked around at the crunching sound on the gravel path. It was Seth, grinning expectantly.

"Joyce. Pearl. This is Seth."

"Ladies." Seth preferred his hand and smiled his best smile.

"Joyce and Pearl are going to help with the Autumn Party."

"Oh." Pearl spoke for the first time. "I thought it was a Harvest Festival."

"Well, Autumn Party, Harvest Festival—it's all the same thing, really."

"Actually, no it isn't."

There was an embarrassing silence. Pearl may have been a quietly spoken woman, but, Eva noticed for the first time, she had the mad look in her eye of a religious zealot.

"So," said Joyce, to everyone's relief. "Tell us what you've got planned so far. Or perhaps we should discuss this inside the house."

Both sets of women's eyes lit up and they nodded enthusiastically.

"Oh, I wouldn't want to disturb Mrs. Prendergast. It's still quite early."

"Nonsense. Myrtle's always been an early riser. I expect she's been up for hours."

"Myrtle!" said Seth. "You're kidding me. No wonder she kept quiet about it."

Eva gave him a withering look. "Ladies. Why don't I show you around the garden?"

As they walked away from Seth and the vegetables, Joyce giggled in that high-pitched way peculiar to some women of a certain age. "Oh dear. I hope we haven't let the cat out of the bag on poor Myrtle."

"Not at all. I'm sure she won't mind."

"Are you sure we shouldn't just knock in on her first. I'd hate to appear rude."

"You know, come to think of it, I don't think she's even home. I saw her heading off about half an hour ago. Probably doing her weekly shop."

"Oh, that's a pity."

The two women looked so disappointed that Eva almost felt sorry for them. But she was under strict instructions from Mrs. Prendergast not to let them anywhere near the house. Her exact words had been: "If you let either of those nosy old bags within ten yards of my home, I'll set Harriet on them."

"What's she going to do? Fart at them until they're both completely asphyxiated?"

"Don't be so cheeky, my girl. I mean it. If you let them anywhere near me, I'll cancel the whole thing. Let me remind you that I'm still the owner of this garden."

Mrs. Prendergast had shaken a crooked finger at Eva. She did have a glint in her eye, but Eva knew she was serious just the same. She'd seen the telltale twitch of the bedroom curtain when the women first arrived. She imagined their reedy voices floating to the uppermost reaches of the house, where Mrs. Prendergast was waiting—watching—checking.

To Eva's frustration, Seth had insisted on following them. She knew that he knew she had meant for him to stay put. How typical of the man. She gave him a look and he grinned back at her.

Eva and the other two women chatted as they walked. It came as no surprise to Eva that they were both retired schoolteachers.

"What's going to happen on the day?" said Joyce.

"Well, I thought we'd have a stall selling fruit and veg and that I could make some soup."

"What kind of soup?"

"Parsnip. We've got a glut of them at the moment."

"I've got a wonderful recipe for honey-roasted parsnip soup that I can give you."

"I already have—"

"Now. Bread."

"What about it?"

"You have to have some homemade bread to go with the soup. Would you like us to make it?"

"Um. Maybe. I'm not sure. Can I get back to you on that?"

"Fine. What else?"

"I hadn't really thought much further than that."

"What about a cake stall?" this from Seth.

"Excellent idea!" Joyce beamed at him. "We can use some of the fruit from the garden. Pies, flans, crumbles. That sort of thing."

"And jams," said Seth.

"Oh yes. Jams, preserves, chutneys. I must say, you are full of wonderful ideas."

"Oh, he's full of it all right."

If Eva didn't know better, she'd swear that Joyce was flirting with Seth.

"Now." Joyce was striding with great purpose toward Emily's sensory garden. "This lavender. I know it's past its best, but it's hanging on in there. I'm sure we could put this to some use. Soaps. Lotions. Scent."

"What about the roses?" said Seth. "They're shedding their petals right now. Could you make something out of them?"

Joyce clasped her hands as if in ecstasy.

"Yes! Your husband has such wonderful ideas." She addressed Eva.

"My what?"

She could hear Seth snorting with laughter behind her.

"Oh, I do apologize. I assumed you two were married."

"Um. No," said Eva.

"Where shall we put the reverend?" Pearl seemed quite oblivious to the conversation going on all around her.

"What do you mean?"

"For the ceremony."

"What ceremony?"

"For the Harvest Festival."

"Right. You know, I think we may have got our wires crossed. It's not going to be a religious event. At least not a Christian one. We hope to have many people here from all sorts of different faiths. We wouldn't want to alienate anyone."

Pearl looked most put out.

"I'm sorry if we've misled you in any way," Eva continued. "Of course the vicar is very welcome to come along. He can have some soup. I'll understand if you don't want to participate, under the circumstances."

"Oh, don't be ridiculous," said Joyce. "Of course we want to participate."

Pearl didn't look so certain.

When their visit was over, Seth and Eva walked the two women to the gate. Seth walked ahead with Pearl while Eva dawdled with Joyce, who stopped every now and then to admire some plant, invariably calling it by its Latin name.

"Can I ask you something?" Eva said abruptly.

"Of course you can, dear."

"Why did you think that Seth and I were married?"

Joyce giggled. "Sorry about that. I don't know, really. Something about the way you are with each other. I think it was the mixture of familiarity and contempt."

36

$\mathcal{P}$RENDERGAST CONSTRUCTION LIMITED was by now considered one of the premier building companies in the capital. This was a testament to Martin's hard work and charm. He'd just been awarded another government contract, which meant that Myrtle didn't see that much of him. This suited her fine. She and Lance got on very well with their lives without him.

She had infinite time to spend with Lance, since Martin had insisted upon hiring a housekeeper and a gardener, as befit his new status as a master builder. She drew the line at a nanny. Although the housekeeper suited her well enough. Myrtle's talent had always been in picking out exquisite items, not in keeping them clean. The garden was a different issue. They'd done little to it since moving in, the project seeming too monumental. It was a sprawling acre surrounded by high, brick walls and dominated by weeds. The only plants of any account contained within were a few old apple trees.

So a gardener was appointed and things started to happen. Myrtle watched in daily fascination as order was created out of chaos. Four quadrants were made. A pond was constructed in the center and gravel pathways enclosed each section. And then there was the planting, which was where the real fun started. The gardener, a generous man in his fifties, allowed

Myrtle to participate. They pored over garden catalogs together and made their selections.

Martin was equally delighted with developments. On his rare days off, he would help with the digging and the carting around of topsoil. Myrtle guessed it reminded him of his childhood on the farm, but she didn't ask him about this. She didn't care about him anymore. It mattered only that he was sober and leaving her alone.

But it was winter now and not much work to be done. The garden lay sleeping, and inside the house, Christmas decorations were in full swing. Martin was due back from a junket in Amsterdam. A few days after that, his mother and brother Sean were coming to spend their first Christmas in Dublin. There was a lot for Myrtle to do, but she was as happy as she could be.

Lance flew back into his father's arms the second he got home.

"What did you get me, what did you get me?"

There was chocolate of course.

"And this."

"What is it?"

"It's an angel for the top of the Christmas tree."

She was small and ceramic, blue and white.

Martin and Lance looked over at Myrtle.

"She's lovely," she confirmed.

Martin lifted Lance up and he placed the angel at the top of their little fir tree. Then they turned on the lights and had the best Christmas ever.

For her birthday that spring, Martin bought Myrtle her very own camera. Because he was still trying hard to please her. And she was pleased.

"Come on. Let's test it outside."

The three trooped outside and found the gardener.

"Would you mind?" said Martin, showing him how to use the contraption. "A family portrait, I think."

They stood in front of the largest apple tree, the entire Prendergast family. The gardener clicked.

"Wonderful," said Martin.

What a lie, thought Myrtle. The image of the perfect, happy family sticking in her craw.

The time capsule was Martin's idea, enthusiastically hijacked by Lance. They planned it meticulously, then buried it the following week, the very day the first batch of photos was developed. They spent a magical afternoon in the garden, the entire Prendergast family, discussing what to include and where to bury it. It was to remain one of Lance's favorite childhood memories.

That night Martin had a glass of Johnnie Walker. Just a small one. He deserved it after being so good for so long.

IT BEGAN AGAIN, that old familiar dance. First came the smell. He tried to hide it, but her sensitivity was heightened. She didn't say anything. Then came the late nights. Then both factors increased with intensity. Still she didn't say anything. She didn't see the point. There was such a dull inevitability to it all. A cycle as natural as the seasons. As winter followed autumn, so drunkenness followed sobriety. He still came home some nights and played with his son. The two adored each other, and thus far, Lance had never seen his father drunk. Didn't even know what drunk was, thank goodness. Although he did comment once: "What's that smell Daddy?"

"Toothpaste."

"No, there's something else too."

Martin had rapidly excused himself.

Then the insults started, insidious at first, later becoming more obvious. The names. The slaps, the kicks, the shoves. Nothing serious. Base-level stuff. Stuff that by now she felt she deserved. At least he was good to Lance. He never lifted a finger toward him, and as long as that situation continued, she could put up with anything.

It became worse—the drinking, the violence. She wondered how he continued to get away with it in the outside world. But she knew that to the outside world, he was charm personified. It added to her sense of isolation, her desperation, the knowledge that she alone knew the truth and that if she tried to share it, she wouldn't be believed.

HE CAME HOME early one evening. The housekeeper was out sick, so Myrtle was seeing to the dinner. The gardener had brought her in some vegetables for the stew that she was making. They chatted awhile about some new planting schemes while Lance played with his cars on the kitchen floor. She hadn't been expecting Martin, not until much later. Her spirits drooped at the sound of his voice.

"Daddy, Daddy!" Lance ran to his father and clung to his leg. For once he was ignored.

What Myrtle saw on Martin's face filled her with fear. He glared at the gardener, who beat a hasty retreat.

"What was he doing here?" The words were spat out of him. It was clear he was moldy drunk and looking for a fight.

"Lance, darling. Why don't you go upstairs and play with your trains?"

"I said what the fuck was *he* doing here?" he roared and slammed his hand down on the counter.

Out of the corner of her eye, Myrtle saw Lance jump out of his skin, then stare at his father in wonderment and fear. He'd never seen him like this before.

Myrtle struggled to keep the tremor out of her voice. She'd rarely seen him so bad.

"He was bringing me some veg. Mary's off sick and I'm making the dinner."

"What were you talking about?"

"The garden. We—"

"You've always got your heads together. Are you fucking him?"

"Martin, please! Don't be so stupid, he's old enough to be my father."

"Don't you dare call me stupid, you fucking whore." He was screaming with rage.

"Lance, go upstairs. Now!"

"Are you making a fool out of me, woman?"

He had her by the throat now, squeezing hard, the back of her head rammed up against the fridge.

"Stop it, Daddy. Stop it!" Lance was screaming now and pummeling Martin's legs with his tiny balled-up fists. Myrtle wanted to tell him to stop but she couldn't utter a sound. It was all she could do to keep on breathing, Martin's hands tightening by the second. She pulled at his hand with her own to no avail. She stared back into his murderous eyes and registered with horror the manic spittle on his lips. If she ever got out of this . . .

"Mummy!" Lance was hysterical now, running at his father and ramming into him with his head.

"Stop it," roared Martin. But Lance wouldn't. Until Martin let Myrtle go, whereupon she collapsed onto the ground in a heap. Martin launched himself at Lance now and slapped him so hard across the face that the little boy was knocked back several feet. Then he descended on his son and started to shake him.

"You little shit!" he roared.

"Take your hands off him."

And suddenly all was silent, all was still.

Myrtle held a kitchen knife to Martin's throat.

Neither of them doubted her capacity to use it.

37

$\mathcal{T}$HE WEEKS DRIFTED by and all was suspiciously quiet. Neither Uri's nor Mrs. Prendergast's lawyers had heard a peep out of Lance. Inquiries were made and the reason became abundantly clear: Lance had checked himself into rehab.

How was Mrs. Prendergast to react? With relief that Lance was getting help for his problems? Or shame that her son had sunk to such depths? Either way, it was a difficult and emotional issue for her. She had to go and see him, of course. How could she not? Although part of her had never been going to forgive him for the way he'd behaved, he was still her one and only son and she his only mother.

Curiously enough, she'd never been to a rehabilitation center before. It was nicer than she had expected. She'd had a vision of peeling paint and terrible toilets and junkies lining the corridors, needles sticking out of their arms. But it was a calm place. Dignified. It reminded her of an active retirement center she'd visited, once and once only.

Lance was sitting at a table, his back to her. The shock was physical. He looked so much like his father from behind. She realized that Lance had grown up to be the same age as Martin the last time she'd laid eyes on him. The identical hairline. The broad expanse of his shoulders.

She sat down quietly beside him. He looked at her and

promptly burst into tears. She didn't know where to put herself. Mother and son had always been in the habit of hiding their weaknesses from each other. Stiff upper lip and all that. She hadn't seen him cry since he was a teenager and she didn't know how to react. She felt overwhelming sympathy and compassion toward him but she wasn't sure how to express this. She settled for a swift pat on the arm. This seemed to make him worse. Whether this was because her action was too much or not enough she couldn't say. But Lance was clearly at the point in his treatment when he cried like a baby at the tiniest thing. Eventually, he was able to get a few words out.

"I'm sorry," he sniffed.

For what? For blubbering all over her? Or for breaking her heart?

"I've been such a shit."

While she had no intention of actively agreeing with him, she couldn't bring herself to deny it either.

"How can you even look at me? After everything I've done. Everything I've said."

"Oh, Lance." She put her hand on his. "I'll always love you no matter what you do. I'm your mother. I can't help it."

This at least made him laugh. They'd always shared the same sense of humor. Dark. Ironic. Gallows humor, Martin used to call it. She surprised herself by thinking of him for the second time that day. Normally she was quite successful at blocking out such thoughts. She'd certainly needed gallows humor living with *him*.

"I take it this means you'll be dropping that ridiculous lawsuit?"

He nodded sheepishly and rubbed at his eyes with the balls of his thumbs.

"Sorry."

"So you should be. I mean, if you needed money, Lance,

you should have come right out and asked me for it, instead of going about everything in such an underhanded way."

"I know, I know. I was ashamed."

"Of what exactly?"

"Of how I lost my money."

"You mean by gambling?"

"How did you know that?"

"Uncle Roger told me."

"Oh."

"Yes. Oh."

"Did he tell you the rest?"

"You mean about the drinking and the cocaine?"

"Oh Jesus." Lance was mortified. And amazed. He looked at his mother in wonderment.

"How do you know about cocaine?"

"How could I not know? I didn't come down in the last rain shower. I read the papers. I watch the news. I saw *Trainspotting*. I know you think I live a sheltered life, Lance, but I've got eyes and I've got ears."

"And you're not—shocked."

"Well, I am a little bit. You don't expect these things right on your doorstep. And from someone who's had the benefit of a private education. But." She paused. How to say this the right way.

"I think a part of me always wondered if it would come out in you. Your father was an alcoholic, and from what I can gather, so was his father before him. You have an addictive personality, Lance. I'm sure if cocaine were available in their day, they would have been shooting that up too."

"Snorting it, Mother."

"Snorting it, then. Don't contradict me. You're in enough trouble as it is. Anyway, the point is, you didn't get it from my side. The strongest thing my parents ever drank was coffee. I don't have an addictive personality. Some would say I have no personality at all."

"I wouldn't."

They were both smiling now. Each with a tremendous sensation of relief.

"So," she sighed. "Are you all right for money now?"

"Yes. Uncle Roger bailed me out. He's paying for this too. But you probably know that already."

"He may have said something."

"He's been unbelievably good to me."

"Yes, well, I think he's always felt a certain amount of responsibility toward you. He thinks of himself as a kind of distant, surrogate father figure."

Roger had turned out to be a bit of a genius when it came to business, building up several successful companies and selling them for enormous profits. He spent most of his time now in semiretirement, in his town house in Maida Vale, with his third wife, Anthea, who was twenty-five years his junior.

"There's something I need to ask you," said Lance, his face darkening. "I had what they call a 'breakthrough' in group therapy the other day."

God, thought Myrtle. It all sounds so appallingly American.

"I'm listening," she said.

"And ever since then I've been having these—I don't know what you call them. Memories. Flashbacks. Almost like dreams except I'm already awake."

"Go on."

Part of her knew what was coming.

"Did . . ." He faltered. "The day Dad left. Did something happen?"

She sighed, her limbs feeling suddenly leaden.

"What do you remember?"

"Did he hit me?"

She nodded her head solemnly.

"Jesus Christ. I must have been blocking it out all of these years."

He sat there shaking his head for a few moments. Then he
looked up at her sharply.

"And you? Did he hit you too?"

"Yes."

"Just that time or other times?"

"There were other times too."

"Christ. All these years and I never knew. Why did you
stay with him as long as you did? It's not like you to take any
crap from anybody."

"That's what we women did in those days. You put up
and shut up. There wasn't much of a choice. If you were unfortunate enough to have married the wrong man, you just
had to make the best of it."

"So why that day? Why did you finally snap?"

"I was in fear of my life, Lance. I hadn't felt that way before. But mostly it was because he hit you too—for the first
time. I never thought he would—he doted on you."

"And to think that all this time I blamed you."

"For what?"

"For driving him away."

"How could I have done that?"

"Well." Lance squirmed uncomfortably in his seat.
"You're not exactly the warmest person in the world." He
threw her an apologetic look. "Sorry."

"That's a fair comment, I suppose. But I wasn't cold with
your father. Not in the beginning at least. I adored him, you
see."

"Did you?"

"Yes."

They were both quiet. Each absorbed in their own set of
thoughts. Each set touching at certain points.

"Mum."

"Yes."

"There's something else I remember from that day."

"What?"

He laughed somewhat nervously. "But it can't be right. It's so far-fetched—my memory must be playing tricks on me."

"What is it?"

"I somehow seem to remember you holding a knife to his throat."

"Yes, Lance. I did."

38

URI AND EVA worked easily together. He was helping her, yet again. His endless patience and generosity amazing her anew.

"You must get tired of my constant questions," she said.

"Not really, no."

"But I'm forever asking you things."

"The knowledge isn't mine to keep. It's for passing on to the next generation. That's you. Then it will be your turn."

She digested this for a while, wondering how far she could push her luck.

There was an unspoken rule in the garden. The "respecting each other's privacy" rule. But he seemed in the mood to be open . . .

"Seth tells me you're from Germany."

He looked up at her briefly, something indefinable in his eyes, before turning his attention back to the sapling he was tending.

"That's right."

"What part?"

"Just outside Berlin."

"Do you ever go home?"

"Dublin is my home now."

"But you must have some family over there."

"Not anymore."

There was something definitive about the way he said it. She knew that their discussion—such as it was—was at an end.

He gradually wandered away from her then, the atmosphere now slightly strained. In any case, he preferred to work alone. It meant that he could perform his tasks uninterrupted and that his daydreams remained undisturbed. Unfortunately, there was the ever present danger that his thoughts might wander into forbidden territory.

He lovingly touched his fantail fig, rubbing a fruit between his fingers, fruit that was soon to be transformed into something even more delectable by the women of the Mother's Union. His own mother used to make something out of figs. What was it again? He closed his eyes and tried to recall.

HE LOVED TO sit and watch his mother bake. He and his sister would stand on chairs overlooking the counter on which she worked: rolling, kneading, mixing, creaming, chopping, peeling, filling, trimming. Sometimes she let them help. Always she let them lick the bowls. Well, he got the bowls because he was the biggest and Hannah got the spoons. If there was one thing better than watching her bake, it was eating the results afterward: challah loaf, bagels, blintzes, honey cake, rugelach, kugel, and tzimmes.

Sometimes Uri would bring these treats to school for his lunch. The other boys did this too but Uri was sure that his mama's were the best.

Then one day, his school was closed down. He didn't know why exactly, but he did know it had something to do with the soldiers. Although what they could have against him learning his letters and numbers and playing chase in the yard, he couldn't work out. It was exciting at first. Like being on holiday. But after a while, Uri missed the other boys and even learning things. Another funny thing happened around that time. Uri was no longer allowed to play in his favorite play-

ground. His mother said that it was closed down but he knew
that this wasn't true because he had seen other children playing there. He thought it might have something to do with the
yellow star on his clothes because none of the children playing
there had stars. He asked his mama if he could take it off so
he could go over and play. But she said he had to wear it. He
thought this was very mean and sulked in his room for a
while. So no school and no playground. Life was very boring.
Uri liked to play with the other boys on the street but sometimes children without stars would shout names and rude
things at them. It wasn't very nice, but not so bad if he was
with his mama or papa. Then he would just hold their hands
even tighter, look straight ahead, and pretend he hadn't heard
a thing.

All this meant that he spent a lot of time indoors and a lot
of the time, the only one left to play with was Hannah—and
she was useless. The only thing she was good at was messing
up his games. So life was pretty dull. Then one day, his parents
said that they were moving. To somewhere called Ghetto.
He'd never heard of it before, but he hoped it had a playground.

His parents didn't seem pleased about moving. Maybe because it happened so quickly that they didn't have time to take
everything. They had to leave all the really big things like tables and beds. Uri got to bring most of his toys with him, so
he was happy about that. And his parents could always come
back for the rest of their things later.

The new house wasn't what he was expecting at all. It was
a lot smaller, for a start. Before, they'd had a whole house and
garden to themselves. Now they had to share a house with
other families and it wasn't even very big. *And* it didn't have a
proper garden, just a yard. Uri didn't have his own room anymore either. He had to share with his parents and sister, and
not just for sleeping. They had to do everything in this room—
cooking, eating, playing. In the beginning, he would ask his

mother to bake him honey cake. She would say she couldn't and then look all nervous and worried and bite her lip. So he stopped asking.

But there were good things too. The best was that now there were lots of boys to play with. There wasn't a playground, as Uri had hoped, but they made up games and they could play on the street all the time because in Ghetto, everyone had a star and there was nobody left to call them names.

Another good thing was that Uri's father was home all the time now. He used to have a job at the Palace Gardens. His was the most important job of all and the other men who worked there had to do what he told them. He had taken Uri to work with him a few times, on the special seat on his bicycle.

Uri liked having his father home, mainly because he told such brilliant stories. Even though he was quiet and normally didn't say very much, his stories were fantastic. It was funny, because his mother talked all the time but her stories weren't nearly as good. Most of Papa's stories had dragons in them because they were Uri's favorites. Except when Hannah was listening too and then Papa had to include princesses and other stupid girl's stuff. But Papa would wink at him to let him know that he was only putting in these parts to keep Hannah happy.

When he wasn't telling stories, Uri's father looked sad a lot of the time. He would stare out the window. Uri thought that he was probably thinking about his flowers and plants in the Palace Gardens. Normally, he didn't like to leave them, even for a few days, so he must be wondering how they were getting on without him and hoping that somebody else would weed them and water them until he got back. Uri would try and cheer him up when he looked like this with little jokes and tickling games.

Then one day they had to leave their new house—even more quickly than the last time. He could take only a few of his small toys. It wasn't a nice day. There were lots of soldiers with guns and they were shouting loudly and making people run to where they wanted them to go. They all ended up sitting in the town square—hundreds and hundreds, maybe even a thousand people. All wearing yellow stars. Then they started moving them in big groups. They were in the second group. After a while, they could tell that they were going to the station.

39

*O*NCE ON THE train, Uri could hardly breathe. He stood awkwardly, pressed up against his mother, his cheek cradled by her hip bone. They had to stand because there was no room to sit down. His father held Hannah in his arms. She had fallen asleep some time ago, her body slopped heavily against his father's rigid form. As an old man, Uri could still recall the haunted expression on his mother's face that day on the train. But every time he looked up at her, she smiled at him and touched his cheek or his hair. This would have embarrassed him normally. He *was* ten years old now, after all. But things like that didn't seem to matter anymore. A few hours earlier, he had seen a boy from his school, a boy who was a lot bigger than Uri, crying like a baby. He wouldn't do that. He looked up at his mother again and returned her smile. She touched her fingers to her lips and pressed them up against his. He hugged her hips more tightly, wishing he could reach up and hug her properly. He could just see through the slats that it was growing dark outside. Elsewhere in the carriage, parents sang lullabies to their children. Prayers were muttered. Uri hadn't known that it was possible to fall asleep standing up. But that's what he did.

THE TRAIN JUDDERED to a halt and they all fell against one another. Uri's eyes felt gritty, as if he hadn't slept at all. He could hear men shouting outside the train. The doors were opened and the people started to spill out, gasping at the fresh air. There was one man who didn't get up at all. Uri and his family had to step over him. Uri wondered how he could stay sleeping with all the noise and activity that was going on around him.

The air outside was very cold. It bit into Uri's skin. His mother wrapped her arm around his neck like a scarf as they were herded quickly along. The guards shouted orders at them. He'd had plenty of experience with these guards at this stage. They always seemed to be angry about something or other. One of them was screaming at everybody to leave their bags on the train. Uri wished he would stop—it was hurting his ears. One old man wouldn't let go of his briefcase, so three of the guards pulled him to the side. There was a lot of shouting, then, a few seconds later, an even louder noise like a gun going off. Uri heard his mother gasp and she covered up his ears. He didn't see the old man again.

When they got inside the camp, it was the men and boys on one side, the women and girls on the other. Uri's mother wouldn't let him go. She smothered his face with kisses and held him so tight against her coat that he could hardly breathe. Then a guard yelled at her and hit her on the side of her head with the butt of his rifle. The last time Uri saw his mother, she was scrambling to her feet, the blood running down the side of her head.

"Be a good boy," she said. "Do everything your papa tells you." Then she picked up Hannah who was crying and grabbing her leg. As they walked away, Hannah held out her hands to Uri's father, like she did when she wanted him to pick her up. But he couldn't go to her. He wasn't allowed. He took Uri by the hand and they joined their queues.

They made everyone take off their clothes. Uri couldn't understand why they did this when it was so cold. It wouldn't have been so bad if it was summer. In the summertime, Uri would go down to the river behind their house in Berlin. He'd strip off all his clothes and jump in. Sometimes there were other boys with him and they would take turns diving off the rocks and seeing who could make the biggest splash. One time a fish nibbled at Uri's toes. It kind of tickled.

He was at the top of the queue now and two men sat behind a desk looking at him. They took down his name and age and then made him turn all around. Then one of them looked inside his mouth. It was a bit like being at the dentist and the doctor all in one go. It wasn't too bad because he could see his father the whole time in the queue beside him. Next they gave Uri some new clothes to put on. They were blue and not the type of clothes you'd normally wear outdoors. Uri didn't think they'd keep him very warm. Then he copied what the boy in front of him had done and went into this big hut. He found it was best to do what everybody else did and not make a fuss. That meant you didn't get shouted at so much. The only time Uri got upset was when he thought about his mother. He tried to put her out of his mind, to not think about the last time he'd seen her with blood running down the side of her face. Maybe somebody would bandage it up for her later. As scary as her blood was to Uri, her tears were even scarier. He'd seen her cry only once before—when she'd had a baby and it had died. She'd had three babies who died. One in between him and Hannah, a girl called Esther. Then two boys after Hannah, Oskar and Jacob. They were both dead when they were born. Uri felt especially sad about them because he would have loved to have a brother to play with. They would remember them in their prayers every day.

When you got to the top of the queue in the hut, you sat in a big chair and a man shaved off all your hair. He was rough. Not a bit like Mr. Rothschild in the barber's Uri went to back home. Mr. Rothschild always chatted to you the whole time, asked you questions about school and what sports you liked, and when he was finished, he gave you a sweet. The man in the shed didn't say anything at all.

Next was the worst bit because all the boys had to go off together in a big group and he couldn't see his father anymore. The guards made them run to another hut. There were loads of huts all over the place and they all looked the same. This one was full of beds, except they weren't like real beds. More like long, wooden boxes that you had to share and try and sleep in. Everyone was very quiet until the guards went away. Then Uri could hear a few whispers. But most of all he could hear other boys crying. Uri squeezed his eyes tightly shut and rolled up into the smallest ball ever.

That night, he dreamed he went fishing with his father and grandfather near his grandparents' home in Heidelberg. Uri caught a small, blue fish that thrashed and glistened in the sunlight. Then, quick as a flash, a kingfisher swooped down, grabbed the fish in its beak, and carried it away. Uri could still see the vivid colors when he first woke up. The dream made him feel warm inside, even though he was cold on the outside. The strangest thing was that his grandfather had died two years before. But in the dream he was alive and smiling and exactly as Uri remembered him.

All the boys in Uri's hut were his age or older. There were no little ones. Uri couldn't work out what had happened to all the little ones. They must have been keeping them in a different part of the camp. Over the next few days, Uri kept an eye out for his mother, father, and sister, but then all the boys got moved to a different camp. Uri was upset because he wanted to stay where his family was, even if he couldn't see them. Unless, of course, they were all being moved. There was no way of knowing. He kept an eye out the whole time they were marched to the train and while they were getting onboard, but there was no sign. All he saw, as the train was pulling away, was that the sky above part of the camp was orange. A terrible stench filled his nostrils, something he'd been smelling on and off since he'd got there. Years later, when he walked the streets of Dublin as a young man, he sometimes thought he could smell it still.

The first day in the new camp, they set them to work breaking up stones. They might have been to put between the railway sleepers. That's what they looked like to Uri. Hard and gray. There were lots of men working there too, not just boys. Uri was overjoyed to see his father among them. For a moment, he thought he was going to cry. He and his father saw each other at exactly the same time. They stopped what they were doing and smiled at each other. But not for long because there were guards all around. But now and then they would look up and smile when the guards weren't looking. What Uri really wanted to do was run over to his father and hug him and be hugged back. Which was strange, really, because he'd never done that in real life. His father was kind but distant. It was to his mother that Uri had gone for hugs. But everything was different now.

The work was hard but Uri was strong and quick. Which was just as well because the guards whipped you if you were too slow. Some of the boys were finding the work more difficult than Uri, but then they didn't have a father to smile at them every now and then. They didn't have the happiness of knowing where their papas were and having them near.

Uri didn't see any women or girls in the camp.

Later on, when they were giving out the bread, he was able to talk to his father for a minute.

"Have you seen your mother and sister?"

"No."

His father gave Uri half of his own bread, which wasn't fair because he must have been starving too. But he made Uri take it. And Uri ate it because he was so, so hungry. He'd never been so hungry in his whole life.

That night, he dreamed he was back at home and his mama was cooking him dinner. It must have been a special occasion because she was making all his favorites: matzoh ball soup, gefilte fish, blintzes.

He ate until he was so stuffed he could hardly move. His mother didn't look the way she did the last time he'd seen her. She was smiling and happy and she laughed a lot. The dream felt very real, and when he woke up, it was if she was with him still. He was to have this dream several times. It was his favorite one.

There was a man in the new camp, another prisoner, called Viktor, although some people called him Dr. Frankl. He was friendly with Uri's father. He wasn't an ordinary doctor, although he did know a lot of stuff and he could help you out if you were sick or hurt. Many of the boys had sores on their bodies. Uri had one on his head. Dr Frankl looked at it for him one day. Uri felt the man liked him on account of his father.

"Hold still," he said, smiling at Uri as he examined his head. He was from Austria but you wouldn't have known it because he spoke German so well.

"Have you had many dreams since you came to the camp, Uri?"

That's the kind of doctor he was. He was more interested in what was going on inside your head than on the outside. The question took Uri by surprise and he wondered if he'd been talking in his sleep and one of the boys had said something.

"Why are you asking me that?"

"Because many of the men have been having very vivid dreams since they got here and I wondered if it was the same for the boys."

Uri told Dr. Frankl about his dreams.

"Did you dream much before you came here?"

"Not as much. And the dreams—didn't have as many colors in them."

Dr. Frankl nodded.

"Hold your dreams tightly to you, Uri. Don't let them go. And don't let go of your dreams for the future. They're important too. You're a strong boy. You have your father with you and he's a good man."

"Dr. Frankl."

"Yes?"

"Do you think my mother really comes to me at night?"

Dr. Frankl looked at him for a long time.

"Yes, I think she does. I think your mother is always with you and always loving you, even when you can't see her. Her love is real, Uri. There's nothing more real."

This thought helped Uri through the winter months. Because it was very hard. Sometimes a boy didn't get up when he was called and they couldn't wake him. They'd all be sent out to work and when they came back, the boy would be gone and they would never see him again. At least working kept you warm.

Uri was worried about his father. He had a bad cough that wouldn't go away. That made him work more slowly and sometimes he got whipped. Seeing this made Uri very sad and angry. He arranged it so that he could work alongside his father whenever he could and help him when he couldn't keep up. And he would make him eat all his own bread. Because of this, Uri was extra tired at nighttime but this was okay, because it meant that he fell asleep straightaway.

One night, he dreamed his brothers were with him. Even though they were dead when they were born, they were alive now and quite grown up. They were still a little bit smaller than Uri but not much—big enough to play with. His two brothers were quite different from each other. Jacob was quiet and shy. Oskar was noisy and laughed a lot. Uri taught them both to jump off the big rock into the river behind their house. It was their home too. Their river too. The boys had never lived in Ghetto. Sometimes he thought that the boys were lucky to be dead, but he didn't let himself think this too often.

Surely the winter would be over soon. There weren't that many boys left now. Most of the ones around his age had already gone.

URI'S FATHER'S GOAL was constant: to reunite his family. For the four of them to be together once more. And for that, he would beat this cough. For that he would beat the Nazis.

Then one evening, the day's backbreaking work at an end, a guard came into his hut and called out his number. He was taken outside, his limbs shaking slightly. Was this it? What was to become of his boy? The guard who had singled him out wasn't the worst of them. Although they all followed the same set of vile orders.

"This way," he said.

"Where are we going?"

"The commandant wishes to speak with you."

For what possible reason could the commandant want to talk with him? Many possibilities buzzed around his head, none of them good.

He was led, not to an office, but to a house at the far end of camp. He'd never been there before. The unfamiliarity made him even more nervous. It was like any house that you might see in an affluent suburb of a German town. Windows with curtains on them. Samuel would never have thought that ordinary windows could seem so extraordinary. The house looked quite incongruous at the edge of camp. Like a jewel in a cesspit.

The guard knocked at a side entrance. They were allowed inside and escorted to an inner door. The guard knocked once more.

"Enter."

The guard ushered Samuel into the room. A thick-set, middle-aged man sat behind an enormous desk.

"You are a gardener, is that correct?"

"Yes, sir."

Samuel looked straight ahead of him at a spot on the wall. He didn't risk looking the commandant in the eye for fear of appearing insolent.

"And you were in charge of the gardens at the Palace, in Berlin?"

"Yes, sir."

"Excellent. You will look after the garden of this house. You will start today. You will be shown a shed at the back of the house where you will find all the tools you need. Any seeds and so forth that you require, you are to inform my household staff and arrangements will be made. Is that clear?"

"Yes, sir."

"Go now."

Samuel felt the opportunity bubbling up in his throat.

"I beg your pardon, sir, but may I have permission to speak?"

The commandant regarded him with a mixture of surprise and annoyance. Samuel could see the guard out of the corner of his eye, getting ready to strike him should it be required. He felt the blood rushing in his ears as he braced himself for the guard's blow and the commandant's refusal. But he said gruffly: "What is it?"

"The garden is large. Usually for a space that size, I would have at least one assistant. My son, who is also in the camp, is my apprentice. We could make greater progress if there were two of us."

He could feel the commandant staring at him.

"Why not?" he said at last.

"Thank you, sir."

"Get him out of here." He addressed the guard before turning his attention back to the papers on his desk.

"Heil Hitler."

"Heil Hitler."

Samuel kept his head well down in order to hide his jubilation. Smiles weren't easily tolerated amongst the prisoners. Not to mention seldom seen. Now he'd be able to spend hours at a time with his son. Talking to him, protecting him, teaching him. And he could hold him. His heart swelled and ached at the thought of his boy. How proud he was of how he had conducted himself—working alongside him, taking up any slack. Doing more work than many men twice his size. Like Samuel, Uri was small but stocky. In a sense, he was a man now. How his mother would . . .

But it pained him to see how thin Uri had become. Viktor had expressed his concern for the boy only recently. Samuel feared he would go the way of so many of the other boys in his group. That one night he would go to bed and never wake up again. Samuel quickened his pace behind the guard. But that wouldn't happen to Uri now because everybody knew that the personal servants had access to better food. And he could easily grow extra vegetables and smuggle them back to the camp. For the first time in months, a ray of light shone into Samuel's gray world. They came to a shed, whereupon the guard stopped abruptly.

"You will stay here," he instructed.

"And my son?"

"Will be brought here shortly."

URI FELT THE familiar sense of foreboding when his number was called. He ran to the guard and saluted briskly.

"This way."

He'd never been to this part of the camp before. His head never stopped turning, looking for his mother. He knew she was out there somewhere, loving him. They took him to this strange-looking house, except the house itself wasn't really all that strange. It was just that it was so unexpected. He was brought around the back of the house through a spacious garden. By now, he was becoming more curious than afraid. Then he saw his father and he didn't know *what* to make of it. And then he saw that his father's face was happy and relaxed. Not smiling. But that expression he had sometimes that let Uri know he was smiling on the inside.

"You will be working here from now on," the guard said before walking a few paces away and lighting a cigarette.

"Is this true?" said Uri.

"Yes it is."

"Together?"

"Yes."

The guard turned away as father and son embraced each other hungrily.

HARVEST

*To forget how to dig the earth
and to tend the soil is to forget ourselves.*

—Mohandas K. Gandhi

40

 *S*UMMER DEEPENED INTO autumn. The garden harldy noticed at first. But little by little, the edges of the leaves burned to an orange crisp. The grass slowed down its hectic growth. Everything had bloomed. Now it was time for the harvest.

It was also time for big school for Liam and Kathy. In Eva's mind, the terrible day had dawned. The great letting go. She fixed a bright smile on her face as she helped him on with his brand-new uniform. He stood in front of her, fully dressed and beaming.

"You look very handsome." She tried not to cry.

Privately, she thought he looked like someone playing at being a grown-up. Unnatural. Ludicrously beautiful. She had to roll the sleeves of his sweater up several times to find his hands.

Liam was too excited to eat his cereal. He was ready to go, branded to within an inch of his life with his Thomas the Tank Engine rucksack and his Bob the Builder lunch box. She held his hand as they left the house and made the short journey to school. She wondered how much longer he'd permit her to hold his hand in public.

The school gates were uncommonly busy after two months of abandonment. Everywhere, throngs of mothers and maroon-sweatered children. It was a beautiful morning that promised to turn into a scorching afternoon—traditional for the start of the school year. At least they'd be off at lunchtime. Eva planned to spoil Liam rotten that afternoon. Provided, of course, he didn't have too much homework. The thought appalled her. Surely five was far too young to start school, too early to institutionalize their precious little minds.

So that morning, as they neared the school gates, swinging their hands between them, Eva's heart was heavy but her smile was bright. It dimmed, however, when she saw who was coming from the opposite direction. It was Kathy, resplendant in her new gear, flanked by Seth on the right and a woman, presumably her mother, Megan, on her left. Kathy was holding hands with both of them, smiling up at each of them in turn. They looked like the quintessential happy family. Eva felt the most extraordinary pang of what she was honest enough to name as jealousy. She knew this was ridiculous. Not only was Megan Seth's ex. She was also a raving lesbian. Which meant that it was hardly very likely that they were going to get back together anytime soon. Unless Megan changed her mind again. Shit. They were all going to reach the gate at exactly the same time.

"There's Liam and Eva," Kathy squealed and, disengaging herself from both of her parents, ran over to Liam, where she started jumping up and down on the pavement. They both giggled, too excited for words. Their parents' reactions were a little more restrained.

"Hello."

"Hello."

"Eva, this is Megan. Megan, Eva."

"Yes, of course. Delighted to meet Liam's mammy at last. I've heard a lot about you."

Did she mean from Kathy or from Seth?

The two women smiled at each other and looked each other up and down a little. Megan was slim and petite and pretty. Exactly the kind of woman who made Eva feel clumsy and whalelike.

"Lovely to meet you too." What a liar she was.

Thank God she'd worn something decent today, so as to make a good impression on Liam's teacher. She was wearing a new skirt, inspired as she was of late to show off her legs. She'd even applied a fake tan. And it wasn't even that streaky. The skirt was floral and floated pleasingly about her knees. Her top was plum colored, tight fitting, and left her arms bare. She didn't need fake bronzer here. Her upper body was naturally tanned from all the hours spent tending her veggies. She drew herself to her full height and found herself pushing back her shoulders. Megan's waist may have been smaller than hers. But she had bigger boobs and longer legs.

They all walked into the school together, the children chattering one hundred to the dozen. The high-pitched noise of all these little people speaking at once made Eva feel as if she were trapped inside a beehive.

Liam and Kathy all but ran into their classroom before descending on a pile of Legos in the corner. Liam immediately struck up a conversation with a boy Eva recognized from his nursery school.

"It's best to go quickly if your children are happy," the teacher addressed the gaggle of anxious-looking parents standing at the doorway, her voice kind but firm. Oh God. So soon. She went over to Liam and crouched down beside him.

"I'm going now, Liamy. I'll be back to pick you up in a little while."

"Okay, Mummy."

"Have a nice time and be a good boy. Remember to say please and thank you."

"I will."

He allowed her to plant a kiss on his cheek.

"Bye, then."

"Bye-bye." His attention was immediately diverted by the

Lego tower that the boy beside him was building. She got up and left, seeing that Seth and Megan were talking earnestly to the teacher. Perhaps they were explaining Kathy's unconventional living arrangements.

Was that it? She walked back down the corridor, feeling like she'd just been disemboweled. She couldn't stop thinking about how today should have been. With Michael by her side, Katie's three-year-old hand in hers. She felt her lone-parent status keenly. It had been so difficult, agonizing over which school to send Liam to. No Michael to look to for his ever practical, ever logical advice. She hoped she'd made the right choice. Prayed she had. Do you approve, Michael?

She quickened her steps out of the school grounds, her vision blurring, wanting to get a safe distance away before the flood came. How embarrassing. She didn't want to do this. Liam was fine. He was happy. It was good that he'd reached this milestone, a cause for celebration. Then why did she feel so wretched? She was thinking of herself and not of her son, which was entirely wrong. So intent was she on curbing her tears that she didn't hear the footsteps behind her.

"Eva." She swung around and almost collided with Seth.

"By God, woman. You're a fast walker." He looked at her face. "Are you okay?"

She nodded, the first tears escaping.

"Is it Liam?"

She nodded again, furiously this time.

"Come here." He put his arms around her and pulled her close. Her body stayed rigid at first.

"This is not very English of you. Not very stiff upper lip."

She laughed and her body relaxed. Then the deluge came. Seth held on tight as her body shook and the shoulder of his T-shirt became soaking wet. A good five minutes they stood there, passersby walking curiously around them, long after, in fact, Eva had stopped crying. She was afraid to lift up her head. What now?

"Eva."

She shook her head and burrowed into his shoulder.

"Eva." His voice was soft as he disentangled himself and placed his fingers under her chin, making her look up at him. She was embarrassed by how red and blubbery her tear-stained face must look. She badly needed to blow her nose.

"It's okay. Everything's going to be okay." Then he kisssed her. Not only did she let him. She kissed him back. But only for a few seconds before breaking away.

"I can't."

"Why can't you? What have you got to lose?"

"Everything. If something were to happen to you . . ."

"So you're going to live your whole life avoiding getting close to anyone in case they get taken away from you?"

"Sounds like a plan to me."

"Sooner or later you're going to have to put your heart on the line. Why not do it sooner? With me."

When she didn't answer, he said: "You could do a lot worse, you know."

"You think so." She couldn't help smiling.

"Eva. I'm offering myself on a plate here. Please don't let me go cold." He held his arms in the air and looked up to the clouds, as if appealing to the heavens. Then he put his hands on his hips and looked at her.

"I won't be on the market forever, you know. There are plenty of hot lesbians out there dying to get their hands on a man like me."

This time she laughed outright. Then she swiped at her wet face with the backs of her hands. Then she blew her nose noisily and unself-consciously.

"Okay. You can walk me home."

"Really? You mean all the way down the street? In broad daylight? Are you sure?"

"Do you want to or not?"

"All right. Hand, please."

She put her hand in his and they strolled along, both feeling a little bit shy, but both smiling. They reached her front door. She opened up as he leaned expectantly against the wall.

"Are you coming in for coffee?"

"I don't want coffee."

"I don't have any."

"Then I'm coming in."

GOD, THIS WAS going to be awkward. But no sooner had she formulated the thought than Seth was beside her, one hand on either side of her head, kissing her again, as if she was some urgent matter he had to attend to. And all her thoughts dissolved as her body responded to his. And it seemed to Eva as if they were trying to crawl under each other's skin.

Eva's clothes appeared to dissolve along with her thoughts. She didn't know how she got them off—or how *he* got them off. All she knew was that she found them strewn about the staircase sometime later. Close to the location of their initial coupling, having failed to make it to the bed the first time around. And after the second time, they lay coiled around each other, thoroughly spent, high on happiness and each other.

41

$\mathscr{L}$IFE WAS SUDDENLY better for Uri. Yes, he was still in the camp. And yes, his bones were still sticking out of his skin like sharp sticks. But he was with his father.

The worst of the winter was behind them now and Samuel's cough was much better. It was still cold, but the housekeeper would bring them out hot cups of soup when the house was quiet. Years later, Uri was to speculate that the housekeeper and her soup may have saved his life.

As Uri watched his father work on the garden, it was as if he was watching him come back to life. His cheeks had a little color in them now and when he smiled at Uri, his smile sometimes reached his eyes. Uri was relieved to get away from the unremitting grayness of the rocks that they'd had to break. They still had to do that sometimes, when it became obvious that there wasn't much for them to do in the garden. But they did so much digging and they made so many ambitious plans for new beds and borders and the like that they were very successful in making extra work for themselves and had to go back to the rocks less and less. The commandant would come out from time to time to see what they were doing. He would ask Samuel lots of questions. Samuel and Uri would stop what they were doing and stare straight ahead of them. The commandant nodded a lot and looked quite pleased as he walked away. Uri felt like telling him that he should be pleased, and did he know how lucky he was to have one of the best gardeners in all of Germany working for him?

Every so often, Uri would wonder who had looked after the garden before and what had become of them. He was going to ask the housekeeper but thought better of it. As he held the garden tools, he thought of those who had held them before him and silently blessed them.

He was newly impressed by his father. He had always respected him but had never realized the full length and breadth of his knowledge. A new bond was forged between father and son as Samuel painstakingly taught Uri the secrets of plants. Uri had to admit that he hadn't been all that interested before, but now—now he could see that there was something to it.

At sunset, they would both go back to their huts. Uri felt guilty seeing the other boys passed out from hunger and exhaustion. He knew what they had gone through and that their day had been infinitely worse than his. But he also felt lucky. Maybe he felt a little too lucky.

URI WAS STARVING all the time. Of course, he had been permanently hungry ever since he'd arrived at the camp, but there was a new quality to his hunger now. Insatiable. His father said it was because he was growing that his body needed more food. Uri could see himself that he had grown a good two inches since his arrival. His trouser ends now floated somewhere above his ankles. At night, he got strange pains in his legs. Not the usual ones. Dr. Frankl told him they were growing pains. Then Dr. Frankl was transferred to another camp and they didn't see him anymore. At least they hoped that was what had happened to him.

The delectable smells that floated out to the garden from the commandant's kitchen window mocked Uri on a daily basis. There were times when he felt he'd go crazy with food lust. One day, when he was pushing his wheelbarrow past the window, he happened to look inside. Sitting on the kitchen counter, completely unattended, was a tray of dumplings. Uri was filled with an uncontrollable craving. He walked on with his wheelbarrow and tried to immerse himself in his work. He got a shovel and he dug and dug and dug. After a while, he took up his wheelbarrow and walked past the house again. There was no harm in looking. They were still there. Still unattended. A trickle of steam rising up from them. He looked down to the other end of the garden. His father was thinning out onions, oblivious to all else. The house was quiet as a tomb. His head turning constantly, Uri put down his wheelbarrow and walked as rapidly as he could down the path. His heart hammered wildly as he inched open the back door, which was, as usual, unlocked. Nothing. Nobody. He went into the kitchen, the tray now looming up ahead of him, just a few sweet feet away. One last look around and he was on it. There were so many of them that no one would notice. He crammed one into his mouth and closed his eyes. It was better than he'd imagined. The softness, the warmth, the sweet, spicy, apple flavor. He crammed another in his pocket and turned to leave. He stood stock-still. Framed in the doorway was the commandant's wife. At first she was silent and they stared at each other. The seconds ticked slowly by—one, two, three—then she started to scream at him.

"What are you doing here? Dirty, Jewish boy in the kitchen. Stealing my food. Get out! Get out!"

She grabbed a broom and started to strike him with it. Uri crouched on the floor, adopting a submissive position, his hands shielding his head. He heard footsteps—running—getting closer—and now he could see the black boots.

"What is it?"

"This boy. This Jewish rat. He's been touching my food. Stealing from me."

A guard yanked him to his feet and dragged him by the arm out of the house. He threw Uri onto the lawn where he lay cowering. Then he tore off Uri's shirt and started to whip him. Once. And again. And again. Uri was vaguely aware of his father's voice. Shouting. Footsteps running. Then the whipping stopped. Uri lay there for a few seconds, anticipating the next strike. When it didn't come he looked up. The guard was on the ground and Samuel was sitting on top of him, his hands around his throat. The guard's face was red, Samuel's hands were tightening. A shot rang out. The crows on the roof of the commandant's house rose in black unison, cawing and croaking their cacophony. Samuel's hands loosened and he fell to the side, a gaping red hole in his left temple.

"No!" Uri screamed and fell on his father, shaking him first, then cradling his head. The guard rolled away from them, coughing and clasping his neck. The guard who had fired the pistol came running over and crouched beside him.

"What is the meaning of this?"

The commandant strode across the lawn. He stood over Uri and his father.

"Who did this?"

The second guard stood up and saluted.

The commandant slapped him in the face.

"This was the best gardener I ever had. What has occurred here?"

"Sir." The first soldier spoke through his coughs. "I caught this boy stealing food from your kitchen."

"Stand up boy," said the commandant.

Uri stood up, his body swaying slightly, his face awash with tears, his mind awash with grief. Through his tears he could see the face of the commandant's wife, screwed up and hard and pressed against the window. Then he heard the click of the gun that her husband was pointing at him.

Uri closed his eyes and awaited oblivion. Nothing happened. The gun clicked again and he opened his eyes.

"Better not," said the commandant. "I've already lost one gardener today." Then he raised his gun and struck Uri across the face with it. Uri fell to the ground, not caring. Someone with big boots kicked him in the back as he walked past.

He lay on the ground, bleeding profusely, until long after he was able to get up. His father's body was gone. He walked unsteadily to the onions that Samuel had been working on and knelt to the ground. Then he finished the job his father had started, his blood mingling with the earth.

Back in his hut, the men he lived with waited for Samuel's return. Until it got too late. Some of them mourned. For others it was too late.

42

*U*RI DIDN'T KNOW if he could fill his father's shoes. Had Samuel had time to teach him enough? Enough to pass his son off as a gardener? Increasingly, Uri didn't care. And then came the day when it really didn't matter anymore.

It was April and the tulips bobbed their pretty red heads in the breeze. But there was no other sign of activity in the garden or the house. There was an almost unearthly silence. Where were all the guards? It seemed that they had vanished overnight. Even the watchtower was empty. Prisoners began to emerge from their huts and stand around in straggly groups, whispering and shaking their heads. As if they were afraid it was all some elaborate trick and that at any moment, the guards could jump out en masse with their guns and their whips and their vicious dogs barking. The silence was broken by strange sounds emanating from the other side of the camp. The sounds were strange because they weren't of the type that the prisoners were accustomed to hearing. Shouting, singing— jubilation. They looked at each other and started moving toward the sounds, slowly at first. Getting quicker.

Uri couldn't believe what he was seeing. Seven giants surrounded by prisoners who were whooping and hugging and kissing them. The giants were dressed as soldiers, but not German. As Uri drew close, he recognized the uniforms as American. Young men. Older than him but not much more than seventeen or eighteen. It seemed that they had cut through the wire. They were there to liberate them.

Uri joined in with the general mayhem and jumping around. But part of him felt that it was all happening outside himself. Liberation. What did it mean? What would happen to him next?

There were lots more Americans outside the camp. They set up tents for the sick. Which was just about everybody. But the sickest went first. Uri watched them stretchering out the half dead. It took three people to lift each one of them. One took the head, another the body, and the other the legs. They had to go slowly so the skin wouldn't tear. He wandered out after them, stepping for the first time beyond the boundaries of the camp. He didn't feel so different. Part of him wondered if he'd ever feel anything again.

One of the American soldiers handed him a package. Uri sat on the ground and opened it. It contained a tin of meat. The soldier crouched down beside him and held the tin in front of Uri's face.

"Spam," he said. Then he made a gesture, bringing his fingers up to his lips. "Eat. It's good."

The American tried to smile at him but didn't quite make it. He was looking at Uri with the oddest expression on his face.

There was chocolate in the package too, and some milk powder. Uri ripped open the wrapper on the chocolate and began ramming it into his mouth.

"No!" Somebody wrenched the rest of the bar out of his hand. Uri cowered instinctively and covered his head with his hands. Another man hunkered down beside him. He was older. He spoke gently to Uri in a language he didn't understand. When the man got no response, he switched to German.

"I'm sorry," he said. "But you can't eat that. Your stomach is unused to such food and it will make you sick. Please spit it out."

Reluctantly, Uri spat the sweet, dark brown heavenly goo onto the grass and wiped his mouth with the back of his hand. The man spoke sternly to the soldier in the language Uri didn't understand. Then he held out his hand and helped Uri to his feet.

"Come with me," he said in German.

Uri followed him into one of the tents. The man spoke rapidly to a woman in uniform. Then he turned to Uri.

"This lady is a nurse. She will look after you."

The nurse bade Uri sit on the makeshift bed. Then she gestured for him to take his top off. Uri did so. He continued to sit there for a long time, waiting for her to do something. But she just stood there staring at him. For ages. She made a funny kind of noise in her throat but she didn't say anything. At last she moved toward him. She prepared a needle and indicated to Uri that she was going to stick it into his shoulder. He let her do it. It only stung a little. Then she walked around the back of Uri and gasped. He knew she must have seen the red weals and he felt ashamed. He watched her as she picked up a tube of cream. She held it up to him and pointed at his back. Uri nodded. The cream felt cold at first and he winced. But soon it started to feel good. Soothing. The nurse's head was above his. He felt her hot tears landing on his scalp but she made no sound. It reminded him of his mother and he started to cry too. Silently, but his shoulders shook. The nurse wrapped her arms around him—gently so as not to hurt him—and he tucked his head under her chin and cried some more. They stayed like that for a very long time. Long enough for some of the humanity to seep back into him.

Later on, the man from before came back into the tent. By now, Uri had worked out that he was a doctor. He told him that he was going to examine him.

"Can I have something to eat first?"

"You can have a cup of tea."

"But I'm starving."

"I know, Uri. But we have to take it slow."

Tea! Were these people trying to starve him too?

The doctor and nurse exchanged glances and the doctor looked at Uri. Right in the eye.

"I know," he said. "Who could do this to a child?"

Uri felt like telling him that he hadn't been a child for a very long time. That he never would be again.

After two hours, they let him have some weak, milky mixture. He signaled to the nurse that he wanted some more but she smiled sympathetically and shook her head. Uri lay down on the bed, hungry and frustrated, and pulled the covers over himself. He didn't think he'd sleep with all the activity going on around him, but he did. He didn't dream though. For the rest of his life, Uri was never to have another dream.

When he woke up, he was allowed a kind of broth. Then every couple of hours, a little bit more. The food got better and more solid. The next day, some potatoes. The day after that, meat. The doctors and nurses stared as he gobbled up everything they put in front of him then looked for more.

It took them four days to fill him up. The doctor smiled as he watched him hoover up the last of his stew. "Is there anything else I can get you, Uri?"

"Yes. My mother and my sister."

43

$\mathcal{S}$ETH AND EVA collected the children together on their first day of school. They were lucky to make it on time. Liam and Kathy accepted their joint appearance as totally natural, which of course it was. They babbled about the morning's goings-on.

"We did coloring and then we played with molding clay."

"You mean plasticine."

"It's called marla."

"No it's not, it's—"

"Hey, hey. Never mind that. What else did you do?"

"We went out to the playground and we ran around," said Kathy.

"Super fast," said Liam.

"Daddy."

"Yes."

"Why is your T-shirt on inside out?"

"It's not."

"It is. Look at all the nobbly bits sticking out. And there's the label at the back."

"I must have put it on like that this morning."

"No you didn't. It wasn't like that this morning."

"I know what it was. I was doing some work outside and I took my T-shirt off because it was so hot. I must have put it back on inside out."

"Oh." She abruptly lost interest.

Seth squeezed Eva's hand.

"Okay, kids. What do you want to do this afternoon? We all have the day off, so we can do anything you like."

"I want to play in the garden."

"Me too."

"Are you sure? You can go anywhere you like."

"The garden!" they chorused, then ran ahead hand in hand, laughing and chattering.

They stopped off at the Good Food Store to buy themselves a picnic lunch—luxurious, celebratory, no holds barred.

"Would you ever tell Mrs. Prendergast to bring over some more of her gourmet pies? They're flying off the shelves."

"Will do, Mrs. Harte."

As they walked across the hot city streets toward the garden, Eva felt a peculiar lightness. A long-forgotten, once-familiar feeling. And she realized she was happy. It did cross her mind for a second to feel guilty and she thought of Michael. But at that moment, she knew with an absolute certainty that he'd be happy for her. She smiled up at the flawless sky and for the first time, felt forgiven. By Michael, and, more important, by herself.

Uri was working alone when they arrived. Despite the sweltering conditions, he was formally clad as usual, in his shirtsleeves—although he had undone his top button.

"Granddad, Granddad!" The two children ran to him and he grabbed them both up in a massive bear hug.

"How was school?"

They chattered to him like a cage of budgies newly released. Then: "Granddad. Will you tell us a story?"

"Yes, with lots of dragons in it."

"After lunch, kids. Here, Dad. Take this drink while it's still cool. You look like you need it."

They set out the food, laughing and talking as they went, the atmosphere pure carnival.

"Where's Mrs. P?"

"She's gone to collect Lance. They're letting him out of rehab today. They'll be back soon."

"What do you mean 'they'?"

"He'll be staying here for a while."

"So she can keep an eye on him?"

"No. Because his house has been repossessed."

"That's serious stuff. So we're going to have to suffer him for a while."

"He *is* her son, Seth," said Uri.

Seth kept quiet.

The sun beamed down, hotter than ever. The children took off their shirts and protested vociferously as Eva slathered them in suntan lotion. They wriggled like little, wet fish in her grasp. Seth lay back on the grass and shielded his eyes.

"Daddy. Why don't you take your T-shirt off if you're hot?"

"You know, I think I will."

"Don't forget to put it back on the right way around this time."

"I won't."

"Mummy. Why don't you take your top off too?"

"It's okay, Liam. I'm not that hot."

"Can I take my vest off too?"

"You can if you like, but you'll have to put on more lotion."

"No thank you. Why don't you take off yours, Uri?"

"I'm too old. I might frighten you with my hairy chest. You might think I'm a bear. Grrrrr!" He held up his hands like claws and made a gruesome face. The children ran off screaming and giggling.

Seth peeled off his top and Eva got to see his tattoos for the second time that day.

"What are those pictures on your skin?"

"They're called tattoos, Liam."

"Where did you get them?"

"A man gave them to me, using needles."

"Did it hurt?"

"Only a little bit."

"My daddy has my mammy's name tattooed on his arm. Look."

Kathy held up Seth's arm for everyone to see.

"I'm having it removed," he whispered to Eva.

"What's that star on your other arm?" said Liam.

"It's called a Star of David."

"But your name isn't David."

"I know it isn't."

"What have you got it for, then?"

"To show that I'm proud of who I am and where I come from."

"Stoneybatter?"

They all laughed except Liam, who looked confused.

"Granddad. Why don't you show Liam *your* tattoo."

There was a change in the atmosphere. Barely discernible, but it was there. Uri sat perfectly still. Then he unbuttoned his cuff and rolled up his pure white, left sleeve to the elbow. Eva froze. It was something she'd suspected from time to time but to see the evidence up close—that was another matter.

"It's just numbers." Liam was distinctly underwhelmed. "Why did you want numbers on your arms?"

"I didn't."

Liam wrinkled up his nose. "Then why do you have them?"

"Some bad men gave them to me."

"What, like baddies?"

"Yes, like baddies."

"Where are they now?" Liam raised his eyebrows and looked slightly alarmed.

"They lived far, far away, a very long time ago."

"So they're gone now?"

"Yes, they're gone now."

"Come on, Kathy. Let's play football."

"Okay."

They ran off in pursuit of the ball and Harriet ran after them in her own arthritic way.

The day was just the same. The sun was still as high in the sky and that sky was just as cloudless. But everything was different. The party was over and Eva felt sick to her stomach.

"I didn't know," she said to Uri. "I'm so sorry."

Uri nodded and rolled down his sleeve.

"You must have been a child."

"I was ten."

She closed her eyes and swallowed.

"Back to work," said Uri. He got up and walked away from them without looking back.

Eva watched him go and turned to Seth. He was sitting up, his chest still bare, his elbows resting on his knees. His brow was furrowed and his expression serious.

"He doesn't like talking about it?"

"No."

"What happened to his family? His parents?"

"All killed in the camps."

"Oh God. Where . . . ?"

"You know what? Do you mind if I tell you about it another day? I don't want him to think we're talking about him."

"Okay. Yes. You're right." She paused. "But let me just ask you one thing. Was he upset when you started getting tattoos?"

"No. He understood my thinking behind it. That I was taking a painful memory and turning it into a matter of Jewish pride. Honoring what he'd gone through in a way. My mother was more upset. But that was because she thought I was desecrating the perfect body she'd given me. She was the same when I used to smoke. Now come here."

"Someone might see."

"I don't care."

IT WAS AN hour later when Lance and Mrs. Prendergast came out to the garden. Lance's air was nonchalant, but in a way that was almost too studied. He examined the plants intently, looking at everything there was to look at, looking at everything, in fact, other than the people. The people—Uri, Seth, and Eva—were standing around in a small circle, chatting. Although the chatter died away when Lance was spotted.

The two drew close. Greetings were exchanged. Lance looked well, Eva thought. He'd put on a little weight and his cheeks had filled out. He'd lost that gaunt, waxen-skinned look. He seemed more relaxed too. Less twitchy and no longer brimming with nervous energy. Although he was somewhat nervous. He met Uri's eyes with difficulty. Then he held out his hand. The others held their breath as they waited to see what Uri would do.

Uri took Lance's hand and shook it.

"I'm sorry," said Lance. "What I said to you before. It was wrong. Unforgivable. It'll never happen again."

Uri nodded in acknowledgment.

"Apology accepted," he said.

Lance's face relaxed into a relieved smile.

"Thank you," he said. "Thank you so very much. That means a lot."

He turned to his mother. "I'll be up in my room if you need me." He put his hands in his pockets and walked back up to the house.

"Thank you, Uri," said Mrs. Prendergast.

Uri smiled at her.

"I think he's going to be all right," she said.

44

$\mathcal{A}$LONG WITH THOUSANDS like him, Uri was sent to a displaced person's camp in Germany. The conditions were better than in the concentration camp, but only just. Crucially, he was no longer in fear of his life or anticipating a beating. But there was never enough food and it was too cramped.

He scanned every female face, every girl child. Sometimes he would get excited by the back of a head. He would run around to the front but he was always disappointed. He did this for weeks. And the weeks stretched into months. His hope was beginning to fade. When one day he had an idea. What if his mother and sister had gone back to their home in Berlin and were waiting for him there? There was only one way to find out. Without saying anything to anyone, he saved up three or four days' rations. Then he packed up his knapsack with what few belongings he had and set off to find his family. It was easy to sneak out. Nobody took much notice of an eleven-year-old boy. He knew he wasn't far from Berlin—he had made some seemingly innocent inquiries to some of the men—and the thought that his mother could be waiting for him, just a short distance away, was too much of a temptation to resist.

It took him a week. It was summer, so there was no problem sleeping outdoors at night. If it was a bit chilly, he'd find a nice, snug barn and fall asleep to the company of animals breathing. He would wash in a stream in the morning, laughing as he splashed his face with icy drops. He was good at finding his way. He'd been on many camping trips with his father and grandfather before the war and they had taught him more than he had realized. He felt at home in the fields and the woods.

But it shouldn't have taken him a whole week. He must have gone wrong somewhere. But make it he did, although he didn't realize it at first. Because all was changed. The house was no longer standing. It was nothing but a pile of rubble— as were their neighbors' houses. There was no one around. Birdsong filled the air. Uri sat on a piece of the old kitchen wall and cried his heart out. Until then, he hadn't known how strongly he'd been clinging to the hope that the house would be standing, his mother cooking in the kitchen, his sister playing in the garden. Throughout it all. Through everything that had happened to him. He'd never felt so alone. He had to face the possibility that he'd never see his family again and it was almost too much for his little-boy heart to bear. When he was all cried out, Uri got up and looked around the rubble, re-membering where everything used to be, imagining it as it once was. Some of his parents' furniture was amazingly intact. The kitchen table. His parents' bed seemed to have fallen through the roof and landed where the dining room used to be. A thousand memories of his family all together. He cried again when he found the shredded remains of a poster that used to be on his bedroom wall. He looked for signs that his mother and sister had been here before—perhaps looking for him. But there were none. He did find a teddy that Hannah had left behind during their hasty move to the ghetto. He re-membered her crying for it one night. There was nothing his parents could do. They weren't allowed to go back. Uri hadn't understood that at the time. He saw now how much his par-ents had tried to shelter him from everything. But now. Less than a year later. There was so much he knew. So much he wished he didn't.

He picked up the teddy and stuffed it into his knapsack. Then he wandered down to the river behind the house. The river was still there, remarkably unchanged. The same water, the same rocks. Just as he'd seen it in his dreams. He stripped off and dived in. He imagined he was a fish, quicksilver and light. Fish didn't have to worry about being Jewish. They were just fish. Or he could be an otter. He rolled, he splashed, he played. He felt nine years old again. But once out of the water, the familiar heaviness descended upon him and he was eleven-year-old Uri once more, with everything that he knew.

He lay on a rock until the sun had dried him off. Then he dressed himself and walked back up to the house. His stomach was starting up its eternal rumbling and he'd had an idea. He walked around the back to the place where his father's kitchen garden used to be. There was a small chance . . . yes! Just as he had hoped. The raspberry canes were laden down with fruit and there was no one to eat it. No one but Uri and the birds. He gorged himself before moving on to the gooseberries. He'd never have considered them before the war, but now . . . When he'd eaten his fill, he stuffed as many berries as he could into his knapsack. Then he headed back to the camp. He had nowhere else to go.

The return journey took him only four days. His raids on abandoned kitchen gardens sustained him as he went. He thought a lot as he walked. Mostly about family. By the time he'd reached the camp, he'd come to a decision. The next day, he approached one of the teachers at the camp's makeshift school.

"What is it, Uri?"

"My father has family in Ireland. Will you help me get a letter to them?"

IT TOOK WEEKS to get an address for Samuel's cousin. They finally tracked him down through one of the Jewish agencies.

Then the letter was sent. Uri wrote it, but the teacher helped him and made sure the return address was legible. Uri felt as if he was sending out a letter in a bottle.

For two whole months he waited, each day checking the post, each day more anxious. He'd never met this man or his people. Would they even care about his existence? Be willing to take in a boy they'd never met?

At last, a reply. With a return address in Dublin, Ireland. Uri went off on his own to read it, his entire future in his hands. He opened the letter and this is what he read:

> *My dearest Uri,*
>
> *I am overjoyed to hear of your survival. I can only assume from your letter that your father and the rest of your family were not so fortunate. Nothing would make me happier than for you to come and live with us. Of course you must come. I will set things in motion immediately. In the meantime, please write often.*
>
> G-d be with you,
Jacob Rosenberg

Uri clutched the letter to his chest and closed his eyes. He was no longer alone in the world.

BUT THE PLAN was to take another three years to come to fruition. Not until 1948 did Ireland agree to take in 150 Jewish refugee children. Their government didn't want to, but their leader, de Valera, made them.

Uri arrived at the port at North Wall a tired, undernourished fourteen-year-old. His new family was there to meet him on dry land. He recognized them from photos they had sent. They embraced him as if they had known him forever and took him back to their home, the first proper home he'd

known in years. It was a heady experience. At first, it overwhelmed him and he didn't know what to do or say. But they
were so welcoming, so kind, so full of unconditional love for
this boy that they had never met that they saved him.

There was his uncle Jacob—because that's what he was instructed to call him—his aunt Martha, and his two young
cousins, ten-year-old David and eight-year-old Sarah. They as-
tounded him, these happy, robust, pink-cheeked people. He
wasn't used to seeing such well-fed Jews. And the children
played so happily, as if they'd never had to endure a hardship
or witness a bad thing in all their lives. Which of course, they
hadn't. Uri vaguely recalled being like that once.

At first, he didn't believe in them, his faith in humankind
smashed almost to nothingness. But little by little, they won
his trust and later his love and devotion.

Jacob was a tailor, and the following year, Uri began his
apprenticeship in that trade. He was hardworking, quick,
and dexterous, and most of all, grateful for being given a second chance. He learned quickly and advanced rapidly. It
seemed as if his luck had turned. He wondered sometimes if
it was possible for a person to use up all of their bad-luck
quota for a lifetime. If it was, then he had certainly used
up—exceeded—his. But he wasn't optimistic enough to really
believe that.

Jacob's business partner—a Mr. Stern—had a daughter.
Her name was Deborah. She would come to the shop sometimes. She had these glossy curls that bounced every time she
laughed, which was often. And her dimples. Uri could have
watched them for hours. She was the most beautiful thing he
had ever seen. He now knew that perfection existed in this im-
perfect world.

"Close your mouth, Uri, you're catching flies," the other
men had laughed at him. Which embarrassed him because he
wasn't normally this transparent in his emotions. Uri was a re-
served, serious, and well-mannered young, man prone to dark

moods but also to great kindness. Had his destiny been different, he might have been different. But that was something that neither he nor anyone else would ever know for sure.

Miraculously, she liked him too. Her light was drawn to his darkness. He pulled her in. It was lucky that she was a forward and loquacious girl, because he might never have had the courage to approach this divine being.

She would come up to him in the workshop and engage him in conversation. This wasn't always an easy task. Uri's innate reticence, combined with the dumbstruck nature of his regard for her, rendered him monosyllabic at the best of times. But she must have sensed that there was something there. Something beyond words. In the same way that Uri saw something beneath the girlish dimples. A depth. A woman deep enough and strong enough to take him on. She might even be his bashert. His soul mate.

So it was that he found himself knocking on the door of Mr. Stern's office one afternoon.

"Come in."

The fear that Uri felt surprised him. A fear he hadn't felt in a long time. Because nothing had meant this much to him in a long time. Once he had thought that there was nothing, no one left to take away from him. But here was someone.

Mr. Stern's face opened out into a smile.

"Uri. What can I do for you?"

The older man leaned back in his chair, glad of the distraction, and placed his hands behind his head. Uri closed the door behind him and, cap in hand, approached the desk.

"Mr. Stern."

"Yes."

"It's about your daughter."

"Ah."

"I would like your permission to ask Deborah to go dancing with me this Saturday night."

Uri waited. And waited. As Mr. Stern regarded him solemnly for what seemed like an age. Finally, he spoke. "You have my permission."

Uri allowed himself to breathe.

"I do?"

Mr. Stern laughed. A deep, raspy chuckle.

"Why the surprise?"

"Because I have nothing."

The answer shocked them both and hung in the air between the two men, waiting for a response. It was a long time coming as Reuben Stern thought back on the years he'd known this boy—now a man. How from the very first day he'd observed his capacity for hard work, his respect for his elders, his loyalty, his integrity. His gratitude.

"I think you have everything my daughter needs," he said quietly.

The two men looked squarely at each other.

"Thank you, sir."

Uri inclined his head and backed toward the door.

"And besides," said Mr. Stern as Uri was about to leave. "You're Jewish, aren't you?"

THAT SATURDAY NIGHT, Uri's heart kept catching in his throat. Every time he looked at Deborah. The first time his arm encircled her waist, her hand resting gently on his shoulder. Many years later, the widowed Uri could still feel the feel of her in his arms. He didn't even have to close his eyes to recall. Deborah was as real to him as if she were still living and breathing beside him.

They were betrothed a year later, but it was another full year before the wedding ceremony itself took place. A year in which Uri worked outlandish hours in order to earn enough to set up a home with his new bride.

The customary week before the ceremony, in which the bride and groom were not permitted to see each other, nearly killed Uri. But made his first glimpse of Deborah on their wedding day, her eyes sparkling with unshed tears from beneath her veil, all the more mesmerizing. As they stood under the chuppah, the seven blessings recited, Uri had the strangest feeling that something was being returned to him. The feminine element that had been missing in his life since that first day in the camp. And in the riotous celebration that followed, Uri laughed as he hadn't done since he was ten years old.

He marveled at the forces that had brought him to this point in his life. An orphan, but with a family. In a strange land, but with a home. And now, setting up his own home and about to start a family.

On their wedding night, Uri told Deborah what had happened to him and his family during the war. Even the part about his father being shot and his own hand in it. He hadn't told another soul up to now. But she was his wife now and part of him. She listened to the grim reality of a life she had only half-guessed at and they cried in each other's arms. Deborah promised Uri that it would be her life's work to heal his pain with her love. She was as good as her word.

They waited a long time for the children to arrive. So long that they'd begun to think they wouldn't come at all. Part of Uri was okay with this—a part he tried to keep hidden from Deborah. Did he really want to bring his children into a world in which so many terrible things could happen? He didn't know if he could survive another loss. But the children arrived in their own good time. Deborah thought them a miracle.

They had two sons, Seth and Aaron. The day that Seth was born, Uri finally knew how much his father had loved him. He'd always thought he'd known, but now he knew it in his soul. And when he saw Deborah with their child, he understood how much his mother had loved him.

The boys grew, as boys do. They gave him unimaginable joy and unimaginable sadness. That they would never know their grandparents and that their grandparents would never know them. He wondered what kind of aunt Hannah would have been. What type of woman would that precocious girl have become?

There were times when Seth looked so like his grandfather, Samuel, that Uri felt as if God were ripping out his heart with his bare hands. Such piercing, such bittersweet pain. And then when Seth began to exhibit a flair for gardening, Uri knew for sure that his father lived on. He taught Seth everything he knew, everything his own father had taught him, and he watched that talent grow and blossom and bloom.

But there was a part of him that could never fully connect with his children. The same part of him that couldn't talk about the past. They felt it and he felt it too. It was at its worst when they were teenagers, their moodiness colliding with his own. They were all so lucky they had Deborah to coddle and correct and act as a big, warm, cuddly buffer among them all.

By the time Deborah died, they had reached an accommodation, Uri and his sons. They gathered around each other and held each other up, urging each other to go on in their own individual ways. Privately, Uri didn't know if he could. Deborah had sustained him for so long that there were days when he felt he could no longer go on living. He was surviving for his sons and in memory of those who hadn't had any choice as to whether they lived or died.

Then one day, about a year after Deborah's death, Uri saw a notice in a local food store. Or was it a sign?

Could it be that for a second time, a garden would save his life?

45

$\mathscr{P}$EARL, THE QUIET but intense Protestant lady, had set Eva thinking. Even if she didn't want the gathering to be religious in the strictest sense of the word, perhaps they could inject a little meaning into it. To have it be something more than a mere "Autumn Party."

The name itself was something they discussed endlessly. The children were vociferously unanimous in favor of "the Autumn Party." Emily, who was now on the phone almost daily with her constant ideas and enthusiasms, wanted to call it "Cornucopia," in reference to the ancient symbol of food and abundance, otherwise known as the horn of plenty.

"I have one of those," said Seth.

"Stop!" Eva hissed, Mrs. Prendergast within hearing distance.

"I don't know what all the fuss is about," the older lady said. "Why can't we just call it a harvest festival and have done with it?"

"That's too traditional," said Eva.

"What's wrong with tradition?"

"Nothing. But it might give people the wrong impression. Make people think that it's something it's not. Like what happened with your friend Pearl."

"She's no friend of mind, dear."

"Okay. But you know what I mean."

Mrs. Prendergast was silent, which indicated that she did in fact know what Eva meant but was in no way going to admit it.

Then Eva suggested, "Fall Harvest."

"No," said Uri, very firmly, surprising Eva, as he normally offered no opinion on the matter, instead listening to their endless discussions with tolerant amusement. Seth looked away, seemingly uncomfortable. It wasn't until she got home and looked up "Fall Harvest" on the Net that she discovered why and her face burned with embarrassment, even though she was alone in her own house: it was a term the Nazis had used to describe a particular phase of Jewish murders.

Mrs. Prendergast had got Eva thinking about tradition. She remembered the corn dollies of her childhood and realized that she had no clue as to the significance behind them. So she looked them up too. She learned that the practice of plaiting the wheat stalks to create a straw figure came from the belief that the corn spirit lived in the wheat and, as it was harvested, the spirit fled to the wheat that remained. By making the dolly, people believed they were keeping the spirit alive for the following year and the new crop. The next spring, the dolly would be plowed back into the earth.

So Eva had a word with Liam's teacher, purchased several sheafs of wheat from the local farmer's market, and had the boys and girls of that year's junior infants class busily making a veritable army of corn dollies.

Another memory from the harvest festivals of her youth was the bread. From the Church of England primary school she had attended she had a clear recollection of a large loaf of bread in the shape of a sheaf of wheat. She consulted Mrs. Prendergast.

"Yes, that's right. It's to symbolize thanksgiving for the harvest. They usually surround the bread with lots of fruit and vegetables."

"Like a display. What a great idea. We could do that. Surround a loaf with produce from the garden. Let people see
what we've been doing. Do you think the Mother's Union
would bake the loaf for us?"

"Well, I could help you with it if you like."

"Really?"

"Yes. I did it a few times when Lance was a child."

"That would be terrific. In fact . . ."

"What is it now?"

Eva's mind was joyfully ticking in overtime. She had a dim
recollection of an essay one of her students had written. It
concerned the Celtic celebration of the harvest. The festival of
Lammas, or the celebration of bread, where all the women of
the village would come together and prepare the bread, this
being seen as a sacred ritual in itself.

"We need lots of bread to serve with the soup. Why don't
we all get together for a great big baking session?"

"Who's 'we'?"

"You, me, Emily, Emily's mother, Kathy . . . well, that's it
really."

Emily was coming up a few days early to help out. She
was bringing Rose and her mother with her. They were all
staying with Mrs. Prendergast, her first houseguests, Eva
would guess, in a very long time.

"So just women, then?"

"I think so. That'd be more fun, wouldn't it?"

"You can use my kitchen if you like."

"Thank you!"

"Or had you made that assumption already?"

"Kind of."

Mrs. Prendergast tried to look grumpy and failed misera-
bly. The matter was settled. Eva began organizing the ingredients that very afternoon.

THE NEWS EVA received the following day caused her to feel both happy and anxious: her mother was coming for the festival. While she was looking forward to seeing her and happy for Liam that he'd get to see his nana, she couldn't help but worry. She supposed this mostly had to do with Seth. Her mother had known Michael and that seemed to matter. Furthermore, he had been her beloved son-in-law, the father of her grandchildren. Of course, she didn't *have* to tell her about Seth. It wasn't as if they were living together, and nobody else knew about it yet.

They had decided to keep it secret, mainly for Liam and Kathy's sake in case it all went pear shaped. So that was it. She wouldn't tell her. Nothing to worry about.

"The Autumn Party" was the title decided upon. A decision greeted with much whooping and jumping up and down by the children. They put flyers all over the neighborhood:

COME JOIN US FOR OUR AUTUMN PARTY,
MUSIC SWEET AND FOOD SO HEARTY,
HOMEMADE SOUP AND BREAD FOR ALL,
COME CELEBRATE THE HARVEST HAUL.

"What music?" said Emily. Eva had just read the flier over the phone to her.

"Hold on. I haven't read the rest of it: 'Bring your musical instruments, dancing shoes, storytelling hats, and hours of sunshine.'"

"Oh."

"Well. What do you think?"

"Um. It's very good. Only . . ."

"What?"

"Do you mean we're just relying on people bringing their own instruments and making their own music?"

"That's right."

"Isn't that a bit risky?"

"How so?"

"What if they don't, and everyone's standing around waiting to be entertained?"

"It'll be fine. People will make their own entertainment."

"If you're sure."

"I am."

THEN EVA'S MOTHER arrived. They went out to Howth, a mutual, almost unspoken decision, a place they'd both loved in their separate childhoods. It was to be beside the sea as much as anything else on this beautiful, golden, windswept, autumn day, Liam running ahead of them in a state of high excitement. The seals were in the harbor, five of them. So close that you could hear them breathing; watch their nostrils opening and closing; see their sleek, glistening bellies as they rolled over and dived under. A dog stood on the quayside, barking dementedly at them. Eva bought a bag of fish scraps from the fishmonger across the way and Liam fed the seals, laughing joyously as they caught the fragments of fish in their mouths.

They bought late-season ice creams—in cones with red syrup—and devoured them on the way to the lighthouse, waves crashing against the walls and roaring into their ears the whole time. Then they doubled back on themselves and walked up the hill to Howth Head, keeping the sea on their left.

Eva hadn't been to Howth since she'd settled in Ireland permanently. It was on the other side of the city now. And she hadn't wanted to come on her own. Eva noticed and her mother commented on how Liam's legs wouldn't have been sturdy enough to make this climb just a year before.

"He looks good," she said. "You both do. My God, Eva. I was so worried about you moving to Ireland. It seemed like such a rash decision to make at the time. But now I can see you were right to follow your instincts. The move has done you a world of good. Both of you. I haven't seen you looking so happy since . . . well, since Michael."

"I still miss him."

"Of course you do. You always will. That's normal."

"And I'll never let Liam forget him."

"And neither should you. But that doesn't mean you can't move on. Both of you. The last thing Michael would want is for you to stay stuck in your grief forever."

That afternoon, Eva took her mother to visit the garden. She was fishing around for the key in her bag when she saw that the gate was standing wide open. This was unusual. Unprecedented, even. She walked cautiously inside. At first it looked as if no one was about. Then Uri emerged from the foilage like a woodland creature. He grinned broadly at Eva.

"What's going on?"

"It's gone through."

"What has?"

"The sale. You're looking at the proud owner of"—he swept out his hand in an expansive gesture—"this."

"Oh, Uri." She kissed him on both cheeks. "That's wonderful. Congratulations. Oh, where are my manners. This is my mother, Moya."

Uri kissed Eva's mother firmly and enthusiastically. He looked like he was in the mood for kissing everyone.

"Does this mean you're going to keep the gates open all the time?"

"Yes. Every day from sunrise to sunset. From now on, this will be a true community garden."

"What does Mrs. Prendergast make of all this?"

"I don't know. I haven't told her yet."

He was too polite to point out that it was no longer any of her business.

Next to arrive were Emily, Rose, and Emily's mother, Bridget. Rose was crawling now and pulling herself up on anything that was available to her, be it stable or otherwise.

Mrs. Prendergast, having forgotten what babies were like, had left her home exactly as it was, much to Emily's fright. She spent the first half of her visit removing breakables from all the lower surfaces.

She seemed every inch the proper mammy now. It was as if Rose had always been a part of her. In a way, she always had. Big pea, little pea. So alike.

Upon their arrival, Emily released Rose into the hungry arms of Uri and Mrs. Prendergast and went directly to inspect her sensory garden. Eva found her on the swing seat, beneath the entangled boughs of the jasmine and honeysuckle, each both past their prime, but beautiful in their autumnal state.

"Do you mind if I sit with you?"

"Please do." Emily patted the seat beside her and smiled. She sighed as Eva sat down.

"It's good to be back."

"Are you staying for good?"

"Yes. Mum's staying for a week to settle us into our new flat. I have Rose enrolled in the nursery at college. Only two years left to go. Then I'll hopefully be able to get a job and support her properly."

"Sounds like you've got it all worked out."

Emily laughed. "Hardly. My God. It's hard work, all this baby stuff. Why didn't you tell me?"

"I didn't want to put you off."

"I can see that now. But—she's lovely, Eva."

"She is."

"I can't believe she's mine. I'm so happy."

"Good! Good for you."

"Mum's been brilliant."

"And your dad?"

"Great." She laughed. "I can't believe it, really. How well it's worked out." A cloud passed over her countenance. "All I put myself through. And Rose. It was all for nothing." Her sigh seemed to come from a deep well inside herself.

"Come on now, Emily. Enough of the maternal guilt. The important thing is how well it's all worked out. Remember how terrified you were of your dad's reaction?"

"Yes. I guess Rose just won him over. You should see him with her when he thinks no one's looking." She laughed. "I think he still feels he has to come across as stern and disapproving in case my little sisters think it's okay to arrive home with their own bundles of joy."

They swung together for a while, lost in the motion, Eva entranced by the way the delicate twigs of jasmine and honeysuckle twirled and wrapped themselves around each other.

"How are things with you?"

"Great."

"And Seth?"

"He's fine too."

"You know what I mean."

"No I don't."

"Fair enough."

46

I KEEP FINDING bowls of goo everywhere. Places you wouldn't believe. The airing cupboard, for pity's sake," Mrs. Prendergast complained in a confidential whisper. But Eva knew from the expression on her face that part of her was enjoying the strange unpredictability of sharing her house with other human beings. Not only did she have Lance back home for the first time in years. She also had Emily, her mother, and baby Rose staying with her.

"What do you mean 'bowls of goo.'"

"Some experiment to do with the bread making."

"Oh, I know what that is. She's making sourdough bread. She'll be trying to capture particles of yeast from the atmosphere."

"For goodness' sake. Can she not buy it in packets in the supermarket like everyone else?"

Each woman had been assigned a different type of bread. Emily, the aforementioned sourdough. Her mother, Bridget, soda bread. Because she made it every morning of her life and was an acknowledged world expert. Eva's mother, Moya, was on poppy seed detail. While Eva and Mrs. Prendergast, as well as being in charge of the loaf in the shape of a sheaf of wheat, were attempting a variety of flavored loaves such as sun-dried tomato, cheese and onion, and raisin. Kathy's job was to squelch down the newly risen bread with the palms of her freshly washed hands. She was also the official licker of bowls and utensils. They felt that between them, they had all the bases covered. Eva just hoped they weren't being overly ambitious.

So they gathered together the night before the party. Five—and a half—women in Mrs. Prendergast's fabled kitchen. Seth called them "the Coven" and Eva privately thought he had a point. There was something about a group of women together. A unique dynamic, fascinating to feel and watch. The way they sat so comfortably, kicked off their shoes, threw their heads back and laughed with abandon. Eva perceived that within this group were the women she had come to love most in all the world. The thought made her smile as she watched Mrs. Prendergast boss everyone about. She hoped this didn't cause a clash with Bridget, who was quite a domineering presence herself and used to being in charge of a kitchen. She seemed quite relaxed so far, however.

There were a few bottles of wine knocking around. Eva wondered if she should suggest opening one of them. On the other hand, she didn't want them all so pissed that they messed up the bread. So she'd bide her time and choose the moment of inebriation carefully.

They all wore aprons. Eva had flowers and kittens on hers. She felt as if she were in home economics class, Mrs. Prendergast the strict and bossy teacher.

"Now, girls," she was saying, relishing her role as the one in charge. "It's probably best if we keep to our own sections of the kitchen at all times."

They were designated a piece of counter each. Everybody had brought their own bowls and bits and pieces that they laid out now. When this was done, Eva announced: "Okay, ladies. Let the great bake off commence."

She saw Mrs. Prendergast's sour look and understood that the old woman had been planning on making such a declaration herself. Oh well. Too late now.

So off they went. Weighing, measuring, sifting, mixing, kneading, rolling, chattering. So much chattering that a passerby might have been forgiven for mistaking the noise for that of a gaggle of excited schoolgirls released on a school trip.

There were quiet times too, every woman intent on her own soulful work. Eva looked up on one such occasion. Emily looked up at the same time. They smiled at each other before turning their attention back to the dough. Eva felt as if she were participating in some ancient ritual. There was something about making bread—the staff of life. The knowledge that generations of her female ancestors before her had done the same. It was a soothing notion. One that filled her with a sense of contentment. Eva hadn't made bread in years, but she had helped her mother sometimes when she was a girl. She was amazed by how it came back to her so quickly, as if the knowledge had been locked away inside the whole time. A secret memory. Coded, in fact, in her very DNA.

They came to the point when most of them had to stop and wait for their bread to rise. Not Bridget's soda bread, which was the first to enter the oven and fill the air with its delectable aroma. They cleared up as best they could and then the clinking began, of chilled wine bottles and glasses. A party atmosphere invaded the kitchen. Mrs. Prendergast produced a tray of nibbles that she'd secretly prepared earlier. They descended on them greedily, in the manner of women who know that no men are present. No pretense of delicacy here.

"I thought we might need these to stop us from munching on the bread," said Mrs. Prendergast. "Looks like I was right."

"Well, smelling all that delicious bread baking is making me feel starving," said Moya. "Especially since I know I'm not allowed to eat any of it."

"Not necessarily," said Emily. "I mean, we're making so much bread that it'd probably be okay to nibble on a bit of it."

"Except if we start, we might never stop," said Bridget.

"Do you think we've made too much?" Eva was suddenly filled with fear. "What if nobody shows up?"

"They will."

"But what if they don't? What'll we do with all the bread?"

"We can take it home and eat it ourselves."

"Or give it to the ducks."

"Don't worry, Eva. It's going to be fine."

"I wonder how the Mother's Union is getting on with the soup?"

Joyce and Pearl and the women of the Mother's Union had volunteered to make the honey-roasted parsnip soup. Eva had taken them around a massive crate of parsnips that afternoon.

"Oh, I'm sure they're on their second gallon already," said Mrs. Prendergast. "Honestly. That woman. You should have heard her yesterday. 'All the honey is sourced locally.' I mean, what did she do? Take down the names and addresses of all the bees?"

Eva giggled as she imagined the scene and the ruthless efficiency that Joyce would apply to it. But she was grateful. So very grateful. Those women had really come up trumps for her.

The atmosphere mellowed as the women sipped their wine. It was during this time that Lance came home and unwittingly walked into the kitchen. He blinked a couple of times, as if caught in headlights.

"Oh. I'm sorry. I didn't know you were all here." This was clear. He wouldn't have come anywhere near them if he had known. The group of women knew their power to intimidate a lone male. They felt their strength in numbers.

"Something smells good."

"Are you hungry, Lance? Shall I make you a sandwich?"

"That'd be great."

"Go through to the sitting room. I'll bring it in to you."

He nodded his thanks and beat a hasty retreat.

"Poor guy," said Emily.

"How's he getting on?" Eva asked Mrs. Prendergast when she came back in.

"Very well." She smiled a smile of genuine happiness. "Although he thinks he isn't because that trollop of a girlfriend of his has broken up with him. Lost interest when she found out there was no more money in the pot. He'll work out soon enough that he's had a lucky escape. Which," she said, suddenly switching a laserlike focus on Eva, "means that he's free, for anybody who might consider him."

"I . . . I . . ." Eva was mortified.

"Oh, I forgot. You're otherwise engaged with Seth." She smiled a wicked smile.

Eva turned the color of beets. Everybody laughed.

"Who else knows?" Eva said in a strangled tone.

"Eva," said Emily. "The dogs on the street know. Even Harriet here knows." She reached out a stockinged foot and rubbed the supine, overweight body of Harriet, who was passed out under the table, having satisfied herself with lickings of flour and rogue pumpkin seeds. Harriet snorted in her sleep and emitted a silent but violent fart that rose up and mingled with the scent of the soda bread, somewhere around ceiling level.

Eva took a glug of her wine, mind ticking furiously, craving the quick fix of revenge. She felt her mother's eyes on her but didn't look up.

"You and Uri seem to be getting on very well lately, Mrs. Prendergast."

"Yes, we are."

"I'd almost say that you're inseparable."

Emily's mother interjected, "I'd imagine that when you get to your time in life, Mrs. Prendergast, it's more a question of companionship."

Mrs. Prendergast turned and faced them all.

"Actually, no," she said. "It's all about the sex."

There was a moment's silence—then the room exploded into uproar and laughter.

"Uh-oh. Little pitchers have big ears," said Moya when the general hilarity had died down, inclining her head in the direction of Kathy, who was sitting in the corner, goggle eyed. She was in that privileged position of a child in the company of a group of adults who had forgotten about her.

"Kathy," said Emily, in a bid to distract. "It's time for you to push your hand into the dough. Remember, I told you it would be your special job. It should be ready by now."

The distraction appeared to work. They peered into their tea-towel-covered bowls. As if by magic, the dough had risen. To Kathy's disgust, they made her wash her hands again.

"I already washed them."

"But you've been licking your fingers."

"No I haven't."

"Yes you have." A chorus.

"Oh!"

But she did it and the first bowl was set in front of her.

"Ready?" said Eva.

"Ready," shouted Kathy.

"One, two, three—go!"

Kathy splatted her hand down into the dough and laughed as the air escaped and the mixture flattened down.

"That felt funny. I want to do it again."

She did it to the remaining mixtures, punching the last two with her little fist.

"Pow!"

The women finished their loaves and dispatched them to the waiting oven.

"I hope someone's sober enough to set the timer," said Eva.

Then they finished their wine as they waited.

It was after eleven by the time all the loaves were baked, including the pièce de résistance, the bread in the shape of the sheaf of wheat.

"Come on, miss," said Eva to Kathy. "Your eyes are nearly falling out of your head. Let's get you home to bed. You have a big day tomorrow."

They all had. Hopefully they wouldn't be too hungover to do what was necessary.

"Plenty of water before you go to sleep tonight, ladies," she called as they were leaving.

"Who's minding Liam?" Emily walked them to the door.

"Seth."

"Really. That's cozy. Will he be staying over?"

"He will not. He'll be taking Kathy straight home."

"Good night, then. See you first thing." Emily kissed Eva on the cheek.

"Good night—cheeky pup." She smiled.

They stepped outside and pulled their coats tightly around their bodies. Eva, Kathy, and Moya. Eva knew that her mother was dying to ask her about Seth. So she chattered animatedly and aimlessly, not allowing her to get a word in. She was grateful too for Kathy's presence. It meant her mother couldn't ask her detailed questions. They were almost home by the time Moya managed to interrupt her daughter.

"Eva. Stop talking for one second, will you? I couldn't be happier for you. I think it's wonderful news. I really like him."

Eva's body relaxed. "Really?"

"Yes, really."

They were home. Seth let them in.

"How are things?" said Eva.

"Great."

"Did Liam behave?"

"Yes. Asleep only half an hour after his official bedtime."

"Not bad. That's better than I normally do."

"Did you have a good time?"

Kathy jumped up and down. "I splatted my hand in the dough!"

"You did?"

"Yes. It was fun."

"That's great. Now leave your coat on, we're going straight home to bed."

"Good night, Seth. I'm going up myself."

" 'Night, Mrs. Madigan."

She surprised him by embracing him warmly, as one might do a future son-in-law.

Seth and Eva smiled at each other.

"Night then. See you in the morning."

"Thanks for babysitting, Liam."

"No problem."

"Daddy. You can give her a kiss, you know. I won't mind."

Seth looked at his daughter in surprise. Then at Eva. She shrugged. He gave her a peck on the cheek. Then, to Eva's delight, Kathy did the same before hugging her ferociously.

Eva stood in the doorway, watching them as they got into the Jeep. She heard Kathy's voice ringing out into the crisp night air.

"Daddy."

"Yes, Kathy?"

"What's sex?"

47

*T*HE MORNING WAS sacred, as was everything in it. Wreaths of mist rose up from the earth. To some, it might have looked like smoke. The landscape was otherworldly. Ethereal. The garden, but somehow not the garden. The apple trees reared up out of the mist like giant, arthritic hands, the earth beneath them sweetened by windfalls. The mist cleared a patch over the lawn, revealing a fairy ring that had appeared overnight. Eva laughed out loud. The sound was uncommon.

She was the first. In a while, other figures would emerge from the mist. One by one. Seth. Uri. Emily. Mrs. Prendergast. Custodians of the garden all. To dress and decorate her on this her special day.

Seth and Uri were the first to arrive, erecting a hut with wooden walls and a living roof, evergreen boughs that wouldn't shed.

"What is it?"

"A sukkah. It's part of the tradition of the Jewish harvest festival. In ancient times, Jewish farmers would walk out of the village each day to tend to their crops. At harvest, they built sheters in the fields to avoid wasting time walking backward and forward. That's where it comes from. Families put these up in their gardens during the festival and ate all their meals out there. I thought we could set up a table and chairs and people could eat their refreshments in it."

"What a great idea."

One by one the women came. Tables were carried out and covered with cloths—yellow, orange, brown, and gold—all the colors of the harvest. Pretty soon they were laden down. The first with the sheaf-of-wheat loaf. The shape was a little uneven. Eva thought she noticed a few of the women of the Mother's Union eyeing it critically. But that might have been her own insecurity. Then they surrounded the loaf with the choicest produce they could find—sunbursts of color—like a living work of art. It would, thought Eva, make you feel quite proud. Then there was a table selling surplus veg and one for surplus fruit. A big sign was erected above: ALL PROFITS TO BE PLOWED BACK INTO THE GARDEN. Certain parties found this funny.

Then there was the table for nonedibles.

"Look what they've done with my lavender!" Emily said, beside herself with excitement, before rushing off to grab Rose again, who this time had crawled under the vegetable table and was pulling at the cloth from underneath in a manner designed to bring everything tumbling down on top of her.

Lavender toilet water, lavender room spray, dried lavender bags for underwear drawers, and liquid lavender soap.

"We tried to make bars of soap, but we couldn't get them to set." Joyce sounded apologetic.

"You don't have to explain yourself to me, Joyce. As far as I'm concerned, you've worked miracles. And the packaging is divine. What lovely little bottles!"

Joyce smiled, like the sun coming out.

"It was no trouble at all."

"Well, I'd say you went to a huge amount of trouble."

"You know, I enjoyed it. We all did. And we're just so delighted to be involved."

The Mother's Union had made the same "range" of products in rose. Eva was starting to feel seriously excited. She could have kissed every one of these women. Perhaps she would before the day was out.

The corn dollies, courtesy of the Low Babies of St. Mary's, came in a startling array of shapes and sizes. Some had one leg longer than the other. Others were bona fide amputees. One even appeared to have no head at all. But each was cherished and each proudly displayed: in Mrs. Prendergast's kitchen, in her sunroom, above the stalls, and from the roof of the sukkah—on either side of a big, colorful sign with the words BRUCHIM HABAIM and underneath, WELCOME. The less-edible-looking apples also served to decorate the roof of the sukkah along with artfully placed fig leaves.

But the table that Eva kept returning to, the table that nobody could keep their eyes off, was the one with all the cakes. It looked fit to topple over, under the weight of so much confectionary: fresh fig filo tart; Greek yogurt and fig cake; rhubarb pie and rhubarb crumble; pomegranate cheesecake, berry brulée tart, and blueberry muffins; black-currant bread-and-butter pudding; alpine strawberry and rose-petal shortcakes; fresh berry pavlova; plum and marzipan pastries; cherry and hazelnut strudle; plum tart and plum crumble; pear and polenta cake; Dutch apple cake and French apple tart; chocolate, pear, and pecan pie; filo-topped apple pie and spiced apple crumble.

Eva wanted everyone to leave so she could dive in and scoff the lot. Again, the ladies of the Mother's Union had outdone themselves. And that was before you got to the jam table: damson plum jam, strawberry jam, bramble jam, bramble and apple jam, bramble jelly, quince jelly, red-currant jelly, crab-apple jelly, damson plum chutney, pickled peach and chili chutney, and fig and date chutney.

What with all the goodies on display, it was amazing that the garden wasn't stripped bare. But to look all around, it was as if nothing had been picked, giving the impression that you could go on picking fruit and vegetables forever and they would never run out, giving a sense of unlimited abundance.

The gates opened at twelve, which meant it was almost

time to organize the teas and coffees and bring out the soup and breads. This was the moment the Mother's Union had been waiting for—the moment they got to set foot inside Mrs. Prendergast's kitchen. They gripped each other's arms and giggled like schoolgirls. Mrs. Prendergast had been up half the night scrubbing the place. She regarded them sternly.

"I'll thank you to remember," she said, "that the rest of the house is out of bounds. If you need to use the toilet, there's a perfectly adequate Port-a-Loo at the far end of the garden."

"Oh chill out, Myrtle."

"I beg your pardon?"

"That's what my grandson says to me. Now let's get this show on the road."

Get the show on the road they did. By five to twelve, everything was set up. The soup was hot, the ladle gleamed. The sun had burned off the last of the morning mist. The gates were opened. They were ready.

48

*T*HE PEOPLE TRICKLED in at first. Then they formed a steady stream. Until before long, a veritable river of bodies flowed in and out of the pathways of the garden. Eva hardly had time to register pleasure at the turnout, so engrossed was she in selling leeks and handing out teas and trying to keep track of her son.

"Has anyone seen Liam?"

"He's over there."

"Liam!"

He obliged his mother by running over, his face lit up with happiness from within.

"Yes, Mammy?"

"Did you just call me Mammy?"

"No."

"It's okay if you did."

"Is it?"

"Of course it is."

"It's just that the other boys in my class call their mummies Mammy."

"That's fine, Liam. You can call me Mammy if you like."

"Maybe I'll call you Mummy at home and Mammy when we're out. Okay?"

He grinned and ran back off to play.

"Stay where I can see you."

A young man, a guitar slung across the back of his shoulder, approached her. She thought she recognized him from the college. He cleared his throat and stared at a pyramid of onions as he spoke to her.

"I was looking for the band."

She beamed at him. "You *are* the band!"

"What?"

Before he could run away, she was over on his side of the table with her arm around his shoulder. "Now. I keep seeing people wandering around with various instruments. It's about time we got you all together."

"What do you mean 'I am the band'?"

"Well, we were hoping it would kind of spring up organically. Look. There's a man over there with a fiddle. Come with me."

Eva gathered up the bemused musicians and organized some chairs. These they arranged in a semicircle on the lawn. They had two guitarists, a traditional flautist, a guy with a set of uilleann pipes, a fiddle player, and a Finnish woman with a bodhrán. Once the band members had got over their initial shock, they entered into the spirit of things. The music began, hesitantly at first, as Eva walked back to the stalls, a very definite swing in her step. She'd secretly brought her tin whistle along. She was itching to play it but didn't want to come across as a plastic Paddy. Still. They had a Fin with a bodhrán. So maybe later. Right now, she was too busy anyway.

She was back at the soup station, currently manned by Joyce and Emily. Joyce was in her element.

"The soup is going down a treat," she said.

"I'm not surprised. I tasted some and it's beautiful. You were right to roast the parsnips first. Gives a much better flavor."

Joyce tried to look modest. "Oh, you don't get to my age without learning a trick or two, my dear."

Eva turned to Emily. "It worked out."

"What did?"

"The musicians."

"Oh. Yes."

"What's wrong?"

"Nothing."

"Then why the glum face?"

"It's silly, really. It's just that nobody is eating my sourdough bread."

Eva looked down into the bread baskets. There did seem to be a higher proportion of sourdough left. Admittedly, it was quite forlorn and lumpen looking.

"It's only because sourdough doesn't rise as much as the other breads and they don't know what it is. They probably think it's normal bread gone wrong. It just needs some advertising."

She wrote a sign in Magic Marker:

GET THE LAST OF THE SOURDOUGH BREAD.

"Write that it's made with genuine rainwater," said Emily.

"Pardon?"

"Eva."

She swiveled around at the sound of her name. It was Seth. She smiled in relief.

"I haven't seen you in ages."

"No. It's going well, isn't it?"

"Brilliant."

"Hello, Eva."

Megan stepped out from behind Seth. "Good to see you again," she said. "I've been hearing so much about you lately. We'll have to make time for a proper chat one of these days."

"I'd like that." What she didn't like was the knowing way that Megan, so small and golden, was looking at her.

"This is Siobhan, by the way."

Aha. The other woman.

A voluptuous brunette emerged from Megan's shadow. She nodded at Eva.

"Anyway," said Megan. "We won't keep you. It's clear you're up to your eyes. Come on, Kathleen."

Eva started at the name. She was surprised by the sight of Kathy, who she hadn't noticed before, running over to her mother's side and taking her hand.

"Kathy's name is Kathleen?" she said.

"Yes." Megan gave her an odd look.

"You know, all this time I assumed it was Katherine. I don't know why."

"I suppose Katherine is more usual. No. I named her Kathleen after my grandmother."

"I see."

"Anyway. Talk to you soon, I hope." Megan threw a furtive look behind her to see where Seth and Siobhan were. They were standing a few yards away, Siobhan listening intently while Seth pointed at the herbaceous border. Megan leaned toward Eva.

"You've got a good man there, you know. Hang on to him. Unfortunately, he had one too many penises for me. Come on, Kathy! Let's take a look at this little hut."

And off they went. Eva's eyes followed them up the path toward the sukkah. The hut was packed, all the chairs occupied, people talking and laughing and eating, clearly taking the welcome sign at face value. Her eyes wandered across to the lawn where the musicians were in full flight. A woman she'd never seen before was leading the children in a session of Irish dancing. Liam was the only child doing his one-two-threes backward. She allowed herself a smile and a moment to relax. If somebody told her this was heaven, she wouldn't be disappointed.

"Eva."

"Yes."

"The Port-a-Loo is blocked again."

Mrs. Prendergast was enjoying herself. Of course, she had no intention of admitting this to anyone. She was in the kitchen, wiping bread crumbs off the counter when Lance came in.

"Can I do anything to help?"

"No thanks. It's all in hand."

"Can I get you some soup? It's nearly all gone, you know."

"No. It's all right, darling. I'm not hungry yet."

"It's going well, isn't it?"

"Yes it is."

"You know, I'm glad you didn't sell the garden to developers, Mum. You did the right thing. I can see how happy it's made you. All the new friends you've made. You've really created something very special here."

She stopped what she was doing and looked up at her son.

"Thank you for saying that, Lance."

They smiled at each other. Then he came around and put one long arm about her shoulders. He hugged her to him.

"See you outside."

"Bye, Lance."

Alone again, she was surprised by the prickling sensation at the backs of her eyes.

"Stupid old woman," she said to herself, and resumed her cleaning.

When the kitchen was once again spotless, she went outside to the hall. Imagine her surprise to find Pearl, Mother's Unionist, floating down the stairs, her head turning this way and that, oblivious to the other woman's presence.

"What do you think you're doing?"

Pearl nearly stumbled down the last few steps.

"Oh Lord. I didn't see you there, Myrtle."

"Clearly not."

"I was just looking for a toilet."

"Something wrong with the Port-a-Loo?"

"Yes, actually. It's blocked."

"Oh. Well, there's one at the end of the hall. Downstairs," she said, with emphasis.

"Oh, thank you so much."

Mrs. Prendergast watched her—making sure she was going directly to the loo and making no detours. Honest to God. Bunch of nosy, incontinent old biddies. She must have been mad agreeing to all this.

But then she went outside and her heart lifted. She could never have imagined such a thing. In *her* garden. Well, it wasn't technically her garden anymore. But *her* garden. *Her* home. And she was part of this. Part of something really good. She felt the prickly feeling at the backs of her eyes again. She'd have to get that checked out. Probably glaucoma.

She stepped into the sun and into the milling throng. It was good to feel anonymous. She meandered along the path, humming slightly, her hands behind her back.

"Hello, Marnie."

She stopped walking. She wanted to believe that she was hearing things but she knew that she wasn't. She turned around and looked up at him.

"Hello, Martin."

"Long time no see."

"Indeed."

"You're looking well."

She didn't reply. She was too busy taking it all in. Same frame. Less meaty now. Same features—craggier than before. Same blue eyes. A little faded but still Martin. He still had most of his own hair and teeth by the looks of it.

"It must be . . ."

"Thirty-one years."

"Is it that long?"

"I've been keeping count."

He smiled and she was back in the jazz cellar in Soho, barely twenty years old, her blue felt skirt swirling all around her, about to be swept off her feet.

Her sum knowledge of Martin up to now was that he was still alive. Lance saw him from time to time, but she didn't ask him questions, as he knew she didn't want to know. The memories kept popping up, one after another, like a slide show. Her eyes grew cold.

MYRTLE HELD THE blade tight against Martin's throat. Nobody moved. It was like some gruesome still life. She was standing above him dramatically. He was down on one knee, his neck twisted awkwardly. The clock ticked on the wall. A dog barked in a neighboring garden.

"Now don't do anything stupid, Marnie." Martin's voice was calm and cajoling.

"I've already done something stupid," she said. "I married you." Then she grabbed a handful of hair from the top of his head. "And don't. Tell me. What to do." She tugged his hair back roughly, several times, to emphasize her words. The blade dug deeper into his throat each time. A droplet of blood trickled down his neck and fell onto the collar of the white shirt that she'd ironed for him the night before. He felt the wetness.

"Oh Jesus, Marnie. Please don't. I'm sorry. Truly I am."

She was amazed by how calm she felt. How strong. She. Myrtle. Holding a man twice her size and breadth at her mercy. She knew it was partly luck. That she had him in such a position that the smallest move from him and she could slit his throat wide open. Like a great, big, horrible, gaping red grin.

She felt as if she were outside her own body, looking down on herself. Amazed by the bloodthirsty thoughts of the woman below her and the level of hatred she held for her own husband. But not appalled. Never appalled. It was just. This was justice. She looked down at Lance. He was hiding under the table, his head in his hands. He couldn't see. Just as well.

"Now you listen to me and you listen to me carefully,

Martin Prendergast. You give me one good reason why I shouldn't slit your throat right now."

"Because I'm your husband."

"Hah! Not good enough." She tugged back on his hair another three times for emphasis. Martin whimpered as the blade bit deep. She could have laughed. What a coward. All this time and she'd never known.

"Please don't, Marnie."

"I may decide to spare your life, but I have my conditions."

"What? What are they? Anything."

"Anything?"

"That's what I said."

"You're to leave this house immediately. You're to go directly to your solicitor and tell him you're transferring this entire property, including the garden, into my sole name. Then you tell him you're giving me a divorce on the grounds of *your* unreasonable behavior. If my terms are unacceptable to you, I have some fresh bruises that the police might be interested in. Not to mention a very sympathetic doctor who will be more than happy to give me a detailed medical report going back years. Now. Do I make myself clear?"

"Yes."

"Is everything all right?" It was the gardener. He was standing at the back door, a turnip in each hand, his face incredulous.

"Yes thank you, Paddy. Mr. Prendergast was just leaving."

She released him and he sprang to his feet and faced her, backing away, rubbing his neck with his hand.

"Mad bitch," he murmured.

She crossed her arms into fishwife position.

"Leave your keys on the counter, please. You won't be needing them anymore. And I'll have you know that I'll be having the locks changed this afternoon, so don't get any funny ideas."

Like a man who'd seen a ghost, Martin dropped his keys on the kitchen counter and backed toward the door. When he reached it, he looked at the gardener, one last time at Myrtle, then turned around and left. Only when he was out of view did Myrtle collapse onto the floor, the knife clanging onto the tiles beside her. Her body began to shake.

"Jesus Christ. I'm calling the police," said Paddy.

"No, don't. Please. He won't be back. Lance. Come here, my darling."

Lance didn't move. Myrtle crawled under the table.

"Lance, it's all right. It's all over. He's gone."

Lance lifted his head and looked around. Then he threw himself into his mother's arms and they rocked together until they'd both calmed down.

"YOU'RE NOT GOING to throw me off your property, are you?"

"I couldn't if I wanted to. It's not my property anymore."

"You've sold the house?"

"No, just the garden."

He nodded. "This is a great setup. I'm delighted to see it being put to such good use."

"Is that so?"

He looked at her sharply. "Yes, it is. You remember how fond I was of this garden."

"Yes, I remember. Fonder of *it* than you were of me."

"Now that's not fair."

"Don't you turn up here after all these years, Martin Prendergast, and tell me what's fair."

"You're right. I apologize."

She inclined her head.

They started to walk along together.

"How did you know about the party?"

"I saw one of the fliers. I moved house a while back. I'm living quite close now."

"I know. Lance told me in case I had the misfortune of bumping into you. You'll forgive me if I don't invite you over for dinner."

He laughed. So familiar. "You haven't changed a bit, Marnie."

"Oh yes I have."

"You know, I have too."

"A leopard doesn't change his spots."

"No. But people do."

"I seriously doubt it. Not where you're concerned."

"Look." He stopped walking and they turned to face each other. "Did Lance tell you that I had a heart attack?"

"He might have mentioned it."

What did he want from her? Sympathy?

"When something like that happens, it makes you think. I know it sounds clichéd, but it reminds you of what's important in life."

She took the opportunity to examine Martin's features for any signs of the ravages of ill health as he stared off into the middle distance.

"There were two reasons for me coming here today," he said. "The first was—well—I couldn't resist coming to see this place again. I'm glad I did. And I'm glad I saw you too, Marnie."

"Nobody calls me that anymore."

"I'm sorry. Myrtle. Because my second reason for coming today was to say sorry."

He tried to gauge her reaction as she remained silent.

"For everything I've ever done to you. Every hardship I've put you through. The hitting." He bowed his head. "Our baby. All the babies you never had. I'm so sorry, Marnie. Myrtle. It's not possible for me to make you understand how guilty I feel. Do you think you'd have it in you to forgive an old man?"

She stared at him for a long time.

And she thought of all those times.

All the bruises.

The hurts.

The scars that still bore witness on her body. The wound across her soul that at times felt mortal.

Over the years, Myrtle had anticipated such a meeting. Rehearsed her speech. All the things she would say to Martin if she ever met him again. How she would make him pay for all that he had done to her. Pierce him with her barbed words. But as she looked at him now, the hulking frame diminished, the eyes full of sincerity, all the anger that she'd counted on, the anger that she'd planned and thought she'd wanted. It all fell away. As if she were shedding a skin—as if she were a giant, upright snake standing right there on the garden path. The old Myrtle slipped away from her and she felt lighter than she had done in years.

"Soup?" she said.

"What?"

"Would you like some soup?"

He frowned. "All right, then."

"This way."

They made their way through the crowds to the soup station.

"Joyce. Any soup left?"

"You're just in time. We're down to the last couple of bowls."

"That's all we need."

"Actually, I always think it's the best part myself. All the nice chunky bits sink to the bottom. Here you go." She handed a bowl to Martin and a bowl to Myrtle.

"I don't believe we've met." She eyed Martin speculatively.

"Oh, how rude of me. Do let me introduce you. Joyce. This is my ex-husband—Martin Prendergast."

Joyce's eyes popped and her mouth fell open. The soup ladle fell out of her hand and onto the ground with a loud clatter. Everyone in the vicinity stopped what they were doing and stared. Mrs. Prendergast clinked her soup bowl against Martin's.

"Cheers," she said.

THE RUMOR THAT Mrs. Prendergast's husband had been resurrected and was at large in the garden spread like wildfire. But he was already gone before it was fully ignited. His ex-wife looked very smug. Eva could tell she was enjoying herself.

"Well. You certainly shocked the Union today. You shocked me too."

"Did I?"

"You know you did."

"Oh well. That's what you get when you listen to scurrilous rumors. Although I must admit, I'm going to quite miss my status as the local black widow. Now I'm going to have to find some other way of frightening people off."

"Where has he been all this time?"

"Spain mostly. Building collapsible apartments. That's where he went after I sent him packing."

"And why did you send him packing?"

"Because he was a violent drunk."

"Oh. I'm sorry." Eva was genuinely shocked. She'd never had Mrs. Prendergast down as a battered wife. Really, the woman never failed to amaze.

"You seem quite friendly with him now. That *was* him, wasn't it? The tall, distinguished-looking man you were with."

"Distinguished." She laughed. "I suppose he is. Yes. That was Martin."

"You've forgiven him, then."

She seemed to consider this for a while.

"It was a long time ago. He's gone through two other wives since me. He's had treatment. I don't think he drinks anymore and I know he regrets what he did. So yes. I suppose

I have forgiven him. After all, if it wasn't for him, I wouldn't have Lance."

"He looks so like him."

"Yes, he does. And if it wasn't for Martin, I wouldn't be living in this house, with this garden. We wouldn't be having this day, with all these people enjoying themselves." She smiled. "In a sense, we have Martin to thank for all this. He was the start of it all."

"That's one way of looking at it."

"I've learned recently that it's the only way of looking at it. You know, I heard this saying and it's so true: that not forgiving someone is like drinking poison and expecting the other person to die. I've decided I don't want to drink poison anymore."

"So you forgive Pearl for using your toilet?"

"You must be joking. Come on, Harriet. You're getting far too excitable."

Eva watched Mrs. Prendergast as she retrieved her retriever. She felt she'd just caught a glimpse of the real woman. It only happened once in a while, before the barriers went up again. But it was something worth waiting for. Something special.

49

THE SOUP AND bread had been devoured and all the cakes and produce sold. The band was unstoppable. Eva, Seth, Uri, Emily, and Mrs. Prendergast came together for the first time that day. None of them could stop smiling. The Autumn Party had exceeded all their expectations.

"Is it time for . . . ?"

"I think so. I'll go and get it."

"Oh, hold on. We have one more thing to do first. Lance!"

"Yes."

"Can you take the photograph now?"

"Sure."

"Over by the apple tree?"

"Perfect."

They collected Liam and Kathy on their way. Then the seven of them arranged themselves in front of the tree. Emily sat on the ground, flanked by the children.

"You have to have Rose too."

Emily's mother handed her Rose, who sat benignly on her mother's lap, still for perhaps the first time that day. Uri and Mrs. Prendergast stood behind them to their left. Uri had his arm around her shoulders.

"Oh, we must have Harriet too. Harriet!"

Harriet settled noisily on the ground on top of Emily's feet, a few of the flowers that the children had twisted into her collar still remaining. Standing behind them to the right were Seth and Eva, Seth standing directly behind Eva, his arms wrapped tightly around her waist, his head resting snugly against hers.

"Okay. Ready?" said Lance. "Everybody say 'vegetables.'"

"Vegetables!"

He took a few shots, just to make sure.

"Right. I'll go straight to the chemist's and get this printed." He looked at his watch. "I should just make it in time."

"Oh, Lance. Get a newspaper while you're at it."

Ever since they'd dug up the time capsule, Liam had been pleading with his mother to bury another one. What better time? A crowd gathered around Seth as he dug the hole.

"Right. Who's going first?"

"Me, me!" Kathy danced on the spot.

"Okay. What have you got?"

"My Little Pony. I'm too big to play with her now, so maybe some other little girl can play with her in the future."

"Very good. How about you, Liam?"

"My yellow digger."

"Are you sure?" said Eva. "It's one of your favorites."

"I want to put it in." Liam pursed his lips definitively.

"Okay, then."

"Emily."

"My contribution is this baby onesie belonging to Rose that she's grown out of. And my copy of *Beowolf*. I spent almost my entire first year of college reading this book and I never want to see the damn thing again. In fact, burying it is probably too good for it but here you go anyway."

"Thank you, Emily. While we're at it, I'm putting in this pair of pruning shears. They were the first tool I bought when I set up my gardening business. I found them the other day when I was clearing out my shed. They're not much use for gardening anymore, but I thought they might be—symbolic or something."

Those gathered around murmured their assent.

"Right. Who's next? Mrs. P."

"I've decided to put the angel back in." Mrs. Prendergast handed Seth the blue-and-white ceramic angel that had been unearthed with the first time capsule. "On the basis that she appears to work."

"Okay. Eva."

Eva took a deep breath and handed Seth a small, ornate pillbox.

"This is a lock of my daughter Katie's hair."

There were a few seconds in which no one said anything.

"Are you sure?" said Emily. "It's a very precious thing to bury."

"Don't worry. I have about a dozen locks of her hair at home. And I like the idea of someone finding a little piece of her in years to come."

"Can I see?"

Eva nodded and Seth handed Emily the box. She opened it and exclaimed at the sight of the red-gold curl, secured at one end by a tiny pink ribbon.

"What a beautiful color. I bet she was gorgeous."

"She was."

"May I?" said Mrs. Prendergast.

The box was handed around and Eva felt proud and emotional as everyone admired the beauty of her daughter's hair. Finally, the box was handed back to Seth.

"Da. You're the only one left. What have you got for us?"

Uri handed Seth a small, threadbare teddy bear.

"Da, are you . . ."

Uri nodded.

"This bear belonged to my little sister, Hannah. I found it in the wreakage of our home after the war. For years I kept it with me in the hope that I might be able to return it to her. Today, I lay that hope to rest."

It was a little while before Seth could speak.

"Thank you, Da. Now if you could just hand me the newspaper and the photo, Lance. Thank you. I think we're just about done."

Seth packed all the objects neatly into the box and closed the lid. Then he placed it reverently in the earth and commenced shoveling in the soil.

Liam burst into noisy sobs.

"What is it?"

"My yellow digger."

"Hold on, Seth."

The box was exhumed and the digger resurrected. Liam replaced the digger with a lesser, dinky car that he had in his pocket. Then the ceremony was recommenced and the time capsule buried once and for all.

Now it was time for the procession.

Uri was master of ceremonies. He narrated the passage of the children as they moved in an undulating line from the gate to the sukkah.

"These are the children of St. Mary's. We're very grateful for all their help with the Autumn Party. You will see that some of the children are carrying lanterns. They have made these themselves." The lanterns were clearly jam jars, of various shapes and sizes, with little bits of colored tissue paper stuck on each in an ad hoc fashion. Every lantern housed a night-light, which glowed colorfully in the gathering twilight.

"The other children are holding an etrog fruit in one hand." These looked like large lemons. Uri had been carefully cultivating them in the far reaches of the garden. Now Eva knew why. "In their other hands, the children are holding bunches of leaves known as *lulav*. These are made up of palm, for uprightness; willow, for humility; and myrtle, for faithfulness. Together they symbolize brotherhood and peace. This procession is part of the tradition of the Jewish harvest festival. It serves as a reminder of the beauty of life. Speaking of beauty, the girl wearing the crown is my granddaughter Kathy.

This is known in Germany as the 'harvest crown' or '*Ernte-krone.*' It's made up of ears of grain, flowers, and fruit. Thank you, Kathy."

One by one, the children reached the sukkah. Those with *lulav* placed them on the roof. Those with lanterns, hung them from the eaves. Kathy kept her crown on. This may or may not have been part of the plan. But, judging by the expression on her face, the crown would have to be prized off her.

There was silence while the children returned to their places in the crowd, alongside friends and parents.

"Now we have a presentation," said Uri.

This was news to Eva. She wondered what it could be.

The crowds parted to allow Seth and Lance through. Between them, they carried a bench. It was clearly homemade. Rustic looking. The seat was a log sawn in half, a large one at that. The remainder of the bench was constructed of branches bound together with split roots. There was a metal plaque with writing. Eva couldn't make it out from where she was standing.

"Eva. Where's Eva? Can you come up here please?"

Eva stiffened. Those around her pushed her gently forward. As she entered the clearing, everyone started to clap. How mortifying. She stood beside Uri and he put his arm around her shoulder and turned her around to face everyone.

"You're looking here at the woman who made this possible. This garden. This wonderful day. Through her vision. Her hard work. Her bossiness."

There was an appreciative laugh from the audience.

"For this, my dear Eva, we thank you from the bottom of our hearts. And as a token of our appreciation, we hereby present you with this bench—to be located at a site of your choosing."

Everyone clapped again.

"It was made by Seth," continued Uri. "So it really is a labor of love." He squeezed her shoulder. "Could you read out the inscription please, Eva?"

She cleared her throat:

For those we have loved and lost,
That they might linger here.

"It's beautiful," said Eva. "Thank you all so much." She nodded at everyone, not trusting herself to say anything more.

"The idea," said Uri, "is that we all have a special place to go to to think about our loved ones who are no longer with us. Now." He gave her shoulder another squeeze. "Where do you want it?"

She pointed. "Over there beside the pond."

"Gentlemen?"

Lance and Seth carried the bench to the designated spot and Eva was released—whereupon she ducked back into the crowd and hid herself the best that she could. She thought that would be it. But Uri hadn't finished.

"If I might have your attention for a few more moments."

He bowed his head and was quiet for so long that people began to glance at one another and fidget. Then he lifted his head and spoke.

"My friends. This day fills me with great joy. It is the culmination of nine months of hard labor. You could say that today signifies the birth of this garden. This creation. Because, really, she is still only in her infancy. She has many years of growth yet to come. And it is up to us to make sure that she fulfills her potential. This generation. And generations to come. May we cherish and sustain her, just as she sustains us."

He bowed his head again, for some time. People weren't sure if he had finished or not. An uncertain round of applause broke out then died rapidly as he lifted his head again. His voice rang out.

"Gardens have always been an important part of my life. This comes from my father and his father before him and who knows how many generations back. Men—and women—who worked the land and participated in her bounty. And now when I see my son working. He's so like my own father that it hurts me"—he put his hand up to his heart—"here. How proud he would have been. And of Kathy. Working on her own little flower bed." Uri smiled warmly, on the verge of tears. "What I'm trying to say is that gardens. That nature. That this garden. Has given me so much. That it very probably saved my life. My prayer is that you allow it to save yours too."

He walked away so that everyone knew this time he'd finished. The crowd clapped one more time then merged in upon itself.

A ʟᴏᴛ ᴏғ people went home after that. But many stayed on, reluctant to let go of such a magical day.

Seth found Uri sitting quietly on the bench.

"Do you mind . . . ?"

"Not at all."

"Nice speech."

"Thank you."

There were a few moments of silence.

"Are you okay?"

"Never better. In fact, there was something I wanted to ask you."

"What is it?"

"Would you come to Germany with me? You and your brother."

This wasn't what Seth had been expecting.

"Well—yes. Of course I will. And Aaron too, I'm sure. But what brought this on? You've never wanted to go back before."

"I know. Perhaps you'll understand when you get to my age. The need to say good-bye."

"Don't talk like that, Dad. You've got years in you yet."

"Maybe so. But who knows? I'd like to show you and Aaron where I grew up. The river I used to fish and swim in. Perhaps visit my grandparents' house down south."

"I'd love that."

"And I'd like to visit the camps. The one where your grandfather was shot. And the one where your grandmother and aunt were murdered."

"I didn't think you'd found that out for sure."

"It's the only possible explanation. There's no record of them. They must have been taken straight to the gas chambers the day we arrived. Those people weren't registered."

Seth nodded and didn't say anything.

"If you think it's too morbid, you don't have to go."

"No. Not at all. It's important to you. To all of us. So I can show Kathy when she's older."

"Yes."

They were quiet for a while.

"You never know," said Uri. "We might find some long-lost relatives. I couldn't trace any of them after the war, but who knows? So many were displaced at the time. It's worth looking into I think."

"Yes. I think it's a great idea. I'll start looking into flights tomorrow."

"Thank you, Seth. Now. I think I'd like to sample some of your poteen."

"Only if I can have a glass of your elderberry wine."

"Deal."

The alcohol was produced. Under its influence, the playing of the band took on a new, more frenzied dimension. And with most of the children gone home for their tea, the adults began to dance. Heavily improvised versions of the Siege of Ennis and the Walls of Limerick. Then a young man crossed two brooms on the ground and danced gloriously around them, his hands hanging loose at his sides, his thigh muscles admired collectively and silently by all the women present. Then a very old man got two kitchen chairs and held on to the backs of them, one on his left and one on his right. Then between those two chairs, he performed the best jig that anyone had ever seen. It even inspired Eva to take out her tin whistle and tootle for a while.

Many songs were sung that night. Emigrant songs by people who had never left the ould sod in the first place. Rebel songs by those without a rebellious bone in their bodies. Love songs.

"This was a brilliant idea," said Emily. "We should have a party to celebrate the change of every season."

"You can organize it the next time," said Eva.

"We could do the winter solstice. And May Day. We could have a May pole!"

"Where are you going to get the Morris dancers?"

"We could do it."

"They're meant to be men."

"We could be the Morrisettes!"

"Hey, Mrs. P. Tell me something," said Seth.

"For pity's sake. Will you stop calling me that? Call me Myrtle if you must. Anything's better than Mrs. P."

"Myrtle! If you didn't murder your husband and bury him in the garden, how come you never let us dig in that little patch at the back?"

"Because—you fool—Harriet's mother is buried there."

"Thanks, Myrtle. That's all I wanted to know."

The party went on until the early hours. None of the neighbors complained— because all of them were there.

LIAM SLEEPS IN his own bed now.

I sleep with Seth, the contours of his body following my own. Of course, every now and then, Liam might have a bad dream and come in to us. As might Kathy. On those occasions, we adults hang off the respective edges of our bed, childish knees and elbows digging into our spines.

But it's joyous. This not being able to sleep. This discomfort. Because every jab, every limb thrown casually across my face, reminds me of how much I'm loved. How my life, once a void, is now full to the brim, brimming over, in fact, with love and life and laughter.

Just like that, my family has been doubled. At first it made me uneasy. I felt I didn't deserve it. This miraculous second chance. But over time I learned to be grateful. And it is this gratitude that has blossomed and transformed my life.

Acknowledgments

I HAVE MANY people to thank:

My editor at Gallery Books, Kara Cesare, for her warmth and professionalism. It is lovely to know that my book is in the hands of someone who really cares about it and believes in it. Likewise Katharine Dresser, editorial assistant, for her valuable insights and input. My gratitude to those on the sales team who came up with the great new title. Also, my thanks to Linda Roberts, senior production editor, for arranging the copyediting, and all those people I may never meet, who have worked so hard on my book, in Gallery Books, Simon & Schuster, and beyond.

A special mention to my U.S. agent, Victoria Skurnick, and all at the Levine Greenberg Literary Agency, especially Monika Verma. Thank you for getting me my first American book deal! And thank you Victoria for your directness and forthrightness.

My editor at Penguin Ireland, Patricia Deevy. Thank you for taking me on in the first place. I've enjoyed your insights, your direct approach, your love of words, and your unstinting dedication to all things grammatical.

Much gratitude also goes to Michael McLoughlin, Brian Walker, Cliona Lewis, and Patricia McVeigh at Penguin Ireland. And to all the people, Penguin and otherwise, I have yet to meet, who will contribute to this book.

My Irish agent Faith O'Grady. I have many things for which to thank you. First, your role in helping me to conceive of the idea for the book in the first place, and for the pep talk that spurred me into writing it. If it wasn't for you, the walled garden would have been a scruffy, corner plot and the deli would have been a dingy corner shop. And thanks for getting me this book deal. Thanks also to Lauren Hadden at the Lisa Richards Agency, for all your help and kindness.

Thank you Hazel Orme for your brilliant copyediting. Your attention to detail astounds me.

Many moons ago, Lenny Abrahamson was kind enough to meet with me and share valuable insight into what it means to grow up Jewish in Dublin. At last, I was able to put that knowledge to good use. Thank you.

Heartfelt thanks to Emma Delahunt. For filling me in on what "the young people" wear, drink, smoke, and do nowadays. Emos and Dubes. Who knew?

I am also very grateful to Emer O'Carroll, who a long time ago gave me valuable information about the nature of adoption in Ireland.

And thank you very much Eithne Hegarty B.L. for your expert legal advice.

And to John and Dorothy Allen for setting me straight on Eucharistic ministers. And to Neal McCormack for telling me about Tin Pan Alley. Special mention must go to Kay in Thomastown Library, for helping me to locate books about the 1950s.

To those family members, friends, and neighbors who make up my inner circle, thank you for being in my world. I'd particularly like to thank both of my parents for sharing their stories about growing up in Ireland in the 1950s.

To Leo and Marianne, I love you both, you little squirts.

And to Rory, my first reader and editor. Thank you for your enthusiasm and encouragement.

Finally, I would like to pay tribute to three beautiful gardens, all of which inspired me: The walled garden at Woodstock, Inistiogue; The Water Garden in Thomastown; and the walled garden at Mount Juliet, Thomastown, all in South County Kilkenny. To those of you who designed, planted, and care for them, I thank you all, especially Paddy Daly of Mount Juliet.

Readers Group Guide and Author Q&A

INTRODUCTION

In Irish author Tara Heavey's first novel to be published in the United States, Eva, a widowed young mother, finds love, friendship, and a sense of family when she starts a community garden in the walled-up plot of a mysterious Dublin mansion. Reluctant at first to open her home to strangers, lonely old Mrs. Prendergrast eventually warms up to the idea of allowing Eva and a crew of similarly world-weary volunteers to rake, hoe, and sow her decaying garden and help bring it back to life. There's Uri, an older Jewish man with a complicated past, and his recently divorced son, Seth, as well as Emily, a quiet college-age girl with something to hide. As each gardener tends to his or her plot of land, secrets are slowly revealed and the past is finally brought to bear.

QUESTIONS FOR DISCUSSION

1. Eva serves as the central character around whom the rest of the characters revolve. What is it about Eva that draws people to her? Why were so many other people willing to put their faith in Eva when she wasn't able to have faith in herself?

2. Many of the characters in this novel have storylines that mirror one another. For example, Eva loses her daughter in a car accident while Emily gives hers up for adoption. Mrs. Prendergrast's parents disown her for marrying Martin just as Emily fears her parents will

do if they find out about Rose. Discuss how these and other parallel plot points help to underline certain themes in the book.

3. There are multiple references to femininity and fertility throughout this story. Some references are positive (the beauty of pregnancy and childbirth, the girl-power bonding of the baking group and the "Mothers Union," and the central character herself: Mother Nature) and some are negative (Martin becomes violent with Myrtle/Marnie both times that she is pregnant, Eva becomes hysterical whenever she is separated from Liam, and Eva and Megan both have extramarital affairs). What do you think Heavey is trying to say about the complexities of being a woman?

4. Uri and Myrtle (Mrs. Prendergrast) both mention having a difficult time expressing their emotions (pages 274, 325). What do you think are some of the problems that make it difficult for these two characters to express their feelings? Do you think their respective experiences with horrific physical and emotional violence played a role?

5. This book deals with some very dark subject matter, from spousal abuse to the death of a child and the Holocaust. Did you think that the book offered a hopeful message?

6. Emily is terrified of what her parents will think when they find out about Rose, and Eva is worried about what her mother will think of Seth. Yet both sets of parents are equally gracious in their acceptance of the new members of their families. Why do you think this gulf exists between the children and the parents in this novel (think also of Lance and Myrtle)? Do you see the situation changing with Liam and Kathy?

7. Why did Mrs. Prendergrast stay with Martin after he caused her to have a miscarriage? What would you have done?

8. How does each of the main characters change throughout the course of this novel? Discuss the course of each character's progression through the novel. Which one did you most identify with and why?

9. The plaque on the bench given to the garden in honor of Eva reads "For those we have loved and lost, that they might linger here." Explain how the garden can simultaneously be about remembering the past while also celebrating life and what's to come.

10. At the end of the novel Uri makes an impassioned speech about the importance of the community garden in his life, saying, "this garden has given me so much . . . it very probably saved my life" (page 366). How do you think the garden "saved" the lives of each of the main characters?

QUESTIONS FOR THE AUTHOR

1. **What kind of research did you do for this novel? Are you an avid gardener yourself or did you have to do some studying before beginning to write?**

This novel is a blend of research, knowledge assimilated over time and flights of the imagination. In preparation for Emily's story, I spoke to a social worker who dealt with adoptions. After that, it was just a case of tring to put muself in her shoes, since I've never had to make such a heartbreaking decision myself. As for Seth, I had seen and heard various interviews over the years with people who didn't discover their true sexual orientation until after they were married. I am thinking of one particular, remarkable such interview with a woman on *Oprah* (yes, we get her over here too), who said that she didn't realize she was gay until she was pregnant with her daughter. Something to do with being filled with so much femaleness. She felt she couldn't be with a a man again. I found this fascinating and used this as part of Seth's wife, Megan's, explanation to him. Eva's story relies most on the imagination. I think I was able to carry this off as she was the character with whom I most identified. Although I would like to point out that I have yet to have an extramarital affair! Neither have I—thank goodness—ever had to deal with the pain of losing a child. Again, it was a question of walking a mile in another woman's shoes. Myrtle's story of domestic abuse was born of the shocking statistic that the primary cause of death among pregnant women in the States was violence at the hands of their husbands or partners. I also did quite a lot of study in relation to life in England in the 1950s. Uri's story required by far the most research. Because when you are covering a topic as important as the Holocaust, you have to ensure that you get your facts right. I read books, researched facts over the internet, and like most of us, have seen and absorbed many programs and films on the subject over the years. As for the gardening, I would love to claim that my garden is as beautiful and awe-inspiring as the one in the book. The reality is that it is a rather messy, sprawling country garden. It's not without charm—old-fashioned roses, apple trees, and yew trees—but the garden of my imagination is so much nicer! I did have to look up certain facts along the way, and my father-in-law, who is a keen gardener, also helped me in this regard.

2. **How did you come up with the character of Eva, who makes some mistakes, but who is also a genuinely kind and caring person? Was it important to you to have such a complex character at the center of your story?**

In my opinion, Eva makes only one bad choice and that is to have the affair. Yes, it was important to me to make her a complex character because that is the reality of human existence. To paraphrase Walt Whitman, we are large; we contain multitudes. I don't feel it is my place to sit in moral judgement on my characters. Merely to tell their stories. In a way, Eva is me. In a way, she is everywoman. And every woman—and man—makes her or his fair share of mistakes.

3. **What made you decide to incorporate the Holocaust into this novel? What do you hope the reader will take away from Uri's part of the story?**

I have always wanted to write about the Holocaust. I was particularly inspired to do so after spending some time in Berlin and visiting the Jewish Museum there. I can't think of a more important topic to address—and to honor. I think that ultimately what I was trying to convey was the triumph of the human spirit. How somebody—a child even—could survive the worst that could possibly happen to a person and go on.

4. **Which character in this novel do you most identify with? Which character is your favorite?**

I most identify with Eva. She is the same sex, of similar vintage, and a mother of young children. (In fact, her son, Liam, is very much modeled on my own son.) Because of this, and also to identify her as the central character, I employed the device of writing her story in the first person, whereas all the others are written in the third person. Whether anybody ever picked up on this, I have no idea! My favorite characters to write were Myrtle (Mrs. Prendergast to you!) and Uri. Perhaps because it was the first time I had tackled the stories of much older people—their lives seemed richer. And also because I found their stories intensely moving to write.

5. **Was it ever a struggle for you to express the thoughts and feelings of characters whose life choices you may not have agreed with?**

No. Because I believe that life is most definitely not black and white. And as a writer, I embrace moral ambiguity.

6. **How do you set out to write a story? Do you start with an idea for a character? A plot? What are the parts of the writing process that you enjoy most? Least?**

I usually write out a mission statement for a book before I start writing it. What am I trying to achieve? What am I trying to convey to the reader? In this book, it was my intention, amongst other things, to inspire the reader and explore the theme of healing through nature. I would normally have just a skeletal plot, which I flesh out during the process of writing. As for my favorite parts of the writing process, there are so many. There is something very magical about what Norman Mailer claed this "spooky art." When the characters appear to take over. When you look back on your day's writing and wonder where it all came from. I also love that point where a novel "ignites." The hardest part of a book for me is always the start. But there is a point where the story takes off and you get into your stride. The sooner this happens the better, for both writer and reader! And it's wonderful to read back over your completed novel for the first time and realize that it works. My least favorite part of writing is definitely the revision. I find the second draft particularly hard to visualize. That's where the editor comes in!

7. **This novel has a very strong message of female empowerment. Is that something you purposefully set out to create and, if so, how**

does the garden factor into the process of self-actualization that each woman goes through?

I didn't consciously set out to portray a strong message of female empowerment. This is the first time I've even thought of it! I suppose it just seems natural to me that women should empower themselves. If the garden factors into all this, it would be in the sense of mother nature being the source of all strength.

8. There are so many interweaving relationships in this story, was it ever difficult for you to keep them all straight? Were there any relationships that you thought were particularly important?

No—and I'm going to let you in on a secret. When I first wrote this book, the stories did not interweave as they do now. I wrote each story one at a time. In other words, in the first draft, you were told Emily's story from beginning to end before I moved on to Seth's story. When my Irish agent, Faith O'Grady, first read it, she thought it was too "episodic" and advised me to break up the individual stories into smaller chunks. I agreed. It was easier than I expected and worked better than I would have imagined. I think that all the various relationships between the gardeners are important in that they help each other to heal. Equally important, I think, is the relationship of each character to the garden.

9. On page 359 Mrs. Prendergrast says, "Not forgiving someone is like drinking poison and expecting the other person to die." Is this something that you personally believe to be true? Is there a difference between letting go of the past and forgiveness? If so, do you think Myrtle actually forgives Martin at the end of the book, or does she just decide to let the past go?

Yes, I honestly believe that existing in a state of unforgiveness is the very worst thing that a person can do to himself. It doesn't hurt the other person a fraction of the amount that it hurts you. Often the other isn't aware of your feelings. In the meantime, you are "poisoning" your body, mind, and soul, with venomous thoughts of bitterness and revenge, which serve only to bring more negativity into your life. Of course, it's not always easy and can often be an ongoing process in which you sometimes can feel as if you are taking one step forward, only to take another two back. But definitely worth the effort. I think that letting go of the past and forgiveness are very closely related, if not exactly the same thing. I do think that Myrtle forgives Martin at the end of the book—for her own sake if not for his. But, of course, both the forgiver and forgivee benefit in the long run.

ENHANCE YOUR BOOK CLUB

1. Turn this month's book club into a gardening club as well. Have your meeting in one of your favorite community parks or gardens, or in the garden of one of your member's homes. If you want to go a step further, bring some seed packets and do a little planting as you discuss the novel.

2. This novel has many cinematic qualities. Discuss who you'd cast in each of the major roles if this book were to be made into a movie.

3. The story takes place in modern-day Dublin. Do some research on this world famous city by visiting www.visitdublin.com.